She was h

Actually, it was rather shocking. Anna Rose was lying naked in a meadow of red clover, but she wasn't in the least embarrassed. Someone—she couldn't quite see his face—was plaiting wild-flowers into her hair. Every once in a while, her lover would toss a flower on her breast, laughing and saying, "Here's a kiss for you, my love, and another."

She kept reaching out to the man—wanting him, needing to love him—but he was just out of her grasp. Still, she knew that soon he would come to her. And that knowledge brought with it peace, calm, and an enfolding warmth.

"Anna Rose." The whisper came not from her dream, but from the real world. She opened her eyes; she saw his face at last. He wasn't smiling, but there was a gentle understanding in his face that made her realize he knew her needs and had come to satisfy them.

"Hugh? What are you doing here?"

"Don't you know, my love?" He leaned down and brushed her lips with his. The kiss made her tremble down deep inside. She pressed her palms against his chest, gently forcing him away.

"Oh, Hugh, what are we going to do?" Her voice was filled with pain and desperation.

"This, darling . . ."

He bent down to taste her lips again, but this time his kiss was far more persuasive. Anna Rose felt her long-denied passions rising, and she answered his kiss eagerly. . . .

Also by Becky Lee Weyrich:

Detour to Euphoria (Loveswept #188)

THE THISTLE AND THE ROSE

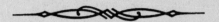

Becky Lee Weyrich

BANTAM BOOKS
TORONTO · NEW YORK · LONDON · SYDNEY · AUCKLAND

THE THISTLE AND THE ROSE

A Bantam Book / December 1987

ISBN 0-553-26891-0

Published simultaneously in the United States and Canada

Bantam Books are published by Bantam Books, Inc. Its trademark,
consisting of the words "Bantam Books" and the portrayal of a rooster,
is Registered in U.S. Patent and Trademark Office and in other
countries. Marca Registrada. Bantam Books, Inc., 666 Fifth Avenue,
New York, New York 10103.

PRINTED IN THE UNITED STATES OF AMERICA

O   0 9 8 7 6 5 4 3 2 1

*With love and gratitude
for my husband Hank,
who always believed in this story
and in me.*

THE THISTLE AND THE ROSE

1

Anna Rose Mackintosh, in her later life—when her chestnut hair showed the glint of silver, but her gray-green eyes still held a lively sparkle—would speak often of how her fate was decided by a rotten piece of wood. She never laughed in the telling, though after many years, she no longer cried.

On the first day of May in 1834, in a barley field near Inverness, Scotland, her world shattered under the weight of a broken wagon stacked with six precious casks of Scotch malt whiskey—*uisge-beatha,* the Highlanders' water of life. The heavy oaken barrels, which had contained all her family's hopes, smashed her dreams as suddenly and thoroughly as they crushed her father's legs, shaping her destiny into something only faintly resembling what her own mind had mapped out for the future.

The mellow, smoky liquid—the final batch from her father's pot still before it was closed down by law in 1814—had been aging in oak these twenty years past to give it a pleasing amber glow and tame its fierce Caledonian bite. The contents of the casks, whiskey as precious as liquid gold, now watered the field where John Mackintosh lay.

Her father's agonized cry—the sound that brought the whole family and even the stranger from Inverness running—silenced all else and put an end to Anna Rose's carefree youth.

Before the accident, Anna Rose had shared the optimism of most adolescent girls. She'd viewed the whole world as a miracle about to take place for her sole benefit. This particular morning, she had awakened in such a glorious mood that she'd felt as if the glow inside her might burst right through her skin. She had sat in bed for a long time, gazing out over the meadows and hugging her knees to her breasts, feeling that if she let go she might fly off in bright, shattered particles. The odd pleasure she felt had something to do with being sixteen, she'd decided.

Later, her father's exciting news at breakfast had left her feeling as if she were poised in midair. She had gone about her chores—gathering eggs, feeding the chickens, and milking the cow—

floating on a cloud of expectations. Even the unpleasantness with her sister Iris had failed to suppress her soaring spirits.

But now, standing in the half-plowed field, staring down at her father's twisted form and the aromatic mud where he lay, Anna Rose thought of the happiness she had taken for granted such a short while ago and it seemed like hard-earned gold stolen by a ruthless thief.

She watched her two brothers and the man from Inverness—Iris's man—set their shoulders to the overturned wagon, huffing and straining to lift the weight off her injured father. Their boots dug into the black furrows. Sweat rolled down their faces. Muscles strained.

"On the count of three, lads, heave!" the tall stranger commanded. "Heave like the very devil! Now . . . one . . . two . . . three!"

The disabled wagon shuddered stubbornly before toppling off John Mackintosh at last. Margaret rushed to her husband and fell to her knees beside him, pillowing his head in the worn linen of her apron.

"Oh, Johnnie, you're near dead," Anna Rose heard her mother whisper through her tears.

"Near dead never filled a kirkyard, Meg darlin'," he said between gasps. "I'll be about me chores again in no time. You'll see."

Relieved as she was to hear her father's voice and know that he was alive, an unaccountable anger welled up in Anna Rose. She knew, as they all did, that his words weren't true. And even if he did recover quickly, as he promised, the whiskey and the money its sale would have brought were gone. Gone too was their dream of America.

Why? Why now did you have to go and get yourself hurt? a self-centered part of her cried out in silent misery. Just when everything was perfect, he'd spoiled it all!

Anna Rose, her usually serene face lined with battling emotions, turned away, ashamed of her own selfish thoughts but unable to stop them. She gazed back across the field toward the sod and stone cottage where she had been born and reared. Her stormy-green eyes blinked back a rush of tears as she willed the scene away. If only she could make the past hour vanish as well. She longed for things to be right again, the way they had been at breakfast.

The Mackintosh clan of Inverness possessed enormous wealth. Unfortunately, very little of it was in the specie of the realm. But

2

Anna Rose, the eldest of the Mackintosh brood, had never realized that fact.

Every morning over porridge, her father, Big John Mackintosh, his bulldog jowls wrinkled in a grin and his slate-colored eyes twinkling as if he knew the grandest secret, would confront his "pretty Meg" and their six stair-step children—Anna Rose, Iris, Cullen, Ewan, Laurel, and Fern—with the same command: "Count off your dearest treasures so we'll start the day rich as lairds." This particular morning, he added, "After you've all had your say, I have a surprise for ye."

Meg, tall and not the least bit stoop-shouldered as most crofters' wives became from heavy farm work, rose from her chair and went to the window of their cottage. Looking out past the dooryard and the stone fences, across the fields and Culloden Moor to the Highlands, lavender-blue in the distance, she whispered, "Spring," as if it were a magical word. Indeed, they all felt the magic of another hard winter gone by and the meadow outside greening under a sun as warm and soft as freshly churned butter.

"Aye," John answered, giving Meg's hand a lover's touch. " 'Tis spring we have this mornin' and a blessin' it is upon us all."

Six dark, curly heads—ranging from the rich, softly waved chestnut locks Anna Rose shared with her mother through shades of russet, mahogany, and oak, to the midnight locks John himself had bequeathed to baby Fern—nodded in agreement around the table.

"Well, bairns, what say you?" their father demanded.

"The proud heritage of Clan Mackintosh is my treasure!" Twelve-year-old Cullen almost tipped over his chair in his show of zealous family pride.

"Well spoken, son!"

The two youngest girls, just nine and seven, whispered in secret consultation. Laurel, though two years baby Fern's senior, was too shy to speak out during these family conferences. So Fern piped up with an air of importance, saying, "Me, yellow butterflies, and sister likes red-clover honey."

"A fine pair of treasures, darlin's," their father agreed, beaming pride and love on his babies as he reached both his big hands out to tousle their dark curls.

Ewan, a sullen boy of ten, given to "the black miseries," as his mother called his gloomy moods, grumbled, "Rain," hoping to dampen the sunny spirits which made him feel uncomfortable—like having a pebble in his boot. His attempt failed.

"Aye now, lad, that's very clever of ye," his father replied.

3

"Without rain, all that sweet red clover on the meadows would dry up and your poor sister'd never taste another drop of honey on her scones."

Anna Rose sat struggling with her choices, trying to think of something grand enough to say to fit her mood. This morning she felt a special rarity in the air. Though most of it came from within herself, even more poured out over her from her father. He always demanded and obviously enjoyed this first-hour accounting, but today something was different. He had the same proud set to his jaw that always came when he talked of the heroic deeds of generations of Mackintoshes long dead upon the moors in battle, the same twinkle that came to his eyes when he told his fantastic tales of castles, kings, and the clan's glory at the Battle of Bloody Marsh far away in a land across the sea called Georgia.

She tried to guess what John Mackintosh might have on his quick mind this morning. Only one thing fired his imagination like the dreams of the past—the promise of the future. And that promise was one he had solemnly made to them all, many years ago. In fact, the grand promise dated from the year of her birth. In 1818 John Mackintosh had mapped out his family's future, and Anna Rose's birth had been the instigation of it all . . . their dream of going to America.

Could it be? Finally? she wondered.

A painful kick under the table captured Anna Rose's immediate attention. She turned toward Iris, ready with a sharp retort for her attacker. But her sister's benign expression stopped her short.

"Papa's waiting, Anna Rose. I have my own piece to speak, but I'll let you go first. Only, please, hurry!"

Please? Anna Rose stared at her sister. Was Iris ill? She'd sooner swallow bitter gall boiled up in a dirty kettle than say one courteous word to her older sister. It took all Papa's bullying and all Mama's pleading to keep Iris civil most of the time. And courtesy seemed something completely beyond her grasp. What could have come over her?

At fifteen, Iris, dark of hair and eye, was that peculiar and irritating mixture of child and adult that produced a sour outlook on life and a malevolence for those closest to her. As for her feelings for Anna Rose, jealousy and total resentment described them best.

"Well, Anna Rose, dear!" Iris prodded too sweetly.

"Uh . . . ." The older girl cast about frantically, so shocked by Iris's uncharacteristic behavior that she couldn't think of a thing to say. Finally, she stammered, "Having a sister . . . three sisters . . . and two brothers . . . and Mama and Papa . . ."

4

"Whoa! Hold on there, Anna Rose! One blessing only to each customer," her father cautioned. "You wouldna want to use up everything all in one morning."

"I'm sorry, Papa." Anna Rose dropped her gaze as she felt all eyes on her. "I got carried away."

"You always do!" Iris chided in her normal, vehement tone.

"Very well, Iris. You've near squirmed through the seat of your chair by now," John Mackintosh said. "I can tell you're fair bursting to share a treasure with us all. Be on with it, girl."

Iris rose slowly, majestically, with a look on her heart-shaped face that would have made a saint weep for all its sweet purity. She brushed at her straight, oak-brown hair and smiled at each family member in turn, then hid her gray eyes from them under lashes that were almost, but not quite, as thick and rich in coppery darkness as her older sister's.

"My treasure's been a secret up to now. But today he's coming to call. His name is Rory McShane and he's first mate on Captain Hugh Sinclair's *Olympia* out of Glasgow."

A general intake of breath around the table was followed by their mother's sharp exclamation: *"Iris Mackintosh!"*

Meg's calloused fingers worried the handkerchief inside the pocket of her apron. She felt as if her second daughter had struck her a blow. Both Iris and Anna Rose were of marriageable age. She wanted them to wed. But she couldn't have either of them hauling home strays as prospects. And a sailor of all things!

Besides the total impropriety of inviting a stranger into their home, Iris knew full well that it was out of the question for anyone to come courting her until her older sister was spoken for. Margaret Mackintosh simply couldn't understand her second daughter. What were young people coming to these days?

Anna Rose felt the tacit clash of wills charging the atmosphere in the room. She was as shocked as anyone by Iris's announcement, but she couldn't endure this awful, strained silence. It was as if waiting for a bomb to explode and knowing she were going to be blown to bits by it.

Their mother looked on the verge of tears and their father's face had gone thundercloud-dark at Iris's statement. He jumped up suddenly and slammed his big fist down on the table with such force that the ironstone dishes danced on the worn white linen cloth.

"I'll have no *slut* in this family!" he bellowed. "Are you hearin' me good, Iris Mackintosh?"

Anna Rose looked up at her sister. Iris was still standing straight with her head held at a defiant tilt, but her face had drained of

5

color and her dark eyes smoldered with a spiteful fire. She was gearing for a family row, there was no mistaking it. Anna Rose felt compelled to head off trouble if she could. Not for Iris's sake—Lord knows, she deserved whatever she got!—or even for her own, but to save the younger children from getting caught up in an ugly scene.

"Papa, please!" Anna Rose cried, touching his arm when it looked as if he might strike Iris. "You haven't told us your surprise yet."

He held his threatening pose for an instant, then slumped back into his chair. "Aye, Daughter." His angry voice softened. "I near forgot, what with your sister claverin' on like a mad one. But what I have to say will put an end to her loose talk once and for all. She'll mend her slatternly ways whether she's inclined to or not."

Anna Rose felt torn. She knew Iris had gone against the rules, and it was far from the first time. But still, Papa shouldn't speak to her so harshly in front of the whole family. She had probably done no more than exchange a few words with the man . . . what was his name? . . . *Rory McShane* . . . when she was in Inverness to sell eggs and butter.

She watched with relief as Iris resumed her seat and her father went to the fireplace, drawn back now to his original purpose. Carefully, he removed one of the large stones below the mantelpiece. From the dark void behind, he drew out a cowhide pouch and held it up for all of them to see. His eyes flashed with excitement once again.

"Who knows what this is?" he asked.

They all knew and answered in unison, except for Iris, "The key to our future!"

The pouch did indeed hold a key, the key to the cellar below the barn. And in that dark, cool place resided six fat barrels of Scotch malt whiskey. Back in the old days, before the law forbade the production of whiskey by crofters, the Mackintosh clan had brewed their share. John Mackintosh, like his father and grandfather before him, had raised the barley, then soaked it, spread it on a stone floor to malt, dried it, ground it, and mashed it before adding the yeast. Then the resulting brew had been distilled twice to attain a high proof and minimum impurities. Last of all came the aging; up to thirty years the water of life slept in its oaken casks. The longer it mellowed, the smoother it became. And the smoother the Scotch, the better price it would bring.

One day of every year of her life, Anna Rose had been taken to the whiskey cellar to view the precious casks. And each year,

6

while the whole family stood there in the cool, dim room, John Mackintosh renewed his pledge to sell the whiskey in good time and to use the money to sail for America. But year after year passed and he never sought a buyer, never named a sailing date.

Now John Mackintosh held the big iron key on high and grinned at his brood. "Aye! You've guessed it, bairns. A buyer's been found to purchase the goods this key guards. Once the transaction's taken place, we're bound for America! For Georgia!" He spoke the last word with gruff tenderness and a hint of awe in his deep voice. "We'll have enough to buy passage for one and all and to purchase a nice parcel of rice lands when we get there. Long before spring kisses the land next year, we'll be with our kin in New Inverness."

"The town's called Darien now, Papa," Anna Rose reminded him. She had to focus on one tiny detail as the entire prospect would take some time to accept.

"No matter the name, lass! It's the land that's important. The rice they grow is like gold right out of the marshes and everyone rides in fine boats from plantation to plantation. Why, I've heard the place likened often enough to Venice with all her grand canals." The dreamy tone faded from his voice suddenly and he bellowed, "What say ye, bairns? Shall we go to America?"

A chorus of excited cries greeted his question. They crowded around him, hugging, laughing, all talking at once. Only Iris hung back, anger, hurt, and rebellion still smoldering in her gray eyes. Obviously, she had more to say on the subject of Rory McShane.

Anna Rose moved out of the family circle to her sister's side and cautioned, "Let it go, Iris. There'll be other boys."

"And just why should I wait for others when it's Rory McShane I want?"

"Don't make trouble now that we're finally going to America," Anna Rose pleaded. Then she added in a stronger tone, "It's not fair, the way you always try to spoil everything."

Ignoring her sister's accusation, Iris hissed, "I'm not making the trouble. He is!" She gave an angry nod toward their father. "Well, the devil take him! I'm going to America all right, but not with the likes of him. And I'm not waiting for him to sell his old whiskey! I'll be gone before the month's out. With Rory!"

"He's asked you to marry him, then?" Anna Rose was truly shocked to think that the relationship might have progressed that far without their parents' knowledge.

Iris paused for a long time before answering. When she finally spoke, her eyes were narrow with cunning.

"Maybe he hasn't asked me in so many words, but I've seen the way he looks me over. He wants me all right. Besides, there are ways a girl can make a man marry her."

"Iris!"

Anna Rose was brought out of her pondering by the gentle pressure of a hand on her shoulder. She was still standing in the field beside the ruined wagon, but the others had gone. All but one.

"You're all right, aren't you, lass?"

She turned quickly to find herself staring into a suntanned, boyish face. It was Iris's caller, Rory McShane. He brushed nervously at a stray lock of wheat-colored hair that refused to stay out of his eyes.

"We got your pa up to the house, your brothers and me. Cullen's run for the doctor. He's broke up pretty bad, but your ma says he'll make it. She's a right brave lady. Handsome, too." He paused, waiting for Anna Rose to say something, but she only stared at him. "You look mighty like her, you know, same bright hair, same eyes that look green as the sea, but with a trace of gray mist to soften the hue."

Anna Rose was having trouble breathing. Strange thoughts and sensations were running through her and getting all mixed up together. Her anger at her father for getting hurt was fighting with pity for him and for herself, and a kind of hopelessness had been creeping in to dull the other feelings. But now, she was only aware of Rory McShane, his hand still resting on her shoulder while he stood looking down at her with the bluest eyes she'd ever seen. He was very tall and lean—"wiry" her mother would have said. Yet she could see the hard seaman's muscles in his arms through the threadbare fabric of his work shirt.

"Hey, you can talk, can't you?" He was grinning down at her in a beguiling, crooked way.

She swallowed hard, fighting against feelings she didn't understand completely. "Of course I can! If I'm of a mind to and there's someone around worth passing the time of day with. What are you doing here, anyway?"

"Well, when we all went up to the house, but you just stayed out here, your ma asked me to come see about you. She said you were awful close to your pa and sure to be upset. She was scared you might faint or something, I guess."

The racket her heart was making drowned out some of his words. "No. I mean why did you come to our farm in the first place?"

He grinned in broader fashion and brushed at his hair again.

"Maybe I came out just so I could meet you and get to talk to you for once. You always walk right past without looking this way or that when you come to the village."

Anna Rose stared at him hard, trying to think if she'd ever seen him in Inverness. If she had, she'd taken no notice of him. But then there was nothing remarkable about Rory McShane. He looked like all the local farm boys—the Grants, the MacLeods, the Farquharsons. Only he was a little taller than most, and those eyes, like a clear morning sky reflected in the loch.

"My sister said you were coming to call on her," she said accusingly.

He drew away from her, affronted. "I never!"

"But Iris told us—"

"Look, I don't know what that Iris has been saying, but I know my manners. Sure, we passed the time of day at her egg stall the other morning, but I wouldn't of come traipsin' out this way, bargin' in without your pa's say. Iris told me Mr. Mackintosh had a staghound bitch that just dropped a litter. I come to see could I buy one of the pups."

Anna Rose felt some of the worry lines easing from her face. Of course! Iris had only imagined Rory McShane's infatuation with her. She'd made up the whole story because she desperately wanted him to find her attractive and to show some interest in her. At her in between age, she needed to be admired by a man. Even one as unremarkable as Rory McShane would do.

Her smile turned into a giggle and then a full, pleased laugh. Rory joined in, though he had no idea what they were laughing about.

"By damn, you're a beauty when you ain't all frowned up. You know that, girl? I like the way your smile starts down deep in your eyes, then spreads all over. And that blush high up on your cheeks, it's nice. Makes a man want to touch you there and feel the glow."

She watched his work-hardened hand sweep up suddenly toward her face. But when his fingertips brushed her burning cheek, his touch was as soft and light as the kiss of a summer breeze. She caught her breath.

He was holding both her hands now, and she was letting him, enjoying the pleasurable, new sensation of physical contact with a man. And maybe, she thought, Rory McShane wasn't so bad after all. There was something about him she truly liked.

Before she knew what was happening, Rory pulled her close against him and closed his arms tightly around her for a moment. Anna Rose was too surprised to protest.

9

At that moment, it seemed to Anna Rose that she and Rory were the only two people in the world, a pair of actors on a bare stage, playing romantic roles only for each other. A mysterious door opened when he held her, letting all sorts of wonderful sensations flood her mind and body. Surely no one else had any part in this intimate drama but the two performers.

But Anna Rose failed to take into account their audience. Iris, who had started across the field to find Rory, saw him take her sister's hands then pull her to him in a brief embrace. Their shared laughter made her cover her ears. Angry tears flooded her eyes.

Anna Rose had it all—the striking looks, the bright spirit, the quick mind, and now she had Rory McShane, too. Maybe Iris hadn't really wanted him. Maybe she had stirred up the fuss at breakfast just to see what would happen. But she'd certainly never meant for Anna Rose to have him. It wasn't fair!

Now she really would marry him! Iris decided.

She whirled away and ran around the side of the cottage so she would no longer be able to see them together. She took refuge in a thicket to cry out her fury and to make her silent vow that Anna Rose would pay for this betrayal. But soon her tears gave way to silent, hateful scheming.

At the same time, Margaret Mackintosh, sitting beside her husband's bed and holding the dazed man's hand, saw the pair together. Her own anger flared at first when she saw Rory McShane touch her daughter. How dare he! But unable to keep them from the impetuous embrace, she could only sit and watch from the window. After a time, her temper cooled to a kind of detached fascination.

She had liked Rory on first sight, that innocent air he had and the way he jumped right in to supervise John's rescue. Then when he explained to her about the puppies, all her misgivings drained away. He hadn't overstepped his bounds with Iris. Yes, Rory McShane was a good lad!

Already, realizing that John would be laid up with his injuries for some time and that the long-anticipated money from the whiskey was gone forever, she had asked the young sailor to stay on with them and help around the farm, raising more barley to sell to the big distilleries. He had agreed. But he'd told her that he couldn't remain indefinitely. Captain Sinclair would sail from Glasgow in a month and he would have to return to his ship for the trip to America.

"America!" she sighed aloud with a hopeless glance at her

10

semiconscious husband. It had been such a wonderful dream all these years.

But now that dream was gone, at least for the time being. What little money they had saved would go to the doctor and to see them through the long period of John's recovery. So New Inverness would remain what it had always been, a hope for the far-off future.

Then suddenly, watching Anna Rose and Rory together, Meg felt the stir of an exciting idea. Young McShane would be sailing for America very soon. Perhaps in the month he would stay with them . . .

"Meg darlin'," John rasped, clutching at his wife.

"I'm right here, Johnnie, my love." She bent over him so that he could see her plainly and whispered, "Hold on darlin'! The doctor should be here soon."

When he reached for her with his uninjured arms, she kissed him slowly, tenderly, with a feeling that had remained constant since their first lovemaking over twenty years ago.

"Don't ever leave me, Meg. I want all my family with me." He whispered the words before slipping back to the other side of consciousness.

"We'll be with you, Johnnie darlin'," she answered to reassure him.

No need, she thought, to trouble him with her plans. He was in no condition right now to listen rationally.

She looked back out the window. There they were, still holding hands, both their faces shining as if they'd just discovered some grand secret unknown to another human soul.

Surely God Himself couldn't fault her for her scheming. After all, it was for the good of the whole family. She wanted more for her children than hard lives lived out on poor, rock-strewn crofts. This could be the start of a new life for them all.

"Yes, it's time Anna Rose settled down," Meg whispered to herself. Her eyes strayed from the couple in the field back to the pain-lined face of her unconscious husband. She cradled his ruddy cheeks in her palms and whispered, "Oh, Johnnie darlin', this isn't the end of our dreams, it's only the beginning."

Then tears filled her eyes and fell to his cheeks as she bent to kiss his still, pale lips.

2

Warm and fragrant as the spring days were on the Mackintosh croft, each setting of the sun brought a chill sea mist from the coast, wrapping around the stone cottage and elevating the smoky peat fire inside to the favored spot after chores were done each evening.

On just such a night twixt the gloaming and the mirk, with smoke rising from the old chimney of the Mackintosh clan's gray stone cottage, the family was gathered round the hearth, resting from one day's toils while they awaited the next day's work.

It had been two weeks since John Mackintosh's accident. He was no better. Indeed, he seemed weaker to Margaret. As she sat rocking baby Fern before the fire, her thoughts were on the fast-fleeing days and her as yet unaccomplished plans for her eldest. She gazed at her children, gathered there before her, all intent on the snip-snip of Anna Rose's scissors. The group looked so content, and their faces, shining in the firelight, wore smiles. All but Iris's. Margaret would have called her expression "conniving." She noticed that her second daughter sat as close as possible to Rory McShane and brazenly pressed against his shoulder at every opportunity.

The worried frown that had taken up permanent residence on Margaret's face the day of the accident deepened. Things weren't going according to her plans. Granted, if Rory showed any favoritism, it was toward Anna Rose. But for the most part, he seemed to regard all of her offspring as mere children.

Their voices rose suddenly in something other than glee, drawing Margaret's full attention back to the hearth gathering.

"It does not look like me!" Iris whined. "You made me look like an ugly old hag, Anna Rose!"

Iris snatched at the silhouette her sister had clipped out of black paper, but Rory, laughing, held it just out of her reach.

"Look at it, Iris," he said, dangling the paper profile between two fingers for everyone to see. "It's exactly like you. See the way the bottom lip pokes out? Poutin' Iris!" he teased. "The spittin' image, girl!"

"You!" Iris shrilled, making a lunge for the offending likeness.

Rory tossed it quickly into Cullen's lap and he passed it on to Ewan. A wild scramble ensued with everyone laughing except Iris. She inflicted her wrath on the lot of them—hitting, slapping, and punching while angry tears streamed down her cheeks.

"Hush now! You'll be waking your father," Margaret Mackintosh scolded. "Let me see that picture."

Her words froze the action and brought immediate silence to the room. Rory retrieved the now torn silhouette from Ewan and handed it to her. She held it up, viewing it thoughtfully.

"It doesn't look like me, does it, Mama?" Iris pleaded.

"Why, dear, it is you, and I think it's lovely. Anna Rose is very talented." She smiled at her eldest, then turned back to Iris, careful to give each daughter equal time and attention. "But she could never make such a charming picture without a pretty subject."

"Come on, Iris," Rory said. "Don't be mad. We were only funnin' with you."

"Well, it wasn't fun for me," she answered, sticking out her lower lip in a pout identical to the one Anna Rose had snipped with her scissors.

"I'm sorry you don't like your silhouette, Iris," her sister said. "I'll do another one for you."

For a brief moment, Iris saw Rory's eyes meet Anna Rose's in understanding intimacy. She jumped up, crying, "I don't want one of your old paper pictures!" Then she ran out into the night, slamming the cottage door behind her.

Margaret Mackintosh heaved a weary sigh. She rose and handed the sleeping Fern to Anna Rose. "Put her to bed, please. I'll have to go see about Iris."

"I'm sorry, Mama. I didn't mean to make her so angry." She and Rory exchanged glances a moment before she hid the bemused light in her green eyes by staring down at the red and black plaid of her skirt. In a quiet voice, she added, "The scissors must have slipped."

"Never mind, Anna Rose." Margaret didn't believe for an instant that her eldest had mistakenly caught her sister's pout, but she had barely enough strength tonight to cope with Iris and certainly none left over to scold Anna Rose. "She's just at that age. There's no telling from one minute to the next when her mood will turn from honey to vinegar."

"Mrs. Mackintosh, let me go find her," Rory offered. "It's my fault. I shouldna have teased her so."

Margaret hesitated. She was bone-weary from tending John and doing a good deal of his work as well, and the air outside would be cold by now. And, too, perhaps Iris might listen to Rory. She knew from the girl's mood that she would have none of her mother's lecturing tonight. In truth, Margaret preferred almost anything at the moment to an unsettling confrontation with Iris.

"Thank you, Rory. Try to talk some sense into her, won't you?"

Rory flashed one of his most endearing smiles. "I've always been a good one for jawing at gateposts, Mrs. Mac."

Rory noticed as he wandered the dark yard that everyone inside was preparing for bed. He saw the lamps flicker low and heard exchanged good nights whispered from within. The cottage seemed to be closing its eyes for sleep as the lights dimmed, then winked out one by one.

He walked the uneven ground, calling quietly, "Iris. Iris. It's me, Rory. Come on out here, girl."

Shivering with the damp chill from the sea, he pulled his rough fisherman's sweater closer about him. Iris had neither sweater nor shawl over her linen shift. She would have to show herself soon since the night air was sure to cool more than her temper.

He stopped for a moment and listened. Somewhere toward the back fence he thought he heard a soft whimpering. Careful to make as little noise as possible, he crept toward the sound.

"Iris, is that you?" he whispered, approaching a thicket.

"Go away!" came the sniffled answer.

"Come on now, lass. I'm not going to leave you out here alone. A wolf might get you."

He waited, but received no reply.

"Or an elephant or a crocodile!"

He heard a stifled snicker from the bushes. He waited, not moving for fear he might flush her from her hiding place and lose her in the shadows beyond.

"You're crazy, Rory McShane! There aren't any such beasts in these parts!"

He edged toward the sound of her voice. "You never know, girl. Are you willing to take the chance?"

A slight movement in the brush revealed her exact location. He made a dive into the bushes and grabbed her. She fought, she scratched, she shrilled her protests, but he finally subdued her.

"What is this?" Iris hissed at him. "Your imitation of an attacking crocodile?"

"No. It's my method of grabbing hold of pretty girls who hide in bushes after dark before they can jump out and grab me. I tell you, it does something to a man's ego to have the female do the attacking, and that's no lie!"

She giggled. "You're an awful tease, Rory McShane!"

"Me?" he cried. "It's you girls who do the teasing. Fair drives a man wild! Why, I couldn't begin to count the number of women who've thrown themselves at me, just begging me to pleasure them." He shook his head and Iris could see the gleam of his grin in the moonlight. "Makes a body weary, it does!" he said with an exaggerated sigh.

"I'd never throw myself at you or any other man the way Anna Rose has been doing," Iris replied with righteous outrage.

Rory caught her shoulders and tried to look through the darkness into her eyes. "What do you mean? Anna Rose hasn't done that."

"Not much! I've seen the way she looks at you. Why, her heart's nearly pouring out melted through her eyes these days. It's purely shameful!"

But Iris's accusations had the opposite effect on him from what she'd intended. Rory was silent, his heart thundering hopefully. Had he been blind these past two weeks? His first encounter with Anna Rose in the field—his only close contact with her—was something that he dreamed of nightly. The very thought that she might feel something for him in return stirred deep, welcome sensations.

He looked up suddenly, realizing that more than his thoughts were stirring him. Grasping Iris's busy hand, he removed it from his britches leg.

"What the hell do you think you're doing, girl? Stop that!"

"Just kiss me, Rory," Iris panted. "Please! I've never been kissed before. Not that I haven't had the opportunity, but I've been saving myself for the right boy. I want you to be my first, Rory darlin'."

He had no time to agree or object. Iris lunged, toppling him backward into the scratchy bushes and pressing her lithe body against his full length. He was too surprised to fight when her lips found his. His first thought was to roll over, out from under her. But he was pinned between the thick branches of two bushes. He might as well have been staked out, spread-eagle, by some warring clan.

"Iris!" He tried to protest, turning his face away from her lips. "Iris, get hold of yourself, girl!"

"Kiss me, Rory. I want you so!"

Her breathy words had an alarming effect on his body. He tried

15

to control his reaction, but there was no way he could stop the blood coursing downward.

Iris's lips moved to his throat, lingering to tickle his Adam's apple. The feel of her kisses on his chest, bared by her insistent hands, forced a moan from him. All was lost! He knew it at that moment. He was only a man, after all, and a man who hadn't had a woman for some time now.

Rory McShane had bedded many a maid in many a port. The first had been a prostitute at a house in Glasgow where his salty old stepfather took him for his initiation into the mysteries of love when he was a mere lad of thirteen. Since that time he'd known the willing bodies of at least a hundred women—all ages, all colors, all shapes and sizes—women who practiced every technique known to man, and some, he suspected, that were made up especially for him. But Iris Mackintosh was a unique creature. Delighted at the novelty of being forced by a tender female, he used none of his strength to resist her.

He shivered as the sweat of lust covered his near-naked body. She pressed her hands down on his chest, wriggling atop him as she pulled the full skirt of her shift over her knees. He groaned aloud when he felt her bare thighs pressing against his sides.

"You're my very first, Rory darlin'!" Her words were a warm, wet whisper in his ear.

When Iris leaned forward, her breasts rubbed his chest, taunting him beyond the point of no return. His hands came up, as if of their own volition, to seek out the soft flesh. His fingers kneaded and teased until her nipples, erect and hard, strained against his palms.

"Oh, now!" Iris gasped. "Take me now, Rory!"

"God, I can't! You're just a kid," he choked out.

"You can! You must!" she pleaded, fumbling at the lacing on his trousers.

The cold air rushed at his burning flesh and caused a momentary contraction of his erection. But the feel of Iris's damp warmth against him soon brought new life and pulsing urgency. His hips jerked upward, finding their mark with the first thrust. Iris cried out and dug her nails into his shoulders. Then, forcing her body down over his, she caught his rhythm and rode him to the finish, collapsing atop him after the hot flood.

Rory dared not move. He lay there, waiting for tears, accusations, hysterics from Iris. He deserved them all, but still dreaded the scene he knew was sure to come. He'd seen it happen before with virgins and he'd sworn not to take another until he bedded his wife on their wedding night.

But instead of cursing him, Iris lifted her head and kissed his lips softly, quickly, then said matter-of-factly, "You'll have to ask Papa's permission before we marry, of course. But I'm sure he won't object. How can he . . . now?"

Stunned, Rory looked into Iris's satisfied face. He couldn't believe what he was hearing. Marry her? She was only a baby! Then he laughed out loud. That was no baby who had ridden the juices from him just now. No, Iris Mackintosh was all woman, a scheming, ambitious, witch of a woman! She knew exactly what she wanted and was not above doing anything she had to to get it. And right now she wanted him—not just for tonight, but forever and ever, amen!

Confusion reigned in his mind. God, he'd made an awful mess of things! He didn't want Iris. He wanted Anna Rose. But she'd never marry him now, not after what he'd just done to her little sister. Then, too, he wasn't all he'd told the Mackintosh family he was. Another man was the first mate on the *Olympia*. Rory was only a lowly seaman, signed on a year ago by Captain Hugh Sinclair from his berth in the Kirkcudbright Tolbooth, the town's derelicts' jail. He'd been put there after a drunken brawl that ended with a local constable being tossed into the muddy estuary of the Dee by Rory and three of his fellow tipplers.

Captain Sinclair, an old friend of his stepfather's, had given him bloody hell for his misconduct, he remembered. Like a towering prophet of doom, the fierce sea captain had bellowed, "So you're in the soup again, you worthless pup! I promised your old dad before he died that I'd see you grown. But at the rate you're going you'll never make it. So we'll just see what a bit of salt air and hard work will do for you. I'll bring you back from America a Galloway *man* or I'll bury you at sea. It's up to you which!"

Rory shuddered, remembering those first, killing months at sea under Captain Sinclair's command. He had survived, but just barely.

"What's wrong, darlin'?" Iris asked, cupping his cheeks in the palms of her hands.

"I was just thinking, girl. There's going to be hell to pay with my captain. I'm supposed to get his permission to wed. Then, too, we sail only days from now and he has strict regulations against wives coming on board to be with their men. If we marry, you'll be staying on here with your family when I ship out."

Iris jumped up, hands on hips. "Not a bit of it, Rory McShane! The devil take your captain! You'll marry me and take me with you or I'll tell Papa how you forced me and then I'll refuse to marry such a loathsome beast and he'll have the sheriff down on you like that!'' Iris snapped her fingers and it sounded like a cannon shot to Rory.

"But, Iris . . ."

She only smiled. She had him right where she wanted him. Of course, she could never carry out her threat, but Rory didn't know that. To confess her tryst with Rory to her stern father would be asking for a trip to the barn and a sound beating once she got there. She felt confident, nevertheless, that within the week she would be a married woman, no longer subject to the total domination of her parents.

"I'm ready to go in now," she said as calmly as if their wedding date were all set and the parson were donning his marrying coat even now. "Papa will be sleeping, but you can speak to him tomorrow."

Anna Rose, concerned about her sister and feeling slightly guilty, hadn't been able to fall asleep. She lay on her cot next to the window. Though a drape hung between the space where she and the two babies slept and the cot Iris occupied—put up because the younger girl insisted on her privacy—she knew that her sister and Rory were still outside.

She pulled back the curtain and peered out into the yard. The landscape seemed frosted with mist and moonsilver. In the distance, she spied two figures coming slowly toward the house.

"Rory found her," she said aloud, relief easing her conscience. She really had cut Iris's silhouette to show her unpleasant pout.

She watched the pair come closer. Iris was clinging to Rory's arm possessively. Anna Rose tried to suppress her surprising jealous reaction. After all, she had no claim on Rory McShane. But then, neither did Iris, she reminded herself, feeling a well of resentment.

"And I'm the oldest!" she said in quiet rage.

She continued watching. Iris's hair, she noticed, was snarled with twigs and her clothes looked damp and rumpled. Rory appeared no less a shambles.

Anna Rose gave a little snort of indignation. He probably had to chase her down and haul her bodily out of the woods, she thought. Wouldn't Iris ever learn to act like a lady?

As if in answer to her sister's unspoken question, Iris reached up and pulled Rory's lips down to hers in full view of Anna Rose's window. Anna Rose gasped and Iris seemed to look directly at her, a smile of triumph on her pouting lips. She let the curtain drop quickly, though she told herself Iris couldn't possibly have seen her spying from the dark room.

Anna Rose flopped down on her pillow. She felt like crying, but she wasn't sure why. Had she thought that Rory's private looks were for her alone? It was a foolish notion. He'd probably been showing Iris the same sort of attention.

But he put his arms around you! some emotional part of her brain insisted, only to have the statement countered by a more reasonable voice in her head that replied, *So what if he did? He's a sailor with a girl in every port!*

"And two in some!" she whispered to herself, reliving the sight of his lips caressing Iris's.

Anna Rose had closed her eyes when Iris tiptoed in a few minutes later. But she wasn't sleeping. She was far too overwrought for that. Her sister was humming softly.

"Are you asleep?" Iris asked, poking her head through the dividing curtain.

"Not anymore!"

"Well, I won't keep you long. I just thought you'd like to know that Rory and I are going to be married."

Anna Rose sat bolt upright in bed. "Married? But how? When?"

"I believe the usual manner is by a parson. As for when, as soon as Rory asks Papa."

"Iris, you aren't serious?"

"Never more so, Sister dear! I told you there were ways." With those parting words, Iris closed the curtain for the night.

Long after her sister's even breathing told Anna Rose that Iris was asleep, she lay thinking, trying to sort out her own feelings. Iris's announcement had been like a physical blow. She hadn't realized until now how much she cared for the boyish, blue-eyed sailor. And it wasn't as if she had never had any other male attention. Several of the crofters' sons had singled her out at the market in Inverness. Some had even called at the house. But not one of them had ever made her feel the way Rory McShane could. All he had to do was look in her direction and her insides went all fluttery.

She lay in the dark with her heart aching. Tears ran down from the corners of her eyes. Iris's announcement made it seem to Anna Rose that the end of the world was close at hand. First, her dream of going to America had been dashed and now Iris was taking the only man she had ever wanted. The future seemed to stretch before her in an endless haze of empty, gray days and cold, lonely nights.

It seemed like hours before Anna Rose finally fell into an uneasy sleep. Her dreams, which had for the past nights been peopled by a cast of two—Rory and herself—were now troubled by a third spirit. Iris, her chin at a defiant jut and her laugh malicious, stood between them. He reached out to Anna Rose, calling her name. She tried to go to him, but it was no use. Iris barred the way each time she tried to seek the safe port of his arms.

She pounded her pillow as she slept, imagining that she was destroying the vision of her sister.

Rory couldn't marry Iris! It wasn't fair!

Anna Rose came wide awake suddenly, her mind calm and lucid. The cold sweat left from her awful dreams turned to a warm sheen on her flesh. Her heart was pounding, but not from fear or anger. Excitement flooded through her in a rush as strong as the flow of a rain-swollen river.

It was all so clear to her. She loved him. It was as simple as that.

Anna Rose Mackintosh loved Rory McShane.

3

The time had come, Margaret Mackintosh decided the next morning. She had waited two long, fruitless weeks for John to show some improvement before she spoke to him. She couldn't afford to wait any longer, to let Rory McShane sail away.

She lay in the big bed next to her husband and watched the first rays of the sun slide through the window to bring out the planes and contours of his familiar and well-loved face. The cheeks were sunken slightly and dark circles shadowed his closed eyes. Although he was only a ghost now of the once robust, life-toughened man she had loved since childhood and had married over twenty years ago, Margaret saw her husband through her heart instead of her eyes. Viewed from that angle, John Mackintosh was the same as he had always been.

But they had never faced a situation as desperate as this one. And Margaret herself had never been forced to make such a momentous decision all alone. Would John understand? Would he give his blessing?

For a long time she watched him, trying to frame the proper words in her mind before he awoke. She had to make her argument convincing. If she couldn't persuade him on the first try, she would have to give up the whole idea. Her daughter's future meant a great deal to her, but her husband meant far more. She refused to run any risks with his health by upsetting him.

Hesitantly, like a shy maiden approaching her lover, Margaret's slender hand crept across the quilted counterpane. She stroked his fingers, then curled her hand into the warmth of his palm. He stirred, shifted, and groaned when the movement shot pain through his body.

"John darlin', are you awake?"

From long years of habit, he reached out at the sound of her early morning greeting to draw her to him.

"No, John, we can't," she murmured, fighting tears. She wanted him, too.

His eyes were open now, staring into her face. He traced a lone tear down her cheek with one unsteady finger.

"Don't cry, pretty Meg. We'll love each other again. You'll see."

"I know, darlin'." She answered him with as much conviction as she could muster. But then a long pause followed while she fought to gain control of her emotions. "It's not just that," she continued. "I have to talk to you, John. I've tried putting it off till you're better, but . . ."

"But I'm not getting any better," he finished for her gruffly. Then his voice softened. "You dunno have to be afraid to say it to me. I know how I feel, love. God-awful!"

She sat up so that she could look at him as she tried to explain about Anna Rose.

"Ah, that's better," he said, smiling as he reached up to cup a linen-covered breast, still firm even after suckling six babies.

She closed her eyes, enjoying the feel of his strong, stroking fingers. Was there ever another love as deep and abiding as she and her husband shared? She doubted it. Yet she could hope for a like affection to blossom between her children and their mates. The thought brought her back to her morning's purpose. Reluctantly, she removed John's hand from her sweetly aching breast, kissing his fingers before she spoke.

"I want you to listen to what I have to say, John. It's very important. It may decide our whole family's future, the future of generations of Mackintoshes yet to come."

He bestowed a broad grin on his wife. "You certainly have me full attention with a speech like that, Margaret darlin'."

"It's time our daughter married, John. Not only is the time right, but the man as well. I've seen the way she looks at Rory

McShane and there's love in her pretty green eyes, no doubt about it."

He frowned, remembering only that he'd first heard Rory McShane's name from Iris's pouting lips. "You're speaking of Anna Rose, of course."

"Of course."

His face broke into a smile. " 'Tis nothing short of a stroke of genius, this match you've come up with, Meg love. They'll marry and then afterward young McShane will give up the sea and stay on here so he can take over my jobs and responsibilities until I'm well again. I see your plan. You're a good, sensible woman, Margaret Mackintosh."

This was the moment she had dreaded most of all. It was one thing to arrange their daughter's future and remove some of the family burdens from her ailing husband, promising him at the same time that his favorite would be close, soon providing him with grandchildren to spoil. But to tell him the rest of her plan was hard indeed.

"No, John darlin', that's not quite what I had in mind," Meg said gently. She took a deep breath while her husband stared at her, his shaggy brows drawn together in a studious frown. "Rory leaves for America before long. I plan for them to be wed by that time. Anna Rose must go with him on the ship to make a home for all of us there. We'll follow when you're able."

He looked away from her, his gaze fixed on some distant point out the window. "Anna Rose . . . leave us?"

Margaret touched his arm, stroked his hand, feeling his sense of loss even more than she felt her own. "It's the only way, John. Can't you see that? If she doesn't go now, she'll end up married to some crofter's son in the district and here she'll stay for the rest of her days."

He caressed her cheek and his smile held melancholy pain. "It's been a hard life for ye, hasn't it, Meg darlin'?"

"No, John," she whispered, turning her head to kiss his hand, "not by your side. But we've all dreamed of going to America for so long, Anna Rose most of all. Wouldn't you like to see her know that dream?"

"Aye, she should have it." He nodded.

"Then you agree?"

"I do. But what about young McShane? He has some say-so in all this."

Margaret Mackintosh leaned down and brushed her husband's brow with her lips. "Do you know of any man who wouldn't want your daughter for his wife?" she whispered.

22

"Not if she's half the prize her own dear mother is." His eyes lit with their old sparkle and longing, but they both knew that was as far as it could go. To break the tension between them and to forestall his wife's tears, John swatted Margaret's behind playfully and said, "He drives a good wagonload into his farm that gets a good wife, Meg darlin'. And mine was a good load, indeed!"

She silenced his Highland platitudes with her lips. For a long time they lay in each other's arms, enjoying their quiet, comfortable intimacy.

That day proved long for Anna Rose. She hadn't slept well the night before, tossing and dreaming over Iris's surprise announcement. Then came her mother's odd request in the afternoon: "Your papa and I would like a word alone with you this evening, Anna Rose, in the bedroom."

Her parents' bedroom, the only separate chamber in the cottage, was their sanctuary. The children learned early in life to respect their parents' limited privacy. A bedroom audience usually meant trouble for the one invited to attend, some felony so awesome that the other family members were not welcome to witness the chastisement.

Anna Rose, her hair combed and pulled neatly back and wearing a clean frock and apron, knocked hesitantly at the door. She was still sifting through her mind, considering all possible sins she might have committed, to prepare herself for what was to come. But she could think of nothing so terrible that she had done. Of course, there was the unflattering silhouette she had snipped of Iris, but that hardly seemed to warrant the harsh punishment she was anticipating. Her mother's request baffled her.

"Come in, Anna Rose." Margaret Mackintosh's guarded tone gave no hint as to what would be discussed.

Anna Rose took a few stiff steps into the room. She looked about as if viewing the chamber for the first time. The huge, carved oak bed, the only fine piece of furniture in the house, looked menacing with its high headboard looming up over her father's sunken form. Long evening shadows crept through the small window next to the chest-on-chest, cloaking the room in purple darkness. Only the yellowy-white halo of light from a coal-oil lamp fought the encroaching night. Its glow cast harsh shadows over her parents' faces, making them seem even more intimidating. Strangers, though she loved them both dearly.

"Well, girl, come over here so I can see you," her father commanded. "You've scarce spent a moment with me since I took to my bed."

"You've needed your rest, John," Margaret explained. "I've kept the children away."

Anna Rose moved to the side of the bed while her parents carried on their exchange. When her father reached out his hand, she took it, surprised to find it smooth against her palm. Two weeks without hard work had allowed his crofter's calluses to heal.

John Mackintosh looked up at his daughter and offered her a sly smile. Deep deep down in his gray eyes, she could see just a flicker of his old good humor. More noticeable were the lines etched by pain at the corners of his mouth. She smiled back, but only because she knew he expected it.

"There, lass, that's better. Your mother's wrong, you know. She shouldn't call you a child any longer. You're a woman now. Look at the way you've filled out and rounded off. Why, when my pretty Meg was your age, you were at her breast already!"

"John!"

Anna Rose glanced at her mother, but Margaret said no more. She seemed to be busy memorizing the plaid pattern of her skirt, her cheeks faintly flushed.

"This was your idea, Meg, and a fine one it is. You wouldna be changing your mind now?"

"No, John. Of course not."

Anna Rose looked from one to the other, confused. "Please," she begged, "have I done something wrong?"

John Mackintosh chuckled and squeezed her hand. "Not a bit of it! You're a joy and a treasure, Anna Rose. It's right alone you've done since the day your mother gave you to me. And I know in my heart, it's right you'll do by the whole family now, Daughter."

As a strained silence followed, Anna Rose could feel her parents' eyes on her, searching, scrutinizing. She cleared her throat and tried to think of something to say. But no words would come.

"Oh, John, just be on with it!" Margaret pleaded in an anxious outburst.

He sighed and shifted in the bed. His smile vanished as he continued staring at his oldest daughter, as if he meant to memorize the coppery glow of her thick hair, the high cheekbones, delicately shaped nose, generous mouth, and the unusual smoky-green hue of her eyes. The dimple he loved, just at the right corner of her mouth, was missing now. She wasn't smiling.

"Your mother and me have decided it's time you married, Anna Rose."

24

"Married?" she echoed, her voice a whisper.

"Time you married and went to America," her mother added. "We can't go now, but you can. Then when your father's well and we've earned enough for our passage, we'll be able to join you. Don't you see? This is the perfect plan. You can go ahead of us and get established. When we get there it will be easier for all of us to pick up our lives again."

"It's a fine plan," her father assured her.

"But marry? Who?" Her mind was whirling. "There's not a man I know of who's spoken his intentions to you, Papa."

"There's one, right enough," Meg Mackintosh answered, studying her apron again.

"Who?" Anna Rose felt a prickling along her spine. Her future was being decided. Was she to be only a bystander in that decision?

"Young Mister McShane," John announced.

"Rory wants to marry me?" Anna Rose couldn't have been more surprised if her father had said the king of England had asked her to share his throne.

"He as much as told me so only yesterday, Anna Rose," her mother answered.

But Margaret Mackintosh almost choked on the words. Lies came hard and only out of direst necessity to her. In truth, all Rory McShane had said was that he wanted to marry someday and that America would be a hard land for a man without a wife. But Margaret felt sure the young man would realize with little prodding what a perfect partner her eldest daughter would be.

Still, she would not pledge Anna Rose to a man she could never come to love. She had to find out the girl's feelings about the plan before she coaxed Rory along toward the altar.

"And how do you find young Mister McShane?" her father asked.

Anna Rose couldn't answer his question simply. *How did she find him?* How could she tell her parents that her heart swelled up ten times its normal size, that her breath came hard, her head swam, and it seemed that everything wonderful in the whole world belonged to her alone when Rory touched her? How could she admit to them that being Rory McShane's wife was something that she had never dared let herself think about? That it was too great a treasure to expect this side of heaven? Granted, they had known each other for only two weeks. But that was more than long enough for Anna Rose to realize that Rory was her love of loves.

"Well, Anna Rose, your father asked you a question," her mother prompted.

"Mister McShane is nice enough," Anna Rose answered, feeling the urge to laugh aloud at her own understatement.

"Then it's all settled," John Mackintosh said.

"All but the asking and the accepting," Margaret added in a soft voice.

Anna Rose wanted to say, "But what about Iris?" She couldn't imagine what had happened in the few hours since her sister had made her intentions known. But what did it matter? Their parents' word was law in the family. Undoubtedly, they had had a long talk with the younger girl and made her see that this match was the right one. There would be someone else for Iris, soon, she was sure.

Anna Rose went into her mother's outstretched arms. They hugged each other with the understanding of two women who have found their men for life.

Rory McShane bedded down early that evening in the sweet hay in the barn. His whole body ached from a full day's farming. But he gave up trying to sleep when he heard his name mentioned in the next stall where Cullen and Ewan were supposed to be asleep already. He listened with a keen ear.

"You don't know what you're talking about, Ewan." Cullen's whisper was so loud that the old plow horse neighed a tired complaint.

"I know what I heard, and they wouldn't have said it if they hadn't been giving it a lot of thought. I heard 'em say Rory's name, plain as you're hearing me say it right now."

"Aw, go on with you! They could have been talking about anything or nothing at all."

"Go ahead, Cullen Mackintosh! Call your own sister 'nothing' if you want! But I heard what I heard. They're planning a match."

"Ewan, you little sneak! What were you doing outside their bedroom window anyway? You're the worst kind of snitch!"

"You take that back!"

"Will not!"

"Take it back, Cullen!"

"Won't! You are!"

When Rory heard the raised voices and the sound of fists pounding flesh, he roused himself out of the hay. It fell to him to see that this scrappy pair of brothers didn't beat each other to a pulp. They were little enough help around the farm as it was. Banged up and bleeding, they'd be no use at all.

"That'll be it, lads!" he said, grabbing each by the scruff of the neck and yanking them apart. "Now, what's all this about your ma and pa discussing me?"

"Thought you were asleep," Cullen mumbled.

"Hard to sleep with a couple of pesky bugs buzzing in my ears. Now out with it! Tell me what you heard or I'll clang your noggins together till your ears ring."

Cullen scowled at his younger brother. Ewan's freckled face broke into an almost malicious grin.

"I'll tell you what I heard and maybe you'll be running for your life, Rory McShane!"

Rory's blue eyes darkened and flashed a warning as he declared, "I ain't now, nor have I ever been, a man to run from trouble, young mister. Stand up and face it is my motto, and it's served me well enough these nineteen years."

"Oh, there's no trouble!" Cullen was quick to assure him.

"All depends on how you look at it," Ewan answered with a knowing grin. "Were it me, I'd rather face the devil himself than a girl!"

"You little hellion!" Rory boomed. "What are you talking about? What girl?"

Rory geared himself for the answer. Obviously, Iris had gone to her parents, telling them the whole sordid tale of last night. He took a deep breath, preparing for the worst. Iris was nice enough, but he didn't want to marry her! Still, in all, he'd done a great wrong and would pay the price like a man, if forced to.

Cullen gave his brother a threatening look, but it did no good. Ewan could hardly wait to tell all.

"Ma and Pa's decided you'd make a good husband. Looks like you're about to get saddled with a wife, Rory McShane!" Ewan grinned again in that devilish fashion of his as he added, "And two darlin' little brothers in the bargain."

"The hell you say! You're talking crazy, boy. What wife?" Rory swallowed hard, preparing himself for the answer he was sure would follow.

"Miss Anna Rose Mackintosh is what wife!" Ewan announced.

Rory, who had been hanging tight to both boys' shirt collars all the while, released the pair so suddenly that they tumbled backward into the hay. They shrieked and chattered at him, both at the same time, but Rory only heard their words as background noise.

Miss Anna Rose Mackintosh. The name wove through his thoughts as prettily as the fat black spider spun her fine silk web in the corner of the barn door. The idea of marrying Anna Rose had been trying all these past days to worm its way into his consciousness, but he'd thrust it back every time it tried to surface. No need for a boy from the docks to go wishing for the moon! he'd told himself.

Cullen and Ewan grew suddenly quiet. They both saw that Rory wasn't listening to them any longer. He staggered like a drunkard toward the door and out into the stable yard, his face turned up to the night sky and his arms stretched out as if he meant to harvest the stars.

"I told you you shouldn't have said nothing, Ewan!"

"Aw, hell, he'll be all right! Besides, it would've been a whole lot worse had Ma and Pa just sprung it on him. A condemned man's got a right to know his sentence, ain't he?"

Rory McShane didn't feel condemned. He felt for all the world as if he had just been given some fabulous treasure that no other man on the face of the earth possessed. He himself—Rory, by God, McShane—a fellow who'd never had anything to call his own. No real family. No home. Since he was just a tyke, nobody except maybe Hugh Sinclair to care whether he lived or died. And now, out of nowhere, this! The prettiest, most loving, most precious woman in the world was about to become his forevermore!

"Anna Rose." He breathed the name with an almost religious reverence.

Ewan must have heard wrong, he decided. Surely, Mr. and Mrs. Mackintosh wouldn't hand over their beautiful daughter just like that to a nobody, a nothing! She was too special, too fine for him.

But, God, he wanted her! That day in the field, his whole body had ached from just touching her hand. And then when impulse prompted him to hold her close, it felt as if the earth were moving under him. There had never been a woman like Anna Rose. For Rory McShane there would never be another.

He wandered on aimlessly beyond the stone fence toward the brown stream that meandered with the road toward Inverness. He didn't see the first stars blinking out of their twilight slumber. He didn't hear the last sleepy notes from the starlings. He didn't smell the rich tilled earth or the first heather there on the hill. He saw Anna Rose, her fresh skin with the hint of freckles dancing across her pert nose, her eyes greenish-gray as a Highland mist on the meadow, her mouth full and pink as the first rose of summer.

Drunk on his own thoughts, he collapsed into a mystified heap at the river's edge, crushing the new clover beneath him so that a cloud of green smells enveloped him. He lay back, feeling like a part of the spring earth, alive, pulsing, awakening. He closed his eyes to better experience the phenomenon.

"Rory?"

At first he thought it was his own mind playing tricks on him, allowing the soft, night breeze to whisper his name. But then he knew it was really her.

He sat up and turned. There she stood, the waxing moon forming a halo behind her bright hair. He felt a knot form in his throat and its mate in his stomach. He wanted to weep. He was that happy to see her.

Anna Rose wondered at her own brazenness. She shouldn't have followed him when she saw him leave the barn. She knew she should turn and run back to the house, but her legs refused to carry her. It was as if their hearts were two magnets, drawing their bodies closer with each fragile moment that passed.

"Anna Rose, darlin'," he whispered. "Come here to me."

She didn't hesitate a moment. She went, letting him take her hands in his, feeling as if he held her pounding heart in his gentle grasp. She could hardly believe any of this was real.

When he pulled her down next to him in the sweet bed of clover, she made no protest. His lips found hers, pressing gently, starting a trickle of ice that quickly boiled to steam in her veins. He kissed her eyelids and brow, her tear-damp cheeks and chin, then captured her willing lips once more. Their warm bodies pressed close, deep in the soft clover. Anna Rose thought she would always remember that fragrance with a pang of love and longing. She would remember how Rory's cool hands felt pressed to her flushed cheeks and how his body seemed to mold itself to hers, making them one.

"I want you so bad, darlin'," he whispered, letting his hands fondle her aching, straining breasts. "But we have to wait till we're man and wife, proper and legal. I won't have it any other way."

As much as she loved him, as much as she longed to have him show her all the mysteries and wonders of passion, the thought frightened her, too. She knew that if he asked for all that was in her power to give, she would not hesitate. She couldn't! But he seemed to be too much in awe to demand more of her. Her arms, her lips, her breasts, were all he required to make him happy just now. And his happiness made hers complete. As he said, they would wait for their magic moment and be ready when it arrived.

"You will marry me, won't you, darlin'?" His question came hesitantly, almost timidly.

Anna Rose once more found her eyes flooding with tears, but could not find her voice. In answer, she kissed him—a deep, lingering kiss that said more than any words she might have spoken.

For a long time they lay embracing in the clover, the moon's silver eye the only witness to their gentle loving. Anna Rose, like many a young girl, had wondered from time to time what it would be like to be a bride. That May night, on the bank of the stout-colored stream, feeling Rory McShane's heart beating against her own, she thought she understood at least part of the age-old mystery. She ached for this welcome marriage and the man who would fill her, who would make her life complete, who would transform her into a whole, awakened woman.

Rory McShane would be that man . . . her husband.

4

Captain Hugh Sinclair tugged the collar of his black cloak up around his ears and muttered a curse on Rory McShane's uncertain parentage. Would that young whelp never learn to follow orders? He should have sent word to the ship concerning his whereabouts over a week ago.

The lad's trail had brought the captain and his ship from Peterhead to Inverness, but inquiries at the town jail, at a certain accomplished lady's house of pleasures, even at the undertaker's, had turned up no clues as to Seaman McShane's whereabouts. Now the *Olympia* stood waiting, ready to sail ahead of schedule as soon as this last sailor could be rounded up and herded on board. And, Captain Sinclair vowed silently, his ship *would* sail with a full crew!

"I'll have the bloody, little bastard keelhauled when I do find him," Sinclair said aloud, setting his broad chest into the rising wind as he turned a corner onto the main street of Inverness.

He glanced up at the sheet lightning that periodically flashed its warnings through the night sky. "There's weather blowing in," Sinclair told himself, remembering the gulls he'd seen at sunset, skrieghing their warning as they flocked inland. "Damned if I'll let the boy get away with delaying our sailing and letting this dirty weather close in on us!"

Just ahead, he spotted a painted wooden sign, crying its complaint as the rising wind worried its hinges. *Skean Dhu*, he read silently. The Black Dagger. A fine-sounding establishment for a town tavern, he thought. Better, at least, than The Headless Queen in Glasgow.

An unsteady customer exiting the pub bumped Sinclair, who righted the man, then asked if he knew Rory.

"Know the lad well, I do!" the tippler assured him, squinting up through one bleary eye. "Smallish lad, wouldna ye say? Comes no more than to your shoulder and wide as he is tall."

"I'm afraid that's not my man."

"Och, well," the fellow said with an apologetic shrug. "We gets 'em all here—moss-troopers, hackbuteers, spalpeens, and all manner of fly-by-nights. Hard for a body to keep one stranger straight from another. But I did hear tell of a new lad in town who's taken on a job at one of the neighborin' crofts . . ."

Preposterous! Sinclair thought, as he heard out the rest of the story.

After the captain thanked the man and let him be on his uncertain way, he stood outside the tavern a moment longer, thinking about what he had just been told. Something about an accident and a stranger filling in to help out one of the local families for a time. Yes, he pondered, that would be like Rory. Never a stray mongrel nor a bird with a wounded wing, but what it wound up on board the *Olympia*, courtesy of Seaman McShane's tender heart. The boy might be lazy, unreliable, worth only half his sailor's pay, but how could one fault a kindhearted dreamer?

Captain Sinclair laughed humorlessly and said under his breath, "You were something of a dreamer yourself at one time, old boy."

He pushed those thoughts from his mind as quickly as they intruded. He was no dreamer these days. He had a ship to command and the last of his wayward crew to collect in time to set sail. His cargo was distasteful to him—human beings, bound for what they considered the "promised land." But he knew from experience that America could be a hard place for the unwary. There were no handouts, no streets paved with gold. And the voyage across the Atlantic was a near hell for most. He wondered how many of the poor devils who had booked passage knew that the owner of the *Olympia* planned to make a killing on this crossing by turning his vessel into a "coffin ship," a term grimly used by survivors who had made similar voyages.

Sinclair had considered throwing the owner's orders back in his greedy face. But, after all, he was only the captain. If he began letting ethics get in the way of his job, he might as well turn in his sextant and navigational charts and settle down in Georgia on the long-neglected land he'd inherited from his vagabond father. He wondered if any of the people on the *Olympia* would be bound for those same rice lands . . . if any of them would survive to see Georgia, if that was their destination.

Sinclair made an angry sound deep in his throat. "You think too much, damn ye! That's your whole problem!" he grumbled, pushing open the tavern door to breathe in a fog of blue pipe smoke and ale fumes.

They all stared at him—the crofters, the sailors from other ships, even the fly-by-nights. It was always so in a Scottish tavern. This was home turf, not to be violated easily by outsiders. Of course, any outsider could become an insider with an hour's friendly conversation and a few rounds of good cheer. Still, the entering of the fold was not a step to be taken lightly. Just as if he were sailing on a new ship, there were certain formalities to be observed before he would be accepted by the crew of The Black Dagger.

"Help you, mister?" the burly proprietress demanded unsmilingly as she swabbed the bar.

Hugh Sinclair could feel forty eyes crawling over him, from his sea boots to his coal-black hair, as he stepped up to the bar and ordered a tankard of ale. The lady barkeep slid the potion down the polished oak to him without sloshing so much as a dram. He hauled it up in his big fist, saluted her, then drank deeply.

"Ah-h-h! That's good!" he said to no one in particular.

Still feeling the hair on his neck crawl from the stares aimed at his back, he swung around quickly to catch the curious at their work. But not an eye in the place was turned his way. He smiled all around and raised his tankard to the seemingly disinterested customers.

"Better to be the head o' the commons than the tail o' the gentry!" he called out in a toast, but only strained silence greeted his cheer.

"Aye, laddie! Here's to ye!" a bull of a man answered back at length, raising his own mug. "You'll be from 'the land of the stranger Gaels' by the look of ye."

"A Galloway man indeed, and proud of it!" Sinclair answered. "Might I buy you a drink, friend?"

"Any man who calls Cully MacCullough 'friend' deserves a drink on the house," the Highlander said. "Elspeth, me darlin', refill the man's tankard." He waved an arm as thick as a gatepost in an expansive gesture. "And all the rest as well!"

"Fine with me, Cully," the woman replied, leaning over the bar to tug at the big man's red chin whiskers. "Just so long as you're buyin'. I'm only a poor widder woman, trying to keep me wee ones from starving. If the wolf weren't right at me door, you know I'd be pleased to see the house in ale."

"Ah, Elspeth love, you're breaking me poor ole heart," Cully answered mournfully. Then, leaning over to whisper in Hugh Sinclair's ear, he said, "The woman has a heart cold as a witch's tit! 'Tis my guess she keeps bags of gold in her root cellar."

"I heard that, Cully MacCullough!" Elspeth said with a wink and a wide grin. "But you'll never find out for sure, will you? My root cellar's the next to last place I'd allow you to visit—after me bed, of course!"

Hugh Sinclair and the entire clientele of The Black Dagger roared their approval of the woman's retort.

Cully elbowed his new friend in the ribs and winked broadly. "A tongue that would clip a hedge, that one!"

The next hour passed pleasantly enough. Cully loved a good story and a good mugful to go along with it. As he put it to Hugh, "It's a dry tale that doesna end in a drink." The others soon gathered round to join in the yarn-spinning, making sure that each tale topped the one told before it. At last, comfortable in the knowledge that he was accepted, Hugh turned to the business at hand.

"Cully, my friend, I'm looking for someone."

"Aye, Hugh, me boy, aren't we all?" He spoke the words with a longing glance in Elspeth's direction.

"No, this would be a lad. A sailor off my ship, but more than that. He's been like my own son since his father died. I promised my friend while he was breathing his last that I'd see his boy to manhood and keep him on the right track. But I'm afraid he's always been one to stray. I heard he may be helping out on one of the crofts hereabouts. There was some sort of accident . . ."

"Ah, you'll be meaning young Rory McShane," Cully answered. "An upstanding lad, indeed!"

"You know him, then?" Sinclair asked excitedly.

"I do!" Cully replied importantly. "I'm invited to his wedding the day after tomorrow."

"His wedding?" Sinclair slammed his tankard down on the bar and jumped to his feet.

"Aye! And a comely lass he's gettin' for his bride, name of Anna Rose Mackintosh."

Hugh Sinclair was already headed for the door. "Can you tell me where to find Seaman McShane right now? I've got to stop this wedding."

But Cully followed and caught the captain's arm, squinting hard at him. "Hold on now! Unless the lad's got himself a wife already, you have no call to be interfering. The Mackintoshes are fine folk, and Anna Rose is the pick of their litter. I'll not see the lad's heart broken by an outsider!"

"Better by me than by some scheming woman!" Sinclair answered with an edge of bitterness in his voice.

Cully's eyes flashed a warning. "Do I detect a love gone wrong in your own past, me friend?"

"That's one tale I'm not willing to tell," Sinclair answered, trying not to think of the girl with the roving eye and roaming affections he'd planned to wed so long ago.

"I see," Cully answered, nodding sagely. "Dinna speak o' a rope to a child whose father was hanged, eh? You'll not allow the lad to wed because you've run afoul of a woman yourself."

"You don't understand, Cully. My ship sails for America three days from now and Rory McShane will be on it. I'll carry no women on the *Olympia*, other than those who have paid their passage."

Cully turned away from Hugh Sinclair and cast his gaze about the tavern. "A kindhearted sonuvabitch, ain't he, mates?"

His words were answered by a general grumbling among the other customers. Hugh Sinclair began to feel uneasy. For a moment he imagined that his own head might soon be mounted above the bar next to the one that had once sat atop the shoulders of a handsome elk stag. But Elspeth saved him.

"Hold on there, boys!" she boomed in a boatswain's voice. "I'll have no bloodletting in my establishment."

"Thank you, Elspeth!" Captain Sinclair said under his breath.

She shot him a hard look. "Widow Gray to you, my fine scoundrel!" she snapped. "Thanks be, my own dearly departed mister had no 'friend' the likes of you or I'd doubtless be a shriveled old maid today! Why, if you knew that sweet girl herself, you'd be beggin' to give the bride away instead of acting the bully to save your young mate!"

Hugh eyed Elspeth closely. "You know this Mackintosh woman, then?"

Elspeth drew herself up with an air of importance. "Well, I should hope I do! Know the whole clan, but Anna Rose best of all. Every market day since she was knee-high she's brought me eggs and butter, right to my door. Saved me a many a weary step, she has. And she'll not disappoint me tomorrow, not even on the very eve of her nuptials."

"Tomorrow, you say?" Hugh's interest was piqued.

"Aye!" Elspeth nodded until her graying red curls bobbed about her plump face. "She'll be here! I've her word on it."

Hugh looked down at the bar and toyed with his empty mug, a plan taking shape in his quick mind.

"I say we throw the bloody bastard out in the storm!" someone yelled from the back of the room.

The tavern patron's suggestion was followed by grumbled agreement from all sides.

"Now listen to what I have to say, all of you," Elspeth shouted above the din. "Captain Sinclair will have a change of heart once he sees young Rory and his Anna Rose being wed. I say, we put him up here until time for the wedding—so as to keep an eye on him—then take him along to the nuptials with us. My guess is he won't be making any trouble for anyone."

"Aye!" the customers chorused.

Hugh Sinclair gave the crowd a challenging glance, scowling under his dark, shaggy brows. But it was only for the sake of appearances. It would never do to let them think he was less than hostile to the suggestion. He had no intentions of fighting them. Actually, they'd played right into his hands. He fully intended to stay put, to be here when the butter-and-eggs girl arrived the next morning. Not only would he see her for himself, this great love of Rory's life, but he'd have a few choice words to say to her as well. He doubted very much that he'd be attending her wedding after that.

As soon as the Widow Gray and her cronies saw that Captain Sinclair had no intentions of resisting their plan, the tavern's atmosphere returned to normal. Elspeth refilled Hugh's tankard and he settled in to a long night of waiting.

He spent the time mulling over exactly what he would say to Miss Anna Rose Mackintosh. One thing was certain, he had to stop this wedding! Rory was too young to know his own heart. Hugh couldn't allow him to ruin his life by rushing into a hasty match that would doubtless sour on him as fast as milk turns to clabber in the summer heat. There had to be a way to get young McShane out of this, and Hugh Sinclair considered himself just the man to do it.

Anna Rose was late leaving the market square to deliver the Widow Gray's eggs and butter. The whole town knew of her coming marriage and everyone wanted to offer good wishes. By the time she'd packed her basket with two large cakes of butter and a dozen fresh brown eggs, Anna Rose was in a grand mood. The state of matrimony, she decided, must truly be wonderful for everyone to share such excitement over it.

Only one person marred the perfection of the morning. Iris, red-eyed and sullen, presided over their stall without a word to her older sister. There had been quite a row in their parents' bedroom the evening before. Although Anna Rose herself had not been present when her mother and father told Iris of the match they'd made, one needn't have been in the room to hear the younger girl's shrieks of outrage. And since that time, Iris had ignored her sister and Rory entirely, as if they were both ghosts she could neither see nor hear.

Before heading off to The Black Dagger, Anna Rose turned to Iris, making one final attempt. "It will be for the good of all of us, you know? And it's not as if I set out to take him from you. Love just happens."

For the first time, Iris looked directly at her sister, but her gray eyes were cold and her face was hard with bitterness. "You might as well save your breath. If I wanted him, I could still have him. But he's not worth it. Believe me, you'll rue the day you promised to marry him." Iris smiled unpleasantly. "Actually, I think the two of you deserve each other. I'll be more than glad to see the both of you sail off to America! In fact, I'm counting the days!"

With that, Iris turned her back on Anna Rose, killing some of the bright day's joy. Anna Rose sighed and lifted her basket, then headed down the road. Her relationship with her sister had never been good. She knew finally that it would never get any better. But she squared her shoulders and lifted her head to the morning breeze. She refused to allow Iris to spoil this day for her.

Hugh had been pacing his small room above the tavern. He glanced at the clock on the mantelpiece. Almost noon! The girl was late. *Fine!* he thought. That was one mark against her. If she never showed up, that would be another. She had promised Elspeth she'd be here.

He stood at the window, one large hand braced against the sill, and stared down at the busy road below. Crofters with wagons pulled by tired-looking horses trudged to and from the market. A group of ragtag children played a raucous game of stickball just below.

Suddenly, Hugh's eyes focused on a lone figure coming toward the inn. The sun struck her hair, making it gleam like bronze fire. She was a tall girl, elegant of frame and carriage. By her bare feet and the stem binding her hair, he knew she was a maiden.

"A bonny lass," he said to himself, smiling as he watched the gentle sway of her skirt in rhythm to her step.

He continued to stare as she drew ever nearer, forgetting for the moment that he had a dire purpose with another maiden this morning. Then, as she paused directly below him at the very door of The Black Dagger, his mind snapped back. This was not just

36

any pretty maid on market day, to be admired as he would. Look at the plaid of the Tonag shawl about her shoulders—none other than the bright red and green of Clan Mackintosh! And wasn't that an egg basket on her slender arm?

As she disappeared below, Hugh rushed into the upstairs hallway. From down in the taproom, he could hear Elspeth's gravelly voice. "Well, my dear, you've come at last! I'd feared you'd forgot me in all the excitement."

A soft, feminine voice, like a gentle rain on a summer's eve, answered her. "I'd not be forgetting your order, Mistress Gray. How many years has it been? It makes me sad to think this will be my last visit. But come next market day, I'll be on my way to America."

"A married woman, too!" Elspeth added in a voice filled with dreams.

"Yes, Mrs. Rory McShane!" came the girl's wistful answer. "Can you believe it?"

Hugh made an angry sound in his throat, as Elspeth added, "The lad has no idea how lucky he is!"

Lucky that I'm going to get him out of this! Hugh thought.

"I've left tea and scones for you in the little parlor, Anna Rose, like always. Do go and help yourself while I put these things away."

"Thank you, Mistress Gray."

Hugh waited only long enough to be sure that Elspeth had left before he headed downstairs. He moved quietly to the door of the parlor behind the taproom. There she sat, sipping tea and smiling as she nibbled daintily at a scone. Hugh had not been mistaken. She was a beauty, the kind of woman every man dreams of, but few have luck enough to marry. Be that as it may, his mission was set.

Anna Rose, alone in the Widow Gray's parlor, was a million miles away. Well, several thousand at the very least. She was with her husband, sailing across a calm azure sea, with America gleaming golden on the horizon before them. She couldn't be sure if it was a sound or merely the feeling of someone watching her that made her start from her daydream. She turned quickly to find a tall, dark-haired stranger standing in the doorway watching her. He wore canvas britches and sea boots and his broad chest was covered with a fisherman's sweater. A sailor off one of the ships in port, no doubt.

"If you're looking for Mistress Gray, she's gone to the pantry,"

Anna Rose offered, feeling uneasy at the way the man looked at her.

"No," he answered in a slow, rough drawl. "I believe I've found the person I'm seeking. You are Anna Rose Mackintosh?"

Startled that the stranger knew her, she only nodded, her teacup poised in midair.

A long pause followed as the man continued his thorough observation of her. Finally, to break the silence, Anna Rose set her cup down with more force than was necessary.

The stranger cleared his throat and moved into the room. "Forgive me for staring, Miss Mackintosh, but you are quite pleasant to look at."

She cared neither for his forthright manner, nor the way his midnight eyes sent little shivers along her spine.

Anna Rose stood up and moved away from him. "Sir, if you don't mind, I'd like you to leave. I don't believe we've been introduced properly."

"Ah, once more you must forgive my lack of manners. I can see now how a lad like Rory could easily lose his wits when in your presence. You've quite disarranged his mind, I'm afraid."

Anna Rose felt more confused than ever. "You know Rory?"

"Indeed! I am Captain Hugh Sinclair, master of the *Olympia*."

Sinking back down into her chair, Anna Rose laughed with relief. "You gave me such a start, Captain. I thought you were one of the tavern customers. And I've been warned to say clear of that sort."

A slow, cynical smile parted Hugh's lips as he thought that Rory had been warned to stay clear of *her* sort as well.

"I hope you'll be at our wedding, Captain Sinclair. Rory would be so pleased. I don't think he knows that you're in town."

Hugh helped himself to the seat across the table from Anna Rose. God, how the girl glowed when she spoke of Rory! He'd often wished some fair woman would sparkle that way for him.

Hugh put his hands on the table and stared down at them, trying to frame his words. At length, he looked up and said, "Anna Rose, I'm afraid that I won't be at your wedding. In fact, if you think calmly and rationally about it, I believe you'll call the whole thing off while there's still time. It would be to your advantage."

Anna Rose felt the blood draining from her face. There was a roaring in her ears from the pounding of her heart. She couldn't be sure she'd heard him correctly.

"I beg your pardon, sir?"

"The wedding, I think you should reconsider. I understand how Rory's head could have been turned by a woman as pretty as you.

38

It's not the first time it's happened. But you'll get no bargain by marrying Seaman McShane. You could have any man of your choosing. Don't tamper with young Rory this way.''

Anna Rose was on her feet, caught between fury and disbelief. "You needn't try to belittle my betrothed in my eyes. I don't want any other man. Rory is the one I choose. And don't you mean *First Mate* McShane, Captain?''

Hugh laughed humorlessly and shook his head. "So he's been at it again, has he? My dear young lady, apparently there are many things that your intended has failed to confide to you, his true status on board my ship being one of them. Rory is no more than a common deckhand. He may never be more than that. I'm afraid his skills at seamanship are sadly lacking, along with his facility for the truth.''

"I don't care what you say about him. I love Rory and I'm going to marry him. We're planning to start a new life together in America!''

His eyes narrowed as he stared directly into her face. "And just how do you plan to get to America, young lady?''

"On board the *Olympia*, of course! Rory has made all the arrangements.''

"*My* ship?" He laughed maddeningly. "Strange then that I know nothing about these 'arrangements,' don't you think?''

Anna Rose was on the verge of tears now. Rory had spoken so warmly of his captain, whom he thought of almost as a father. How could this cold man say such things about her Rory? She didn't want to hear any more. She refused to listen!

Turning quickly, she headed for the door. But Hugh caught her wrist and brought her up hard against his chest. She could feel his heart beating next to hers, feel the heat of his loins. She fought to get out of his grasp, but it was no use. The man had her at his mercy.

Anna Rose stared up at him, as afraid as she was angry, but oddly fascinated. There was a sort of magnetism about the man. No wonder Rory was taken in by him. She stopped fighting him as she watched his heavy-lidded eyes narrow. His lips drew back in a hard line, then moved to form words.

"Has he bedded you?" he demanded.

Anna Rose gasped. How dare he? She refused to dignify his question with an answer. She said instead, "I don't see that that's any of your concern, Captain!''

"Perhaps not, but Rory McShane is my concern. I won't see him hurt. I can't believe a woman like you could care so deeply for a mere lad. There's a fire in you that won't be satisfied very easily. It will take a man, a *real* man, to give you what you need, Anna Rose Mackintosh."

Her fury flared. "And I suppose you consider yourself man enough?"

"Perhaps, Anna Rose," he whispered huskily. "Perhaps I am!"

Her face was flaming. Her whole body was burning. Never had any man spoken to her this way or treated her in such a fashion. And all the while he held her against his hard body, forcing her to feel his heat, his need for a woman . . . for *her*, she realized with a horrible sense of fascination. She couldn't deny that his nearness brought changes in her—frightening, dizzying, dangerous changes. Her breasts ached, her thighs throbbed, her legs had grown almost too weak to hold her.

"Please, Captain . . ." Her words trailed off.

He laughed deeply. "Mrs. Rory McShane, eh? Well, we'll see, won't we? I don't think you'll go through with it. I believe you are wise enough to see that it would be wrong, for all of us."

She wanted to deny his words, to tell him that she had no idea what he meant, but she had no breath left, no will of her own as he held her. His face hovered over hers as she felt his warm breath on her lips. Her head was spinning, her whole body trembling.

An instant before he would have captured her lips in a kiss she both longed for and dreaded, Elspeth Gray called from the taproom, "Anna Rose, are you still here?"

Hugh Sinclair released her, but with great reluctance. The woman had fit in his arms as if she were born to be there. Only once before in his whole life had he met such a prize as Anna Rose. She, too, had wed another. Somehow, someday, he would have Anna Rose for his own, he vowed wildly. Were she to be the bride of any other man alive, he would move heaven and earth to stop the wedding. But she belonged to Rory, *she loved Rory*. Could he bring himself to do it? Only time would tell the outcome of this meeting.

"I must be going now, Mistress Gray." Hugh heard Anna Rose's lilting tones from what seemed a great distance away. And then she was gone. He was alone in a room that suddenly seemed darker, drearier for want of her presence. He slumped down in the chair and ran his fingers through his hair, sighing wearily.

As for Anna Rose, she all but ran from the tavern and from the strange man who had awakened some dark longing in her soul.

"Rory, Rory, Rory . . ." She repeated his name over and over as she fled back to the market. He would be waiting for her at the croft. Rory with his gentle nature, Rory with his simple ways, his loving words for her alone. Two days and they would be married. Nothing on earth could stop that. Nothing else on earth mattered.

She would force Captain Hugh Sinclair and his lies and his accusations from her mind. She decided not even to tell Rory she had met him. He was dangerous. He was wicked. He was like no other man she had ever met, and, she hoped, like none that she would ever meet again.

Even Iris's sour countenance seemed a welcome sight when she reached the stall in the marketplace. With great effort, Anna Rose forced a smile for their customers. When the sun finally began to set and she and Iris headed home in the wagon, she was almost calm once again.

5

The morning of the wedding arrived bright blue and shining clean. Anna Rose had awakened at dawn to watch the night give blazing birth to her wedding day. As was the custom, she walked out onto the meadow in the early light and washed her face in the May dew. Never again would she perform this maiden's ritual, and her wish this morning was not the one she had whispered for years: "Let my lover find me!" but a new version: "Let my husband love me!" The very words sent a thrill of anticipation through her.

Now the hour was approaching. Already she wore her bride's gown of white lawn and lace. Her hair, combed and gleaming, hung down her back in a single, thick braid, and her head was crowned by a halo of heather, thistle, and rosebuds.

She stood waiting by her bed, hearing from outside the sound of pipes and fiddles being tuned and balladeers testing their voices. Wagons and carts rumbled into the stable yard as the guests for the "penny wedding" arrived. There would be forty guests in all, the number allowed by the Kirk. Every one of them would bring food, drink, or pennies to pay the pipers.

All was in readiness. Only Iris's disappearance threatened to spoil the celebration. She might have been counted on to pull one of her tantrums today of all days! Anna Rose tried not to think about it, even as she tried to ignore her thoughts of Rory's captain.

"Daughter, are you ready?" Margaret Mackintosh said from the other side of the curtain.

"I think so, Mama. Any news of Iris yet?"

41

"Don't fret about your sister!" her mother commanded. "We aren't going to let her spoil this fine day. She'll slink home with her tail between her legs, right enough. And she's not too big for a switching, when that time comes. I've had all of her bullheadedness I intend to take."

"You know she wanted Rory," she answered wistfully. Anna Rose still had difficulty realizing he would soon be hers.

"But he wanted you! Come along now. You have to let your papa see you before we go out to the others. And, for goodness' sakes, smile, girl! You look as if you're going to your own funeral instead of your wedding."

"Yes, Mama." Anna Rose let a smile light her face as she pushed all thoughts of Iris to the back of her mind. Her mother was right. There had never been anything serious between her sister and Rory. It had all been a figment of Iris's imagination. But the love that had blossomed between herself and the blue-eyed sailor was very truly real, in spite of what Captain Sinclair thought. She had every right to smile, to laugh, to rejoice on her wedding day.

Rory McShane waited in the yard, from time to time stopping his restless pacing to speak to an arriving guest. He knew why he was so ill at ease. It was that Iris! At first, he'd been relieved when she'd lit it out after hearing the news of his plans to marry Anna Rose. It was easier not to have to face her today. Damn, he felt guilty! But, what could he do? He didn't love her any more than she loved him. What bothered him most was his fear that she might try to get even. What if she turned up and told all just in time to spoil his marriage to Anna Rose?

"Rory!" a familiar voice hailed.

He turned quickly, too surprised to believe his ears. Hugh Sinclair? Could it be?

"Captain!" he cried delightedly. "How the hell did you find out I was getting married?"

"Never mind that. I've come to tell you that you aren't! I don't know how you got yourself into this mess, but I'm here as usual to bail you out. She is with child, I presume."

Rory only laughed and shook his head. "I've yet to touch the lass. But soon, I hope, she'll be carrying our first of many sweet babes."

Hugh Sinclair stared hard at him. He didn't believe a word of it. He knew Rory McShane for the ladies' man he was. Twice before the lad had headed for the altar half-cocked. Hugh had extracted the boy from those messy affairs, and somehow he would save

42

him again. Three times, after all, was supposed to be a charm. Maybe Rory would learn his lesson after this near-miss. Besides, Hugh had more reason than ever for talking Rory out of this match after his own meeting with Anna Rose.

Hugh glanced about, eyeing musicians, wedding guests, and the waiting parson. Things had gone a bit further than he'd meant them to this time. But he'd get his young friend out of here somehow and haul him back to the ship where he belonged. As for Anna Rose . . .

"Captain, I love her!" Rory's words broke into Hugh's thoughts.

Hugh took Rory by the shoulders as if he meant to shake some sense into him. "You can't be serious, lad!"

Rory steered his captain toward a quiet corner near the barn. They sat down on a bale of fresh, sweet hay.

"I want Anna Rose Mackintosh more than I've ever wanted anything in my whole life, Captain. I swear, this marriage is going to make a new man of me. But I'd like your blessing." He waited for Sinclair to answer, but the man only stared at him, frowning a thundercloud of misgivings. "Wait till you see her. She's a wonder. I love her, Captain. Don't go against us, please."

"See here, Rory, it's only your best interest that I have at heart . . ."

Just then the skirling of the pipes rose to a new pitch. Both men looked up. Out of the front door of the stone cottage came the most beautiful woman Hugh Sinclair had ever set eyes on. The barefoot girl he'd held in his arms at The Black Dagger had been transformed into a vision. He gazed, transfixed, as Anna Rose moved among the crowd with a curtsy, a smile, and an extended hand for each guest. She caught his eye, frowned for a moment, then bestowed a pleading gaze on him with her liquid, gray-green eyes. His resolve to stop the marriage crumbled. He swallowed several times, trying to find his voice.

"She makes a lovely bride, Rory."

"Aye, Captain! Can you believe she'll be my wife?"

"Frankly, no!" Sinclair answered. He thought the whole matter through for several minutes. In spite of his beginnings, Rory was a good lad. Hugh had promised to watch over him as if Rory were his own son. And if Hugh had a son, he'd want just such a woman as Anna Rose Mackintosh to be the lad's bride. Hell, who was he trying to kid? The truth was, if Hugh himself ever took a wife, he could do no better than Anna Rose! He forced the thought away quickly. He had no right to deprive these two of their happiness.

"Very well. I'll give you my blessing, but we sail tomorrow, on schedule!"

"Tomorrow?"

"You heard me, lad. And you'll be shipping out alone."

"But, Captain, I can't! I promised Anna Rose I'd take her to America. I promised her whole family."

Hugh Sinclair glanced again at the lovely, fragile-looking bride. She might look the frail female, but something about the set of her shoulders and the proud tilt of her head bespoke a wealth of strength and maturity. Hadn't she shown him the depth of her determination at their first meeting?

New resolve gripped him suddenly. He couldn't do this to Rory. Anna Rose Mackintosh was too great a prize for either of them to leave behind. Sinclair searched his heart for another solution.

"What do you plan to do after we reach America, Rory?"

"I was figuring on jumpin' ship, turning landlubber again. See, me and Anna Rose want to get us a place in Georgia, and, well . . ." Rory looked down at his feet, blushing from the high collar of his black wedding suit to his carefully combed hair. "She loves kids and so do I. I figured we'd get right to work on it."

"Then I take it you really haven't started already?"

"Captain!" Rory protested. "I'd never! Not with Anna Rose, not till after the vows are spoke." He squirmed uneasily, thinking again of Iris and his less than scrupulous behavior where she was concerned.

"All right, lad. I have a plan, if you're willing to trust me."

"You mean Anna Rose can come?"

Hugh Sinclair slapped the happy bridegroom on the back and gave a hearty laugh, secretly pleased at the thought of having such a lovely woman close at hand during the long voyage to America. That, at least, would be some consolation. "Aye! Now go to your love and do what has to be done. We three have a ship to catch!"

Suddenly, the pipers' music changed. Anna Rose, who had been greeting guests, felt more than heard the altered tones. The deeper notes throbbed through her, bringing a sweet ache to her heart and tears of happiness to her eyes.

She glanced uncertainly toward Hugh Sinclair, fear clutching at her that he still might make some move to mar the day. He wasn't smiling, but, when he saw the pleading look she gave him, he nodded to her ever so slightly. A great weight lifted from her at that moment. The time had really come!

She looked around, but her search for her groom was brief. Rory was there at her side, his boyish face as solemn as the wedding song, his hand extended to receive her own. She reached out to him hesitantly, almost as if the joining of their hands would seal the sacred bond. His fingers clasped hers with such a warm, caressing touch that she felt the gentle contact deep down inside.

"You'll truly be my wife, then, Anna Rose?" He asked the question softly, so that only she would hear.

She wanted to throw her arms around him and smother him with kisses in answer. But she controlled her impetuous urge. Instead, her quiet tone matched his as she replied, "Yes, Rory, and love you well, I will!"

As her groom led her toward the waiting parson, Anna Rose felt as if she were crossing some invisible threshold. She was no longer a girl, but a woman grown—a woman cherished by the man she loved with all her heart and soul. She held her head higher and gripped Rory's hand with a new strength, born of loving and sharing.

And just as we are this minute, Anna Rose thought reverently, *so we shall journey through life together, clinging to each other from this day forward*.

Then the parson began his preamble to the joining and the bridal couple focused their attention on him. The wedding took place according to the solemn custom of the country. Rory and Anna Rose, both kneeling on a white satin pillow during part of the ceremony, exchanged their vows of everlasting love and faithfulness beside the brown stream's flowing water, an age-old symbol of eternity. Between them they held a Bible, pledging their troth on its holy words.

Margaret Mackintosh smiled on with pride. Watching from the window beside his bed, Anna Rose's father found himself weeping at the beauty of the occasion and the thought of losing his favorite child. The younger Mackintosh children fidgeted, twisted, dug the toes of their good shoes into the earth, and, in general, behaved as children will at weddings.

Only Iris watched, unseen, from a distant hillock, her heart filled with hateful schemes. Maybe she was carrying Rory's baby and maybe she wasn't. But she *would* have a child. And, when the time was right, she would tell Anna Rose and Rory her own opinion regarding the identity of the baby's father.

"Oh, you'll pay all right, dear sister!" The words hissed from her lips. Then she turned toward Inverness, calculating her next move.

But Anna Rose was aware of nothing outside the shining aura of happiness about her and her groom. This was a moment of pure magic and total joy, a moment she would always remember.

The instant the parson said his final amen the fiddler broke into music for the bridal reel and the pipers soon wailed in.

Anna Rose felt the touch of her new husband's hand on her own all the way to her heart. The music was sweeter, the sunshine warmer, her friends and family more dear than they had ever been in her life.

Rory led his bride to the center of the circle of guests and musicians to have the first dance. It was a traditional kissing dance in honor of the wedded couple. When Rory leaned forward and touched Anna Rose's lips with his, her heart provided its own music. But in the next instant, they were whirling and twirling, putting on the show of their lives.

Hugh Sinclair was sure that Anna Rose was oblivious to the fact that his eyes followed her every move. She couldn't know the long-suppressed emotions and urges that her dancing—the very sight of her—stirred in him. Nor could she guess the doubts raging in his heart. Was he arranging to take Anna Rose to America for her husband's sake or for his own?

He'd sworn off women long ago, when the great passion of his life turned sour. Granted, he still had the needs of any red-blooded male, the kind that could be satisfied in any port. But love and a wife were thoughts he had long since put from his mind. So it was totally baffling to him how the mere sight of young Mrs. McShane, her lithe body swaying to the music and her gray-green eyes shining with love for her new husband—could so affect him. She aroused sensations he thought he had long since forgotten. He tried to tell himself it was pride he felt, the pride of a father on his son's wedding day. But the emotions that Anna Rose awakened in Hugh were far from appropriate for a father-in-law.

"Captain!" Rory called. "Come take your turn with my bride."

Sinclair's great urge to do just that, in more than the dance, proved too much for him. Pretending not to hear Rory's invitation, he stalked off toward the barn where ale was being served to the men.

Anna Rose, in spite of all the excitement of the day, had been quite aware of Captain Sinclair's close scrutiny. The way the man looked at her was at the same time intriguing and almost frightening, just as it had been at the tavern. She wondered what he was thinking, why he kept staring at her with such an odd expression of joy and sadness in his night-black eyes.

"Captain!" Rory called after him.

Anna Rose laid a hand of caution on her husband's sleeve. "Please, Rory," she begged, "leave your captain be."

She was confused by her reaction when Hugh Sinclair failed to hear Rory's second summons. Both relief and disappointment mingled within her. She forced herself to dismiss the man from her mind. This was her wedding day. She would allow neither Iris's behavior nor Captain Sinclair's bold, unsettling gaze to intrude upon her happiness.

Anna Rose smiled up at her tall husband, staring into his clear blue eyes. He made love to her with the gaze he returned, and, suddenly, she felt herself trembling in his arms as a deep longing rose within her.

"Oh, Rory, my dearest," she sighed.

The next moment, his lips came down to touch hers, transporting her to a place far away from the rest of the world, locking the two of them tightly, warmly, in a secret universe all their own.

The pipers and the fiddlers played on and on. The women spread great roasted piles of game, fat loaves of bread, and cakes glistening with sugar and honeyed nutmeats on groaning boards set in the shade of a copse beside the stream. Anna Rose, of course, danced every dance, with little time to think of food, drink, or even her new status of wife.

"I'll wear my slippers right through," she called to her mother as her partner whirled her past.

When the couple came round again, Margaret Mackintosh replied, "Then I'll fetch you another pair, Daughter." They both laughed, and the bride danced on.

Meanwhile, the groom and his captain had found a quiet spot, away from the happy throng. They sipped their ale while they discussed the business at hand, sailing for America.

"You have money to pay her passage, of course," Hugh Sinclair said.

"Her passage?" Rory's head shot up quickly and a flush of embarrassment suffused his cheeks. Then his gaze dropped to the toes of his boots, avoiding the captain's eyes. "I hadn't thought of that," he muttered ashamedly.

"And did you think I'd take her on out of the goodness of my heart, Rory? Lad, you *don't* think! That's your whole problem." Captain Sinclair realized suddenly that he'd been storming at the boy and forcibly lowered his voice to a gruff roar. "Even if I wanted to give her free passage, I've the *Olympia*'s owner to answer to."

"There's the money her folks are owing me for the past weeks' work I've put in." Rory shook his head and swiped at his stray forelock, at the same time squaring his shoulders. "But I'll not take it! They'll be bad off enough when I leave, with no one but those two scamps, Cullen and Ewan, to see to the running of the place."

Hugh Sinclair eyed his young friend with renewed respect. He still thought Rory had been foolish to take a bride when he hadn't a Birmingham copper to his name or any plan of action. But, a certain amount of dignity shone through when he set his jaw and straightened his spine. However, it took more than a loftiness of spirit to put bread on the table.

"That's very noble of you, Rory, but it's not going to buy your bride a berth on the *Olympia*. Were it my own ship, I'd bring her along without another thought or a farthing paid. But, as I've already pointed out, the owner's agent will be waiting at the South Street docks when we reach New York. He'll count every head—man, woman, child, and rat—that comes off the ship. Her passage must be accounted for."

"I know," Rory replied lamely. Then he looked up at Hugh Sinclair with his most beguiling smile. "You wouldn't want to be giving me a wee advance on my wages, now would you, Captain?"

Sinclair let his expression go dark and threatening. It would be the simple way out for him to pay Anna Rose's fare, letting her husband off the hook. But no! Now was the time for Rory to learn responsibility, if he was ever going to. Besides, against his better judgment, Hugh had advanced Rory over half his wages for the upcoming voyage already. Enough was enough!

"I promised your stepfather I'd see you grown, not wet-nurse you through life, boy! If you're man enough to take a wife, you should be man enough, by God, to take proper care of her!"

An uncomfortable silence stretched between them. Both men found their eyes straying to the spirited bride, who was doing her best at the moment to keep up with a rather drunken Cully MacCullough. Elspeth, the barmaid, stood by, cheering them on in a lusty voice. Anna Rose's face was prettily flushed. Her eyes glittered with happiness.

"A bonny lass," Sinclair said as much to himself as to Rory.

"Aye!" the groom replied. "Bonny indeed."

In the same quiet voice, the captain said, "There's a way, lad."

Rory looked up, but said nothing. He knew the explanation would come, all in Hugh Sinclair's good time.

"You said yourself you won't be with the crew on the return trip. You mean to head south and settle. Now think this over before you say yea or nay. I've heard of a certain absentee landowner in the very area you mentioned who is looking for a new man to oversee his acres and his workers. He might be willing to pay your indenture. I know what you're thinking, that you don't want to be bonded over to any man. But you'll get where you're going and be able to have Anna Rose with you. When your seven years are up, you'll be given tools, supplies, perhaps even your own plot of rice land free and clear.''

Hugh Sinclair saw no need to tell Rory, who would proudly refuse any charity, that he himself was the landowner and that the plantation where the young couple would go was his own neglected acreage near Darien, Georgia, land he had inherited and not seen since he was a boy.

"Well, Rory?"

The lad looked pained. "Would Anna Rose have to know?"

"She's your wife, man! Do you mean to begin your life together with secrets between you?"

Rory winced, thinking of the one great secret that must forever remain his alone. He only hoped Iris would never tell. The sooner he got Anna Rose on the ship, away from her sister, the better he would feel.

"Well, lad, what say you? Will you do the noble thing or hide the secret from your bride?"

"I want to do right by her. But for now," he begged, "couldn't I just sign the papers without her and her family's knowing? I'll tell her all about it before we reach America."

Sinclair sighed with relief. "You're willing then?"

Rory looked away from the captain, back toward his pretty bride. "I've little choice in the matter, have I?"

"There's one other thing, Rory."

The lad knew what was coming and he dreaded to hear it.

"The redemption papers." Sinclair's voice was grave. "You'll have to sign them as well, you know, to make it all legal."

"Aye," Rory whispered with a shudder. He'd viewed the auction of redemptioners on the New York docks. It was not an uplifting sight.

"Come now, my boy!" Sinclair said, slapping him good-naturedly on the back. "Nothing's going to happen to you in the crossing. You've made the trip before. Anna Rose will never be auctioned off as a bondwoman to redeem your debt, even if the worst should happen. You have my solemn word on that."

Rory still felt uneasy about it, but his friend's promise relieved him somewhat. "You'll take care of her, if anything should befall me? You'd even go so far as to marry her before you'd see her suffer?"

Sinclair frowned at the thought, which both troubled and

enticed him. "I hardly think you've a right to be deciding such matters for your bride. But, indeed, I would marry your Anna Rose to keep her from harm, lad. You've no cause for worry there."

Rory offered his hand and the two men shook on it. "Then it's a deal. You're a good friend, Hugh Sinclair."

"Rory, love!" Anna Rose called. "Come dance the last reel with me."

Hugh Sinclair's gaze darted toward the bride at the unexpected sound of her voice. Their eyes met. She blushed and quickly looked away. But not before she'd set Hugh's pulses pounding. God, she was a lovely creature!

"You come here first, darlin'," Rory called to her. "I've someone you haven't met yet, and news to tell."

So, Anna Rose thought, the time had finally come when she must face Hugh Sinclair again, the man with the bold stride and the bolder glance. She had begun to think that her husband had had second thoughts and meant to keep them apart for all time, probably for good reason. Of course, Rory knew nothing of their earlier meeting. She certainly hadn't told him and she gathered that the captain had chosen to keep his own counsel on the matter as well.

Anna Rose knew Hugh Sinclair did not approve of their marriage. Rory had warned her that they might see trouble from that quarter. She had been certain of it when he showed up at the wedding. Even Cully had confided to her that the captain had come here meaning to put a stop to the ceremony. But so far the man had kept very much to himself. She was glad. She wanted no disturbance on her wedding day. Besides, the way he had of staring darkly at her from afar was most unsettling, reviving thoughts of their other distressing encounter.

She smiled at her husband when she reached the two men, but she couldn't force herself to meet Hugh Sinclair's gaze. She felt shy with him, as if he knew the deepest secrets about her, secrets that even her husband didn't know.

"Darlin', this is Captain Hugh Sinclair," Rory said, beaming. "He'll be taking us to America."

Anna Rose dropped a pretty curtsy to the ship's master. He took her hand and brought it to his lips. Surprised, she looked up. His obsidian gaze, dark as night and sharp as a claymore's edge, held hers. She felt oddly weak under his intense scrutiny.

"Mrs. McShane, this is an honor." He said the words as if they were the first he had ever spoken to her.

She smiled at him gratefully. "Why, Captain, you're the very first to call me by my new name! Thank you. I love the sound of it.''

He released her hand with obvious reluctance, and she quickly slipped it into Rory's warm grasp.

"What is this news that can't wait, Rory?" she demanded.

"You'd better sit first, love," he said, hoisting her up onto a nearby stack of hay. "The captain's not here only to see us wed. He came to fetch me back to the ship. We sail tomorrow!"

"Oh!" Anna Rose cried. "Tomorrow?"

"Indeed we do, Mrs. McShane," Hugh replied. "So as soon as your celebration is done here, we'll be leaving for the *Olympia* to set sail for America."

"Then everything's been arranged?" she asked, eyeing Hugh warily.

"It has," he replied.

Both men stared at her expectantly, waiting for the good news to take hold and bring joyful exclamations.

Instead, Anna Rose's face fell suddenly. "But . . ."

Neither Rory nor his captain could guess what she had been about to say. Her cheeks flushed. Her lips moved, but she seemed unable to continue.

"What is it, Anna Rose?" Rory asked with genuine concern.

She gave Hugh Sinclair a nervous glance, then leaned down to whisper into her husband's ear.

Sinclair watched the frown smooth itself from Rory's face as his bride spoke. At the same time, Rory began to smile and his blue eyes sparkled with something akin to delight.

"Don't worry, darlin'," he whispered back to his bride. "We'll figure out some way."

But his words didn't prove much comfort to Anna Rose. How was their wedding night to be accomplished on board a ship ready to sail and overrun with sailors and immigrants? She didn't like to think of herself as anxious—that wouldn't be the least bit ladylike—but they'd be weeks in the crossing. She didn't think she could live with the anxiety of facing her wedding night and a new land all at once. Besides, she'd heard whispered tales among the older girls at the market that being with a man was more joy than trial, that what passed between a husband and wife in the privacy of the bedchamber was special. Certainly the love shown openly between her mother and father, after all their years of marriage, seemed proof of that. And, too, Rory, even with the slightest touch, stirred certain longings deep inside her that demanded to be satisfied.

"Maybe we could stay ashore at the inn tonight and board just before sailing in the morning," Rory said, thinking aloud.

Captain Sinclair suddenly realized the cause of Anna Rose's distress. He had been correct in his earlier observation; she was a woman of passion. Taking Rory by the elbow, he steered the groom a few feet away from Anna Rose so that their conference would cause her no further embarrassment.

"Rory, it's the wedding night that's worrying her, isn't it?"

"Aye. And I'll have to admit, me too! I hadn't looked forward to finding much privacy in the cottage here with her whole family, but the ship! God and all the old people will be watching our every move!"

"I'd like to let you put up at the inn tonight, but that's impossible. We must leave with the tide at first light tomorrow."

The disappointment showed plainly on Rory's face.

"But suppose I let the two of you have my own cabin tonight. Only for one night, mind you, but it will be easier for her. The first night's always a little rough on the bride, or so I've heard."

"Captain, you're a prince!" Rory shouted, throwing a bear hug on the other man. Then he yelled to his bride, "Darlin', it's all set! We'll bed down in the captain's cabin on board the *Olympia* for our wedding night!"

Everyone heard and cheered, much to Anna Rose's embarrassment. She could do nothing but cast a dark look her noisy husband's way and lift her head proudly, pretending to ignore the wedding guests' good-natured, but slightly suggestive, remarks.

She turned her eyes away, only to meet those of Captain Sinclair, who offered her a knowing smile.

The leave-taking was not easy. John Mackintosh put on a brave face, though Anna Rose could tell that he'd been weeping earlier. He clasped her gravely in his big arms and said, "You're a special one, Anna Rose McShane! And I couldna be prouder of you. Remember, wherever you and your husband go, that the land is what matters over everything else, except your love for each other. It will be hard at first. But look always to the future."

"I'll remember, Papa," she answered, fighting tears.

"Go then, with my blessing and God's. When we meet again, it will be in a fairer land."

Anna Rose could hardly bear the parting. By a "fairer land" had her father meant America or heaven? Somehow she knew the answer without asking and the pain tore at her heart.

Her mother and little sisters did not try to hide their tears, and even Cullen and Ewan sniffled a time or two. Only Iris missed the farewells. No one knew where she was or when she might return.

"Don't worry about Iris," Margaret Mackintosh told Anna

Rose. "She'll no doubt turn up before nightfall. And she'll be the first on the boat when the rest of us head for America. God, grant it will be soon!" she prayed softly.

"I'll send money, Mama," Anna Rose promised.

"Not and deprive yourself, you won't. We'll be fine. Now don't you worry. These big, strappin' lads of mine will learn how to work at last."

Margaret Mackintosh placed the Bible that had been a part of the ceremony into her daughter's hands. "I've pressed sprigs and blossoms from your wedding crown inside to remind you always of this day and of your home and family. Take care, my child, and know always that our thoughts and prayers are with you."

Moments later, the cart taking Anna Rose away was headed down the narrow, twisting road toward Inverness and the sea. She rode in silence, scarcely daring to trust any words past the lump in her throat. But as they wound along their way, and the salt sea air freshened in her face, Anna Rose felt thoughts of the past slipping away, replaced by plans for the future. And that future began here, now. She reached out and took Rory's hand in hers, giving it an affectionate squeeze. He smiled and leaned over to kiss her cheek.

"I'll be a long time loving you, Anna Rose McShane," he whispered.

"And I'll be just as long, my darlin'."

They had all but forgotten the captain was there until he said, "Ah, to be young again, and in love!" Hugh Sinclair sighed, offering Anna Rose a sly wink.

"You've been in love, then, Captain?"

She asked the question more to make conversation than out of any true curiosity. Still, there was no denying that Hugh Sinclair was a devilishly handsome man. She wondered that he had no wife and family. She guessed his age at something over thirty. Most men were well settled by their third decade, with bairns waist-high or better. Had he managed to escape the blissful bonds of wedlock by taking to the sea?

"Aye, lass," he answered at length. "I've known love, and more heartache than I care to remember because of it."

"I didn't mean to make you sad, Captain."

"Sadness lives with the man who's known an unfaithful woman," he said with an edge of bitterness in his voice.

"Your wife?" Anna Rose knew she was prying, but now she was curious. And, too, he seemed to want to talk about it.

"It didn't go that far, the saints be praised! We were altar-bound when my ship returned. But she couldn't find it in her fickle heart to wait that long. She ran off with a whaling man from New

Bedford, who left her with child when he sailed away on his final voyage. He was killed on a Nantucket sleighride, the boat smashed to smithereens by the fluke of the monster he'd harpooned. She came to me after his death and offered herself and his child to me for the taking. I loved her still, God help me! But once burned . . ." He let out another long, weary sigh. "Ah, Lil was a comely lass. Perhaps I should have married her. But I suppose it's better this way. Some things aren't meant to be."

Sinclair had been rambling on, indulging himself, since the lass seemed willing to listen. But when he looked at her and her eyes were bright with threatening tears, he said, "Here, now! None of that, Mrs. McShane! This is your wedding day—no time for weeping over ancient history. Some men are born to the sea and never meant to wed. That's the way it is with me, I suppose, and I'm not unhappy with my lot."

But even as he said the words, he knew that if ever a woman the likes of Anna Rose came into his life—willing and available—he would cast aside his seafaring ways in a minute to become whatever she desired him to be. Much ocean had slipped under the bow since any such thoughts had entered his mind. What was the girl? A witch off the moors? How could she stir a heart that had been nothing but dead ashes for the past ten, long years? Since he'd first spied her coming toward The Black Dagger, she'd haunted his thoughts. And why now did his mind keep going to the bunk in his cabin, that lonely, celibate bed, and thinking that after tonight it would never be the same? He knew that from now on whenever he laid his weary bones down at the end of a long day at sea, he would be conscious of Anna Rose's having been there, of her having known love for the first time in his own berth.

"There she is, Anna Rose!" Rory shouted gleefully. "The *Olympia*! Isn't she a beauty?"

"Oh, Rory! She's magnificent!"

Captain Hugh Sinclair, jolted from his dangerous reverie, almost laughed out loud. One would have thought that the pair of them were looking out at one of the sleek, American-made clippers of the Black Ball Line, instead of gazing upon this ancient, English tub—short, squat, and dirty. This would be his last employment with a Liverpool owner. He had captained enough years to move up in the world, perhaps buy his own ship with the money he'd saved and invested in New York. Even though he dreaded the voyage ahead, he would travel easier knowing that things would be different from now on.

Sinclair glanced over at the shining face and sparkling green eyes of the bride. He felt a lump in his throat suddenly and his pulses raced hectically. Having Anna Rose on board would help, too, he admitted to himself with a twinge of guilt.

Rory hopped off the cart and took down the bit of baggage he and Anna Rose had brought with them, leaving the captain to help his bride out of their less than fancy carriage.

"I can manage, Captain," Anna Rose said, shy about having this man touch her even if it was only a matter of courtesy, after the way his contact had affected her at the tavern.

"Please, let me," he insisted.

His fingers gripped her waist gently but firmly, and he lifted her out as if she were weightless. Though he set her on her feet with great care, the heel of her shoe lodged between two cobbles and she stumbled when he released her. His arms were around her again instantly, and he drew her close to steady her, almost as close as he'd held her that first time.

For the briefest moment, Anna Rose's cheek rested against his chest and she could feel the furious pounding of his heart. She looked up at him, directly into his troubled black eyes. Like a shock wave, it hit her. She realized in that instant that her husband was not the only man who saw her as desirable. Captain Hugh Sinclair's whole face read like the pages of a book, a tempestuous romantic novel. All his stored up love and pent up longing lay naked for her eyes alone. He had taunted her mercilessly at the inn. But his expression now frightened her even more. Still, at the same time, his gaze sent an odd thrill through her. It was as if their contact had unleashed some magnificently dangerous power within him, some force that had remained long dormant until this moment.

She took a step back, pushing out of his arms. "Please, no, Hugh," she whispered, wondering at her choice of words and her use of his Christian name.

"I can wait." His answer made her feel all the more wary and puzzled.

Then the spell was broken by a gang of noisy sailors from the ship. Anna Rose was cheered, hailed, and ogled while Rory was congratulated with handshakes and slaps on the back. The mob of sailors swarmed around them, blocking all else from view. Although Rory kept his arm protectively around her, silently threatening any shipmate who would dare touch his wife, the men seemed set on bestowing their good wishes on Anna Rose as well.

"Leave her be now, all of you!" Rory commanded.

"But we ain't had a go at kissin' the bride yet, Rory-boy!" a particularly large, rusty-bearded tar yelled.

Anna Rose cringed back against her husband, but the sailor

meant to have his kiss. It seemed that there was nothing Rory could do to stop the man.

The unshaven, dirty face loomed over hers, bearing down, the thick lips aimed point-blank for her protesting mouth. At the last second a stern voice commanded, "Belay that, Seaman Guilcher!"

The big man backed off at the sound of his captain's order. The others followed until they stood at a respectful distance and Anna Rose could catch her breath again.

"The party's over, my lads. Back to work with all of you!" Hugh Sinclair shouted. "We've only a few hours before we weigh anchor."

Anna Rose offered the captain a grateful smile, but he didn't return it. The look in his eyes was not far different from the lustful expression she had seen on the face of Seaman Guilcher.

"It's all right now, darlin'," she heard Rory saying. "Come on, love. I'll take you on board."

Though she could no longer see Hugh Sinclair as they climbed the gangway, she could still feel his eyes on her—caressing her, following her every move. Even if he was Rory's friend and superior, she knew she would have to keep her distance from him during the crossing to America. There was something in the man's expression that both beckoned her and warned her away.

"Step lively, Anna Rose!"

At the sound of her husband's voice, she forced her thoughts away from Hugh Sinclair. She smiled warmly and clasped Rory's outstretched hand.

"Lead the way, my darling."

6

The captain's cabin was not luxurious by shipboard standards. Like the vessel itself, the quarters were small, dark, and cramped. But Anna Rose, having nothing with which to compare it, thought the room a marvel, with its built-in chests and table and the oversized bunk below velvet-curtained windows. This was more space than all four Mackintosh sisters had shared at home.

After seeing her to the cabin, Rory claimed some "pressing

duties.'' Or perhaps he only left her so that she could prepare for his return and what would follow, thought Anna Rose. At any rate, she welcomed the quiet time alone. She knelt on the bunk, staring out the windows to sea. Squinting her eyes, she imagined she could see America, far off in the distance. But slowly darkness descended. At last, she had to give up her game of make-believe and return to the real world.

She opened the satchel her mother had quickly packed for her before they had left for the ship. Underneath the carefully wrapped packets of meat, bread, cheese, and the jars of honey and jam, she found a new, white nightgown. It was made of the softest linen and every stitch had been sewn in by her mother's loving hands. She had watched Margaret Mackintosh work on the fine garment for years. She could almost hear her mother's words right now: "I hope the occasion of its wearing brings you as much joy, Daughter, as the making of it has brought me."

Lighting one of the whale-oil lamps bolted to the bulkhead and drawing the curtains, Anna Rose shed her plaid skirt and waist. She poured water into the copper basin and bathed her face and neck, then slipped quickly out of her underthings and into the gown. It felt soft as swans' down against her bare skin, and the heather scent of the fabric soon filled the cabin as well.

A light knock at the door sent her hurrying to greet her husband. But it wasn't Rory. It was Hugh Sinclair.

"I don't mean to disturb you, Anna Rose."

He didn't say anything more for what seemed the longest time. He only stood there, looking at her, as if his gaze had melted away the snowy linen covering her form. She bit her tongue to keep from ordering him away from his own cabin, to keep from telling him that he was very much disturbing her!

"Captain?" she said at last, hoping to prompt him into stating his business.

He smiled in a nice way and said, "I liked it better when you called me Hugh."

"That was only a slip. I shouldn't have. I don't think it's proper. I don't feel comfortable."

"Then call me whatever you like. One name is as sweet as another from some lips, Anna Rose."

His staring was making her nervous. Suddenly, she realized she was wearing nothing at all but her thin nightgown and the lamp was burning brightly directly behind her. She stepped out of the golden path of light and reached to the bunk for a blanket to cover herself.

"Will Rory be here soon, Captain?"

57

His face stiffened. "That's what I came to tell you. He's been held up for a bit. But I thought you might like something to eat before . . ."

She was glad she had stepped into the shadows, where he couldn't see her face. She felt the blood rising and receding like the tide.

"Thank you, but my mother packed something for us. I'm sure we'll be fine."

Again, he offered her a strange smile, as if she'd made some jest without realizing it.

"I'm sure you will. But I won't let you refuse a bottle of my best French wine. Not on your wedding night."

"That would be lovely, thanks," she answered, having never tasted a drop of spirits in her life, but wanting desperately to end this conversation. "Now, if you'll please excuse me, Captain."

"Of course." He started to go, but turned back to her. "Anna Rose, if you need someone to talk to . . . later . . . I'll be on deck."

She really had no idea what he meant, but she thanked him and replied, "I have my husband to talk to, Captain."

"Then I'll say good night. And sweet dreams, Anna Rose."

He was gone before she could reply, leaving her with flaming cheeks and an uneasy fluttering in the pit of her stomach.

Anna Rose had time to work herself into a nervous state while waiting for Rory to arrive. She'd thought through carefully the few rudiments she knew about men, love, and the marriage bed, and she'd come to the distressing conclusion that she knew very little at all. How did one start? And what led to what, and how long did the entire procedure take? Would Rory know? Or would he expect her to have some knowledge, if not experience? Surely not! But then he would need to know something about what they were going to do. And how could he know anything unless he had done it before?

"Oh, no!" she cried aloud. "He couldn't! He wouldn't have! Not with another woman before me!"

She paced the cabin, too upset to be still. She had to stop thinking about it. Surely, nature would take its course and direct them. After all, men and women had been involved in begetting since the dawn of time. And judging from the world's present population, she thought, it couldn't be all that difficult.

Anna Rose realized that in her nervousness she'd been pulling at the threads in the seam of her gown. She forced her fingers to be

58

still. She sat down in one of the chairs at the small round table and took several deep breaths.

When another knock came at the door, she didn't jump up and fling it open as she had before, but instead called out cautiously, "Who is it?"

"Your husband, Anna Rose," came the long-awaited answer.

Her heart gave a mighty leap, but her legs refused to carry her to the door.

Rory was inside before she could move. He brought the captain's wine and two Waterford crystal goblets with him. He kissed her rather shyly on the cheek, then popped the cork from the bottle of champagne and poured some into each glass.

Raising his goblet to her, he said, "Drink up, love! You're going to need it when you hear what I have to tell."

Anna Rose did as he ordered, feeling a sudden urge to sneeze when the bright, little bubbles tickled her nose. The wine burned her mouth and throat at first, but left behind a curious, warm tingling that raced through her blood.

"Are you ready for this?" Rory asked, after he drained his first glass and refilled it.

"Ready for what, Rory? What's happened?"

"Damnedest thing I ever heard tell of! That Iris!"

"Iris?" Anna Rose frowned, suspecting suddenly that Iris had found a way to spoil her wedding after all. "What about her?"

"Married! That's what! This very day, the same as us! Seems when she ran off, she came into Inverness. She met up with a sailing man from another ship and the two of them spent the night together!" These last words were whispered, as if Rory didn't want anyone to hear of her shame. "Well, then this morning, she hauled ole Jaimie Kilgore off to the first preacher she could find and they tied the knot, tight as could be!"

Anna Rose, hardly able to believe her ears, had been trying to get her husband's attention. When he paused for a breath and another sip, she jumped right in. "Rory, how do you know all this is true? Who told you? And where's Iris now?"

"Iris and her new husband told me and that's why I figure it's true. After I settled you in here, I went down on the docks and I ran right into 'em! As to where they are now, headed out to face your ma and pa, they said. See, Jaimie's shippin' out in a few days, too, but he's got the word from his skipper that Iris can't come. So she'll have to butter up your folks so they'll let her stay with them until Jaimie comes back for her."

Anna Rose was stunned. She didn't know what to say. Iris couldn't love the man! She'd only just met him. She knew Iris's marriage was a mistake. And, worse yet, she felt it was all her fault. If she hadn't taken Rory . . .

"Come on, darlin', it's bedtime," her husband insisted, interrupting her thoughts. He took her hand, gently tugging her up from the chair.

"Rory, wait!" she protested. "Give me a moment."

"Anna Rose, we have waited," he answered softly, brushing his fingers over her cheek with clumsy tenderness. "But we're married now. There's no need to wait any longer. I want you so, darlin'."

She wanted him too. She ached for him to hold her again as he had that night on the riverbank, to kiss her with deep warmth and caress her until she cried out his name. But the news about Iris had come like a numbing blow. How could she abandon herself to total happiness and joy with her new husband when she knew that Iris was miserable and trapped in a hastily concocted marriage to a stranger? She needed time to adjust to the idea, to try to assuage the guilt that pained her so.

"What'll happen to her, Rory?"

"Who?" He had forgotten all about Iris already, intent as he was on bedding his bride.

"My sister!"

He went to her and hugged her gently. "Lord, darlin', Iris is the last person you need to worry about. If there was ever one who could take care of herself, it's her. Besides, Jaimie's a good man. Handsome too, with hair and eyes as black as pitch. He'll do right by her."

Anna Rose let her husband's words soothe her. Leaving her family and the land she'd known all her life was hard enough. She wanted with all her heart to believe that Iris's sudden marriage would not bring further grief to her mother and father.

"Better now?"

"Yes, Rory. I'll be fine."

She turned away for a moment to wipe her eyes. When she looked back at him, Rory had pulled off his shirt, laying bare his dark-tanned, hairless chest. When he started unfastening his trousers, Anna Rose averted her eyes. She went quickly to the lamp, extinguishing it. From somewhere in the darkness his hand reached out for her and she felt his tender caress, first on her arm, then cautiously as his fingers stroked her breast.

"It's all right, darlin'. If you'd rather have it dark, I understand."

She didn't answer him. She waited, frozen in silence, feeling his nearness, longing to be held. Finally, the wordless darkness forced his name from her lips.

"Anna Rose," he whispered, folding loving arms around her, "I'm here. I'll always be here for you."

"Rory, I do love you so!" she half-sobbed.

"I know. I know," he soothed. "And I love you, too, Anna Rose, more than anything or anyone. Let me hold you, darlin'."

He pulled her tightly against him, finding her lips with little effort. Anna Rose felt a new kind of warmth fill her body. Her first shock at feeling his nakedness pressed to her, with only the thin separation of linen between them, soon gave way to a burning need. As his tongue teased her lips, seeking entrance, she realized no knowledge of the act was needed. What they were about to do would come as naturally as breathing and, because of their love, would be as beautiful and innocently sweet as the first smile of a newborn babe.

Ever so gently, as if he feared she might bolt like a skittish doe, he led her toward the bed. When her head touched the pillow, she became instantly aware of masculine scents mingled arousingly about her. Her husband gave off an aroma of salt and sea air and a certain musk all his own that had aroused her from the first. But from the bed itself came the stronger odors of pipe smoke and brandy, reminding her of the other man whose bed they were about to anoint. It seemed almost as if Hugh Sinclair were there with them, insinuating his powerful presence upon their loving, watching their every move with his darkly accusing eyes. She forced herself to banish those thoughts from her mind.

Rory was beside her now. Slowly, cautiously, he bent down, kissing her face, her neck, and finally her parted lips. As they shared a solitary breath, Anna Rose felt her need rise to new heights. She returned his caresses, his kisses. She wanted him, oh, so badly!

He reached down suddenly, toying with the hem of her long gown as if uncertain what to do about it. Silently, she begged him to remove this final, thin barrier between them, but she dared not voice her wishes for fear her new husband would think her brazen. But when he raised the gown to smooth a hand up her leg from knee to quivering thigh, he met no protest. As his hands explored her virgin flesh, she sucked in breath from his mouth and clung to him, arching her breasts against his warm, smooth chest.

The cool air from the open window made her shiver when it blew over her exposed legs, thighs, and belly. Rory's hands followed the path just kissed by the breeze. She moaned softly. This first sound from her encouraged him. He tugged the gown higher, exposing her breasts. When his lips suddenly closed over one nipple and he suckled hungrily, she gasped aloud. Never had she felt anything like this. Her whole body seemed filled with burning liquid. She ached, she actually hurt deep down inside. And some instinct told her that only her husband could take away this sweet, mysterious pain. He was her master at this moment. She could do nothing but wait for him to give her what she must have to exorcise the ghost of her innocence and satisfy her longing.

His mouth shifted from one breast to the other. She bit her lip and dug her fingers into his back to keep from crying out for him. Her hips, she realized, were moving in a sensual rhythm of their own accord. His back, under her hands, was hard and lean. She could feel his ribs. To keep her mind off the wondrous, forbidden things he was doing to her with his hands and mouth, she began running her fingers along each rib, counting them mentally as she went.

Suddenly, Rory pulled his lips away from her breast and cried, "Oh, God, Anna Rose! That feels too good. I can't wait!"

All in one motion, it seemed, he pulled her beneath him, pried her thighs apart, and thrust deeply. In an instant, he had been transformed from a gentle lover into a man who could no longer deny his passions.

The sharp pain of total penetration forced a cry from Anna Rose, but the sound never slowed Rory's hard pace, as if he were a seaborne storm battering at a defenseless coastline. But the instinct that drove Rory to seek out a pinnacle of ecstasy carried Anna Rose helpless in its wake. She met each thrust with answering fury, anxious to know these uncharted seas of passion and claim them for her own. Her pain was beginning to vanish in a rising crest of pleasure when Rory gave his final spasm within her and rolled away.

"God, you're wonderful, Anna Rose!" he gasped, still holding her close. He gave her a last, lingering kiss, then turned on his side and said, "Best get some sleep now, darlin'. Dawn comes early aboard ship." Within seconds, Rory was sleeping beside her.

Anna Rose lay stunned, disbelieving. What had she done wrong? She'd followed her husband's lead. She'd let him do what he wanted with her. She'd even been enjoying the things he did, as much as it shamed her to admit it. But now it was over. Just like that! She was left aching with longing.

Climbing out of bed, she covered Rory's naked form with the sheet, then lit the lamp. Quickly, she washed the blood from her thighs, then she put on her nightgown again. The wine bottle still sat on the table, half full. She poured a glass and sipped it slowly, pondering her dilemma. Apparently, there was something about being a wife she didn't understand. The second glass went down faster while she told herself that tonight was her punishment for having a part in Iris's misery. The third was gone before she had time to think at all—before she even realized she'd taken a sip. She stood up and the room seemed to move about her.

"I'm seasick," she said quietly. "That's what it is." She staggered and fell against one wall. Her head was spinning, her vision blurred. "Some air, I need fresh air! Go out on deck. I'll feel better."

Captain Hugh Sinclair paced the dark deck. It was well after the midwatch. He'd tried every trick he could think of to banish from his mind all thoughts of what was going on in his cabin. But nothing worked. Everywhere he looked, toward Inverness or out to sea, he saw a lanky lad in his bunk, bedding a young woman who must be one of God's own gifts to man. And try as he might, he couldn't stop his own arousal at the thought.

What would love be like with Anna Rose? Would she be shy and pliable or would she bite and scratch like a tavern wench? Those bright lips would have to taste sweet. And her breasts, small compared to some he'd known, but just to his tastes, a handful, no more. He dared not think beyond that point. Any further and folly became fatal fascination.

He continued his rounds until he spotted a dark figure ahead of him, leaning over the railing. He hurried his step to check it out.

"You, there, sailor! What's going on?"

Anna Rose turned quickly toward the sound of the captain's voice. She had forgotten that he'd said he would be on deck. Oh, she didn't want to see anyone now! Especially not Captain Hugh Sinclair.

"It's only me, Captain. I came up to get some air." She tried to stand straight and tall, but the champagne and the slight pitch of the deck caused by the rising tide worked against her. She took a few stumbling steps and landed in Hugh Sinclair's arms.

"Are you all right?" he asked.

"Shertainly!" she slurred. "I've better been never!"

He gave a hearty laugh and tightened an arm about her waist to support her.

"You liked my wine, I take it?"

"Lovely, lovely wine, Captain!"

"And where is your husband?"

"You shouldn't have mentioned him. Now see what you've done!" The tears began. She couldn't hold them back. "Rory's sleeping like a log—like an old bear in a log," she managed, sobbing between words.

"There, there, Anna Rose, it can't be all that bad."

He pulled her into his arms—a warm, soft ball that smelled pleasantly of heather and good wine—and let his shirt soak up her tears. What could the lad be thinking of, to let his wife get into this condition? Now, here she was, exactly where he'd wanted her, in *his* arms, but what was he supposed to do with the besotted, weeping bride?

"Anna Rose, listen to me." He put a finger under her chin and tilted her face up to his. Her eyes were wide, glistening with the most beautiful tears he had ever seen. He longed to kiss them away. "Don't you think you'd better go back to bed and sleep it off?"

She was suddenly angry. "Go back to bed? For what? He's a good one for getting me ready, but then he doesn't do anything about it! Besides, he won't wake up. He doesn't care how I feel. Just takes his pleasure, then nighty-night. It's not fair! I've got feelings—needs—too!"

"Hush now, Anna Rose!"

Hugh truly did not want to hear any more. He might have been speculating before over what was happening in his bunk, but hearing the details from the disappointed bride was almost more than he could bear. Much more of this and he would likely take it upon himself to sooth her frustration in his own fashion. Better to take her back to her husband before . . .

"Come along now, Anna Rose. I don't think you want to talk this way. I'll take care of you. Just hold onto me and I'll see you safely back to bed."

She looked up into his face, grinning, her bright eyes wide with childish trust. "Hugh will take care of Anna Rose," she mumbled. "Everything will be all right. Right, Hugh?"

"Right." He steered her toward the cabin.

"And will you tuck me in and kiss me good night, Hugh?"

"Anna Rose, stop it!" He was scowling at her now, but her bleary, well-wined vision refused to recognize his expression as threatening. "Don't tempt me!"

"Tempt you? *Me?*" She stood on tiptoes, offering him teasing, pouting lips.

"I warned you," he said, his voice a husky snarl.

But he gave her no time to change her fogged mind. His lips came down hard on hers, stealing the kiss he'd wanted ever since that day at the tavern. When she responded instinctively, he tightened his arms around her until he could feel the erect nipples of her breasts pressing hard against his chest. At the same time, he forced her mouth open, sucking the breath from her lungs, battling her tongue with his own.

The kiss went a long way toward sobering Anna Rose. She realized suddenly what was happening. It might feel right, but it was all wrong. She fought him, breaking his grasp, finally. She stood gasping for breath, her whole body quaking from its close contact with Hugh Sinclair's and the fury she felt for herself as much as from his actions.

Pretending a composure she didn't feel, she said, "Thank you for seeing me back to the cabin, Captain. I'll say good night now."

"Until tomorrow, Anna Rose."

He was still standing in the passageway smiling at her when she closed the door.

She stumbled through the darkness to the bunk and clasped her sleeping husband tightly, shaking all over.

What had she done?

"I'm sorry, Rory," she whispered through her tears.

But he slept on, unaware of her clandestine, albeit accidental, meeting with Hugh Sinclair, or her apology for their kiss.

7

Anna Rose felt the morning light before she opened her eyes. It was like a white-hot needle, piercing her skull to embed itself in her throbbing brain.

"Oh-h-h," she groaned, still not daring to look at the day. "What happened?"

She jerked fully awake when an all too familiar, but totally unexpected voice answered, "A simple case of too many champagne bubbles all exploding at the same time."

"Hugh! I mean, Captain Sinclair!" she cried, sitting up so quickly that vertigo set in. "What are you doing here?"

"Odd as it may seem, Anna Rose, you're in my bed, which just happens to be in my cabin, where I stow my clothes. I need a shave and fresh linen."

She made a frantic grab for the blanket to cover herself, but the effort was too great, the pain too severe. What did it matter anyway? Bits and snatches of memory were returning—her midnight excursion to the deck after Rory fell asleep, Hugh Sinclair's sudden appearance, her tears, his arms, and then their kiss. Those memories, too, hurt mightily. She wanted to crawl through a porthole and drown herself. She felt like the lowest form of life. And Captain Hugh Sinclair wasn't helping matters any.

"Must you always stare at me that way?" she lashed out.

"What way, Anna Rose?" he asked, quietly amused. "I've been staring at pretty women all my life. It's a habit I've never been able to break. Actually, I've never even tried."

"Pretty?" she groaned. "I must look like last week's warmed-over hash. I don't think I've ever felt this bad before in my life. I wish I were dead!"

"There, there, my sweet child, this too shall pass."

He's laughing at me! she thought. *The nerve of the man!* First, he'd sent his accursed wine, then he'd taken advantage when she was not herself, and finally he'd arrived in time to gloat over her wretched condition. The bounder! The blackguard! The . . .

". . . bastard!" Though she hadn't meant to, she blurted the rest of her thought aloud.

"Oh, dear! What a temper!"

She thought she'd scream if he didn't wipe that holier-than-thou smirk off his face. She glared back at him, seething silently.

"And what language, Anna Rose! Surely you didn't learn that back home on the Mackintosh croft. You must have overheard it from a member of the crew. I shudder to think what colorful gems will be spilling from those delicious lips by the time we reach New York."

He had moved close to the bunk, and now lifted a hand toward her, one finger reaching as if he meant to trace the trembling line of her mouth. She turned her head quickly to avoid his touch.

"I'm sorry," she murmured. "You made me angry."

"In that case, I'm the one who should apologize. I didn't mean to upset you. But then you did ask for it, didn't you?"

"Ask for what?" she snapped.

"You wanted to marry Rory. You wanted to go to America. You drank too much wine. We do eventually have to pay for our mistakes, you know, Mrs. McShane."

She wanted to throw something at him, instead she shot back, "Marrying Rory was not a mistake!"

"That's not the impression you gave last night," he countered.

She slumped back, defeated, and mumbled, "It was your bloody wine."

He caught her chin in his palm and forced her to look up at him. She thought he meant to steal a kiss from her again. She couldn't let that happen. But somehow she felt powerless before him, a meek child in the presence of a domineering adult. However, the feelings his touch stirred were hardly childlike.

Where was Rory? Why didn't he come and rescue her? Her lips quivered and a hint of moisture gleamed at the corners of her stormy-green eyes.

Hugh Sinclair knew he should release his hold on her, should never have touched her in the first place, but something perverse in his nature enjoyed this torture he was inflicting on himself as much as on Anna Rose McShane. Maybe he was being too rough on her, but she didn't have to be so beautiful, so femininely soft and sweet-smelling, so goddamn vulnerable that it made him ache to hold her every time he came near her.

He should have stopped the wedding. He would curse himself forevermore for holding his peace. He'd known from the start that Rory was all wrong for her. Anna Rose was *his* kind of woman— hot, impulsive, lusty—quick of word and action, warm of heart and body.

Unconsciously, he made an angry sound deep in his throat and Anna rose shrank away from him.

If he dared tell her the truth, she'd know that his anger was pointed inward, not at her. He was the one who was really vulnerable, the one who had let his guard down just long enough to allow a woman to steal into his affections. Still, he had every right to be furious with her. Who invited her into his life, and into his heart?

He scowled down at her and said, "Oh, come on, Anna Rose! You aren't going to cry again?"

She'd been planning to, but now she changed her mind. she used all her willpower to remain calm so that she could meet his challenging stare. The hard slate-gray glitter of his eyes and the curl of his lips made her want to shy away, but she kept her gaze steady. She determined not to break eye contact until he did.

"That's better," he said, releasing her at last. "How's your head?"

"Aw-ful!" Her dry throat cracked the word in two. "Could I have a drink of water?"

"No! That's the worst thing you can do when you've had too much champagne. I'll fix you something shortly. Close your eyes!"

She was staring at him again, but this time, dumbfounded. What was he up to now? He stood next to the bunk, hands on hips, a purposeful look on his face. She certainly would not close her eyes!

As she watched, he shrugged and his hands slid forward suddenly to his belt buckle. He unfastened it, then he began working at the buttons on his trousers.

"Hugh! What do you think . . . ?"

"I asked you to close your eyes, Anna Rose, but I leave it entirely up to you. I'm about to drop my trousers and change. You're a married woman, though. If you want to watch, be my guest!"

She closed her eyes . . . immediately . . . tightly.

A silence followed, filled only by the rustle of canvas against flesh and the thud of his long, booted strides across the cabin. Anna Rose sat rigid on the bunk, twisting the sheet with nervous fingers while she strained her ears to try to make out what he was doing and where he was exactly at all times. She heard the splash of water, the scrape of a razor against whiskers, the opening and closing of drawers. And like an unsighted person, her nose was quick to detect the faintest scent in the air—bay rum and shaving soap, stale wine, and the lingering musk left from her own lovemaking with her husband only a few hours earlier.

From time to time she had the unmistakable feeling, the prickling along her spine, that he was staring, examining her thoroughly while he had her at this disadvantage. But she dared not steal the tiniest peek from beneath her lids for fear of what she might see. She sat silent and unseeing for what seemed an eternity.

"I didn't tell you you had to stop talking, Anna Rose. You could keep me company, you know."

She had never felt more at a loss in her life. It was as if she were being forced to sit passively while the whole world made silent sport of her. Without sight, she felt naked, vulnerable, totally out of touch with reality.

"Anna Rose, say something!" he insisted.

"I can't think with my eyes closed," she blurted out, and immediately felt her cheeks warm with a rush of blood.

What a stupid thing to say! she thought. And it was made all the worse because he didn't laugh or respond in any way. Hugh Sinclair just let her sit there in dumb darkness. Finally, she could take it no longer. She forced herself to open one eye and take a quick look. What she saw made her feel even more foolish, then made her furious. He was fully dressed and apparently had been so for some time.

"Welcome back!" he said with a crooked smile. "I was beginning to think you'd dozed off."

"Hardly!"

"Well, now that you can 'think' again, I'll tell you that we weighed anchor six hours ago. Our first day is half over. And your husband has been at his duties since well before dawn. I might add, he's whistling at his work and looking well pleased with himself after last night. Obviously, you performed as expertly below decks as above, Anna Rose."

He turned toward her, looking her full in her blushing face as he complimented her on her honeymoon night performance. Once again Anna Rose felt the sincere need to leap out a porthole, or slap Hugh Sinclair's handsome face. Instead, she met his slightly amused expression with defiant fire.

Wanting to remove herself from his cabin without further embarrassing delay, she replied, "I'll have our things out of here within the hour, Captain Sinclair, if you will only direct me to our new quarters."

When Hugh saw her grimace with pain as she jumped out of bed, he said, "There's plenty of time for that. I'll mix you up a sure cure for what's ailing you. Then you rest until the ailment and the cure wear off. I wish I could offer you better quarters, but we're packed as tightly as herring in a barrel. I've seen to it, though, that you'll be bunking in with a nice woman from Glasgow, Mrs. Tierney. She'll look after you."

"What about Rory?" Anna Rose asked uncertainly.

"As you are just another passenger from now on, he is just another jack-tar. He'll string his hammock with the others in the crew's quarters. I know it's not the most desirable way to begin a marriage, Anna Rose, but there's no help for it. If I let Rory take up passenger space to be with you, I'd never hear the end of it from the other men, nor would he. Besides, every berth in steerage is filled. I'm sorry. But you both knew what you were getting into."

Hugh felt bad for having to point the facts out to her so bluntly, but the new Mrs. McShane had to toughen up and start seeing the world realistically if she was going to make it in America as Rory's wife. If it were up to him, he would gladly give up his quarters to the newlyweds. But the very thought of such a charitable move was sheer folly. This was no honeymoon cruise. He had a ship to run and passengers to deliver to New York, and he had a feeling Anna Rose would have thrown such an offer back in his face anyway.

Still, he softened his tone as he added, "At least the two of you are married and you did have last night together."

Anna Rose turned from him. Why did he insist on dwelling on the night before? Couldn't he let it rest? She wanted to scream. She wanted to run from the cabin, to hide from him with his handsome, all-knowing face and his verbal jabs as passionately violent as the physical thrusts she'd withstood and encouraged from Rory. But that was different. He was her husband. What claim had Captain Hugh Sinclair on her?

"We'll be quite all right, thank you," Anna Rose replied simply. What else could she say—that Rory didn't tell her about this? That there were a lot of things she hadn't been told before her wedding? She thought with sudden panic that maybe she should never have left home. No, it was too late for second thoughts. She was committed, now and forevermore. She would make her marriage and her new life work!

Anna Rose did as the captain ordered. She drank the foul concoction he mixed from secret ingredients out of his spirits chest, then she lay back while the fiery potion kicked up a dizzying maelstrom inside her. She was sure he'd poisoned her. But after she'd slept for another hour, she awoke with her head its normal size and shape and her usual vim and vigor restored.

Quickly, she gathered up the few articles she owned and packed them back into her satchel. She dressed carefully in her plaid waist and skirt again, her long russet braid picking up the deep red in the pattern. She checked her appearance one last time before leaving the captain's quarters, anxious to look her best when she met her new bunkmate.

She looked forward to meeting Mrs. Tierney and to sharing a space with the lady. What she had envisioned was a small, neat cabin with twin berths, one above the other. She had already made up her mind that she would insist upon sleeping overhead so that the older woman wouldn't have to be climbing up and down. What actually awaited her took her totally by surprise.

The ship was crammed from stem to stern with passengers bound for America. Temporary flooring and bunks had been erected in the tween-decks. The space was dark and airless, filled with the stench of unwashed bodies and the cries of seasick children. Smoky lanterns provided the only dim light, and their fumes further fouled the air. Anna Rose's heart sank. How would any of them survive the crossing living like so much human ballast?

"Oh, lovey, you must be the new bride," a dumpling of a woman with a turban of steel-gray hair cooed. "I'm Mrs. Tierney, and it's my own pleasure to meet you, Mrs. McShane."

"Anna Rose, please," she answered, still reeling from the shock of her new surroundings and the thought that thirty-odd passengers would be forced to share the cramped space.

"Well, if that's not a name to match the face! Pretty as a primrose, you are, lass. I'm sure we'll get on famously." She pulled Anna Rose close to her ample bosom in a welcoming squeeze and whispered, "Captain Sinclair, he said I was to look after you—said you was special. If I was your new husband, I'd be keeping an eye peeled for that handsome scamp!" She winked broadly, making Anna Rose squirm.

But surely no one on board had witnessed her intimate moment with the captain the night before. She prayed not! Then a new and more frightening thought struck her. How would she ever face Rory if he found out what had happened? Her conscience ached with shame. It would have been bad enough if Hugh Sinclair had forced his unwanted attentions on her. But she seemed to recall that she had invited that kiss. Yes! Out of the bubble-filled fog enshrouding some of last night's events, she could hear his warning echoing: "Don't tempt me, Anna Rose!"

With the memory of those words other things returned to mind, uncomfortable things that set her stomach quivering and her cheeks stinging. She remembered how intimately demanding his tongue and lips were and how expertly he aroused her senses. She recalled, too, that Hugh Sinclair's arms were tender in their strength, holding her as if she were as fragile as a china doll. She forced her thoughts away, willing the captain into a far corner of her mind. She must keep him there!

Only half-listening to Mrs. Tierney's interminable, one-way conversation, Anna Rose went about stowing her belongings, with her mind on her husband and what she would say to him when she saw him next. But before she could get her thoughts collected, he was there beside her.

"Anna Rose, love," he whispered. "I had to find you and tell you how grand last night was, darlin'."

He leaned down to kiss her, but she shied away, very aware that the other passengers were staring and listening.

"Rory, please! Not here in front of everyone."

The smile dissolved from his face and deep hurt swam in the sea-blue of his eyes. "Beggin' your pardon. I thought you'd be happy to see me."

"I am, darlin'," she managed, laying a comforting hand on his arm. "It's just that I'm not used to things, married things, yet. You'll have to give me a little time to adjust."

"But it was good for you last night, too, wasn't it?" His

expression begged for her approval with the same eagerness that a puppy pleads for a pat on the head.

"Of course it was, Rory," she replied, but found she couldn't meet his open gaze.

"I'm working out a deal with the cook." His whisper was so low that Anna Rose could barely hear him. "He's going to let us use the pantry from time to time, for some privacy. Not tonight, but soon, I promise. I've got to go now. The captain wants to talk to me."

The moment Rory disappeared, Mrs. Tierney cackled, "The pantry! Your husband's not only eager, but resourceful as well. You'll be able to raid the larder while he's tossing your skirts, lass!"

Anna Rose colored deeply. She didn't think the others could have heard Rory's remarks to her, but they all heard Mrs. Tierney's exclamations. The new bride looked up to find every face in the compartment staring at her, beaming.

A long week of rough seas, confinement below decks for the steerage passengers, and the first case of shipboard fever passed before Rory was able to take Anna Rose to their promised rendezvous. By that time, she was weary and almost sick herself from helping care for the little girl in the next bunk while she existed on meager rations of beans, hard bread, and stale air—the same poor fare that all the passengers shared when they couldn't go on deck to cook. But the child was better now and no new cases of fever had been reported. Even if Anna Rose was only swapping the close quarters of the steerage deck for those of the pantry, at least the change would be a relief.

She'd missed Rory desperately. She found herself lying awake nights, listening to the crash of the sea and longing to have his arms around her, making her feel safe and wanted. Being single and without a man was one thing. Being married and alone was quite another, she discovered.

Looking back on it now, there was something so innocent and right about the way he'd loved her on their wedding night. It was as if they belonged together and had been married forever. As for her disappointment their first night, she had a feeling that was her fault. It would be different next time. She would see to that. No more shy maiden! She knew what to expect now and felt she could guide things along to a more satisfactory conclusion.

"Land, child! You look like a bride all over again!" Mrs. Tierney enthused. "Why, that pale muslin is almost as delicate as

72

your skin. Course, it lacks the blush of your cheeks, but it does become you."

Anna Rose thanked her friend. She knew the dress brought out her best points. The fitted bodice lifted her breasts and even hinted at a cleavage where she was sure none existed. The fit of the waist snuggled her to becoming narrowness and exaggerated the swell of her hips before flaring into gathers, which ended in a wide sweep about her ankles. By daring design, she had discarded all of her petticoats but one, and her feet, shod in flimsy, black slippers that laced up her calves, were stockingless. She stuffed a tiny pouch of crushed lavender into her bodice and smoothed her damp palms down her skirt.

"I'm ready!" she said as much to herself as to Mrs. Tierney.

"Then go to it, girl. Let that man of yours know how much you love him."

Mrs. Tierney gave Anna Rose a motherly peck on the cheek and sent her on her way.

Anna Rose found Rory waiting on deck to show her to the pantry. He paced, just as he had before their wedding. She noticed that his rebellious forelock was slicked down with pomade. He looked scrubbed, combed, brushed, and eager.

"Evenin'," he said, with a twitch of his lips upward that she now knew passed for a smile when he was nervous. "A fine calm sea tonight. No clouds on the horizon. Wind barely ten knots."

Anna Rose slipped her fingers into the curl of his hand and tickled his sweaty palm with her nails. "Rory darlin', I didn't come up here for a weather report, though I might enjoy gazing at the stars for a time."

She drew close to him and looked up as if she were studying the twinkling constellations for some secret navigation of her own. Rory breathed in her halo of lavender and his eyes fixed on the little, throbbing pulse in her neck. He had a sudden urge to kiss it, but glanced about and found there were shipmates in the rigging staring down at them. He'd taken enough ribbing from his mates already, having his new bride on board. No need, he figured, to give them more ammunition for their taunts.

"Come on, Anna Rose. Let's go below. We don't have that much time. I've got to go on duty at midwatch."

She stood rooted to the deck and forced him to stay, too. "Rory, I'm not one to be rushed through life. You're going to have to learn that about me right now. I like to take things slow and easy, to enjoy myself along the way." She paused and looked him square in the eye. "Do you understand what I'm telling you?"

She watched his Adam's apple bob several times before he

could answer. When he did find words, he spoke them downward toward his boots. "You're talking about our wedding night, aren't you?"

She didn't answer, but lowered her eyes as well.

"I'm sorry, Anna Rose," he whispered. "I don't know what came over me the other night. I just couldn't hold back. It must of been the wine."

Yes! That blasted wine! she thought. It had done odd things to both of them. All the while, she was trying desperately not to think of what it and its donor had done to her.

"I'm ready now, Rory," she said at length.

He placed her right hand in the crook of his arm and led the way down the ladder.

The cook had conveniently vacated the galley so that no one witnessed their entry into the pantry. Anna Rose breathed a sigh of relief once they were inside with the heavy door closed against intruders. It seemed to her that eyes had followed her and lips whispered about her every day since they set sail. To be away from all the others was a luxury in itself. And to be alone with her husband at last, well . . .

Rory immediately caught her in his arms and all but smothered her with his anxious lips. As he pressed his body against hers, she felt the rising heat of his excitement. This would never do! She brought her hands up between them and planted her palms firmly against his chest until he released her.

"Not so quickly, Rory. Please!" She smoothed her hair back and took a step away from him.

"But, Anna Rose, I only want—"

"I know what you want, darlin', and I want the same thing. I just want us both to enjoy it longer. Slowly now, please!"

"Should I spread the blanket?"

She smiled, suddenly shy. "That would be nice, Rory."

She almost laughed as she watched him spreading the blanket, ever so slowly and carefully. She started to tell him that was not what she wanted done slowly, but thought better of it. At least the dear boy was trying. When he finished, they had a cozy bunk on the floor, hemmed in by barrels of salt pork and flour. Still, it was their own.

"Should I blow out the lamp, Anna Rose?"

She glanced uncertainly at the flickering wick. Sooner or later she would have to see her husband, and she would have to allow him to see her.

"Perhaps just turn it down a bit," she answered, and he grinned in spite of himself.

The blanket spread and the wick trimmed, there were no more preliminaries to occupy them.

"Now, Anna Rose?" Rory asked with a boyish smile.

She returned his sweet look. "Now, Rory darlin'."

He came to her slowly, as she'd directed, slipping both his hands about her tiny waist. She felt the warm pressure of his fingers sear her through. He looked down into her eyes for a moment before his head lowered and his lips touched hers softly, tentatively. She let her hands slip up his back and tugged him closer to her breasts.

"Slowly, darlin', slowly," Anna Rose murmured against his lips when she felt his excitement rising.

Rory's kiss moved from her mouth, down her chin, to the sweet spot he'd spied throbbing so temptingly earlier. When his tongue flicked the pulse point, Anna Rose sighed and her knees seemed unable to hold her weight.

"Come lie with me, darlin'." Rory whispered the invitation so close to her ear that a shiver ran down her spine.

She did as he asked, nestling in his arms, and making no objection when he began toying with the little buttons of her bodice. She held her breath, anticipating the wonderful feel of his fingers on her bare flesh as he undid each button, ever so slowly. Anna Rose had driven her point home. Now she thought she would die before he finished the task and found her aching breasts. Her own fingers busied themselves with his shirt and his smooth, hard chest was soon bare. Summoning all her courage, she let her hand stray to his belt, meaning to unfasten it.

"No!" he said firmly, stopping her. "We're going to keep things safely in their place until the right time comes. No more getting ahead of myself like the other night. You just lie back and let me take care of things, darlin'."

Anna Rose lay back while Rory did as he promised. With infinite tenderness, his hands caressed her breasts. She could feel them swelling to his touch. Her nipples puckered as if begging for his kiss. And soon his warm mouth found them, pressing lightly, tasting, nibbling. Anna Rose cried out once and then again.

"Sh-h-h, darlin'," he murmured against her sensitive skin, and she felt his words in the deepest parts of her.

He raised her carefully and slipped the blouse from her shoulders, so that they were both naked to the waist. In a moment's embarrassment, she crossed her arms over her chest, hiding what there was no need to hide from the loving, appreciative eyes of her husband. With firm but gentle pressure he forced her arms to her sides and held them there, lowering his chest over hers to tease her nipples with his own. Anna Rose stared up into his eyes, watching the reflection of her own yearning in their warm, blue depths, and feeling things she had never imagined were within the human grasp of emotions.

Rory sat up abruptly, but his eyes never left her, traveling from her face, down her neck, to her breasts.

"You're beautiful, Anna Rose," he said quietly, matter-of-factly.

Then his gaze moved on to her waist and beyond. She could almost read the question in his eyes. She didn't want him to have to ask permission to remove the rest of her clothes. Somehow that would spoil things.

"Rory," she said quickly when she saw his lips move to speak, "help me off with my skirt, please."

An expression of gratitude lit his face. His hands went to her waist, circling, pressing, testing the feel of her flesh in his fingers. Anna Rose closed her eyes, fighting the embarrassment she felt, and waited. But he didn't remove her skirt right away. She felt his hands on her legs, untying the laces of her slippers. He removed one and then the other, caressing her calves, her ankles, and her toes. His warm touch radiated upward, centering and intensifying somewhere beneath her lone petticoat. Then she felt a tug at the waistband. She lifted her hips to allow him to pull the skirt away. Something deep inside her shuddered deliciously when the air and his gaze touched her belly, her thighs, her legs.

"God!" he breathed. "Oh, God, Anna Rose! I never saw anything so beautiful in all my life."

She kept her eyes closed, remembering how all her other senses had been heightened that day in the captain's cabin by her lack of vision. Now, too, it was the same. She could actually feel the heat radiating from Rory's body as he eased himself down to her. She could smell the mingled scents of the pantry itself, but stronger, sweeter, was the aura of their own desire hovering in the air. And when Rory touched her bare flesh—almost as if his fingers were begging permission for the rest of him to approach her—she could feel his very nerves, tingling against her own.

She gasped with a sudden rush of desire. Her body arched upward to meet his, and the pleading words she heard so distinctly seemed to come from a stranger's lips instead of her own.

"Rory, darlin', take me!"

"Not yet, Anna Rose. You're not ready. Just lie easy."

Lie easy, he said! How could she when the blood was sizzling in her veins and the ache deep inside her made her feel as if she might explode into a burst of stars at any moment? But she breathed deeply and did her best to lie still and give all her sensations up to him.

His wet kisses burned all over her body. His teasing, fondling fingers seemed set on learning her innermost secrets. He held her and stroked her and whispered a litany of love words deep into her ear until she could not retain her composure. She thrashed in his arms and begged for him to enter her.

He did, but with careful restraint, riding her gently, as if she were an unbroken mare bound to be skittish. But Anna Rose went against her own rules, quickening their pace, rushing pell-mell for the finish. She felt her senses soaring. She strained and reached for the heights, quivering on the very brink until she felt his hot plume engulf her and send her spiraling upward into the soft black velvet of ecstasy.

"Oh, love me, Rory!" she cried, not allowing him to withdraw or even slacken their rhythm so anxious was she to hold onto the delicious, delirious feeling.

"Anna Rose darlin', it just gets better every time," he murmured as their frenzied pace slowed at last.

She lay very still after a time, feeling the heat drain from her body. Rory leaned down to kiss her and stroked her tousled hair with his hands.

"I swear to God, I never knew anything that good!" Rory said, staring at her as if she were some miracle come to pass.

She could only nod. Her voice felt as if it were trapped somewhere deep inside her—as if it dared not venture out and break the spell of the moment.

Rory swallowed hard. He had been dreading this moment. But he'd promised the captain he'd make a clean breast of things. He had to do it quickly, before he lost his nerve.

"Anna Rose, there's something I have to tell you." Rory's tone of voice disturbed her. "I should have confessed it all before we were wed, but I just couldn't run the risk of losing you."

She frowned, trying to think what he might be leading up to.

"I reckon you know by now that I misrepresented myself to you and your folks. I'm not first mate on this ship. I'm hardly higher up than the captain's cabin boy. Just an ordinary swab without a copper to my name. See, that's the whole problem. I couldn't ask your ma and pa for money to pay your passage. So I bound myself over to get you on board."

She didn't know what she'd expected, but certainly not this. "You mean you'll have to serve out an indenture when we get to America?"

"That's right, but it won't be so bad. The captain's seen to it that we'll go to Georgia, just like you wanted, and after my seven years are up, we'll have our own place, free and clear."

"Seven years, Rory? Why, that's forever!"

"No, honest, Anna Rose. You'll see. It'll pass before we know it. You'll be busy tending our babies and I'll be working and learning to grow rice. We'll be rich as lairds before you can turn around good, just like your papa wanted for you. Then we'll send for the rest of your family to come live with us. I have it all worked out in my mind. Everything will be just like I promised, darlin'."

Anna Rose was pulling on her clothes. She felt confused, disoriented. Once again, all her plans and dreams were torn asunder. She felt the same unreasonable fury rising that she'd experienced the day of her father's accident. It struck her suddenly that her husband and her father were cut from the same bolt, both dreamers and drifters, without the slightest notion of what the real world was all about. She looked at Rory McShane as if seeing him for the first time.

His eyes shifted away quickly. "I'm sorry, Anna Rose. Yell at me if you want. I deserve it. The captain already gave me bloody hell for keeping secrets from you. I was wrong, I know that now. Can you ever forgive me, darlin'?" He looked back at her with such pleading misty-blue eyes that her anger began to cool. "I love you so damn much, but I'm not fit to wipe your slippers, much less be your husband."

"Rory McShane, you hush that!" she ordered. "I won't listen to such nonsense about my own dear husband!"

Anna Rose took Rory in her arms in the next moment, cooing reassurances to him and comforting him as if he were the injured party. He seemed so bereft by his deception that she couldn't bring herself to scold him and make him feel even worse. She would be the strong one, if she had to be, and help him through this bad time. She would help him through all the bad times for the next seven years, for the rest of their lives. At that moment of decision, she felt a new kind of love well up for him. She cared all the more because of his childlike vulnerability.

"It's all right, Rory. I understand," she said finally. "But please don't keep anything from me ever again. Husbands and wives shouldn't, not if they really love each other."

"I know that now, Anna Rose, and I promise. No more secrets!" He was kissing her fingers, distracting her attention, when he added, "There's just one more thing, but it's really not important. Just remember, when we dock in New York, if the agent should ask, you're a 'redemptioner'."

"A what?" Anna Rose had never heard the word before, but she didn't like the sound of it.

He repeated the word and added, "It's just the kind of fare you're making the trip on. Don't worry, darlin', it's nothing bad. But they'll probably ask when we get to New York."

She wasn't sure why, but Rory's words didn't ring quite true. Perhaps it was the way his gaze sidestepped hers as he said the word. She filed "redemptioner" away, determined to ask Mrs. Tierney about the term later. The woman knew all and never hesitated to tell it.

A pounding at the pantry door sent both of them scrambling to get into their clothes. Rory was dressed first and helped Anna Rose finish buttoning up. His hands, straying casually over her breasts as he tried to manage the tiny buttons, made her shiver slightly. She felt the beginnings of the return of longing. She caught his hands and brought them to her lips, kissing them fervently, wondering how long she would have to wait before they could share another intimate evening in the pantry. But now that she knew what love was really like, she could wait. She could exist on dreams of tonight, if need be, though reality was far sweeter.

"Hurry up in there, you two!" the galley chief yelled. "The captain wants his late supper!"

Anna Rose and Rory embraced quickly then stepped away from each other before Rory unhooked the latch. The mountain of a cook stood right outside, waiting. Anna Rose felt his watery eyes roam over her for several seconds.

"You'll be namin' it after me, I'm hopin'!" the fat cook said.

"What?" Anna Rose asked without thinking.

The man bellowed a laugh, then said, "Why, the baby you've just made beside my pork barrel, of course! Me and the rest of the crew's been layin' odds it was a take. My bet's on March 2, 1835. Nine months to the day from your roll in my pantry."

Anna Rose felt her heart lurch. Her face paled before the red tide engulfed her. *The whole crew knows!* she thought, humiliated.

She didn't even wait to tell Rory good-bye or to let him show her back to the steerage compartment. Her slippered feet flew up ladders and down, across the smooth deck, along the dark passageways. She was aware of heads turning to stare as she dashed past. Once someone called her name—Captain Sinclair, she thought—but she didn't slow down to look. She could think only of her embarrassment, her need to be alone, to hide.

As much as she loved Rory, and she truly did, she could not

abide this public knowledge of their every move. She determined to explain to him at their next meeting that they would have to live apart until they reached America.

That night, her resolve made, she cried herself to sleep.

8

Anna Rose McShane made a pretty picture, kneeling there beside the coal fire on deck, frying her breakfast of bacon and oatcakes, Hugh Sinclair mused. He'd been standing on the poop deck watching her surreptitiously for some time. The early morning sun touched her long, thick braid and made it blaze like polished bronze. Her periwinkle skirt flared out about her on the deck like a morning glory just opening to the fresh dew. Yes, the woman was as pleasing to the eye as she was to the other senses. *Too pleasing,* he thought, forcing himself to turn away.

But the sight of her husband approaching her called the captain's attention back. He knew of their rendezvous in the pantry the night before. He only hoped the young scoundrel had taken the opportunity to explain everything to Anna Rose. From what he saw—Anna Rose shaking her head vigorously and Rory making pleading gestures—Hugh Sinclair guessed that the lad had told his wife about his own indenture and the signed redemption papers.

The captain was quite correct in assuming that Anna Rose knew of her status as a redemptioner, but since he was too far away to hear their conversation, he was wrong about why the young couple were disagreeing.

"I'm sorry, Rory, but that's the way it must be."

"Not be together as man and wife until we reach land again?" Rory's voice was a whine of pain. "Anna Rose, you can't mean it!"

It hurt her to look at her husband's face. He seemed as near tears as any man she'd ever seen. But Anna Rose straightened her spine and stood her ground. She would not be humiliated, not even for the sake of love.

"It won't be that much longer, darlin'. Then we'll have the rest of our lives together," she added, trying to coax him out of his gloom.

"Maybe not, but it'll seem forever, loving you the way I do and wantin' you so, Anna Rose."

In spite of the sailors looking on, she reached out to give her husband's hand a reassuring pat. Her voice was only a bare whisper as she said, "I love you, too, Rory. And, you'll see. The time will pass for us. We'll be in America starting our new life together before you know it, darling."

In spite of her encouraging words to Rory, the dejected sag of his shoulders and droop of his head as he turned and walked away nearly broke Anna Rose's heart.

Rory had explained to Anna Rose that the crossing would take approximately four weeks in good weather or up to ten if the Atlantic turned ugly. After the first rough week, traversing the Pentland Firth north of Scotland where, Rory had told her, the tides ran at thirteen knots, the next fortnight proved pleasant enough. Granted, the tween-decks accommodations were nothing to rave about, but with calm seas and sunny skies the steerage passengers were allowed time in the fresh sea air to exercise and to cook their meals at the small brick-lined coal fires on the foredeck.

Anna Rose proved more than an able cook and she gave thanks daily that Rory had purchased ample supplies—bacon, biscuits, tea, sugar, flour, oatmeal, barley for broth, and essence of peppermint—before they left Inverness.

But when she had thanked her husband for his thoughtfulness, saying, "Rory darlin', you're a wonder! All these supplies you bought!" he'd looked at her oddly and said nothing.

"I never dreamed that the ship's meager rations for the passengers would go bad so soon. Why, nothing's been fresh since our first day out!" Anna Rose had continued. "All but the salted meat is now rotten, the butter's rancid, and the bread's moldy and infested with weevils. Even the drinking water tastes terrible. Cook adds more vinegar to the brackish stuff every day. Without the tea and peppermint you purchased, I'd die of thirst."

Rory had only nodded, allowing Anna Rose to give him full credit. He had bought nothing; such preparation would never have crossed his mind. He guessed correctly that it was the captain's doing. Obviously, he'd wanted Rory's bride to be as comfortable as possible on the crossing. Hugh Sinclair had known full well that the young sailor hadn't the price of his wife's passage, much less the cash to purchase supplies. But Rory allowed Anna Rose to thank him, basking in her praise. He would thank the captain later, privately.

As the days passed and many of the passengers became ill from diarrhea, fever, and scurvy, Anna Rose remained healthy. Only a few times in the heat of the night had she been forced to resort to a dose of peppermint to settle her qualmish stomach. It was a good thing, because soon the fair weather deserted them and every drop of essence of peppermint on the ship was sorely needed to dose the sick.

In the stormy seas, all the steerage passengers were confined below decks. The single hatch that had offered a meager portion of fresh air from above was closed. Lamps were forbidden for fear of fire. And, of course, no one could go on deck to cook a meal. They had to survive on stale bread and brackish water. The hours seemed endless, with only fear, hunger, and the shared misery of seasickness to pass the time.

Anna Rose found out soon enough that her services as nurse as well as cook were needed by her bunkmates. She was glad she had paid close attention to her mother's ministerings to her brothers and sisters for her sickroom experience came in handy now. The young ones on board seemed to suffer the most. All the babies had colic, some had fever. There was little anyone could do to comfort them. Still, Anna Rose did her best, taking over when the weary mothers, most sick themselves, were ready to drop with fatigue.

After two howling days of stormy seas, Anna Rose and all the others had taken to their bunks, unable to stay upright with the awful rolling and tossing of the ship. The compartment was pitch-black although it was midday. She tried to sleep, having been up all the night before with one of the sick babies. But the ocean's screams and the heat and closeness of the compartment refused her any rest.

Her mind wandered to her husband. What was Rory doing right now? How was he faring up above, in the very jaws of the tempest? What if he were swept overboard by one of the waves battering the ship?

She couldn't bear to think about that. And she mustn't let herself. Worrying could do no good. Instead, she forced her mind to their last night together in the pantry. She relived it all: the feel of his hands upon her bare flesh, the flickering lamplight that played over his lean body, the smells of tallow and fish and rum for the sailors' grog mingled with the earthy musk of their joined bodies. She went over their quiet conversation, and she remembered something that had slipped her mind. She'd been so busy these past days, she hadn't thought to question her bunkmate about the word that was puzzling her. Suddenly, she felt she had to know right then.

"Mrs. Tierney?" she said, leaning over the side of her bunk. "Are you sleeping?"

"In this sea?" her friend answered. "Not likely, dear. I'm only trying to stay in my bed."

"Please, tell me something if you can."

"Certainly, child. What is it you want to know?"

"What is a redemptioner, Mrs. Tierney?"

"*Redemptioner,* you say?" The older woman's voice betrayed her distaste for the word. Anna Rose was almost sorry she had asked.

"Yes, ma'am. What exactly does it mean?"

"Surely, you're not telling me, Anna Rose, that you are a redemptioner?"

Mrs. Tierney's shocked tone made Anna Rose want to deny the fact. But Rory had told her it was so.

"Please, Mrs. Tierney, I need to know."

"Well, if you must!" The woman sighed wearily. "You see, dear, there's three different classes of us down here, though we all suffer alike. There's those that had the fifty dollars passage money, but not enough to buy better accommodations. That would be me, dear. Then there's the indentured servants, signed on for a number of years to the person in America who paid their way. And last and least, God help them, there's the redemptioners, who had no money nor anyone willing to guarantee the price of their crossing."

Anna Rose was frowning. She still didn't understand. "Then who pays for them?"

"That, my child, is decided by fate alone once we reach New York. You see, the captain takes these poor unfortunates on account. He makes the wretches sign indenture papers to him. Then as soon as the ship docks, there'll be an auction. To redeem the price of their passage, the captain hands over those papers and the hapless redemptioner to the highest bidder, no questions asked. There's some at these auctions who come to purchase servants for honest work. But there's them, too, that would buy a pretty woman for other duties I won't mention."

Anna Rose felt a sudden wave of relief. She had signed nothing. As for Rory, he was part of the ship's crew. He would be paid for his passage, not charged.

Mrs. Tierney wondered at Anna Rose's silence. "My dear, do you understand what I'm telling you?"

"Yes. Thank you. You've relieved my mind greatly."

"Then you were only asking out of curiosity. Praise be! It would be an untold horror to have to stand on that auction block the minute you reach New York and be ogled and bid upon by any sort of man with the will and the wherewithal."

Anna Rose forced a laugh. "Can you see my husband's face if that should be my lot? No, that can't be what Rory meant."

"Eh? What's that you say, child? Your husband is the one who mentioned this to you?"

The ship was tossing so that Anna Rose had to grip the wooden sides of her narrow bunk to keep from being pitched to the deck. The stale, hot air of the compartment filled with moans, prayers, and the cries of frightened children. Over and above these sounds, the darkness screamed with the terrifying crash of the waves against the hollow-sounding bow and the ominous groaning and creaking of the *Olympia* as she strained to stay afloat.

For a time, all conversations subsided. Then a lull set in. Anna Rose released her painful grip on the rough wood. She was able to think again, to speak.

"Yes, Mrs. Tierney, it was Rory himself who told me to remember, should anyone ask, that I'm a redemptioner. But, you see, that can't be. I never signed a thing."

"The saints preserve you, child, and him! It's clear to me now what your husband's done. He's signed redemption papers in your behalf. A husband can do that, you know. A wife is no better than property when it comes to business matters. Should anything happen to him on this crossing, your fate is sealed. You'll be no better than a slave to some unknown master, serving out the years of your husband's indenture." Mrs. Tierney's sad voice trailed off in a mumbled prayer for her young friend's salvation. Then she added in a mournful tone, "But maybe there's nothing to worry about, dear. In this storm, I doubt even the rats on board will live to see America."

Anna Rose lay rigid in her bunk, her eyes closed against the awful darkness. Slowly, the full impact of Mrs. Tierney's words sank in. Unfortunately, it all made sense to her. Rory had told her he'd signed himself into bondage to pay her passage. But should anything befall him in the days to come, she would be the one left to redeem the debt. A new kind of terror filled her. Every moment since the storm had begun, she had feared for Rory's life. But now, she realized, there was even more to be afraid of.

How could Rory have done such a thing? He had no right to treat her future so casually. And what kind of monster must Captain Sinclair be, to force his friend into such an unfair bargain? She had mistrusted the man from the first. Now she knew why.

Suddenly, Anna Rose felt deathly ill. The pounding she'd taken during the storm had made her ache all over. The close compartment made it difficult to breathe. She was burning hot and her throat was so dry she felt as if she could drink a bucketful of the vinegar-laced water. Her legs cramped from having had so little exercise recently. Even her clothes touching her skin caused pain. But worst of all was the dizziness—the awful, never-ending vertigo she had been experiencing off and on for the past few hours.

She closed her eyes, suddenly too weak and exhausted for anything but sleep.

Hugh Sinclair, weary and soaked to the skin, entered his cabin for the first time in two days and nights. The storm was a monster, the fiercest he'd seen in many a year. But it looked as if the worst was over and the *Olympia* was still afloat.

He threw off the oilskin cape and went to his spirits cabinet. Normally, he never took a drink while underway. However, the situation was anything but normal at the moment. The dirty sea wasn't the only thing that had bedeviled him for the past days. Seaman McShane had made matters even worse.

He sloshed whiskey into his glass and drank it down, feeling the warm amber burn his throat in a pleasing way. When it hit his empty belly, he sagged into a chair.

"Damn that boy!" he cursed, his thoughts still on Rory.

He'd had his hands full all through the storm keeping the foolhardy lad from getting swept overboard. The boy was too brave for his own good. Each time an order was shouted to go aloft and secure the rigging or to lash down the long boats, McShane had been the first to volunteer, risking his neck in the most casual fashion.

Didn't the boy realize he had a wife to think of now? What did he expect Anna Rose to do if she lost her husband before she reached America? A lone woman in a new country, without friends or money, would face a short and miserable life. As for Hugh's promise to take care of her should anything happen to Rory, he had made that pledge only because he was sure nothing would. Not that he wouldn't be delighted to take charge of her, but it was senseless for her husband to endanger himself so recklessly, without a thought of the consequences.

The captain uttered a weary sigh and shoved his empty glass aside. He reached down and tugged off his heavy, wet boots. A few hours of sleep, that's what he needed. They'd passed through the worst of the weather and the ship would be all right. The *Olympia* might be an ugly little tub, but she could hold her own in the heaviest sea.

He stripped off the rest of his wet clothes and fell on his bunk, face down, expecting sleep to take him immediately. But it evaded him. His mind still caught on the problem at hand—Rory and his bride.

He remembered the first time he'd met the lad. Dirty, half-starved, and wily as a professional thief, Rory had picked his purse on the docks in Glasgow. It could have been Hugh's ruination. The stolen pouch, fat with gold, was not his but had belonged to his ship's owners. He would have been the one called upon to produce the money or go to jail. He'd tried for days to find the thieving little rascal. But the boy seemed to have vanished. Finally, when it had looked like the end for him, he'd gone to a pub, intending to get royally drunk.

He could see it as clearly as if it had happened only yesterday: himself on his binge at The Headless Queen when the big-eyed moppet turned up, purse in hand. He closed his eyes, remembering:

The pub was dim and smoky, reeking of stale whiskey and overripe fish. The two other customers in the place were only dark shapes, silently hunched over their tankards. Hugh himself felt as if he were drowning in ale and his own misery.

Suddenly, a movement in the shadows near the door caught his eye. He squinted hard, making out a skinny form, dressed all in rags. The dirty-faced child moved stealthily closer, unaware that Hugh had spied him. When he was close enough, he tried to sneak the familiar pouch up onto the bar beside Hugh without getting caught. But Hugh wasn't that drunk. Quick as a flash, he nabbed the little scamp by the scruff of the neck and tried to shake his teeth out.

"Please, mister!" the wide-eyed urchin whined. "I brung it all back to ye. All but enough to buy a wee morsel of bread for me old dad. He's dying, you see. I couldna let him go on a empty belly."

Hugh kept a firm grip on the lad while he counted the gold. The boy had told the truth. What little was missing, Hugh could replace easily from the change in his own pocket. That was a relief!

He turned a stern gaze on the pitiful creature, sympathy overcoming his anger. "You're no kind of thief at all. What made you bring it back, lad?"

The boy, who called himself Rory, shrugged. "I told you. I didn't need so much. I wouldna steal a man's fortune on purpose. Only enough to keep the wolf away."

"What does your old dad do, lad?"

"He was a sailing man in his better days. But it's been a long time since he was at sea."

"Take me to him!" Sinclair ordered, and the boy, kept in tow by an iron grip, had little choice. Hugh planned to give the man a healthy piece of his mind and warn him that he'd better keep an eye on his light-fingered son.

The section near the docks where Rory lived was the worst part of Glasgow. The narrow alleys were strewn with filth and the rats had more to eat than the people who lived there. Rory showed Hugh into a dark back room that reeked of whiskey, urine, and some festering disease. The mound on the sagging bedstead proved to be a man, Rory's dying stepfather.

"You there, I've brought your boy home," Hugh said.

The man made no move, no reply.

Rory immediately set up an awful racket, keening a lament, sure that the old man had expired during his absence.

"Light that candle, lad," Hugh directed, wanting to give the wailing child something to do to shut him up. "He's not dead. You'll see."

"The weak light from the smoky tallow candle proved a revelation to them both. Rory's keening stopped as he saw his stepfather was not dead. And Hugh Sinclair realized at the same moment that he knew the poor fellow, had sailed with him, in fact.

"Black Jack McShane? Is that you, man?"

"Aye," came the weak answer. "And who be you?"

"Hugh Sinclair. Remember? We were mates aboard the *Nancy Q* out of Liverpool."

"God help us all! Can it be? And you lookin' foin and dapper as ye please! Still sailin'?"

"Aye. Captain of the *Siren Song*, soon to set sail for America."

Black Jack coughed wretchedly then until Hugh thought he had breathed his last breath. Finally, in a whisper of a voice, he said, "It's good to see you, Hugh me boy. And a better time you couldna have come. I'm dying. Rory here will come to no good without someone to keep him in hand."

"What about his mother?" Hugh asked, anticipating the unwanted obligation that was about to be foisted upon him.

Black Jack raised his head and spat on the dirt floor. "The bitch! I woulda married her and taken the wee bastard for my own and her in the bargain. But she dumped the boy and ran off. Ain't seen nor heard of that one these past three years. There'll be no help from that quarter."

"The boy's real father?" Hugh was grasping at straws, sure of the answer before he asked.

It came as no surprise when McShane answered, "He's got none. Only what the sickness hasn't eat of me already. I'd be gone by now had the lad not found a bit of bread and whiskey to keep me going a few days more. But I won't have him stealin'! He ain't much to look at, but Rory's a good lad."

Hugh Sinclair steeled himself for what was sure to come next. How could he agree to take charge of this scruffy, undisciplined ten-year-old? On the other hand, how could he refuse his old shipmate?

Another coughing spasm stayed McShane's request. Hugh could tell that every word the dying man spoke racked his body with pain. To save him further anguish, Hugh said quietly, "I'll take the boy in hand, Black Jack. You've done me many a good turn in your day and now Rory himself has saved me from prison or worse."

The dying man reached out unsteadily to Hugh and said, "Bless you! There's not many I'd ask and fewer who'd agree."

As Black Jack McShane drew his last faltering breath and then eased over to the other side, Hugh reminded himself that there had not been many men like him. The old seaman had once possessed a strong body, a sharp mind, and a stout heart. He had saved Hugh's young neck more times than he could recall, and now it was time to repay the debt.

After all, Hugh thought, weren't he and young Rory McShane kinsmen of the bar sinister? Bastards both!

Hugh recalled now with a grimace how he'd had to pry the sobbing boy's arms from around the corpse. A few dollars in the right hands had insured that Black Jack received a proper burial. A bath, a new suit of duds, and a hot meal for his empty belly had seen to it that Rory McShane, forevermore, would be tied to Hugh Sinclair as closely as any faithful dog ever heeled to its master. And so they were linked to this very day, by obligation and affection, if not by blood.

Hugh tossed in his bunk, feeling the last remnants of the storm buffeting the ship. His thoughts went to the poor unfortunates locked away in steerage. He'd had to send his sailors down only hours ago to remove three dead from their miserable midst, two little children and one man who had been too old to attempt the crossing in the first place. The stench below, the sailors had told him, was unbearable.

And Anna Rose was down there—beautiful, delicate, sweet-smelling Anna Rose. How could she bear it? How could Rory stand knowing what she was having to endure?

Maybe Rory could, but Hugh couldn't!

He rose from his bunk and went to his writing desk. Quickly, he scrawled a note, then called for the cabin boy. "Take this down to the tween decks and see that it is delivered into Mrs. McShane's hands."

The lad saluted, said, "Aye, aye, Captain sir!" and was gone.

Hugh was packing a few things in a satchel when the cabin boy returned only minutes later.

"Out with it, boy!" the captain ordered impatiently.

"The lady thanks you, sir. But she says she must refuse your kind offer. There are sick to be tended below and she must stay there."

Hugh's face contorted with rage and frustration. Anna Rose was just being stubborn. He'd explained in his note that he would vacate the cabin, move in with the first mate. There was no need for her to stay below with the other passengers when it was within his power to make her more comfortable. He would speak with Rory. He would order her husband to make Anna Rose take his cabin. If she were *his* wife, he would never allow her to suffer!

The captain was pulling on his clothes, getting ready to go find Rory when the cry from above reached him: "Man overboard! All hands on deck!"

9

Anna Rose, although physically still on board the *Olympia,* was mentally somewhere far away. Her spirit seemed to float cloudlike above the thatched roof of the old gray stone cottage, out over the meadow and the glen, then on to the hazy Highlands beyond.

She could smell the good earth and the fresh-cut barley. She could see the purple of the thistle blending with the lavender-gray of the mists drifting over the hills, and the white roses, looking like stars as they climbed the trellis near the cottage door. She smiled in her fitful sleep, hearing her mother's soft singing and her father's gruff laughter mingled with the high-pitched voices of her brothers and sisters at play.

Home! Always the same, yet ever different. It was a kaleidoscope of love and warmth and security, a safe harbor in the turbulent sea of life.

But soon a dark cloud consumed the calm scene. Anna Rose tossed in her bunk as she felt the cold of a harsh wind from the north. Lightning flashed and dead leaves swirled up to sting her face. She moaned softly. The fever was back, burning her up, consuming her totally in its flames.

She had roused enough sometime earlier to read the captain's note by the flickering light of the cabin boy's lamp. It had been kind of Hugh Sinclair to offer her his compartment. But even if she had been willing to forsake the others and move to more comfortable quarters, she was far too ill at the moment. The fever and chills alternated. She drifted, without a will of her own, in and out of consciousness.

When her dream shattered, she became aware once more of the heat and the noxious odors and the nauseating wallow of the ship, of babies crying and mothers pleading with them to be quiet or with God to deliver them. Then another sound aroused her, that of boots thudding on deck overhead and loud voices calling excitedly. She groped her way back to reality just as one of the sailors entered the tween-decks area and shouted, "Every able-bodied man on deck. Man overboard!"

The "able-bodied" among the steerage passengers were few and far between. Still, those who could drag themselves from their bunks answered the call. They might be little help with the rescue efforts, but the promise of fresh air above was enough to move them to action.

Someone was shaking Anna Rose, calling her name over and over again. She turned her head toward the sound and forced her heavy lids open, trying to focus her uncertain vision.

"Anna Rose, please, wake up." It was Mrs. Tierney. "They've opened the hatch at last, dear. You must come up on deck for some air."

"What's happening? Have we reached America?" Anna Rose mumbled with extreme effort.

Mrs. Tierney helped her friend down, wrapping a moth-eaten blanket about her shoulders to stave off a chill. "No, dear. We've many leagues to go yet. Some poor fellow's gone overboard, I'm afraid. There'll likely be no help for him, but at least you'll be able to clear your head. You've been raving something fierce in your sleep, dear. You've had me half out of my mind with worry."

Anna Rose staggered slightly and her friend lent a supporting arm. She had heard nothing past the woman's statement that one of the crew had gone overboard. "Rory!" she cried.

"Hush, child! Don't even think such a thing. You'll have yourself swooning with worry."

Anna Rose was shaking all over, but the chill came from deep in her heart, not from the fever. She knew as surely as she knew her own name that it was her husband who was drowning.

Mrs. Tierney, feeling Anna Rose's sudden tremor, halted their progress. "Perhaps you're not strong enough to go up after all."

"I'm just tired," Anna Rose insisted, frantic to be above. "I'll be all right, really I will."

"Of course you will, dear," Mrs. Tierney soothed. "But go carefully. You're as weak as watered-down ale."

The progress of the two women was painfully slow. Anna Rose proved anything but steady on her feet, and the sea was still tossing the *Olympia* about as if she were a toy boat made of balsa wood. But as they climbed the ladder, a sudden blast of clean, moist sea air swept over them. In an instant, the foul stench of the steerage compartment vanished. Had it not been for her concern over Rory's fate, Anna Rose would have felt revived and alive again. But as it was, she hardly noticed the fine air.

She came out on deck, turning her face up to the cool ocean spray. The deck was crowded with crew and passengers, all running this way and that. She caught a sailor's arm as he rushed past her, lifeline in hand. "Where is he?"

"Don't know, ma'am. We ain't spotted him yet." Then he hurried on.

Anna Rose felt her heart sink. Although the storm had passed, the sea was still churning. There was little chance that the man would survive the waves. Her only hope was that Rory was still safe on deck somewhere.

Bracing herself against the bulkhead, she shielded her eyes from the misting rain and scanned the ship for any sign of her husband. He was nowhere to be seen. She cast her gaze to heaven, offering up a silent prayer. Her answer came immediately.

When she spied a figure, far up in the rigging, her heart all but stopped, then raced with a hectic beat.

"Rory darlin'," she breathed, her eyes filling with tears of relief.

Seaman Rory McShane clung to the ropes in the shrouds high above the pounding waves that had the deck all awash in spindrift. He was damned if he'd stay below like the others, running everywhere and making no progress whatsoever in spotting their shipmate who'd gone over the side. From his vantage point high in the rigging, Rory, spyglass in hand, could scan a full 360 degrees in search of the unfortunate fellow.

He clung to his perch, one arm locked around the mast, while he surveyed the wild waves below. So intent on his task was he that he never spied Anna Rose when she came on deck.

The wind was freshening again. The sails filled with a sudden blast that made a sound like the shot of a cannon. The spar beneath Rory weakened by the fierce winds of the storm, groaned against his weight. The ropes tightened. And in the wake of the wind, the heavens opened again, dousing all on deck with a new downpour.

Suddenly, Rory saw a dark form in the water, fighting the swells to stay afloat. He squinted through his glass, then gave a mighty shout. "He's there! Man overboard! Off the starboard quarter!"

At the shout from above, Captain Sinclair looked up. His hat, pulled low on his forehead, kept the rain out of his eyes. He could see the figure, dark against the shrouds. "Rory!" he breathed. "Damn his skin!"

A moment later, he spied something else that made his jaw tense and his palms go clammy.

Sinclair didn't wait to pass his order through the first mate as was shipboard custom. Cupping his hands to his mouth, he yelled, "Seaman McShane! Come down! Now, carefully, lad!"

All the others, ship's company and passengers alike, were at the starboard rail, their full attention on the man in the water, the man whose life Rory had saved by spotting him. They had a line out to the sailor and even now a rescue boat was being lowered into the foaming sea. No one at the railing ever guessed that the drama they were playing out was second to the one unfolding high above their heads.

But Anna Rose was there beside the captain; she saw and heard the same as he. The relief she had experienced moments earlier had vanished with the ominous creaking of the spar. She knew exactly what was happening. She also knew there was nothing she could do, nothing anyone could do. Her husband, at the moment, was there before her very eyes—alive and well. Still, there was no way to save him. He might as well have been dying of some fast-killing disease or have been claimed by the treacherous sea himself.

Her frantic fear gave way to acceptance. All was lost. There would be no long years of happy marriage, no sons to watch grow to manhood, no home to share in the rice lands of Georgia. Their love had struck suddenly and would end in like fashion.

Feeling a cold hand close over her heart, Anna Rose called her husband's name, reaching vainly toward his distant figure. Her voice was all but drowned out by the rising whine of the wind and the sickening, heart-rending sound of wood groaning, sighing, splintering ever so slowly but surely.

"Goddamnit!" the captain cursed under his breath. It was an oath of helplessness. He knew, as did Anna Rose, that it was too late.

"Rory?" she called again.

"Anne Rose . . . darlin-n-n' . . ."

The wind took the doomed man's words and played with them, flinging them this way and that as a child might toss a ball.

It all happened so quickly. Yet to Anna Rose the separating wood, the sagging spar and sail, and Rory's body, pitched forward to free-fall toward the deck, seemed to be taking place in grotesque and excruciating slow motion. His cry mingled with her own wail and that of the wind until all sound ended abruptly with the thud of his body striking the deck.

Numb with horror, unable to utter a sound, Anna Rose stood staring at the crumpled form only a few feet away. He had landed on his back, arms outspread. His right leg was twisted cruelly beneath him, while his torso angled oddly toward the left. His eyes and mouth were open. He seemed to be staring up at the broken spar that a moment ago had held him, surprised at the great distance he had come in only seconds.

"Rory?" Anna Rose said in a whispery voice. "I'm here, Rory. You'll be all right."

Hugh Sinclair put a hand on her arm, trying to stop her, but it was no use. She jerked out of his grasp and screamed, "No! Leave me alone! I must go to him!"

The next moment she was kneeling beside the twisted body of her husband, cradling his head in her lap as she smiled down into his staring blue eyes.

He was still breathing, just barely. His lips moved, allowing a trickle of blood to escape down his chin.

"Don't try to talk, darlin'," Anna Rose cautioned.

"Got to . . . before it's too late. No secrets between us . . . Anna Rose, love . . . me and Iris . . . ."

As he spoke her sister's name, Rory's body jerked in a violent spasm, then sagged as he expelled his final breath. His unseeing eyes remained open, staring up at his wife. But the blue had dulled to a hazy hue.

Anna Rose wiped the blood from his chin with the hem of her skirt and rocked his lifeless form gently. "There now, isn't that better, darling?" she crooned. "We'll be in America soon and everything will be just fine. We'll have our land and our children and each other . . . the rest of our lives together, Rory. It's all going to be the way you said, the way we . . . ."

Hugh had been standing back, listening to her words while pain ripped at his heart like a vulture tearing the flesh from a living being. He was conscious that all the others, having whisked one shipmate from the very jaws of death, had gathered about, shocked to silence by Rory's sudden demise. But the captain didn't turn to see them. His whole consciousness was filled with the woman—weeping pitifully now—as she kissed and cradled her dead husband.

Mrs. Tierney went to her and tried to bring her away. Anna Rose seemed not to hear her friend. She only gripped Rory's body more tightly as if she thought she might coax him back to life through sheer determination and the great love she felt for him.

The captain couldn't let this go on. Death on board ship came all too often. Sailors took it in their stride. Had the other man drowned, he would have received a solemn farewell at the beginning of a normal day's work, with little to-do made over his passing. But Rory's fall had been so unexpected, so sudden. And no one could comfortably deal with the fact that his wife had witnessed his death and was even now fondling his broken and twisted corpse. It was unnatural, unwholesome, a sight to discomfort the most hardened seaman.

Hugh turned and motioned to two sailors, both pale with shock. "Get a tarp for the body."

"Aye, sir." They hurried to obey his orders, anxious to put an end to the grisly scene.

When Anna Rose refused to allow the men to cover Rory's body, when she cursed them and screamed at them, it was time for the captain to take matters in hand.

He gripped Anna Rose's shoulders and forced her to her feet, even as she cried out in protest. Hugh felt her body go rigid against him, then a moment later she sank in a faint in his arms.

"Do as I ordered!" he commanded. Quickly, the sailors covered the body.

He turned to the chalk-faced woman standing near. "Mrs. Tierney, I'll need you're help with her. She's not only overcome with grief, but burning with fever. Why didn't someone tell me she was ill? How long has she been sick?"

"For days now, Captain, but she kept going, helping the others who were worse off than herself. She's a brave girl, our Anna Rose. But the past night and day she's been out of her head and confined to her bunk, poor dear."

Hugh Sinclair looked down at the woman in his arms. Her face was totally bloodless except for the bright blotches left from her crying. Her eyes were closed, her lips puffy. She seemed hardly to be breathing at all, yet she shivered against him.

"Come with me. Quickly!" he said to Mrs. Tierney. "I'm taking her to my cabin."

Mrs. Tierney followed as ordered. It was good that the child would have a clean, comfortable place to recover, else she might have died with so many of the others. But deep down inside, a new fear was nagging at the woman. Anna Rose McShane was a redemptioner. And now with her husband gone, death itself might be preferable to what Captain Sinclair was saving her for.

The Widow Tierney crossed herself and followed the captain to his cabin.

For two weeks, Anna Rose struggled against the demons of hell. In scant moments of near consciousness, she was aware that she was being cared for by a grim-faced man and a kindly woman. She thought she knew them, but somehow she could never quite put names to the dim faces. From time to time she was also aware of a vast emptiness inside her, a physical ache more painful than any induced by her illness. But she was unable to identify its cause. Sorting things out seemed totally beyond her. When she tried, she became more confused. Soon weariness would overtake her and she would allow herself to drift off again.

Toward the end of the second week, Anna Rose began to rouse from the clutches of her illness. For brief periods, she was perfectly lucid and in between times she slept the natural sleep of the weary. When she awoke either Mrs. Tierney or Hugh Sinclair was always there to spoon hot barley broth between her parched lips and to talk to her soothingly, assuring her that the voyage was almost over and she would indeed live to see America.

One clear calm night, she awoke to find Hugh alone watching over her. He looked as weary as she felt. His dark-tanned face was lined and his gray-black eyes as dull as quarried granite. But he wasted no time in calling for a cup of broth, which he proceeded to force upon her, all the while talking in quiet, reassuring tones.

"You've slept through the worst of the crossing, Anna Rose. A smart one, you are! The first storm we met was only a warm-up to these past few days. But, as my father used to say, 'There's good in all that's ill.' Thanks to the winds that tried to sink us, we'll reach New York ahead of schedule. Three days from now we'll be making port."

Anna Rose obligingly finished her broth. She had no appetite yet, still, the warmth of the soup felt good inside her and she was beginning to feel stronger from it. But with her renewed health came a flood of pain, the horrible memory of Rory's death. So far, neither the captain nor Mrs. Tierney had spoken of what had happened. She guessed correctly that Hugh Sinclair had warned the other woman against bringing up the subject.

"Captain," Anna Rose said, interrupting his uninteresting recital of wind velocity and storm damage, "what about my husband?"

She watched the forced pleasantness fade from his face. For a moment or two he shifted his gaze, unable to meet her eye to eye. Obviously, he had known this moment would come, and he had been dreading it. When he looked at her again, his jaw was set in a firm line and he wore a stern but calm expression.

"We consigned Rory's remains to the deep, Anna Rose." His voice was quiet as he spoke, like that of a person presiding over a funeral, she thought. "I read suitable passages from the Book so his soul would rest easy. When we reach New York, I'll have flowers cast on the waters for him, if you wish."

Anna Rose felt a strange calm descend over her. The captain—Rory's friend—thought of everything. Had her husband been able to dictate his own passing, he would have wanted it to overtake him suddenly. And had he been allowed to plan his own funeral, he would have desired it simple. What more could a woman ask for a dearly beloved husband? What good would it do to waste tears and strength in mourning now? What fortitude she had left would be needed to make her way in the New World.

"He was a good friend, Anna Rose," Hugh said at length, not sure what her long silence meant.

She nodded. "And a good husband."

Even as she said this, she remembered that his last words had concerned her sister. What had he tried to tell her about Iris? She would never know now.

Anna Rose realized suddenly that Hugh Sinclair was holding her hand, caressing the back of it in a soothing and consoling manner, the way a close relative might stroke a widow at her husband's wake. His touch, taken in that way, was comforting.

"Anna Rose, I made Rory a promise on your wedding day."

She looked up at him quizzically, thinking back to that fine May morning when it had seemed to her that the whole world shared her happiness.

"I told Rory that should anything befall him during the crossing, I would see to you when we reached America. I intend to keep that promise one way or another."

His words turned her cold. She no longer felt soothed by his touch and quickly drew her hand away. More than the memory of her husband's death came back now. She remembered, too, that she was a "redemptioner," bound to serve out her husband's seven years' servitude to the highest bidder. Yes, Captain Hugh Sinclair meant to see to her all right! Mrs. Tierney had explained exactly how.

"I'm tiring you," the captain said. "You should sleep now."

Anna Rose sank back on the pillows and closed her eyes. But she only pretended to sleep. As long as Hugh Sinclair remained in the cabin with her, she would feel uneasy. And she had a plan. If Rory had signed the redemption papers, they must be here in the captain's compartment somewhere. She would find them and destroy them. Without papers of bondage, he could not put her up for auction, she reasoned.

Anna Rose was sleeping, or so Hugh thought. He had spent enough time with her these past two weeks to know her every sound and move. He had memorized her face, the curve of her breasts underneath the blanket, the rich color of her long hair glowing against the white pillows like a flame burning brightly in the snow. He could tell when she was dreaming pleasantly by the soft smile that curved her lips, and when she was troubled by nightmares she whimpered like a small animal caught in a vicious trap. These evil night-stalkers visited all too often. It was these times when he felt closest to her, when he would go to her and stroke her forehead and whisper reassurances. During one of her worst times, he had taken her into his arms and rocked her and whispered to her until she grew calm. He had kissed her tenderly and, foolish as it was, he had gloried in her unconscious response.

A wry smile twisted his lips. He could calm Anna Rose, but he could do nothing to calm himself. The more he was with her, the more he realized that for the first time in his life, he truly loved a woman, as a husband should love only his wife.

And therein lay his dilemma. He wanted to fulfill his promise to Rory McShane by marrying his widow. It was not only the sensible thing to do, but the route that would prove most pleasing to them both; he felt sure of it. However, he knew that a good Christian woman like Anna Rose, gently reared, would demand her period of mourning before she could bring herself to consider another proposal. Nor would she marry him for the convenience of the situation. She would have to love him with all her heart—as much as she had loved Rory—to consent to be his bride. With her dead husband still firmly in possession of her affections, there would be no room yet for another.

So what would he do with her until she reached the time in her life when she could look ahead instead of back? The first thing he would do, of course, the minute they reached New York, was pay her passage and tear up the document he had forced Rory to sign. Never had he planned to auction Anna Rose into servitude if anything like this happened. The signed redemption papers had been for Rory's benefit alone, concrete reminders of the lad's obligations.

A knock at the door interrupted Hugh Sinclair's reverie. "Come!" he called.

The first mate stepped into the cabin, doffed his cap, and said, "Cap'n sir, I've written this notice you requested to go in the New York papers. Would you be wantin' to look it over?"

Sinclair took it, glanced at Anna Rose to make sure she was still sleeping, then mumbled the words aloud, checking the notice's accuracy.

"A few Scots and Irish Redemptioners are landed from the ship *Olympia,* Captain Sinclair from Glasgow, and are for sale on reasonable terms: one millwright, one weaver, one baker, several likely females suitable for house servants and maids, with some few boys and girls. The terms of sale and time of servitude may be known by attending the public auction at the docking place of the *Olympia* on the second noon after arrival in the port of New York."

"Is it all right then, sir? The wording, I mean."

"It's fine," Sinclair replied. "See that broadsides are printed and posted about the city as soon as we dock. And have copies delivered to the *Journal of Commerce* and the *Post.*"

Captain Sinclair had been mistaken. Anna Rose was not sleeping. She had heard every word of the advertisement he had just read and the words chilled her through, especially the part about "likely females." From what Mrs. Tierney had told her, she guessed that few of these would be blessed with the duties of house servant or maid.

Turning her face to the wall, Anna Rose opened her eyes, determined now not to sleep. She must be wide awake and keen of wit so that the moment the captain left her alone she could be up. She must find those papers and destroy them. Without Rory's signature that turned her over to Hugh Sinclair, the man had nothing to sell. And Rory, God rest him, would not be signing away her life ever again.

Nor would any other man control her life from this day on! She meant to take charge and make her own way. She hoped she would love again; she might even marry again. But what happened to her from this moment forward would be on account of Anna Rose Mackintosh McShane's decisions and no one else's!

So she vowed as she lay silent and still in Hugh Sinclair's bed, awaiting her chance to set herself free.

10

The night was fine, clear, and calm. Overhead, the sky looked like a bowl of cobalt crystal, studded with sparkling gems. The faint wind that pushed them ever westward was perfumed with the scent of land drawing nigh. The whole ship seemed to have taken up new spirit with the cry of "Land ho!" from the lookout in the crow's nest just before sunset. Although they were still some way out, on a far corner of the deck several of the sailors were singing songs of home to the plaintive notes of a mouth organ. And many of the steerage passengers had come up to get their first glimpse of the distant smudge on the horizon that would be their new home.

But the *Olympia*'s captain took little note of any of this. Hugh Sinclair paced the deck, hands clasped tightly behind his back, head bowed, and brow furrowed.

What to do about Anna Rose? The question continued to nag at him. By tomorrow this time they would be in New York. Before they made port, he had to come up with an answer.

Anna Rose was much stronger now, almost totally recovered from her bout with the shipboard fever that had struck her down. She was a woman of great constitution, with a will to live that had carried her this far and would continue to sustain her. Undoubtedly, High thought, she could survive all alone, if she had to. But there was no need for that. He was more than willing to take her on as his private and most welcome responsibility. If only he could convince her that Rory had wanted it this way and that she should submit to her dead husband's wishes.

He stopped at the railing—the very spot where he had encountered Anna Rose on her wedding night—and stared down into the dark sea, as if seeking guidance from the ghost of Rory McShane.

"Damnit!" he cursed softly, striking the rail with his clenched fist.

His final decision came suddenly. There was no other way. He would go to the cabin, wake Anna Rose, and declare himself. If need be, he would wave the redemption papers under her nose and threaten her with the auction block should she refuse his alternate proposal. But one way or another, he would make his plan work.

He turned with a purpose now, and strode across the deck toward the cabin that had been his own until Anna Rose took ill.

It was lucky for Anna Rose that Captain Hugh Sinclair wore heavy boots and was anything but light of foot. Had this not been the case, he would have caught her rifling through his desk, searching for the very papers that he planned to hold up against any arguments from her. As it was, she heard him coming and slipped quickly back into the bed, pretending to be sound asleep when the door banged opened.

"Anna Rose," he boomed. "Wake up!"

Her eyes flew wide in surprise, not at his sudden appearance, which she had anticipated, but at his stern voice. She had come to expect only gentleness and concern in his now familiar tone. He might bully his sailors as the need arose, but with her he was always the soul of patience and kindheartedness.

"I'd like a word with you," he said more quietly.

"It's quite late, Captain." She stifled a feigned yawn. "Can't it wait till morning?"

"No!" he answered bluntly. "Tomorrow at first light we'll navigate the Narrows into New York Bay. I'll have little time, come sunrise, to discuss anything besides ships's business. This being a personal matter, it must be settled tonight."

"Very well then." Anna Rose propped up in bed and pulled the covers up to her chin.

She waited and watched while he paced, while he fidgeted with the inkwell on his desk, while he poured himself a glass of vinegary water, sipped at it, spat it out, then paced again.

"Well, Captain?"

When he turned to face her, his features were set in a determined cast. He seemed sure of himself now, ready to discuss his important matter, whatever it might be.

"Anna Rose," he began, "you're in a ticklish situation— young, widowed, penniless, and about to be cast adrift in a strange new land. It wasn't what Rory would have wanted for you."

She looked down, avoiding his searching gaze. Would she ever reconcile herself to the reality of her husband's sudden death? She doubted it. The mere mention of his name caused her pain. "Nor was this fate what I wanted for myself, to be truthful, Captain."

"Exactly my point! You need looking after, Anna Rose. You need a roof over your head, someone to provide for you, someone to belong to."

Anna Rose winced at his final words. She guessed now where he was leading. A bond slave most certainly *belonged* to the master from what she'd heard from the other passengers. During the period that he or she had to serve, an indentured servant could neither buy nor sell anything, could not marry, could not leave the house without consent, and a woman who became pregnant without her master's permission during her time of service was compelled to work out another full term of indenture for the hapless misfortune of becoming a mother before she was free to do so.

Obviously, Hugh Sinclair knew all this and his conscience was paining him. He wanted her to ease it by telling him that she fully accepted the conditions of the paper Rory had been coerced into signing, that she was perfectly willing to be auctioned off in New York for the comfort of room and board in exchange for her hard labor and total loss of liberty. Well, hell would freeze over first!

"Captain, if it's the money for my passage that's bothering you, I'll find work and pay you, but—"

"Damnit, Anna Rose, you aren't making this easy!" He was pacing again, trying to find the right words. When he turned back to her, his face was still set, but his color was high. "I'm not a man to put these things well. I've had little practice at it. You see, I promised Rory that I'd look after you if anything should happen to him. The lad was like a son to me. I won't shirk my duties now that he's gone. I know you loved him well. And I know he's not been long departed. But sometimes necessity takes precedence over propriety. I believe that this is just such a case. I'll pay your passage, you needn't worry about that. Then you'll exchange the name McShane for that of Sinclair."

He paused, waiting for an answer. He knew he'd put it to her bluntly, but it hardly seemed fitting to speak of love just now, when he heard her every night, sobbing her dead husband's name while she slept. Her expression, blank, staring, uncomprehending, told him nothing. He cursed himself silently. He'd botched it, he was sure.

He'd wanted to tell her so much more—how her hair looked in the moonlight, how her eyes shown with all the lights of a warm spring morning, how her voice was like a soft caress, how he loved her as he had never loved another woman. He'd wanted to speak of the long nights he'd spent tending her while she was ill and how on more than one occasion he had been tempted to take her in his arms while she slept. He'd wanted to hold her, to love her. He wanted that still.

But those words would have offended her. Besides, he was not a poetic man. No, he had chosen the only route he could take by offering her his name in exchange for her freedom from bondage. She was a cunning woman. Surely she could see the sense of his proposal. As for talk of love, that could wait until later, until his words could be accompanied by appropriate actions.

She was still staring at him in that odd way when he asked, "Anna Rose, have you heard a word I've said?"

She nodded slowly, taking time to form the proper response. "I've heard, Captain. But I find what I'm hearing hard to believe. Rory had no right to decide my future for me. And I thought the day of buying wives was a long time past. Or is it only a *likely female* you're in need of?" She shook her head suddenly, furiously. "Either way, I'm afraid I must refuse your generous offer."

"Anna Rose, you don't know what you're saying."

"I know full well, Captain." She kept her voice calm in spite of the turmoil of her emotions. She was fully aware of the tender care he had given her during her illness. She'd seen the Death Angel hovering all too near in her fevered nightmares. Were it not for Hugh Sinclair's determined ministrations, she might not be here at this moment, refusing him. He was certainly a fine specimen of a man, one any wife would be proud to have as her husband. But not this way, not to pay off a debt or to be a charity case, without one word of love having passed between them. And, too, there were other things to be considered. She had made a vow never again to depend solely on any man for her survival. She meant to stick to that. She was young, strong, and quite handy at a number of things. Surely she could make her own way. When and if she took another husband, she wanted him for love, not pity.

Her voice was toneless when she spoke, masking all the emotions battling within her. "I'm afraid it's too soon for me to think of marriage again, if that's what you're suggesting."

"You know it is." He answered her in a bare whisper. He had slumped down into a chair, his forehead resting on his palm as if he were suddenly very weary. "Anna Rose, you know it is!"

"But my man's been gone such a short time. It wouldn't be right." She felt tears welling up and tried desperately to fight them back. "I need to mourn him properly."

Hugh was on his feet again, hope welling up once more. Coming to the side of the bunk, he reached out a hand and touched Anna Rose's hair in a gesture that was like a benediction. "I understand that. Truly, I do. And I promise you'll have that time after we're wed. I'll lay not one finger on you to claim you as my wife until you feel you're ready, be it a month or a year, Anna Rose. You have my solemn promise."

In spite of her sincere resolve, she was sorely tempted. How easy it would be to fall back on old ways, to put her life and her future into strong and capable hands once again. But she'd always thought a man's protection a means of security, and look where such ideas had got her so far: her father lame and dying, her husband dead already. No, a man to look after her was no guarantee that all would be well. And her father and Rory had loved her besides. To Captain Hugh Sinclair she was no more than a charity case, a poor widow that honor bound him to look after because in a weak moment he had made a hasty promise.

"It wouldn't be right," she answered quietly, avoiding his dark gaze.

He was angry now and frustrated beyond his limits. "And what's not right about it? Tell me that! I've made you an honest offer."

"Only because you promised my husband. No, I won't be wed that way." Her voice had reached a pitch to match the captain's. She forced it lower when she added, "I have some pride, after all!"

"Pride!" he sneered. "That and fifty Yankee greenbacks will pay the owners of this ship for your passage! Alone it will buy you nothing but loneliness, grief, and hunger."

"I've known hunger before," she answered quietly, thinking of the frequent lean years back on the croft in Scotland.

"All the more reason that you should never have to suffer again. Be reasonable, Anna Rose."

Before she could answer, he hurried on. "I own a fine old Dutch house on Wall Street, made of sturdy Holland brick with three floors and high dormers to hold the heat in the bitterest winter and catch the sea breeze in the summer. It's a comfortable enough house, but it wants a woman's touch to become a home. I can see you now, presiding at table or waiting on the high front stoop for me to come home from work at day's end. Aye! Can't you see it?" He nodded and smiled at her for the first time. "It's a pretty picture, Anna Rose."

"My father and Rory had a habit of painting pretty pictures, too." Shaking her head furiously, she added, "No more than castles in the air." Then she turned away, not wanting him to see her tears and guess how tempted she really was. "I'm sorry. No," she finished curtly.

He paused, wondering if he dared threaten her to get his way. Frustration won out over reason. "Anna Rose, you must understand that there's only one alternative to my proposal."

Her head shot up and she felt the blood draining from her face. Sure enough, when she looked he was holding the redemption papers in his fist—the only legacy her dead husband had left her.

"No, Hugh!" she gasped softly.

"I'll leave you to think it over." He rose, heading for the door, then turned and added, "You have until eight bells tomorrow to decide and give me an answer." Then he gave her the ghost of a smile and said, "You know what I hope it will be, Anna Rose."

With a feeling of hopelessness, she watched him stuff the redemption papers back into his breast pocket before he left. Unless she could think of a way out, she would either be auctioned or wed within a few hours. Neither prospect was of her own choosing.

If only Rory hadn't signed those papers. If only he hadn't asked Hugh to look after her . . . to *marry* her . . .

Her head drooped and she let out a single choked sob. "Oh, Rory, why, my dearest? Why?"

"My dear, I'd take you along with me if I could. But my son and his wife have only a wee cottage in Petticoat Lane and six babies to provide for."

Anna Rose had confided her plight to Mrs. Tierney. The bright-eyed little woman was all concern. However, she could offer no solution.

"And, still, there's your passage price to be paid. Where you'll come by that I have no notion." She smiled encouragingly and patted Anna Rose's arm as they stood at the railing watching the lower edge of Manhattan Island draw ever nearer. "Are you sure you won't take the captain's offer? He's a fine man. A woman could do far worse."

Anna Rose was hardly listening. She stood mesmerized by the sight before them, the many tall-masted ships, like trees in a watery forest, and beyond those graceful leafless trunks, *America!* Oh, how she wished her family were with her at this moment! She cast her eyes down for an instant and stared at the water. If only Rory were by her side. They'd dreamed such beautiful dreams together of this moment.

But quickly she wiped away the tear at the corner of her eye and squared her shoulders. This was no time for sentimentality. She was on her own. She must rely solely upon her own resources to make her way. Her long-pondered decision had come near dawn.

She would not burden Captain Sinclair as an unwanted bride and she refused to be auctioned to the highest bidder. She was counting on the confusion when they docked to provide her with a chance to escape. Once away from the ship, she was certain she could lose herself in the streets of New York, find work, and survive.

"I only wish there was some way I could help."

Mrs. Tierney's words cut through her thoughts. Anna Rose turned and stared at the woman as if seeing her there for the first time.

"Mrs. Tierney, there is! When you leave the ship, allow me to carry your bags. I'll be taken for your servant with no questions asked. Once we're past the agent, I'll vanish."

A bright smile lit the other woman's face, making two deep dimples that reminded Anna Rose of thumbprints in newly-risen bread dough. Her eyes twinkled with excitement as she said, "You're a cunning lass, Anna Rose McShane. Aye, you are that! And a beauty as well. You'll find your fortune, child. I have no doubts in that regard."

Anna Rose, her decision made, stared out over the water to the Battery and beyond. She could hear her father saying, "Wait till you see America! All the streets are paved with gold, so I've heard. Ah, bairns, what a life we'll lead!" With the memory of John Mackintosh's words came a sudden wave of disappointment. Even from this far away, Anna Rose could see that the gilt-paved streets were yet another of her father's follies.

Although Anna Rose remained very much on his mind, Captain Sinclair had little time to consider what her decision would be, or what he'd do if she refused him. The New York harbor was a busy place with ships coming in from sea, down the East River, and the wide, single-masted Hudson River sloops sailing out of the North River that lay to the west of the island of Manhattan.

He was forced to keep a sharp eye peeled for smaller crafts as well. Individual merchants, here as in any port around the world, made a habit of rowing out loaded with wares to entice the sailors even before they reached shore. They took their lives in their hands as they skipped along the wave tops between the tall ships, plying their trade.

The captain passed orders on to his first mate for the sail to be shortened as they made their way past the Battery to find a berth in the East River at South Street. There the American agent of Slattery and Smythe, the ship's British owner, would be waiting to collect passage money before the *Olympia* was loaded with cargo and sent back across the Atlantic.

But this old lady of the sea would have a new master for that trip, Sinclair mused with a feeling of relief. He had transported his last shipment of *human ballast*. He planned to take a well-earned vacation for a time and see to some of his investments in New York. One of his first appointments ashore would be with Michael Flynn, the shrewd agent who watched over his holdings in the city. Then, if he was lucky, he might even be using some of his free time to take a honeymoon.

His gaze strayed from the bustling harbor for a moment to the comely young woman at the port rail. The early morning sun was glinting off Anna Rose's chestnut hair, making the light shimmer around her head like a halo. She was dressed in a neat white blouse and the bright plaid skirt she wore so often. He wondered suddenly how she would look with her tresses waved and piled high, wearing a becomingly low-cut gown of the latest Paris style. She would be an asset to any man of business, he thought practically. Then he smiled, thinking that on a more personal level she would be a cherished treasure to her husband, making his after-business hours the most pleasant to be imagined.

He gave one last lingering glance to Anna Rose before dismissing from his mind all worries in that quarter. No longer was he concerned about her answer. She could refuse him all she liked, but his new plan would still work. The solution had been right there before his eyes all along. He would not press her into marriage before she was ready. That would be foolhardy. He would simply pay her passage himself and inform her that she was bound over to his personal service for the next seven years. Then he would set about making those years the most pleasant she had ever known. She would marry him, sooner or later!

Although inherited slaves worked his Georgia rice fields, Hugh Sinclair had never seen fit to purchase any of the black Africans that made up almost a quarter of New York's entire population and were advertised for sale regularly in the city's papers, nor had he ever before contracted for a bond servant. But, after all, he had as much right as anyone else to hold papers on a fetching bondwoman. And Anna Rose would receive much better treatment with him than in the hands of some grog shop owner or the proprietor of one of the infamous establishments in Cherry Street. Not that he would ever allow that to happen, but even the thought of her in such places made him shudder.

Still, it wouldn't be easy to make her see the sense of his plan. When she realized that she literally belonged to him, he expected an explosion of that quick temper. He would have to handle her carefully. He hoped when she saw his handsome house and understood that it would be her home as well, she would relent. If he could make her come to love him, then he would tear up her redemption papers and gladly sign his own bond papers—a marriage certificate—in the blink of an eye.

He could make no sense of what had come over him lately, but for the first time in years he longed to settle down. Perhaps he'd spent too many lonely nights at sea. Or maybe it was simply that at a certain age a man required a wife and family. Whatever was behind the urge, he knew that he was bound to marry soon. Thinking back, this transformation had begun back in Scotland at the wedding. And since that day, Anna Rose McShane had been the woman he desired, the only woman he thought of marrying.

The passengers lined up at the port railing, anxious to be off the ship and standing on American soil for the first time. Anna Rose carefully positioned herself and Mrs. Tierney in the very center of the group. Were they to go first down the gangplank, the agent would take special note of them. Were they to wait until last, the man might delay them simply because they brought up the end of the line. But squeezed into the middle of the impatient, jostling passengers, they should be passed along without delay or questions.

Mrs. Tierney was obviously nervous over her part in Anna Rose's escape plan. "Dear, why don't you tell the agent you're Brigid Dunwoody since she passed in the crossing, God rest her. She wasn't a redemptioner, so her name will be among those of the paid passengers. You'll be safe."

Anna Rose shook her head. She had talked with the second mate a few days earlier, questioning him closely about the procedure once they reached port. She knew that would never work.

"No, I couldn't," she told her friend. "You see, the first sailor off the ship delivers to the agent a list of passengers who died in the crossing. The man would be sure to recognize the name and detain me. But, if he's told I'm your serving woman, it might work to my advantage. No one cares much whether a servant is listed or not. If my luck holds, the agent will think it's an oversight and let me pass."

They were nearing the short, heavy-jowled man who held the lists in his beefy hands. He wore thick, wire-rimmed spectacles perched on his bulbous nose and seemed to be having difficulty reading the names even with his glasses. A new scheme began forming in Anna Rose's mind. She waited for the perfect moment, just as the last passenger before Mrs. Tierney was cleared and ordered to move on. Then she gave her friend a slight shove, knocking her into the agent, who fumbled his lists and dropped his glasses. Fate, indeed, was on her side. The spectacles hit the cobbled quay and took a bounce toward her. Anna Rose needed only to shuffle her foot slightly to crush the lenses.

"You clumsy wench!" the agent shrilled at Mrs. Tierney.

" 'Twasn't me, your honor," she protested. "I was shoved from behind. Me own servant gave me a stout push." She turned and glared at Anna Rose as she snapped, "You'll be getting the strap from the mister once we get home, you bungling chit!"

The man squinted hard at Anna Rose, but could make out only her hazy outline. "Stupid girl!" he snarled. Then to Mrs. Tierney, he said, "Why would you bring such a twit all the way across the ocean to serve you?"

The older woman, acting to the hilt, offered the ruffled agent a placating smile. "I've a kind heart that will be my undoing some day." Then, leaning close to the man as if she meant to keep her remark strictly between them, she whispered, "Brigid here is a bit simple, sir. Without me protection she'd be sure to fall in with a bad lot."

Anna Rose did hear Mrs. Tierney's words and cringed inside. Obviously, her friend had no idea that simpletons were returned to their homeland more often than not without ever being allowed to set foot on American soil. But, much to her relief, the agent seemed only interested in moving the line forward.

"Your name?" he demanded of Mrs. Tierney.

She replied quickly and gave him a fictitious identity for Anna Rose. The agent shuffled his papers and mouthed an oath.

"I can't read this without my glasses." Then, shoving the papers into the hands of one of the *Olympia*'s sailors, he demanded that the fellow check the list for the names of Mrs. Tierney and her serving girl, Brigid.

At this, Anna Rose bit hard on her lower lip to keep from smiling. This particular sailor, who had been a close friend of Rory's, could neither read nor write. She had written a letter for him to his sweetheart early in the voyage. Now, she was sure, he would return the favor.

The tall, broad-chested seaman frowned authoritatively and nodded. "They be right here on your list, gov'nor. Would you be wantin' me to check the names off for ye?"

"Never mind! Just wave them on through."

The sailor offered Anna Rose a bow and a smile as she passed the agent. She gripped his hand for a moment in silent thanks, then hurried on into the bustling hubbub that was South Street . . . New York . . . America!

It was only moments later that Captain Hugh Sinclair, the duties of docking accomplished and the anchor down, looked about to find Anna Rose. But she was gone, vanished from the railing where he'd seen her last. Nor was she with the group of redemptioners on the dock where they had been herded by the agent as they disembarked.

Perhaps she'd gone below, remembering something she'd left in the tween-decks compartment. He strode across the deck and down the ladder. But the only thing left by the passengers in that area was their foul stench. No one was there in the gloomy place. Nothing moved except a rat that scurried across his boot.

"Blast it all!" Sinclair cursed, storming back out into the bright sunshine, where the odor of the city's garbage-strewn streets and the sewage-slimed river replaced that left behind by the steerage passengers.

On deck again, he scanned the great mobs of people jamming South Street. The bowsprits of the many ships docked along the wharves jutted far out, nearly touching the storefronts and warehouses across the street and blocking much of his view. He scanned the confused scene below—mule-drawn wagons being loaded or unloaded, sailors from every land in the world and whores from almost as many. Agents, ship owners, footpads, and beggars, all were there. But no Anna Rose.

He saw that already the boarding house runners were upon his passengers, first inviting politely, but using force if a person refused. These men were ruffians paid by owners of cheap dwellings to entice newly arrived customers. They met every ship. If the new immigrants refused their offer of "good clean rooms," the runners would steal their baggage or one of their children and dash away, holding these items for ransom until the owner agreed to take the room, at double the mentioned price, of course.

Still, there were worse places for a recently landed and unwitting foreigner to wind up in New York, such as Five Points, the old brewery, or one of the Cherry Street houses. He felt a sick rage at the thought. The immigrants arrived with little more than the clothes on their backs, and if they weren't wary, they'd have even those stolen within the first week.

He had to find her!

Suddenly, he froze in place. Was it wishful thinking or had he really spied her? He held a hand up to shade his eyes from the bright sunlight. There she was! He couldn't mistake the coppery glow of her hair or the long braid swinging down her back as she shouldered her way through the crowds, heading south toward Whitehall.

"How in hell did she get past the agent?"

That didn't matter now. All that mattered was that he reach her before she lost herself in the city.

Grabbing his hailing trumpet, Hugh boomed her name.

"Anna Rose! Anna Rose McShane! Come back here!"

He thought she paused for an instant and glanced back in his direction. But by the time he was off the ship, hurrying as best he could down South Street, there was no sign of her.

Finally, when he knew there was nothing he could do, he slouched against the ballast-stone front of a ship chandlery to catch his breath and mop his sweating brow. A deep sense of loss swept over him.

Turning finally toward the direction in which she had disappeared, he whispered, "God help you, Anna Rose, for only He can now!"

11

Anna Rose heard Hugh Sinclair's booming call even over the babble of languages being spoken, shouted, and sung all around her. She glanced back at the ship, but only for an instant. She couldn't have stopped if she'd wanted to. The flow of pedestrian traffic on South Street was as swift and determined in its movement, ever forward, as the strongest current in the Atlantic. Anna Rose had no idea where she was going for she was merely being swept along with the human tide.

She'd bid a hasty farewell to Mrs. Tierney, whose son had been waiting to greet her at the dock. Before they parted, the two women had embraced and murmured their amazement that they had survived the voyage and their thanks to God that they were finally in America.

Now, suddenly, in the midst of so many people, Anna Rose felt desperately alone for the first time in her life. Someone had always been there—her family, her husband, her fellow passengers, her captain. But no more! She was as alone as if she had been cast adrift in a small boat in the middle of the ocean. Indeed, the city of New York seemed as utterly strange and frightening to her as the raging sea at the height of a storm.

Trying to escape the crowd so that she could stop for a moment to collect her thoughts, to think where to go now and what to do next, she turned off South Street into Broad. As she whipped around the corner, she ran headlong into a heavyset man who reeked of strong tobacco and Irish whiskey.

"Whoa there, missy!" The man caught her by the shoulders to steady her. "In a wee bit a hurry, ain't you? And where might you be headed?"

Anna Rose's first impulse was to draw away from the stranger. But looking up into his face, she saw his warm smile and what passed for a kindly light in his pale blue eyes. Nothing about the man seemed so threatening. She could at least ask directions of him, she decided.

"Your pardon, sir," she begged with a slight curtsy. "I'm just off the ship and still a bit wobbly on land. And I'm afraid I don't know my way about."

"Ah, I should have guessed it!" he answered with a wink. "I was just this very minute heading down to the docks to greet the incoming. And now, bless you, you've saved me the trip. You'll be needing a place to stay, am I correct?"

Anna Rose nodded. That was her first priority, after all.

"Well, then, might I recommend the fine establishment run by Mistress Hattie Tibbs in Cherry Street, a clean and proper boarding house with meals provided twice a day and only the best clientele. And at a most affordable price, I assure you. Only four pence the night or six pence with supper."

Anna Rose thought of the few coppers in her purse. "I haven't much money, sir. I'll be needing to find work right away, too."

"Aye!" He grinned broadly, showing uneven, yellowed teeth. "A fine strapping lass like yourself won't stay long idle in this land of opportunity. I'll be betting Mistress Tibbs can find you this and that to do around the place to help pay your room and board."

The fleshy boarding house runner, Crowder Quigley by name, strained to keep smiling until the muscles of his face ached. He'd caught hell and the end of her broomstick already from Hattie Tibbs this morning for having pulled too long at the bottle last night and overspending his time in bed with one of her girls. But if he could bring her this bit of prime fluff, he'd be in her good graces again for certain. And hadn't he been a lucky so-and-so to run slap into her? He couldn't think how his competitors at the docks had let this one slip through their greedy clutches. But, no matter! Their loss was his own good fortune.

When Anna Rose hesitated, thinking over his offer, he eyed the satchel clutched in her right hand. If need be, he'd snatch it and make her chase him down until he had her where he wanted her, on the very stoop of number 13 Cherry Street.

Anna Rose decided finally that some guardian angel, maybe Rory himself, must be watching over her. Here she was in a foreign land not an hour yet, almost penniless, no family or friends, and out of the blue comes a kindly stranger offering room, board, and honest work. She'd be a prize fool to turn down such an offer.

She smiled at the man. "Mr.—?"

"Crowder Quigley," the runner supplied, doffing his cap in gentlemanly fashion. "But me friends all calls me Quig. And you, milady?"

"Mrs. Anna Rose McShane."

The man's shaggy brows drew together. "And your husband, ma'am?"

"Passed," she answered, lowering her gaze. "In the crossing."

Quig suppressed a relieved smile and clutched his cap over his heart in a show of respect. "It's sorry I am, Mistress McShane, to hear such sad tidings. But that's even more reason for you to take rooms with the Mistress Tibbs, she being widowed three times her own self. She'll be more than a mite understanding of your situation."

"I believe you're right, Mr. Quigley."

"Quig," he corrected, reaching out to take Anna Rose's satchel in hand.

He led the way to Cherry Street, taking Anna Rose for many blocks up Front Street and then west across Water Street. Anna Rose didn't know what she'd expected, but New York came as a great shock to her. The houses and businesses were tall, some three stories or more, and set one upon the other without so much as a garden patch between. She thought back to Scotland and its wide fields and broad moors, not even a single neighbor within hailing distance. Even those who lived in Inverness had more space to themselves than the people here.

What small area the New Yorkers had they shared with the hordes of animals that roamed free to scatter refuse, to further snarl traffic, and to add to the ever-rising din as barking dogs chased squealing pigs and bleating goats.

"Aren't there any stock pens hereabouts?" Anna Rose asked

Quig as they passed a raucous pack of evil-eyed mongrels snarling at a large hog that was rooting through a pile of spoilt vegetables.

Quig looked at her in surprise. "And what would we be doing with all the garbage if 'twere not for the swine that clean the streets?"

Anna Rose glanced back over her shoulder. She couldn't see that the hog was doing anything other than scattering the smelly mess. She supposed Quig's attitude was due to his Irish heritage. Every crofter in Scotland knew that in Ireland the farmer's family and his pigs shared the same roof. She shuddered at the thought.

"There's meadows on up Broadway where some take their cows to graze," Quig added. "But pigs is pigs. They see to theirselves. You don't bother them, they won't bother you none."

Anna Rose had to walk fast to keep up with Quig. The day was too hot for such haste. She felt sweat trickling down her sides and between her breasts, and her petticoats clung to her legs. The mid-July heat was fierce, and as the sun beat down on her bare head, Anna Rose could feel the hot dirt of the street right through her thin slippers.

"How much farther?" she asked.

"No more'n a block now."

Moments later, Quig led the way into Cherry Street. The narrow way was lined up one side and down the other with old wooden houses that looked as if they might fall down at the least breeze off the river. Most shades were drawn and there was a significant lack of activity in this street compared with the busy roads they had passed through.

Anna Rose felt an immediate sense of relief. As the roll of the Atlantic had made her seasick, so the noise and smell and crowds of New York made her feel landsick. It seemed that the buildings of every street were closing in on her. The loud sounds of hawkers' cries, squealing animals, shouting people, and even the church bells tolling the hour had made her head throb painfully. But worst of all were the heat and the smells. She had thought nothing could be worse than the tween-decks compartment of the *Olympia*. But New York had its own distinctive rotten odor, provided by the ubiquitous fly-swarming garbage heaps and the raw sewage tossed into gutters, all baked to nauseating ripeness under the broiling sun. The hot, foul scent of the city caught in her throat with every breath she took, making her long for the cool fresh air of the open sea or a frosty mist from the Highlands.

"So there you be, Quig, you no good sneaking sonuvabitch!"

Anna Rose glanced up in alarm when she heard the woman's harsh tone. The Widow Tibbs was as round as she was tall, with a florid face, beady eyes, and wisps of gray hair straggling from beneath her dirty mobcap. She stood atop the stoop of number 13 Cherry Street, waving a brush broom threateningly at Crowder Quigley.

"You'll be holding your tongue except to beg my pardon, woman, when you see what I've brung you." Quig stepped back and swept off his woolen cap, bowing in Anna Rose's direction as if he were presenting her at court.

"A-a-w-w!" Mrs. Tibbs exclaimed, smiling as she drew back to get a better view. "And ain't she just a beauty, Quig. Me apologies for mouthin' off at you so. You've done fine to bring the lady here."

"Mistress Hattie Tibbs, may I be presentin' to you the recently widowed and even more recently arrived Mistress Anna Rose McShane," Quig said, a twinkle in his watery eyes.

Widow Tibbs bustled down the steps and grasped Anna Rose in a suffocating hug, muttering, "You poor child! All alone in the world, you are. And ain't it just a cruel place, too. But don't you worry none. Hattie will take good care of you, dear."

Anna Rose struggled to free herself from the woman's unexpected embrace. It was one thing to be welcomed to America, but quite another to be smothered by such an enormous amount of bosom, and the smells of rancid lard, onions, and gin.

"Please, ma'am," Anna Rose managed, "I need work and a place to stay."

Hattie eased her hold, but kept a firm grip on Anna Rose's hand.

"Well, of course you do, dearie. And Quig here has brought you to the very place. We'll work fine together, you and me. Now, I can't pay much at first, just your room and the food you eat. But later, after you learn the trade, you'll be wearing satins and laces, I promise you, and you'll have real gold jingling in a fine silk purse."

Anna Rose smiled in relief and gratitude. She had certainly turned the right corner at the right time. Although Mrs. Tibbs hadn't explained what trade she taught, Anna Rose was sure she could learn. Quig had been right; America was certainly the land of opportunity.

Almost two weeks passed before Anna Rose had a chance to write home, and even then she had to guard her words carefully. Perhaps she was naive, but she was neither blind nor stupid. Women who wore fine clothes, entertained all night and slept all day . . . music and laughter from midnight till dawn, and other more telling sounds from the rooms on the second floor. It had taken Anna Rose only a day or so to realize that she was not in the upstanding boarding house she had at first imagined 13 Cherry Street to be. Still, the work she did, though hard, was honest.

Every day since her arrival, Mrs. Tibbs had kept Anna Rose busy from dawn until long past nightfall, scrubbing floors, washing linens, and running errands all about town. By the time she'd cleaned up after supper each night, she was too exhausted to do anything but collapse on the narrow cot in the attic room she shared with her two roommates. These young girls, Mavis and Lena, were part of Anna Rose's reason for staying on, for she couldn't bring herself to leave such poor innocents in the clutches of the greedy madam.

Thanks to Hattie Tibbs and her never-ending errands, Anna Rose was becoming familiar with her new city. She could find her way alone now to the Fly Market at the foot of Maiden Lane, where Mrs. Tibbs sent her to buy fish every Friday. She felt equally sure of herself as she dealt with the merchants at the Old Swago on Broadway, the Bear Market in Greenwich, or Peck Slip at the foot of Ferry Street, where she bargained with the farmers who brought their vegetables over by boat every morning from Brooklyn.

She knew that the best price on Geneva, as Mrs. Tibbs called her gin, was to be found at Fraunces Tavern, the very same building where General Washington had bid farewell to his men following America's victory over England.

For wine and delicate pastries, and for the chocolates Mrs. Tibbs enjoyed even more than her Geneva, Anna Rose went to the Swiss-born Del-Monico brothers in South William Street. It seemed to her that the two brothers, Giovanni and Pietro, along with their nephew Lorenzo, occupied the only scrupulously clean spot in the city. The Del-Monicos conducted a thriving business at their little shop with its six rough pine tables, and they took great pride in their tiny restaurant, a giant step up from how they had begun in 1827, with a mere board set up across two barrels and a sign out front that read Delmonico's. Giovanni explained to Anna Rose that the sign painter had made a mistake, leaving the hyphen out of their family name. Pietro had added, "But you see, young lady, it was cheaper to change our name than to pay for a new sign. So our restaurant is Delmonico's."

At that, the two brothers roared with laughter and insisted that Anna Rose help herself to another bonbon, on the house. She looked forward to these twice-weekly visits with the jovial Del-Monicos.

But earlier today Mrs. Tibbs had sent her out on a new errand, to the quillmaker in Pearl Street. While there, with a few of the pennies she had left, Anna Rose had purchased quills, parchment, and ink for herself. Now tonight she sat in the little attic room, trying to think where to begin in telling her family all that had happened since her wedding day.

It seemed so long ago!

She began by assuring them that she was fine and as happy as she could be under the circumstances. Then she explained those circumstances—Rory's death, being careful to mask the deep grief that still plagued her, then Hugh Sinclair's proposal, her refusal, and finally her chance meeting with Crowder Quigley, who had brought her to 13 Cherry Street. From there, the telling became more difficult.

> Mrs. Tibbs is an uncommon person. I suppose one might call her kind, in her own way. She runs this boarding house for women only—no men and no children allowed. Although, there are two girls, Mavis and Lena, who help me with the cleaning, washing, and cooking and share my quarters. And they are both mere children of eleven and twelve. They claim to be distantly related to Mrs. Tibbs by marriage.
>
> New York is like nothing you've ever seen before. So many people, all of them going in different directions, and so much noise. At first, I felt awed and somewhat afraid of the great city. But now I feel a part of it, as if I had lived here forever. This is, indeed, a fine, brave land!
>
> Father, the streets here are not paved with gold as you thought. But Mrs. Tibbs promises that soon she will teach me a trade that will line my pockets well enough. I hope I start earning a decent wage soon. I have a feeling I may need it.

Anna Rose paused. Should she confide her suspicions to her family? She was all but sure she was carrying Rory's child. Mavis and Lena had already guessed. She had gained weight in the past weeks. Her breasts were swelled, her waist thickened. She could end her letter with a pleasant surprise. But no. Her family would only worry about her more than ever. Instead, she wished them all happiness, assured them once more that she was fine, then signed her letter.

"You'd better be blowin' out that candle, Anna Rose," Mavis said from her bed in a sleepy voice. "Tomorrow's the day we have to restuff all the mattresses. 'Tis hard work, I'll tell you."

116

Anna Rose turned and looked at the thin red-headed girl. "Mavis, what will the other women do tomorrow?"

"Who cares what they do? They'll probably sleep while we work like always."

"Not if we're restuffing their mattresses."

Mavis sat up and rubbed her eyes. "You're right. I clean forgot. Mrs. Tibbs closed the place tonight. No gentlemen invited. That way the *ladies* will get a good rest. Then they can be up and out like normal folks to go shopping tomorrow while we work. Now, can't we get some sleep, Anna Rose?"

She turned a curious stare on Mavis who had settled down again. If she and Lena were truly related to Mrs. Tibbs, as they claimed, why were they treated like slaves and forced to live in the airless attic? She worried about both girls. They were so thin and pale. Their drawn faces gave them expressions of perpetual surprise, and they had the large, tired eyes of old women who had seen too much in their long lives.

"Mavis, who are you, really? Where did you come from?"

The girl sat up again, glaring at Anna Rose. "Have you lost your wits? It's past midnight! And what do you mean by such daft questions? Besides, I don't like talking about such things."

"I wouldn't pry, except that I worry about you both. You remind me of my own little sisters back home."

"We're like your own sisters?" Mavis sounded touched, but still wary. "You miss them, don't you, Anna Rose?"

She nodded. "It's hard to give up one's family, to have no one."

"I'll give you that," Mavis answered quietly.

Then the whole truth came tumbling out. Mavis and Lena were children of the street. They had no idea who their families were or where they had come from. They remembered only that they had roamed the city like the pigs and the dogs, scratching through garbage heaps to keep from starving. They had begged, stolen, and lied to survive until Mrs. Tibbs took them in. She'd promised them food and a bed. But both Lena and Mavis were old enough now to understand that very soon Mrs. Tibbs would take them "into the trade." They claimed they could hardly wait.

" 'Tis better than scrubbing and washing," Mavis said, "by a damn sight, Anna Rose. And we'll not have to worry about starving to death ever again."

The young girl's attitude shocked Anna Rose. "You can't mean what you're saying!"

"Goes double for me, what Mavis says," added Lena, who had been awakened by their discussion. "How'd you like to be out on the streets when your baby comes. Not enough to eat so's you've got no milk to feed it? Then you got only three choices, like my own ma had, I reckon: dump the baby and hope it survives, leave it on some wealthy stranger's doorstep and pray it gets taken in, or keep it and watch it starve to death. I don't blame my ma one bit for washin' her hands of me. A baby's more burden than blessing among the poor of this city."

Anna Rose flinched at the girl's cynical words. How could any mother abandon her child or hand it over to strangers?

Until this moment, she'd been so happy about having Rory's child. But now she wondered bleakly, where would she go and what would she do, if she had to leave Cherry Street before her baby was born? And when Mrs. Tibbs found out, would she allow Anna Rose to stay on? What good was a woman with child in a house where men came to purchase feminine favors?

The girls went back to sleep, and Anna Rose blew out the candle and climbed into bed feeling sick and alone. She lay awake most of the night, deciding what to tell Mrs. Tibbs. But nothing seemed right. The truth was that Hattie Tibbs was not a kindhearted soul, after all. She had led a hard life and because of that she felt little sympathy for others. If they could help her, fine. But, if they couldn't, she had no room for them in her house or in her heart.

The street below came alive before Anna Rose ever closed her eyes.

"Milk, ho! Milk, come!" cried the milkman. Then the shrill voice of a chimney sweep: "Sweep, ho! From the bottom to the top without a ladder or a rope!" And the sandman: "Here's white sand. Choice white sand. Here's your lily-white Rockaway Beach sand for your floor!"

When the repeated call of "Straw! Straw! Straw!" drifted up to the attic, Anna Rose shook the other two girls awake and they all dressed quickly in the plain muslin shifts Mrs. Tibbs called their "uniforms."

All day long, as the three of them slaved away in the August heat—tearing open mattresses, burning the old straw, washing the covers, and restuffing them with clean straw—Anna Rose worried about her unborn baby and wondered if Mrs. Tibbs would let her stay on. By sunset, when the last mattress was finished and back on the bed and it was time to start supper, she had found no solution.

Anna Rose, Mavis, and Lena regularly took their meals in the kitchen instead of at the dining room table with the madam and her ladies. Just as the three of them were finishing, Mrs. Tibbs entered the room and spoke to Anna Rose.

"Let the girls tidy up tonight. I'd like a word with you in my parlor. Immediately!"

The woman was gone almost as quickly as she had appeared. There was no telling from her tone or expression what she wanted to discuss, but Anna Rose felt a cold lump in the pit of her stomach. She wondered suddenly if she would soon be without a roof over her head. Would she be sleeping in an alley this very night? She would for certain if Mrs. Tibbs had guessed that she was pregnant.

"Don't look so pale and fretful, Anna Rose," Mavis said. "She couldn't know yet. Your belly's still flat as can be."

Anna Rose wondered suddenly if either of the girls had told anyone.

As if Mavis had read her thoughts, she said, "We didn't tell, Anna Rose. We wouldn't do that. Honest!"

Anna Rose forced a smile and reached across the table to squeeze the girl's calloused hand. "I know you wouldn't. Now I'd better go and see what she has to say."

She rose and went to the mirror that hung over the washtub. She smoothed her hair and wiped a smudge of grease from her cheek. To her own eyes, her face looked flushed and rounder than ever before. She noted, too, how tightly her bodice hugged her breasts. Yes, Mrs. Tibbs could have guessed. She needed no whispered clue from anyone, but only to look at Anna Rose to see the changes in her. With a sinking heart, Anna Rose headed for the parlor.

Mrs. Tibbs smiled brightly when Anna Rose entered the room. The parlor was decorated in pink and gold, with velvet chairs and a brocade love seat. Mrs. Tibbs, her eyes glittering sharply, was dressed as if to match the room, in a pink satin gown garishly trimmed in gold braid and lace.

"Well, Anna Rose?" she said with a touch of expectancy. Anna Rose squirmed slightly, all too sure now that the woman knew her secret.

"Please, ma'am, I hardly know what to say."

"You've guessed what I want to talk to you about? Bright girl! Pleased then, are you?"

"Shouldn't any woman in my position be?" Anna Rose replied, surprised at Hattie Tibbs's friendly tone.

Mrs. Tibbs's voice softened. "I had hoped you would see it that way, but I couldn't be sure, you being so recently widowed and all. One never knows until the moment actually arrives."

"But it won't be for some months yet." Anna Rose felt confused by the conversation. She had expected to be tossed into the street with a curt dismissal. But Mrs. Tibbs actually seemed warm and solicitous, not at all her usual gruff self.

"Months? La, dear girl, do you want to go on scrubbing floors and changing linens forever? I think not! Likely your husband taught you all you need to know at first. I've decided to start you this very night. One of the girls has took ill and there'll be an extra big crowd here soon since we were closed last night."

Anna Rose was staring, uncomprehending. "Ma'am?"

"Here's your gown now. Hurry along to your room and change, then come back down here. The gentlemen will start arriving shortly."

Mrs. Tibbs rose and stepped behind a Chinese screen, bringing out a dress of scarlet satin trimmed in black lace. At the sight of it, Anna Rose's uncertainty gave way to realization. She felt her hands begin to sweat. Her head felt light and her body heavy.

"But, ma'am . . ."

"Anna Rose, there's no time for discussion. I'll send Mavis up to help you dress. Now do hurry!"

Anna Rose, scarlet gown in hand, climbed the stairs to the attic as if her feet were made of lead. *What now?* she wondered. This was a far worse predicament than she had imagined. Being cast into the street was one thing, but being ordered to entertain a strange man was quite another. Of course she could pack her things and leave immediately. But with hardly a penny to her name, how would she survive?

"It will be all right," Mavis assured her as she helped Anna Rose into the disgracefully low-cut gown. "You'll see. The gentlemen are no doubt as kind as they are generous."

"Too bad you aren't a virgin," Lena put in with a savvy beyond her years. "The men pay more. In one night, you could make enough to retire. That's what Mrs. Tibbs is saving me and Mavis for—the right gentleman with the right offer."

Anna Rose was near tears, not only for her own sake, but for these poor children, being fattened, as it were, for the kill.

"There's a thought," said Mavis, brightening. "The gown would fit me. I could take your place, if you don't want to do it, Anna Rose."

Moved but horrified at her young friend's suggestion, Anna Rose knew then what she must do. But as she stood staring at her image in the mirror, her full breasts overflowing the red satin of the tight gown, her thoughts strayed to Hugh Sinclair and she felt a sudden pang of regret. Here she was about to be sold against her will to a stranger for only a night when she had refused Hugh's decent proposal of marriage. He had offered her so much, so sincerely. She had been a fool to reject him, even if he had resorted to threatening her with those dreadful papers. He had even understood her grief and offered her all the time she needed to mourn for her dead husband. How could she have been so foolish? How could she have imagined that life would come easy to her here in New York, that she needed no one? And all that prideful thought about turning Hugh down because he failed to mention love! Where was it written, after all, that a man must love a woman to make an honest offer of marriage?

A grim smile touched her lips as she eyed the red satin dress. What a dreamer she was! As bad as her father and Rory! Perhaps she deserved this fate. At any rate, there seemed no way to avoid it.

Besides, it was too late to change her mind now. She could hardly go crawling back to Hugh Sinclair, penniless and beaten down. If ever she did return to him, she wanted to go as a woman in full control of her life, with her head held high and honestly earned gold in her purse to repay him.

But for now, she must concentrate on survival. She must figure out a way to get through this night.

12

Hugh Sinclair sat at the head of the polished mahogany dining table in his old Dutch mansion on Wall Street, entertaining three guests. Gone were his rough seaman's clothes, exchanged for the civilized dress of a New York gentleman—bottle-green velvet waistcoat and trousers, ruffled shirt, and gold brocade vest. From over his dark head, candlelight gleamed from the chandelier, sparkling on French china, Irish crystal, and heavy American silver. The light cast its glow, too, over the woman at Hugh's right, making her flaxen hair gleam with golden highlights and the diamonds at her creamy throat glitter like blue-white fire.

Madelaine Townsend was a beauty, he had to admit that. And there was no denying the way she could stir a man's blood with a mere glance of her blue-green eyes.

Hugh had guessed earlier, by the way Michael Flynn looked at her, that his business agent had set his cap for the lovely Miss

Townsend. He found the man's newly acquired and excellent taste astonishing, since more often than not, Flynn was known to squire ladies of a lesser caliber about the town. He was glad to see that Michael was finally coming to his senses.

The dinner conversation remained light and sociable for a time. At one point, Madelaine laughed quietly at one of Hugh's wry remarks, then reached out a slender hand to touch his velvet coat sleeve. "Oh, Hugh, you can be so amusing!"

Feeling her delicate touch as if she had gripped and stroked some vital part of him, Hugh drew his arm away quickly, before his other guests—her father and Flynn—had time to notice. What was happening to him these days?

He'd known Madelaine for years and she'd never had this effect on him. She'd been a mere child when he first transacted business with her father, old Phinias, the wine merchant. He had been conscious of Madelaine growing and maturing over the years. On rare occasions, he had even escorted her to the theater. But they were friends, nothing more. She'd always been like a little sister to him. Now suddenly, for the first time, he was seeing her as a truly desirable woman—cool on the outside, but warm on the inside. So cultured and refined. The kind of woman one courted lavishly and eventually made promises to. Yes, Madelaine Townsend would be the kind of wife other men would envy.

Wife? What in hell had come over him? Had he somehow contracted a shipboard fever that affected the brain? Was he suffering the symptoms only now that he was on land again?

Hugh turned his attention to his other guests, trying to avoid Madelaine's lovely eyes and his own thoughts. He noted that Flynn was glaring at him like a jealous lover.

Hugh tried to turn the talk to business, a deliberate attempt to ignore the lady beside him and to keep his mind off other things. But it was no use. Madelaine, with the skill of a born hostess, maneuvered the conversation from the prices of French wines to the prices of Paris gowns. Hugh found himself admiring her all the more for her artful tact and smooth control over the men at the table.

He knew what was ailing him. It was a sudden, inexplicable urge for a woman all his own. However, recognizing the problem was one thing, while solving it was quite another. Desiring a wife and a family might not be fatal, yet there was certainly no cure for it short of marriage. But whom would he marry now that the woman he desired had disappeared?

This was all Anna Rose's fault, he concluded. She had opened up doors that he had shut and locked years ago. But as soon as she'd forced him to acknowledge his need, she had vanished before his very eyes.

He'd spent the past days searching the city for her, without success. Fearing the worst, he'd even gone to the houses in Cherry Street. For a brief moment yesterday, he'd thought he had a lead. A blowzy, cold-eyed woman named Hattie Tibbs had told him she thought she'd seen the woman he described at one of the houses down the street. But it had been a dead end. Further inquiries turned up nothing. He'd been both disappointed and relieved. As much as he wanted to find Anna Rose, he didn't relish the thought of discovering her in a whorehouse.

The hand was touching his sleeve again. "Hugh, do tell Michael about that quaint penny wedding you attended in Scotland. The story is most amusing."

Hugh thought back to Anna Rose's wedding and a twisting pain gripped his heart. He could still see her as she had been that day—so fragile and lovely that the mere sight of her made a man ache to hold her, to protect her. It was hardly the type of story he cared to relate to dinner guests, especially to Michael Flynn.

"A wedding, you say?" Flynn's voice was touched with irony. "Why, Hugh, old friend, I thought you shunned such affairs with a terrible dread. Are you perhaps mellowing with age?"

Hugh frowned warningly at the man. He knew the direction the conversation was about to take. Michael Flynn had a way of making cruel jests that often embarrassed more civilized guests. And marriage was one of his favorite targets for ridicule.

Flynn, with his dark good looks, was handsome to a fault. But, as Hugh often told him half jokingly, it was a definite case of beauty being only skin-deep. There was a coarseness and a truculence about Flynn that often offended people who didn't know him well. But Hugh and Michael went far back, and the very characteristics that made him poor company also proved to be his strongest assets as a shrewd businessman.

The two men were near the same age, Hugh being only two years Flynn's senior. They had met twenty years before, when they shipped out together from Liverpool bound for the Indies on an ill-fated vessel named *Lady Fortune*. It was the first voyage for both men. But for Michael Flynn, it might have been Hugh Sinclair's last.

The scrawny Irish seaman, with hair as black as the devil's pitchfork and ink-blue eyes that could pierce a man through, had exhibited a strength and ingenuity few had thought him capable of. When they ran into a full-fledged hurricane in the South Atlantic and the *Lady Fortune* foundered, it was Flynn who launched a lifeboat at the last moment and rowed it alone for hours in the storm-tossed sea, picking up survivors. Hugh himself had been more dead than alive, unconscious with the pain of a broken leg, when Flynn hauled him in from the shark-infested waters.

But that hadn't been the end of their ordeal. For ten days, the six survivors in the small boat had drifted with no land in sight. They had no food, no water, no tarpaulin to shelter them from the blazing tropical sun.

The whole episode remained only a horror-filled blur in Hugh's mind. The shattered bone in his leg had pierced his flesh, allowing infection to set in. As long as he was conscious, there was pain, and often with it came chills caused by his raging fever. He could still recall the wrenching cramps caused by his empty belly, the near-blindness brought on by the unrelenting glare of the sea, and the feeling that he was being roasted alive. But beyond those remembered sensations, his memory of the whole ordeal seemed little more than a vivid nightmare from long ago. Bits and snatches came back to him from time to time. Whether they were real or only imagined, Hugh had no way of knowing. Still, he saw the images plainly. Flynn forcing bits of food between his sun-split lips . . . but they'd had no food. Flynn dribbling water into his dry mouth . . . but there had been no water. Flynn telling him that all the others had died and ordering him to live.

Hugh Sinclair had never been one to disobey an order. And here he was today, twenty years later, alive and well, with only a slight limp and an occasional dream to remind him of those dreadful days. Despite all the quirks in his character, Michael Flynn had saved Hugh's life and thereby won his lasting allegiance. And the man also had an inbred talent for business that had worked to Hugh's advantage.

"I say, Sinclair, have we lost you?" Flynn asked. "You seem totally adrift while we all eagerly await your story of the penny wedding."

Hugh offered Michael a smile and a nod. "I won't bore you all with the details. It was merely a country marriage, a crofter's daughter and a young seaman from my crew the day we sailed from Scotland. But the bride was lovely, the groom anxious, and the dancing exhausting. They honeymooned on the *Olympia*."

Flynn's eyes narrowed and a smile curled one side of his mouth. "And the wedding night? How did that go, my friend?"

Hugh flashed a look of caution at Flynn, warning him off the subject as he nodded slightly toward Madelaine. "Ah, now, how would I be knowing about such things? I suppose it went well enough."

"And the happy couple now?" Madelaine asked in all innocence. "Are they making their new home together here in America?"

Hugh looked down at his plate, toying with the last of his thick slice of beef. "Sadly not, dear lady. The groom met his death in the crossing. The bride is alone somewhere here in the city."

He heard a sudden intake of breath from Madelaine. "How dreadful!" she gasped. "Has she no family here?"

"None," Hugh replied, tugging nervously at his ruffled cuff.

"Well, Sinclair," said Flynn, becoming bored with the subject, "you haven't told us how long we'll be allowed to enjoy your company this trip. Is this a welcome home dinner or a farewell sup?"

Hugh, relieved to end the discussion of Anna Rose, grinned and replied, "I'm home to stay this time."

"Do you really mean it, Hugh?" Madelaine asked, making no attempt to hide her delight.

"Of course he doesn't mean it, Miss Townsend," Flynn scoffed. "The man is as much a part of the sea as the sea is a part of the man. When Captain Hugh Sinclair cuts himself shaving he bleeds brine. He's not like me. I tried it once and gave it up for saner, more lucrative pursuits. But Hugh Sinclair give up the sea? Preposterous!"

"Don't listen to a word he says, Madelaine," Hugh replied. "I am perfectly serious this time. When a man reaches my age, it's time he found his land legs and stood on them long enough in one spot to put down some roots."

Flynn uttered a sarcastic laugh. "You can't mean wife, family, and all that rot?"

"It's something to think about, my friend," Hugh answered seriously.

"Oh, I have thought about it!" Flynn paused, casting a meaningful gaze at Madelaine. "But you?" He laughed again. "I can't imagine the great captain tied down to home and hearth."

"In spite of what you may think, Flynn, I've given it a great deal of consideration. What would be left of me if I died tomorrow? Nothing but worm fodder and a cold granite stone with my name inscribed. A man needs sons to carry on and daughters to look after him in his old age. As for what I'll do, I haven't decided yet." Hugh turned toward Madelaine, who smiled eagerly at him. "Perhaps your father will offer me a place in his business. I know wines, and I've acted as my own supercargo on my ships so I have the merchant's instincts as well."

"Papa?" Madelaine asked excitedly, glancing to the other end of the table where her portly father was quietly consuming a mountain of delicacies.

"Well, certainly!" Old Phinias looked up and swiped at his full mouth with a damask napkin. "Of course, Sinclair. Capital idea!" The man's bald head bobbed several times before he went back to the business at hand, an enormous joint of rare beef.

"Then it's all settled!" Madelaine declared.

"Well, not quite," Hugh cautioned. "I've been away from America a good while this time. I need to look around, see the lay of the land. Then, too, there's my rice plantation down in Georgia. I've been an absentee planter for years. I have an overseer on the place, of course, and a neighbor keeps an eye out for me, sending periodic reports. Still, I feel I should take a trip down there and see the condition of the place for myself. But I'll certainly keep your father's offer in mind, and I'm very grateful."

Only a slight dimming of the glitter in her eyes betrayed Madelaine Townsend's disappointment. She had loved Hugh Sinclair since she was a child, when he was the dashing ship's master who brought hogsheads and pipes of Madeira, Catalonia, Teneriffe, Fayal, Malaga, and London Particular to her father from across the sea. He had always remembered to bring her something as well—a hair ribbon from Spain, a china doll from England, a string of shells from Madagascar. Now it was clear to her that he had only been a kindhearted man, taking pity on a motherless child. But when she was very young, she'd imagined that he was in love with her, wooing her with gifts so that she would know he was only waiting for her to grow up before they could marry.

In fact, she remembered her tenth birthday well, as if it were yesterday instead of a decade ago. Hugh had just returned to New York, and she'd insisted that her father include him in her birthday celebration. Hugh had arrived with a lovely handcrafted silver Claddagh ring from Ireland, the pair of hands that formed the band holding a crowned heart, the symbol of close and lasting friendship.

With childish adoration in her voice, she'd asked, "Does this mean we're engaged to be wed, Hugh?"

He'd flashed her that warm and easy smile she so loved and answered, "I've waited all these years, my little beauty. Now you're almost grown up. And when the time comes for you to seek a husband, I've informed your father that I'm to be placed at the head of your line of suitors."

Madeline could still remember how the little friendship ring had felt warm on her finger, how she'd drifted through those next

126

months dreaming of becoming Hugh Sinclair's bride. Then the dreadful news had come, in a letter to her father, and she'd wanted to die.

Hugh had announced his intentions to marry someone else. She had forgotten the woman's name because she had no desire to remember it. Nothing in all her life had hurt her as much as the thought of Hugh Sinclair's taking someone else as his bride. During those dark days, Madelaine had spent long, lonely hours in her room writing sorrowful poems to her lost love. She had cried and cried, she had lost weight, she had contemplated suicide or a nunnery. It was the blackest time of her youth.

But when word came that the marriage was off, that Hugh's betrothed had betrayed him with another man, Madelaine Townsend learned something about herself. She was, indeed, growing up. She had expected to be happy at the news of Hugh's broken engagement, but instead she only felt a new kind of sadness. Hugh Sinclair had been hurt very badly. She cared far more for his feelings than for her own. It was then that she realized she was no longer a child, that she cared for Hugh with a woman's true and lasting love.

Now, at last, Hugh Sinclair had decided to give up the sea, to take a wife, raise a family, put down roots. His words were music to her heart. She knew that he didn't love her in the way a man must love a woman to ask for her hand. And the competition would be stiff. New York was filled with women seeking husbands like Hugh—wealthy, handsome, worldly-wise. But she would be there when he needed her. She would *make* him love her! she vowed with a secret smile.

"Time we said good-evening, Madelaine dear." Her father's voice brought her out of her reverie.

"It's early yet, Phinias," Hugh protested.

The old man laughed. "Not for a merchant, dear boy, especially one my age. You'll come to supper on Sunday, Hugh? We've plans to discuss. And Madelaine's confided in me that our cook's making her special venison roast, your favorite."

"I'd be delighted," Hugh answered, glancing at Madelaine as he accepted. Her look stunned him. She was absolutely glowing. What had happened to the skinny little girl with braids and eyes too large for her face, who had trotted behind him like a pup all those years? Well, that little tomboy was gone forever! And, if his guess was correct, she would never walk behind any man again.

Hugh moved toward Madelaine and said a quiet good night. Then he lifted her hand and kissed it, European fashion. Did Americans still follow the courtly custom? He had no idea, he'd spent so little time here in the past years. But the quaint rite gave him immeasurable pleasure as did Madelaine's slight blush at his action.

Michael Flynn stayed on after the others left, pleading the need of company. A restless person by nature, he seemed even more so tonight. He poured himself another brandy and sipped it as he paced the library, where he and Hugh had moved after the Townsends' departure.

"What shall it be tonight, Sinclair? A game of cards at Fraunces Tavern, a late show at the theater, or is your blood boiling for more amorous sport after sitting next to Madelaine all evening and gazing on those fine, succulent orbs her satin gown displayed so well for your gratification alone?"

Hugh turned and stared at Flynn. Sarcasm was his second nature, but he seldom turned it on a lady.

"What's stuck in your craw tonight, Flynn? You seem unusually on edge and caustic."

Flynn shrugged and sipped his brandy. "Oh, there's nothing wrong with me. But you'd better watch it, my friend. If ever I saw a steel trap cunningly concealed to catch unwary prey, tonight it lay beneath those smiling eyes and that blue gown. Be warned! Madelaine Townsend is out to snare you."

Hugh shook his head and laughed out loud. "That's the brandy talking. Why, there's not a scheming bone in Madelaine's body!"

Now it was Flynn's turn to laugh. "You're daft, Sinclair! Every girl child is born with the knack. When a woman reaches twenty and there's no husband in sight, her instincts become a lethal weapon."

"Maybe it's not the brandy," Hugh said, eyeing Flynn closely. "Maybe you're just plain crazy! Madelaine and I have been friends for years, good friends. No, more than that! We've been like brother and sister. Besides, she could have any man she wants."

"Exactly! And she wants you!"

Hugh sank down into his chair with a sigh. "Well, I'm afraid she'll be disappointed."

"Oh, she certainly wasn't disappointed tonight!" Flynn was pacing again, waving his hands for emphasis, sloshing brown spots of brandy on the Turkish carpet. "All that talk about settling down, roots and all. Have you lost your wits, man? You don't say that sort of thing in mixed company, and stay single for long. Why, you'll find yourself married before the year's out!"

Hugh sighed deeply. "I sincerely hope so, Michael. It's my fondest wish."

Hugh's thoughts, as they so often did these days, had turned to Anna Rose. Where was she? How was she? When would he find her? One thing was sure, the very moment he did find her, he would insist on their marriage. Thoughts of her continued to gnaw at him night and day. All the talk of her wedding to Rory tonight had only intensified the ache of loneliness deep inside him.

When Hugh looked up, Flynn was standing over him, glaring down. "You've been keeping secrets from me, then? You have someone else in mind as a bride?"

"It's no secret, Flynn. But I've been so busy these days since I returned that we haven't had time for a decent man-to-man. And this woman is certainly not a topic for conversation in 'mixed company,' as you say."

Flynn sank down in a chair across from Hugh and leaned forward, his eyes narrowed in anticipation of some sordid tale. "You have my fullest attention. Please tell all! Might I suggest you start with the woman's name and place of residence."

Hugh nodded. "Anna Rose McShane is her name. As for where she lives, I only wish I knew. At this moment, it seems she may be lost to me forever. But she must be somewhere here in New York and, by God, I intend to find her!"

"No need to shout, Sinclair. I'm sure He heard you and will lend any help He can. I'll assist you also, ask a few questions around town and cross a few palms. You'll have your ladylove back in no time. Now do continue."

Soon Hugh Sinclair heard himself spilling out the whole story to Michael Flynn. After all, what were friends for? He told Flynn of his first meeting with Anna Rose, then of the wedding, of the way he felt when he knew she was losing her virginity to another man in his own bunk, of their kiss that night and their confrontation the next morning in his cabin. He said things he had never put into words before about the final days on board ship when she was so ill and out of her head . . . how he'd felt as he tended her needs, bathing her fevered flesh and all the while cursing himself for wanting to take her while she was helpless and in his power.

"And you didn't?" Flynn cried. "What's come over you? Now I know you're crazy! You'd been at sea how long without a woman? And there she was in your own bunk and out of her head? Honestly, Sinclair, sometimes I find your twisted sense of nobility quite hard to understand!"

Hugh smiled wryly at his friend. They were as opposite as men could be in their thinking and their life styles. Michael Flynn was a ladies' man, always had been and always would be. He swore he would never marry, and Hugh believed him, absolutely. Flynn considered females mere property to be used for his personal gratification. When he heard that Hugh actually had in his possession redemption papers on this woman he desired, Flynn was incredulous.

"What a setup that would be! A woman you actually profess to love and you *own* her for years to come. The possibilities of such a situation are staggering. Why, she could never refuse you! You could teach her all those devastatingly fascinating tricks you've learned from the doxies all over the world and make her perform to your specifications." He rolled his eyes and shuddered. "I can't stand it! We must find her! But before we start the search, I need a bit of relief tonight. Your tale of woe has put me in quite a state, old man."

"And?" Hugh asked suspiciously.

"And, I know of a house on Cherry Street where two virgins can be had for the right price. That's one apiece, dear boy, and a sure cure for what's ailing both of us. Grab your cane and hat and let's be off."

Hugh had to admit that the idea was tempting. He and Flynn were well-known and well-liked in New York's red-light district. They'd shared many a romp there over the years. But the thought of such sport tonight seemed like empty entertainment, with Anna Rose so much on his mind at present. He knew he would find little pleasure in another woman's arms.

"Not tonight. But you go along, Flynn, and have a good time. Besides, I'm in no mood to deal with a virgin."

"That couldn't be sour grapes, could it, your own true love having been deflowered by her husband?"

Hugh glared at Flynn. He was making a joke, but it held little humor.

Michael Flynn recognized Sinclair's hard stare and read the threat on his face. He held up his hands before him as if to fend off an attack. "All right, all right! I'm going. It's your loss. But I promise you a full report on tonight's proceedings tomorrow. Every blessed, gory detail of the big devirgination! God, I'd better hurry! I'm about to lose control just thinking about it."

The two men said good night. Hugh started for his bed the moment Flynn closed the front door. It had been one hell of a day! He'd walked for miles about the city, stopping strangers and feeling like a fool when he questioned them about Anna Rose's whereabouts. He'd never realized there were so many people in New York until he began searching for just one.

He'd come home dog-tired and late. He hated having to rush

before a dinner party. By the time his guests had arrived, he'd been hot and weary and out of sorts. Only Madelaine's cool, poised presence had made things better. But now that bothered him, too. What if Flynn was right? What if Madelaine did want to marry him? He knew she had been infatuated with him when she was a girl. In fact, he'd felt quite flattered by her adolescent crush. But surely by now she had outgrown that. If not, he would be forced to refuse the position her father had offered him. He was too fond of Madelaine to lead her on when he had no intentions of asking anyone but Anna Rose to be his wife.

He laughed humorlessly as he crawled into bed. Life suddenly seemed altogether too complicated ashore. Maybe the best idea would be to run away back to the sea.

Michael Flynn loved New York after dark. At midnight the city came alive and its people came out. And, too, the darkness hid all the filth and the ugliness. But most of all, he loved the feel and the sound of the place at night—the clink of tankards in the grog shops, the riffling of cards being shuffled and dealt, the jingle of gold at the gaming tables, the sighs and pleas of the Cherry Street ladies. Yes, New York was his town and night was his time.

As he made his way north from Wall Street and east to Cherry, he thought about all he had learned tonight. He never went to dinner parties for the food or drink or even for the companionship. He went for the gossip he thrived on and made use of. Well, he'd certainly gotten an eyeful and an earful tonight!

He'd been furious when he realized that Madelaine Townsend was out to get Hugh Sinclair. In the past year, Flynn had put a lot of time and effort into building a relationship with that young woman. Of course he found her devastatingly attractive. What man wouldn't? But like most women of her class—the upper crust of New York society, the ones the lower classes called the "topping folk"—she'd no doubt turn out to be a cold fish in bed, in spite of all her lush curves and inviting glances. No, neither love nor sex was the driving force in his pursuit of Madelaine Townsend. Position and money! Those were the only two things that counted. And marriage to the right party could provide both.

He'd had his share of good fortune, wheeling and dealing in the land and money markets. But this past year it had been misfortune that seemed to be riding his coattails most often. First, there was the real estate deal in Brooklyn that had fallen through. Then, he'd made that disastrous miscalculation speculating in foreign paper. But he never gave up hope that his next bonanza lay just around the corner—maybe the cotton he was stockpiling in a warehouse down in Savannah or the shipment of slaves from Cuba he'd invested in. He was a man of all trades, sly as any thief from Five Points. Right now he needed a stake desperately. He'd counted on winning this time by speculating in the marriage market. But what chance did he stand if Madelaine Townsend had set her sights on Hugh Sinclair?

Indeed, Sinclair was a fool when it came to women. Why on earth would he want some milkmaid from Scotland when he could have it all—lovely Madelaine, control of the Townsend wine fortune, and his sweet little widow on the side?

Some men wouldn't know luck if they tripped right over it, he thought glumly.

Suddenly, Flynn found himself standing in front of 13 Cherry Street and his spirits were lifted considerably. Yes, this was exactly what he needed tonight! That old bitch Hattie Tibbs, he was sure, would demand his last farthing in exchange for the tender child she'd been saving in her attic, but he owed himself some prime entertainment. He'd been working too hard of late.

The place seemed unusually quiet tonight, but then it was the middle of the week. Things livened up in Cherry Street on weekends. He glanced up at the small attic window and saw a candle flickering. He smiled. Hattie Tibbs was too tight with a penny to burn a good wick if no one was in the room. So the young girl he'd come for must still be untouched and available. The evening would live up to his expectations, he was sure.

Anna Rose stood at the attic window, behind the candle's glow, and stared down at the street. She noticed a man there, but he was no more than a dark shadow. She had other things on her mind.

She had to get away. Mrs. Tibbs had been up only moments ago. She had been furious when she found that Anna Rose had removed the red satin dress and had tossed it, crumpled, on the bed.

"Get dressed immediately!" she'd shrieked. "I have gentlemen waiting downstairs. I'll be back for you in fifteen minutes. Be ready!"

Now, here she stood, dressed once more in the flashy gown of a whore and wishing she could die before Mrs. Tibbs returned.

"It will be all right, Anna Rose. Truly it will." Mavis, her young face solemn with concern, touched her friend's shoulder, trying to console her. "I've heard from the others that the men— most of them, at least—are kind. And it will be over before you know it. Mrs. Tibbs doesn't allow the men to stay all night unless they pay extra."

Slowly, Anna Rose felt her apathy draining away to be replaced by angry resolve. She turned and faced Mavis and Lena.

"I will not do it! She can throw me into the street; I don't care!" Her voice was shrill with emotion. "And neither of you should submit to this either. It isn't right!"

Lena turned a cold stare on her. "That's fine for you to say! You've got a family and a home you could go back to. Me and Mavis, we've got nothing, nobody. You live in the streets for a time and see how you like it—shivering with cold, eating garbage or starving. You'll see. You'll come crawling back to Mrs. Tibbs, begging to service her clients."

"Be quiet, Lena!" Mavis snapped. "It's different for Anna Rose. She's been married. She's having a baby."

"All the more reason to be willing to work unless she wants her wee one starving right along with her. But she's such a fine lady!" Lena brushed at her thin, pale hair and strutted across the room in imitation of one of the topping folk. "She can't lower herself down to where the rest of us are. Believe me, I'm glad to be here!"

Anna Rose stared at Lena. She sounded so bitter, so jaded for her tender years.

"If you think Anna Rose is a fine lady for not wanting to sell herself to a man," Mavis shrilled at Lena, "then you'd better include me in that as well. I've only been biding my time here, doing honest work. But before Mrs. Tibbs hands me over to one of her groping customers, it's off and away I am! I've seen how prostitutes end up, Lena. You should be thinking of that before you're so quick to follow the trade."

The younger girl's mouth dropped open and her ice-blue eyes went wide and staring. "You, Mavis? You'd leave here? Leave me all alone?"

"If you won't come with me," Mavis told her. "I fought the mashers off in the street from the earliest I can remember. I was a virgin when I came here and I'll be the same when I leave. And if ever a man takes me against my will, I'll finish myself rather than live with it."

Her jaw set and her dark eyes flaming, Anna Rose looked at Mavis. "Then you understand how I feel, child?"

"I do and I'll help you. There's a secret passage that opens by the chimney. I heard once that these old houses were built that way so the folks could hide in case Indians attacked. Come with me. I'll hide you away and I'll skin Lena alive if she breathes a word to old lady Tibbs." She glared menacingly at the younger girl. "After the house is all quiet, I'll help you sneak out and I'll go with you. Lena, it's up to you. You can come with us or stay."

The small closet behind the chimney was dark and dusty. Anna Rose squirmed about, trying to get comfortable, until she heard Mrs. Tibbs enter the room. Then she froze.

"All right, Anna Rose, your first gentleman caller is here."

Silence followed her words, then, "Where is she?"

"Gone, ma'am," Mavis answered quietly, avoiding the woman's hard gaze.

Anna Rose peeked through a knothole in the closet door and saw Mrs. Tibbs advancing on Mavis, her long fingers curled into talons. She grabbed the girl by the shoulders and began shaking her.

"You're lying, you little bitch!" she yelled. "Where is she? You tell me, or so help me, I'll . . ."

Suddenly, Mrs. Tibbs released Mavis and stepped back, smiling. "Never mind." Her voice was quiet now, dripping with feigned sweetness. "She ain't gone far, that one. And she'll be back. Meanwhile, Mavis dear, we'll give the gentleman what he's near dying for. Says, he does, that he's got his heart an' his cock set on a virgin. Even paid me the full price in advance, he did. I was going to slip him Anna Rose and save you for later. But seeing as how she's gone and you're not getting any younger . . ."

Anna Rose, through her peephole, watched all the blood drain from Mavis's face. The girl began to tremble. Even cold-blooded little Lena looked concerned for her friend.

"Let me go, instead, Mrs. Tibbs," Lena begged. "I been waitin' for the chance."

Mrs. Tibbs brushed the younger girl aside. "No man would be wantin' a scrawny thing like you. But Mavis here's even showing some tits." She stepped back and eyed her intended victim head to toe. "Aye, Mavis, you've a cherry just right for the picking. Ripe, but not too ripe." She gripped the girl's arm. "Come along with me now," she growled. "The gentleman's waiting."

"No, please!" screamed Mavis, tears streaming down her face. "I can't! I won't!"

Mrs. Tibbs jerked her around and slapped her face. "I know you for the sneaking little wench you are, girl. You either hid Anna Rose or you helped her run off. You've stolen from me what's rightfully mine. Now I mean to make you pay. You've this one last chance to tell me where she's gone to or else . . ."

Mavis clamped her lips tightly shut. It was obvious that she had no intentions of betraying her friend even if it meant the fate she most dreaded.

"Very well," a grim-faced Hattie Tibbs snapped, "you've made your own bed, girl!"

As the woman dragged Mavis toward the door, Anna Rose made her decision. She couldn't allow the girl who had befriended her to make such a sacrifice. She shoved the closet door open and stepped out.

"Turn Mavis loose," she commanded. "I'm here."

13

Michael Flynn felt much better. An expensive night of entertainment always lifted his spirits. He'd decided to go all out tonight, requesting one of Mrs. Tibbs's large rooms and champagne to put his virgin at ease. Now he paced the worn, wine-colored carpet, listening for approaching footsteps in the hallway outside.

Finally, he sat down on the love seat in front of the window and poured himself a glass of wine. He sipped it slowly. Not the best, but not bad, either, he decided. As the bubbles tickled his throat and the alcohol warmed his blood, he decided that his fortunes might be about to change. After all, Hugh Sinclair was a stubborn man. If he swore he had no intentions of marrying Madelaine Townsend, then he wouldn't. It was as simple as that! That would leave the field wide open for Flynn's own pursuits.

As for this other woman, Anna Rose or whatever her name was, Flynn had connections all over the city. His vocation as speculator and his avocation as gambler provided him with close acquaintances from the loftiest offices in the Government House to the meanest hovels of Five Points. If anyone could find her, he could, for the right price of course. And he swore to himself that he would begin his search the first thing tomorrow. The sooner Sinclair had his true love back, the sooner Flynn would be free to pay serious court to Madelaine. For, until Sinclair was out of the picture, the lovely Miss Townsend would shun all other suitors.

The door opened suddenly and Flynn jumped to his feet.

"Here she be, sir!" Hattie Tibbs shoved a chestnut-haired beauty into the bedroom, then made a swift exit, closing the door firmly.

Michael Flynn could only stare for a moment. The lovely woman he'd paid for was young, but not as young as he'd expected. The few other times he'd indulged his passion for virgins, the girls had been scarcely more than twelve, without the slightest hint of a curve about them. But this one was as shapely as any mature woman, her full breasts hardly concealed by the ruff of black lace at the low neckline of her scarlet gown. Her face was pale—*embarrassment or fear?* he wondered—but her smoky-green eyes stared at him without wavering. Where on earth had Mrs. Tibbs found such a prize?

"Good evening," he said, wanting to break the strained silence between them.

She neither nodded nor smiled.

"Come! Have some wine. It's quite good."

She shook her head—his first clue that she'd heard him. But still she remained stiffly in place.

When she refused, Michael grew angry. Considering the price he'd had to pay for her, she had no right to act so cold. Deliberately trying to bring a rise from her, he moved closer, appraising her from all angles as if she were a heifer at a cattle auction. He smiled, pleased with himself, when his actions brought a flush of embarrassment to her throat and cheeks. At least the woman was aware of his presence.

Anna Rose was acutely aware of the man's presence. She could feel his blue-black eyes crawling over every inch of her. She stood straight and proud, determined not to let him know that she was frozen with fear. But still, her mind was working, trying to form a scheme for escape. She would not allow this man or any other to have his way with her simply because he had paid for the privilege!

He touched her bare shoulder and she jumped, surprised at the iciness of his fingertips.

"You needn't be nervous, my dear. I won't harm you."

She tried to move away from him, but he caught her arm and pulled her close, his full lips almost brushing hers as he said, "But I won't abide any sulkiness from you."

He kissed her hard on the mouth. Anna Rose did not react or respond in any way outwardly, but inside she was gripped with horror. She only glared at him when he released her, saying, "You're not very obliging, are you?"

"Then why don't you demand that Mrs. Tibbs return your money?" Those were her first words to him, cold and hard and angry.

He threw back his head and laughed. "Well, you do have a tongue! But surely you jest! The old bitch would fight to the death before she'd let a farthing out of her clutches. No, my dear, we'll simply have to make the best of things, you and I."

As he said those last words, his hand crept up her arm, drawing her gown down from her shoulder. Once more, Anna Rose shrugged away from his touch.

"Perhaps it would be better if we got to know each other first," he suggested, suddenly intrigued by her cat-and-mouse game. "I'm in no hurry. We have all night. Sit down!"

Anna Rose sank down on the love seat, grateful to relieve the weakness in her knees. Try as she might, she could figure no way out of this.

"Now, that's better, isn't it?" He was smiling at her from where he'd perched on the side of the bed. "Won't you reconsider and have some champagne?"

"No, thank you," she said stiffly.

"Well, never mind. Perhaps we should start by introducing ourselves. I am Michael Flynn. And you, my innocent dear, are . . . ?"

Anna Rose, still searching for some solution to her dilemma, ignored his question. Suddenly, she had a plan. She faced him squarely and said, "You've been cheated, Mr. Flynn. I'm neither innocent nor a virgin as you were told."

He didn't look all that surprised. "Ah, but you are a delightful woman, and a little experience always helps things along. I'm glad you've been honest with me. Now we can dispense with some of the unnecessary preliminaries."

Anna Rose's heart sank. "But Mrs. Tibbs said you paid for a virgin. There are none here," she lied.

He smiled and winked at her. "We both know better, don't we? I've seen that pair of waifs in the attic. And since I have seen them, and now you, I know that I got the better part of the bargain."

He moved quickly to take his place beside her on the love seat, wrapping his arms around her. Anna Rose struggled to free herself from his grasp.

"Please, no!" she cried. "I am here by mistake."

He gave a cynical laugh. "Aren't we all?"

Anna Rose had managed to struggle out of his unwanted embrace. Now she pressed her palms against the fine fabric of his coat to keep him at arm's distance.

"That's not what I mean. I'm in this house, in this room, in this dress by mistake. I came here from the ship thinking this was a boarding house."

He smiled at her. "But you stayed, didn't you? And now here you are with me. If that is a mistake, I consider it a very lucky one."

"I meant to leave as soon as I had money enough. But Mrs. Tibbs tricked me tonight. She never mentioned what she was planning until it was too late for me to get away."

He put his hand under her chin and turned her to face him. "None of that matters to me. There's no way out of this, you know. Why don't you just relax? Enjoy. You might start by telling me your name, as I asked earlier."

Feeling defeated, Anna Rose dropped her gaze, not wanting this man to see the tears forming in her eyes. She felt hopelessness setting in. She'd really believed she could talk her way out of this. But the man seemed set on his mission. She swallowed several times, determined that her voice be steady when she tried a final time to reason with him.

"Mr. Flynn, I am recently widowed . . . and . . . and I am with child," she stammered.

"You poor dear!" His words held a strange sort of sympathy, but she could tell by the glow of his smile that her confessions had only encouraged him. "Well, then I must treat you very gently, mustn't I?" His hand crept across the front of her gown as if to feel her child.

"You can't mean to go through with this," she pleaded. "How could you live with yourself afterward? As for me, my name, Anna Rose McShane, would be ruined forevermore."

He drew back as if he had slapped him across the face. "What's that you say? Your name's Anna Rose?"

She nodded.

"Damnit, woman, why didn't you tell me that in the first place?" he exploded, jumping up from the love seat.

Anna Rose, her nerves raw and her composure about to crumble, mumbled an incoherent answer, but it was clear he wasn't listening.

Michael Flynn was on his feet, pacing the room, rubbing his chin thoughtfully with one hand. His dark eyes held a faraway look. So this was she! The very woman Hugh Sinclair had loved and lost. This, too, was his chance to get back on his feet financially. Oh, he wasn't thinking of ransom or blackmail or anything so low as that. No, Sinclair was his *friend*, after all. But the man would gladly pay his expenses when he launched an all-out attempt to locate Anna Rose McShane. Of course, now that Flynn had the very woman, Sinclair's money would go directly into his own purse. There would be no middleman to pay. And while those expenses would make all the difference in Flynn's life right now, Sinclair would hardly notice the small drain on his accounts. Flynn would simply hide Anna Rose away until he had the amount he needed. Then he would deliver her to Hugh Sinclair, further cementing their relationship.

There was something else to be considered, too. Flynn was willing to bet that if Hugh Sinclair didn't find Anna Rose soon, he would succumb to Madelaine Townsend's charms and propose marriage. That would be the perfect time for Flynn to spring his surprise—the missing Anna Rose. When she reappeared, Sinclair would break off his engagement. And Flynn could conveniently comfort Madelaine and undoubtedly persuade her, on the rebound, to become his bride.

Yes, it would work!

Flynn glanced at Anna Rose. She was sitting quietly with her hands folded in her lap, obviously wondering what was going on in his mind. She was a tempting sight. If his whole future weren't at stake here, he'd have the gown stripped from her and her ripe body beneath his in an instant. He felt a sudden surge of blood at the thought. No, that would spoil everything. If Hugh Sinclair found out Michael Flynn had bedded his woman, the whole deal he had so carefully put together in his mind would fall apart. He must control his baser urges for now.

"Anna Rose, my dear, did you by any chance arrive in New York on board the *Olympia*?"

Her head shot up, and her misty-green eyes widened. "Why, yes! How did you know that?"

"Because Captain Hugh Sinclair is an old friend of mine. He's mentioned you to me. He's very anxious to find you."

Anna Rose couldn't believe what she was hearing. The man knew Hugh! She was saved! Then just as suddenly as relief had flooded through her, a new dread gripped her. Going back to Hugh now and accepting his proposal would only be exchanging one kind of bondage for another. She carefully concealed from Flynn the mingling of fear and hope that crept into her heart.

"Have you come here to return me to him?" she asked in a controlled tone.

"Not if you don't want to go. But you can't stay here." He swung around, gesturing toward the bed. "This is no place for you."

She offered him a hint of a smile. At least on that they agreed!

"Then you won't force me to go back to him?" she asked warily.

He smiled to reassure her, trying to gain her confidence. "No, Anna Rose, I won't even tell Hugh I've seen you, if that's the way you want it."

"That's the way it must be for now," she answered quietly.

As much as she longed to see Hugh, she couldn't face him yet. There were too many things on her mind, including Rory. Emotionally, she wasn't ready yet to deal with another man, not even Hugh Sinclair, as much as she'd thought of him these past weeks. She needed to talk to Hugh, calmly and objectively, about his true feelings and hers. But that was impossible right now.

There was the baby to be considered, too. Hugh might withdraw his proposal when he found out he would be taking on the responsibility of two.

Also, he still had those redemption papers in his possession. If she let Mr. Flynn take her to him, she would lose all control over her own life. She would be forced to go along with anything Hugh decided since the papers gave him legal ownership of her, body and soul. She would be no better off than some black African slave, with no control over her own destiny.

She looked back up at Flynn. "What exactly are you proposing then?"

"That I take you away from here, find you a place to live, see that you have food and shelter and protection for your baby."

She eyed him suspiciously. Why would a stranger do all that for her? She'd trusted one man too many already in New York. "And?" she prompted.

Flynn felt his collar growing tight. This woman might be young and relatively inexperienced, but she was nobody's fool. She had no reason to trust him and it was obvious that he was going to have to put forth more effort if he wanted her to accompany him.

"And nothing, Anna Rose. As I told you, Captain Sinclair is an old and dear friend of mine. He's been half out of his mind worrying about you. I merely mean to see to it that you have a decent place to live until you decide it's time to tell him where you are. Wouldn't you do the same for a friend?"

Anna Rose mulled over his words for a few moments. Yes, she decided, she would. New York might be a strange city in a strange country, but wasn't friendship the same all over the world, after all? Besides, Michael Flynn was a far cry from Crowder Quigley. He seemed reliable and caring—the kind of fellow Hugh Sinclair would number among his close associates. As for his being here at Hattie Tibbs's establishment, she was well aware that men of all classes had common needs.

A sudden rush of relief overwhelmed Anna Rose as she made her decision. This nightmare was over at last! She ran to Flynn and threw her arms about his neck. "You are a good man! Thank you!"

He held her for a moment, smiling at the warm feel of her

breasts pressed to his chest. He pulled her even closer for an instant before releasing her.

"There, there, Anna Rose, don't cry. Everything will be just fine now."

The summer progressed from one hot, sultry day to the next. Anna Rose suffered every morning from the usual sickness associated with her condition and every night from the smothering humidity that seemed to cling to the city like a moist cloud to a mountaintop. But her spirits were higher now, and even the discomforts caused by the season and her swelling body were easier to withstand.

In fact, everything seemed fine for the next month. Not only Anna Rose, but Mavis as well had escaped Mrs. Tibbs's clutches. Once Anna Rose had explained the young girl's plight to Flynn, he was able somehow to ease her way out of the Cherry Street house. Lena might have come too, but she refused, fearing the streets of New York more than anything that might lie in her uncertain future with Mrs. Tibbs.

Michael Flynn found them a room in a house on William Street. The space was even smaller than the attic room they had occupied before, but they managed nicely, knowing a new kind of freedom and control over their own lives.

Flynn provided enough money for them to get by, but he warned them that they would both have to find work. That proved no problem. Mavis was immediately hired on as cook at the boarding house, while Anna Rose, falling back on one of her old talents, took to cutting silhouettes of passersby on William Street. Soon, between the two of them, they were almost able to pay all their expenses. But still, they relied on Flynn to make up the difference. He remained willing enough to help out, secretly using a small portion of Hugh Sinclair's money to provide for their needs, while pocketing the rest. Both women insisted that the money be only a loan until they were on their feet and could repay him. Flynn feigned reluctance, but agreed.

One especially hot afternoon in late August, when the steam and stench from the street below seemed to be rising from the garbage heaps directly into their open second-story window, Anna Rose suggested they go out for a walk. "Surely there has to be a breath of cooler air at Battery Park, Mavis."

Mavis was quick to agree to the outing. This was her one afternoon off and she didn't relish the idea of spending it locked away in their hot quarters. Besides, she had noticed that Anna

Rose was unusually restless today. Maybe she could walk off some of her tension.

"A fine idea!" Mavis said. "The exercise will be good for the baby for sure. But you wear your hat. Too much of this summer sun on your head and you'll be swooning on me before we're halfway there."

Anna Rose had every intention of wearing the broad-brimmed straw hat she'd bought from a farmer at Peck Slip market. But the sun was not her main concern. She had a destination in mind on the way to the Battery. There was a certain house on Wall Street she wanted to see. But she couldn't run the risk of being recognized when she walked past.

Hugh Sinclair was the cause of the restlessness Mavis had noted in her, for he had been on Anna Rose's mind frequently these past weeks. She had to admit she was lonely for a man. But not just any man. Time and again as she lay awake in the heat of the night, she went over every detail of her brief marriage to Rory. She felt the loss of her husband deeply, as any wife would. Still, they had had such a short time together; they had made love but twice. Their whole time—from their meeting the day of her father's accident until that awful moment of Rory's death—now seemed like a strange dream in her mind. Were it not for the baby she was carrying, Anna Rose could almost imagine that it had all happened to someone else. Day by day, hour by hour, she found that her memory of Rory was fading, being replaced by that of Hugh Sinclair.

What was it he had said to her—the strange remark, so puzzling and disturbing, that he'd made on her wedding day as he lifted her from the carriage? Still confused, but no longer disturbed, she remembered his words: "I can wait." Had he planned even then that someday they should be together?

"Are you coming, Anna Rose, or will you just stand there daydreaming all afternoon?"

Anna Rose plopped the straw hat on her head and tied a scarf around it, knotting it under her chin. "Ready!" she announced.

Their landlady, Mrs. Vannatta, a sturdy Dutch woman with iron-gray hair and an unsmiling face, was sweeping the stoop as they came out. She gave them a silent nod at first, then caught Anna Rose's arm.

"Have you laid eyes on Mr. Flynn of late, Mrs. McShane?"

The woman's question took her by surprise. Michael Flynn was never consistent in his visits, popping in when the spirit moved him. But, come to think of it, he hadn't been by for over a week.

"Why, no, Mrs. Vannatta! I wonder where he's been."

"Well, you might remind him that the rent's overdue when next you see him."

The woman said no more and went back to her sweeping. But the warning had been there in her tone. There were too many homeless people in the city for a landlord to have to abide overdue rent.

"What do you 'spose he's been up to these past days?" Mavis asked nervously as they entered the street.

"Heaven only knows! Business most likely. He's always mentioning one 'speculation' or another, as he calls them." She quickened her pace, wanting to put some distance between Mavis and herself and the landlady's veiled threat. "Have you any money left over this week, Mavis?"

The girl's laugh was humorless. "On what old lady Vannatta pays me? Not a copper after we bought that sheeting for our bed."

Anna Rose sighed. "We should have guarded our pennies more carefully. And we certainly could have slept on the bare ticking a while longer."

"It ain't healthy for the baby," Mavis protested.

"It isn't healthy," Anna Rose corrected. "But that's neither here nor there. If the rent's not paid, we'll be sleeping in the filth of the street."

"What about your money, Anna Rose? You were doing so well."

Anna Rose shook her head. "Not this past week. It's the heat. People don't want to stand on the street in the blazing sun to have their silhouettes cut. Yesterday, I even spent what little savings I'd meant to send back to my family."

"Your cravings?" Mavis asked softly.

Anna Rose nodded, her face painted with guilt. "Honestly, I couldn't help it, Mavis. I felt I'd die if I didn't have some raw oysters and chocolate bonbons."

Mavis groaned, then laughed. "It's no wonder you wake up puking every morning."

They had arrived at the corner of William and Wall streets. Anna Rose turned right.

"Where on earth are you going?"

"I thought we'd take a different way for a change, down Wall Street to Trinity Church. Then we can walk down Broadway to Bowling Green and the Battery."

They took this walk often and always went straight down to South William to say good-day to the Del-Monico brothers as they passed. But Mavis didn't question this change in route. No doubt

143

it was another of Anna Rose's whims, like the raw oysters and such.

But when Anna Rose slowed her pace to something less than a stroll, Mavis demanded, "Are you looking for something?"

"A house," Anna Rose confessed, squinting into the sun as she scanned the far side of the street.

"What's the number?"

Anna Rose shrugged. "I wish I knew. It's an older place of Dutch design, made of stone."

Mavis looked about, seeing dormered Dutch houses all about, each one almost identical to the next. "You need the number."

Anna Rose dropped the hand from her eyes and shrugged hopelessly. "I know." The disappointment was plain in her voice. But before the words were out of her mouth, she gave a small cry of delight. "There!"

Mavis looked ahead, where Anna Rose was pointing. A carriage was drawn up in front of one of the lovely old homes. A tall man, handsomely dressed in buff trousers and a scarlet coat, and obviously well-to-do, had climbed out of the coach and was reaching inside to give another passenger his hand.

"Who is he?" Mavis wanted to know.

"That, my friend, is Captain Hugh Sinclair."

"Mr. Flynn's acquaintance?"

Anna Rose smiled, suddenly aware of the calmness that came over her at the mere sight of him. She hadn't been mistaken these past weeks; she did feel something for him. Maybe more than she had been willing to admit to herself up till now. Suddenly, she wanted very much to run to him, to tell him she was safe, to explain everything she'd done and why. She was sure he would understand. Never mind the redemption papers or her own previous misgivings. Rory had chosen properly for her. She would marry Hugh! And her baby would grow up in the lap of luxury, in a fine stone house on Wall Street, with a wonderful father and a loving mother.

Anna Rose touched her friend's hand, her own trembling with excitement and nervous anticipation. "Stay here, Mavis. I'll be right back."

But before Anna Rose had taken two steps, the other passenger emerged from the carriage, a beautiful, golden-haired woman, with skin like delicate china and eyes that were lovingly trained on Hugh Sinclair. Anna Rose noted with a sinking heart that he returned the woman's gaze in kind.

Anna Rose caught her breath, and her hand flew to her throat. She didn't want to look, but she found she couldn't force her eyes

144

away. Hugh possessively slipped one arm about the woman's tiny waist. Even from across the street, Anna Rose could see the smile lighting his face. She watched Hugh glance up and down the street, as if to make sure no one was looking. Then he leaned down and brushed his companion's forehead with his lips as he whispered something to her. Her laughter was as clear as the chiming of a crystal bell.

"Oh, Hugh, darling!" Anna Rose heard her say. The words twisted like a dagger.

As she watched High Sinclair lead his lady up the stairs, Anna Rose felt the same terrible sensations she'd experienced as she watched Rory's fall from the shrouds.

She hadn't known until just moments ago that she truly loved him. Now, when her world might have come together, it had shattered instead. She turned away, feeling numb and infinitely weary.

"Lord, help us, Anna Rose!" Mavis cried when she saw her friend's pale face and unsteady step. "You aren't going to faint, are you?"

Anna Rose took Mavis by the hand and hurried down the street. "No, Mavis. I promise you I won't. Not here, not now. But I must get away. I need to sit down for a while, someplace where it's dark and cool."

Mavis led Anna Rose into the shadowed sanctuary of Trinity Church. The place was quiet, dark, cool, with only sunlight filtering through the stained glass of the tall windows to chase away the gloom. They sank down into one of the back pews.

Anna Rose was hardly aware of her young friend beside her, holding her hand and patting it solicitously. She knew only that she felt twice-widowed now, as if her last hope were gone. She wanted to cry and cry and cry, until her tears washed about her, carrying her far away. But the tears refused to come, and her heart broke silently. For the first time since she was a very little girl, Anna Rose wanted to hide away in a dark place and never come out again.

As hard as she tried to erase the vision, she kept seeing Hugh's handsome face, hovering over that of his lovely companion, his lips brushing her brow, his eyes shining love. She knew the man well enough to understand that this was no casual affair. She would ask Michael Flynn about the woman next time she saw him. But she knew what his answer would be: Hugh Sinclair was about to be wed.

"Anna Rose? Anna Rose!" Mavis's whisper roused her from her thoughts. "It's coming on dark. We need to get back. It wouldn't do to be out on the streets too late."

Anna Rose stood up at her friend's bidding and followed her from the church. But she refused to return the way they'd come. Instead, they took the longer route up Broadway. Anna Rose had suffered too great a blow to endure passing Hugh Sinclair's house a second time.

14

Anna Rose moved through the next weeks like a shadow, with Hugh Sinclair frequently, painfully, on her mind. But he was only one of many problems. Michael Flynn was still unaccounted for. There was still no money. And Mrs. Vannatta's looks grew more threatening every day that the rent went unpaid.

In spite of the sweltering September heat and the growing discomfort of her pregnancy, Anna Rose spent hours each day in William Street, her basket, containing scissors and black paper, over her arm. But money was scarce since customers were few. Those who could afford to had left for the country to escape the heat and stench of the city. The poor, who were forced to remain and suffer the climate, spent their meager wages on salvation, not silhouettes.

It was after one of these long, fruitless days that Anna Rose laboriously climbed the stairs to find a letter propped against the door. Her heart soared as she thought *money from Flynn!* Then her spirits sank as she soberly realized it was more likely an eviction notice from Mrs. Vannatta.

But it was neither. She felt an ache of love and longing and homesickness wash over her the moment she recognized her mother's handwriting. She had entrusted her own letter to her family with a sailor on a ship bound for Inverness. He had promised to deliver it personally and bring back news from home. But that had been so long ago. She'd almost given up hope.

Sinking down to the bed, she tore the letter open.

> My dearest Anna Rose,
>   How my heart went out to you when your letter was
> delivered into my hands this morning. The young man

who brought it is here waiting for my answer, so this shall by needs be brief.

Your family said good-bye with such high hopes on your wedding day. And now to hear that dear Rory is gone. It saddens me beyond words. What will become of you now, my child?

Anna Rose had asked herself that same question a thousand times in the past weeks. Now, reading her mother's tear-stained words, her own emotions welled up, further blurring the ink. She dabbed at her eyes and read on.

Your father is as well as we could hope. He will not walk again. But his spirits remain high even as his strength seems to ebb away, minute by minute. He misses you terribly, Anna Rose. My fondest wish is that he might live to be reunited with his favorite bairn.

Your brothers and sisters are all well, growing like weeds in the meadow. They all send their love and best wishes to you. Never a day goes by that they don't talk of joining you in America. But I fear it will be a while yet before their dreams become reality.

Your sister Iris is here with us, awaiting her husband's return from the sea even as she awaits the birth of my first grandchild. I had hoped the approach of motherhood might temper her nature, but, alas, Iris remains Iris.

Your sister says she has made her Jaimie swear an oath that he will give up the sea after this voyage and take her and their child to live in America. So you may see Iris very soon again, Anna Rose. It pleases me to think of part of the family being together. Iris will write you of her plans in time, I am sure.

I must not keep our messenger waiting any longer. Please take care of yourself and write to us when you can. Your letter has meant so much to all of us.

Always your loving mother,
Margaret Mackintosh

Anna Rose read the letter over and over again, thinking how much she would love seeing her family again, even Iris. She imagined that she could smell the clean, fresh scent of the Highlands on the paper. She closed her eyes and could see again the tiny cottage, the green meadows, and the meandering brown stream—all the places she loved so well.

She reached for her Bible, the same one on which she and Rory had pledged their troth, and opened it to the back, where she hid her most precious keepsakes. There was a sun-colored lock of her husband's hair, a pressed rose from the cottage door, and dried thistle and heather from her bridal wreath. There, too, were the silhouettes she had cut, one likeness for each family member. She spread the paper profiles out on the bed, placing her mother and father at the top, then, in order of their ages, Iris, Cullen, Ewan, Laurel, and Fern. She touched each one in turn, and sent along a wish across the miles.

Two other silhouettes were there, one boyish, the other weathered and craggy from sun, sea, and gale. Rory and Hugh. She had clipped these carefully during the crossing to America. Tears once more filled Anna Rose's eyes. This time she made no attempt to staunch the flood. She found she was crying more these days. Perhaps, she thought, because there were more things to cry over than ever before in her life. It suddenly seemed overwhelming to think that she should have lost both the men she loved, and both so needlessly.

She had cried herself out and was putting away her treasures when Mavis came in the door, her face solemn.

"Our time's up, Anna Rose," the girl announced in a grim tone.

Anna Rose needed no explanation. She knew exactly what Mavis was talking about.

"She actually told you?"

The girl nodded. "We've two more days. If the rent's not paid in full by then . . ."

"It's out on the street we go, with nothing but a garbage heap to pillow our heads at night," Anna Rose finished dismally.

"It's worse than that," Mavis added. "Old lady Vannatta's threatened to call the law on us. We'll have the roof of the debtors' prison over our miserable heads!"

"She wouldn't!" Anna Rose cried. Then in a quieter voice, belying her panic, she said, "We have to find Flynn."

"His friend in the fine house on Wall Street might know where he is," Mavis offered.

"No! I couldn't go to him!" Anna Rose quickly objected, knowing she couldn't seek Hugh's help now. It would be too degrading to reappear under these circumstances, especially since she knew there was now another woman in his life. It wasn't a hasty decision. She had thought of that possibility almost hourly these past days. The thought of going to Hugh held more appeal than she liked to admit to herself. But still she remained strong-willed against such a plan.

Mavis looked at her oddly when she said no more. "Well, what will we do then?"

"We'll locate Flynn, Mavis. Don't you worry. He promised to help us. He won't let us down."

Even Hugh Sinclair couldn't find Flynn. Only two people knew where he was at the moment, the man he'd cheated at cards and the jailer who brought his rations once a day. Flynn himself wasn't sure where he was. He'd been drunk when he was arrested. But better off drunk and in jail than free and dead, he'd reasoned, when he had been led away without protest.

The player who'd caught him palming cards at the gaming table at Black Sam's Saloon had been ready to cut his heart out on the spot. Only the hulking figure of Sam himself had prevented the execution. Flynn, fogged as his brain had been at the time, had recognized the guarded jail cell as the only safe sanctuary in the city when he'd been tossed in and locked up with little ceremony.

But that was almost a month ago. By now he figured the danger had passed. Although he had grown rather fond of the rats that shared his cell, especially the large one with the bent tail, he had taken his ease in this place long enough. He had things to do on the outside, deals to transact and monies to be collected. The very day of his incarceration he had hinted to Hugh Sinclair that he had a lead on Anna Rose. The man had been elated and had promised a large draft to cover the expense of hiring more men to search for her. But, of course, Flynn had been unable to collect. If he didn't get out soon, Anna Rose might be gone and his entire plan would fall through.

"Jailer!" He banged on the bars with his tin cup as he yelled for the man. "When do I get out of here?"

A burly guard with a thick, untidy beard lumbered toward the cell. "You'll be hushing that racket now, mister, lest you disturb the other tenants."

"I'll be quiet when you answer my question," Flynn snarled back. "When do I get out?"

The man smiled a wide, toothless grin. "You've a few more days to enjoy your free room and board before I turn the key and throw you out on the mercy of the streets again."

Flynn slumped down on the pile of dirty straw that served as his bed. He knew it would do no good to argue with his jailer. All he could do was wait out his time and pray that Anna Rose stayed put.

Anna Rose would have liked nothing better than to stay where she was. But on the next evening, true to her threat, Mrs. Vannatta called in the law.

Mavis rushed up the stairs, her eyes wide with fright, and burst into the room. "I heard her, Anna Rose! Cool as you please, she told the officer to be here first thing in the morning to haul us away!" Her words stopped in a keening wail of despair.

"Mavis!" Anna Rose shook her to stop her noise. "Mavis, calm down! Get hold of yourself!"

"I can't! That cold-blooded bitch! She's not even going to give us a chance to pay up." Mavis howled her righteous anger now. "She'd toss her old mother out in a blizzard if she was a minute late paying."

Anna Rose, her shoulders sagging visibly, felt cold all over. She had let herself believe everything would turn out fine, that Flynn would show up in the nick of time, rent money in hand. But Mavis's words forced her to face facts.

"What'll we do, Anna Rose?" the frightened girl asked.

Anna Rose glanced helplessly about the room, taking stock. She hadn't really appreciated its comfort and coziness until now. The place had even begun to feel like home to her. But she'd left other homes, and she could leave this one. She had to! She started bundling up their few belongings. Mavis, silent now, followed her lead.

"I wonder how it would feel to have a real home again," Anna Rose mused with a weary sigh.

Mavis stared at her solemnly and said, "I guess maybe I'm the lucky one. I never had a home to miss. Where'll we go now, Anna Rose?"

Anna Rose had no answer. She only knew that they would wait until everyone in the house was sleeping, then slip out quietly into the streets.

They did just that, sneaking away like thieves in the night. It was the only way to avoid sure arrest and debtors' prison. Even so, Mavis warned that the law would keep hounding them, that nowhere was truly safe.

By dawn, they were footsore and exhausted. All night they had roamed about the city, ducking into dark doorways when anyone approached, jumping at sounds and shadows until their nerves were frayed. Anna Rose knew she had to form a better plan for them.

She had thought about little else these past few days. Until this moment, she had been undecided. But in an instant she made up her mind. Pride be damned! It was the only way.

"We're going to Captain Hugh Sinclair," she told Mavis. "He'll give us both work and a place to live."

Mavis's brown eyes grew wide. "That man with the fine house on Wall Street and the lovely golden-haired wife?"

Anna Rose felt a twinge of pure pain as she corrected, "She's not his wife."

Mavis chuckled. "Well, maybe not yet. But I saw the look that passed between those two. It's a love match for sure. You mark my words, they'll be man and wife soon enough. And the lady will be needing a full staff, including you and me."

The pain in the vicinity of Anna Rose's heart intensified. Mavis was wrong. She had to be!

Hugh Sinclair sat alone in the library of his home, indulging himself with a glass of brandy. It was early for a drink, not yet ten in the morning, but then this was the morning of a very special day. And along with his brandy, he was still nursing a few misgivings.

He had no apprehensions where Madelaine was concerned. No, she was a lovely and lovable woman. She would bring light into his once dark world. And he did love her in his own quiet way. What bothered him most was the speed with which everything had happened. He had hardly spoken his words of denial to Michael Flynn before he found himself proposing to the woman he'd said he had no plans to marry.

But then love took strange, meandering pathways more often than not. True, it was Anna Rose who had awakened in him the need to marry, but she was gone now. Maybe forever. He was not getting any younger, and as he had confessed to Flynn, he longed for a family of his own, children who would be proof to future generations that Hugh Sinclair had indeed existed. A man owed himself that much!

He still thought of Anna Rose, and he doubted that she could ever be banished totally from his consciousness. But it was clear she wanted no part of him. Not only had she turned down his offer, but she had fled from him and hidden herself successfully in the city, he was sure, all this time. He could hardly blame her. He'd been a damn fool to threaten her with those papers. Still, in the heat of the moment, it had seemed the thing to do.

Hugh sighed and turned toward the window, as if willing thoughts of the woman he'd lost to depart by that route and stop haunting him. It was no use. He had felt a glimmer of excitement and hope when Flynn confided that he might be on her trail. But what if he did find her? He doubted that her attitude had changed.

He had long since realized that no woman can be forced into loving any man, another reason he'd decided Madelaine was the woman for him. She truly loved him!

He looked down at the redemption papers lying on his desk. He still had plans to use them, but in a much different way. Even after he and Madelaine were married, he would insist that Flynn—providing he turned up again—continue his search for Anna Rose. When he found her, Flynn would be directed to turn over the papers to Anna Rose. She should not have to live with the threat of being auctioned into bondage always hanging over her like a shadow of doom. Hugh hoped that his show of good faith would allow them to remain friends, at least. After all, he had promised Rory he would look after her and make sure she never wanted for anything. Even after his marriage, he meant to honor that pledge.

"Begging your pardon, Captain." Sinclair's aging butler had crept silently into the room.

"Yes, Chadwick? What is it?"

"The men have finished chaining off the street from here to Trinity Church. It's almost eleven. I thought you might be wanting to get dressed."

Hugh laughed. "I do need a wife, don't I? If for no other reason, to keep me from missing important appointments."

A twinkle of remembrance came into the white-haired butler's eyes. "Aye, sir, but there's many a more pleasant function a wife can perform."

Sinclair clapped the old man on the shoulder and winked at him. "You're as wise as your years, Chadwick. And don't think I'm not looking forward to those 'more pleasant functions'! I never thought I'd see this day. But now that it's here, I'll admit I'm anxious to enjoy every minute of it."

Anna Rose and Mavis, all their belongings tied up in the sheets that had cost them their bed, reached Wall Street to find the block between Hugh Sinclair's house and the church chained off to traffic.

"What on earth?" Anna Rose said, frowning in annoyance.

"Could be somebody's about to make a speech. Or maybe it's a funeral. But most likely somebody's took bad sick," Mavis added. "The city always chains off the street for quiet when there's serious illness."

"Oh, no!" Anna Rose cried. "Hugh?" She moved toward the heavy chain, ready to go under and hurry to his house, but a workman stopped her.

152

"Sorry, ma'am. No one's allowed beyond this point. You'll have to watch from here."

Anna Rose stared at the man. "What do you mean? Watch what?"

He grinned at her. "Thought you knew. There's to be a wedding procession from here to the church and back. No traffic allowed, wagon, horse, or foot."

"But I need to get to one of those houses across the street. I'll be inside in only a moment."

He shrugged and spewed a stream of tobacco juice into the dust at Anna Rose's feet. "Sorry! You'll have to wait."

Already the sun was beating down, making her feel dizzy. "How long?"

"Don't rightly know for sure. But I been told the wedding's at high noon. So I reckon the procession'll be startin' any minute now. I 'spose I could let you through after they move on down to the church. Don't seem wise to keep you standin' out here in the hot sun." The man's gaze dropped to the swell of Anna Rose's belly beneath her faded cotton gown. "My own woman's carryin' our first and she gets a mite light-headed in the heat. Her ankles swell up like sausages, too."

Anna Rose backed away, not wishing to hear any more of another woman's intimate ailments, especially from this crude, tobacco-chewing stranger.

"What's happening?" Mavis asked when Anna Rose returned to her side.

"A wedding. But we won't have to wait long. He'll let us through as soon as the party gets to the church."

The two women stood watching as a fine yellow carriage, pulled by six white horses, drew up near Hugh Sinclair's house. The driver was liveried in shamrock green and his gold epaulets glittered in the bright noon sun.

"Must be someone important," Mavis whispered.

Anna Rose wasn't listening. Her mind had traveled back to her own wedding day and the funny pony cart that had transported her from her reception to the ship docked at Inverness. Her eyes misted at the thought. That seemed so long ago, so far away, as if it had never really happened at all.

Mavis gave her a quick jab. "Anna Rose! Anna Rose! Look! The bride's coming out!"

Sure enough, a slender figure gowned in white and silver lace, a long veil covering her face, came down the steps of the house next door to Hugh's. A heavyset, balding man in a high, stiff collar escorted her to the waiting carriage.

"Land, if that ain't a sight!" Mavis said dreamily. "If ever I find me the right man, I want to get married in a ocean of white foam just like her. And did you see all the glittery stones in her crown? Diamonds, I'd be willing to wager." She shook her head. "It just ain't fair!"

"What, Mavis?" Anna Rose asked, only half-listening. "What are you talking about?"

"Well, some has it all and then there's those like us that's got nothin'."

Anna Rose was about to give her young friend a stern lecture on the evils of envy when a new sight caught her eye and her full attention. Hugh's front door swung open. She could see a white-haired servant just inside.

So Hugh was invited to the wedding. Well, of course he would be since it was his next door neighbor getting married. But that would certainly put a crimp in her plans. Since he was going to the wedding and probably a lengthy dinner reception afterward, it would be late evening before she got a chance to speak with him. What would she and Mavis do in the meantime? They couldn't just stand about in the street.

"Anna Rose, look!"

Mavis's cry brought her attention back to the scene. She looked, but she could hardly believe what she was seeing. Hugh came out of his house, resplendent in his groom's finery, and got into the carriage with the bride.

Wild, illogical thoughts raced through her brain. Hugh, as a good friend of the bride's family, was seeing her safely to the church where the groom was already waiting. Hugh, being a ship's captain, would perform the ceremony. She even tried to believe it might be a proxy marriage—she'd heard of such things—with Hugh standing in for the groom. But Mavis's next words made her admit to herself the truth.

"I told you Mr. Flynn's friend wouldn't be long in making that lovely lady his bride, didn't I, Anna Rose?"

As the shiny yellow carriage started off down the street, Anna Rose caught Mavis's arm and pulled her in the other direction.

"Aw, I wanted to see!" the girl complained. But it was obvious her friend was set on getting away as quickly as possible.

"Come along!" Anna Rose ordered crisply. "There's a police-man watching us! No, don't look back, Mavis!"

Despite Anna Rose's warning, the younger woman glanced over her shoulder. Sure enough, an officer was staring at them and moving closer through the crowd. No doubt Mrs. Vannatta, when she'd discovered they'd left in the night, had given out their descriptions to aid in the search. And they weren't a hard pair to spot—a very pregnant woman and a skinny, brassy-haired girl.

"Mavis, you know the city. Where can we go? There has to be someplace where we can hide out until it's safe."

"There is a place. Turn up Broadway at the next corner." Suddenly, Mavis glanced over her shoulder and lowered her voice to a whisper. "And, Anna Rose, step lively! I think he's still following us."

Quickly, Anna Rose took the lead, forcing her way through the throng of people. If there was a place in the city where they would be safe from the law, that was where they must go, at least for the time being. She headed in the direction Mavis indicated.

"Slow down, Anna Rose!" Mavis begged. "I can't keep up, and no woman in your condition should be hurrying so. We're safe now. The constable's not following us any longer. Can't we sit down and rest?"

Anna Rose hadn't realized how fast she was walking. She felt numb through and through. All her life she had dreamed of coming to America. This land, this dusty, filth-strewn earth beneath her feet, had been in her prayers every night for as long as she could remember.

"The place of opportunity . . . streets paved in gold . . . the promised land!" She could still hear all those hopeful words on her father's lips. What a cruel joke! But then, her father could not have known how everything would go against her.

Bitter tears stinging her eyes and bitter hurt twisting her heart, Anna Rose stopped stock-still in the street. Suddenly, it hit her! She had been feeling sorry for herself, blaming this new land for all her disappointment and unhappiness.

"You have to go after it, if you really want it!" she cried aloud as several passersby stared at her.

"What's that you say?" Mavis asked.

Anna Rose smiled and took her young friend's arm. "We're going to make it, Mavis! I know we are. We just have to try harder. Now tell me where we're headed since we have no money, no roof over our heads, and the law snapping at our heels."

Mavis hardly knew what to think of Anna Rose's change of heart. She'd seen the tears just a moment ago, and she knew that her friend had every right to shed them. But she felt bolstered by Anna Rose's sudden enthusiasm, unreasonable as it was.

"Those that got no other home goes to Five Points. It ain't lovely, mind you, but there's always a place to sleep. And the law's after almost everyone there, so there's no snitching from anyone."

"Then lead the way, my girl!"

Anna Rose's momentary enthusiasm cooled when they reached their destination. Five Points was indeed an unlovely place, an intersection of five streets—Orange, Anthony, Cross, Mulberry, and Water—all converging on the incongruously named Paradise Square.

Years before, Mavis explained to her, the square had been a shallow body of water called the Collect Pond, a gathering place for unsavory colonies of indigent immigrants and freed slaves. As more and more vagrants put up rude shacks, the Collect waters, where women had always washed their laundry in summer and skaters frolicked in winter, became unfit for anything except breeding disease. Sewage and the bodies of dead animals collected from New York's streets had clogged the once-clean water, turning it into a great cesspool.

To rid the city of the contaminated eyesore, the Collect Pond was drained and the remaining dry land turned into a recreation area for the poor with taverns and shops all about. But water seepage soon ruined the site, and the city closed the area to any further building. The vagrants crept back to use the property as they would.

Now Five Points was a place of gangster mobs, brothels, and "nickel-a-shot" grogshops. Policemen patrolled it seldom and only in pairs, never after dark. The converging streets around Paradise Square were lined with decrepit frame houses and ancient brick buildings, long since abandoned by their owners. These wretched structures served as homes for the homeless.

"This is where me and Lena used to live before Mrs. Tibbs took us in," Mavis explained.

Anna Rose grimaced, but vowed silently that she would rather live in Five Points the rest of her life than humble herself to the man she loved. She had lived through Rory's death, and she would survive Hugh's marriage and Five Points as well. Besides, it was only temporary. As soon as it was safe, she vowed, Mavis and she would both find work and a decent place to live. She couldn't have her child born in these miserable surroundings.

"It's not far now, Anna Rose, the place Lena and me stayed. They'll take us back in for sure."

Mavis led the way down a narrow, garbage-strewn alley, shooing aside pigs, rats, and ragged urchins alike. Fires burned along their path, and hunkered down around the scattered blazes were men with dirt-streaked faces and dull, hungry eyes, watching their progress in silence.

Anna Rose spied a woman in rags, her hair tangled and filthy, huddled in a sagging doorway. She clutched a tattered bundle to her breast. As they drew nearer, Anna Rose saw that she was holding a baby, a newborn by the tiny size of it. The child whimpered fretfully as it sucked at the woman's exposed breast. Both mother and baby were bone-thin. Anna Rose clutched her belly as she felt a shudder of horror race through her.

"Not *my* child!" Anna Rose swore softly to herself.

It was at that very moment that Anna Rose made a drastic decision. Remembering Lena's words about the fate of the city's poor children, she vowed that she would find a good home for her baby and allow strangers to raise it, rather than see it suffer. But that would never happen! She would never allow it to!

He looked much like a bum from under the docks. His fine clothes were filthy and disheveled after his time in jail. And the black beard on his face would have disguised him even from his own mother, if the poor woman had been there to see him.

As soon as the jailer had turned the key releasing Flynn to freedom, he'd rushed at a full trot to Mrs. Vannatta's house, only to find a strange man in the room formerly occupied by Anna Rose and Mavis. At least his rough appearance had saved him from the landlady. She'd hardly taken note of him as he brushed past her on the stairs. So the money he knew he owed her was still jingling in his pocket.

Flynn's second destination had been Sinclair's house. He'd wanted to reassure the man that Anna Rose's trail was still fresh, even if it wasn't. He also needed the money Hugh had promised, now more than ever. He might truly have to hire some help to find her, if his plans were to work out.

But he never got in the door. Chadwick didn't recognize him and gave him no time for explanations. The nearsighted old servant merely informed him that beggars were to go to the back door and that he would have to remove himself immediately from the premises as a wedding party would soon be returning to the house.

"Who's been married?" Flynn demanded.

Chadwick raised a brow, indicating that it was hardly any of his affair, but, true to the butler's gossipy nature, he quickly replied, "My master, Captain Sinclair, and Mistress Townsend. Now, be gone with you!"

Flynn jammed his hands into his pockets and strode off down Wall Street, kicking spoilt cabbages and dog dung out of his path, trying to think what to do next. He damned his luck and Hugh Sinclair a thousand times over. Madelaine Townsend was out of his reach now. The financial comfort and social position he might have enjoyed as her husband had vanished like a puff of smoke in a strong wind. But there was still Anna Rose, somewhere out there. And Hugh Sinclair would still be willing to pay a good price to find her, Flynn was sure of it. He stopped for a moment and scanned the busy intersection around Bowling Green as if he might catch sight of her. Of course, that was foolishness, he told himself. She could be anywhere in the city.

Rather than renting a bathtub to be taken to his lodgings, he walked the few blocks to one of the public bathhouses to clean up and shave. As he scrubbed away the grime with hot water and strong soap, a new plan began to form in his mind. He had just enough money left to buy a new suit of clothes to make himself appear suitably prosperous. Then in a day or two, he would honor the bride and groom with a congratulatory visit. But first, he would give Hugh time to deflower the lovely Madelaine in proper fashion, so that there would be no turning back from their vows. And while he was a guest in the house on Wall Street, he would take the opportunity to have a quiet chat with Madelaine Townsend's new husband.

Yes, he thought, this might all work out even better than he'd hoped.

A dashingly dressed Michael Flynn felt exceedingly pleased with himself as he climbed the stairs to the residence of Captain and Mrs. Hugh Sinclair two days later. He'd even had enough money left over after purchasing a suit to buy them a wedding gift—a small walnut money box. The appropriateness of his token pleased him. He meant to get even with Hugh Sinclair for wrecking his plans. Once he finished with the man, the great captain would need a place to keep his small change because that's all he'd have left.

Flynn had no difficulty getting past old Chadwick this time. He found the Sinclair house brimming with guests this afternoon—the newlywed couple's first "at home" since their marriage. It seemed to Flynn that everyone who was anyone had come to wish the couple well. Chadwick showed him in and furnished him with a tall-stemmed glass of wine.

Flynn caught sight of Mr. and Mrs. Sinclair, holding court in the front parlor. Madelaine was absolutely glowing, dressed in a becomingly fashioned afternoon gown, as she stood beside her tall husband, clinging to his arm. With a lascivious smile, Flynn moved toward them, thinking that Sinclair must have done a good job of initiating his innocent bride into the wonders of the

158

marriage bed to have her look in such full bloom so soon after the fact.

But Flynn's smile faded as his eyes traveled to Madelaine's diamond tiara, a gift from the groom, he thought with disgust. The rich always took pride in such vulgar ostentation! he mused.

"Flynn!" Hugh hailed over the heads of his guests. "Where have you been? I've tried for weeks to reach you. I'd hoped you'd be at our wedding."

Michael Flynn forced his best smile. "I'm sorry I missed it. I had sudden business that took me away from the city. I've only just returned."

He was beside the bride and groom now, taking Madelaine's soft, cool hands in his and leaning down to kiss her cheek. His blood stirred at the rose scent of her delicate skin. His eyes strayed down to the low neck of her "second day" gown, a stunning creation of sapphire silk. He felt a sudden, overwhelming fury at the thought of Hugh Sinclair's taking this woman from him. How often he'd fantasized about having her as his own, of covering her slender body with his hard flesh.

"Madame Sinclair, you're looking more radiant than ever," Flynn said, bowing slightly. "I hate to intrude upon these festivities, but may I have your permission to speak to your husband alone for a moment? I promise it won't take long."

Madelaine rose on tiptoe to kiss Hugh's ruddy cheek. "I suppose I can spare him. But only for a short while, mind you, Mr. Flynn," she replied, her adoring eyes focused on Hugh. "You will be brief, won't you, darling?"

Michael flinched. So he was still "Mr. Flynn" to her while Hugh was suddenly "darling." He should have let the sharks have Sinclair all those years ago, he thought in sudden anger.

"Come along to the library, Flynn," said Hugh, after promising Madelaine he'd only be gone a moment.

When the two men were safely locked away from the others, Flynn leaped upon his subject.

"What about your Anna Rose? I thought she was the love of your life."

A pained expression crossed Hugh's face. He'd tried hard not to think about her these past few days. Surely, Madelaine was enough to satisfy any man. And he was married to her now, with no need nor right to allow his thoughts to stray.

"Anna Rose has her own life to lead," he told Flynn. "Besides, she made it perfectly plain that she wants no part of me. If I ever find her again—and I pray that I do—I hope she'll accept my friendship and any help I can give her. Her husband was almost like a son to me."

A sly smile slipped across Flynn's face. "Are you saying Anna Rose was like your daughter, then?"

Hugh shook his head. "Hardly! But now I'm married to Madelaine. Everything is different."

"Still, you'd like to find Anna Rose?"

"Of course I would!" His answer came too quickly, too emphatically, he knew. He added more soberly, "I'm very concerned about her. New York is no place for a young woman to have to fend for herself."

"Very well, then, I'll continue the search. But the money you promised . . ."

Hugh walked to his desk and opened a top drawer. "I've written out a bank draft. If this isn't enough, let me know. I want her found at all costs."

Flynn's smile was genuine when he saw how much money Sinclair was handing over. "I'm almost certain I'll find her within the week. My sources have spotted her. It's only a matter of catching up with her and explaining that you merely want to help. I'm sure she'll believe that."

Hugh frowned. He wasn't sure at all. Then a thought struck him. "One thing more," he said as he pulled some papers out of his desk drawer and handed them to Flynn. "These are her redemption papers. Give them to her. Explain that I paid her passage out of respect for her husband and concern for her. Tell her that she's no longer bound to anyone. She's free. Once she sees the papers and understands that I am sincere, perhaps she'll realize I'm no longer a threat to her."

Flynn accepted the papers with a trembling hand. He couldn't believe his good luck. "I promise you, my friend, when the time is right, she'll see these papers."

The two men joined the other guests and Madelaine. After Flynn had presented his gift and stayed a reasonable time, he said good-bye. "And I'll get right to that matter we discussed," he assured Hugh.

And, indeed, he planned to. With Hugh's generous funding, he should have no trouble locating Anna Rose McShane, the woman he now intended to marry.

He'd have the last laugh on Hugh Sinclair yet!

15

To Anna Rose it seemed that overnight the late summer heat turned to fall's hint of chill, and then, just as suddenly, that mild season gave way to the biting, dead-white winter. And still they were stranded in Five Points.

That was a harsh winter, the one of 1834. The skies seemed perpetually gray, while temperatures plunged down and down, and all the while a constant wind as sharp as a dagger cut through the shivering city.

Those fortunate New Yorkers able to pay the wood peddlers sat before their slow-burning hickory fires, cozy and undisturbed by the tempest outside. But in the Five Points district, the poorest of the poor huddled against the icy blasts with little more than old newspapers and rags and the warmth of their own shared body heat to keep them from freezing to death.

Christmas came and went in the slum without so much as a gift or a "God rest ye merry!" exchanged. Then the old year died, making way for 1835. But the wretches shivering in the hovels of Five Points gave no thought to the old Dutch custom of celebrating New Year's Day. They only hoped to survive the first day of January so that they might live to see the second.

Anna Rose, huge with child now but growing thinner every day, let her thoughts drift to Hugh Sinclair when she heard the church bells tolling in the new year. He was often on her mind these days. At last she realized that her fate as his bond servant would have been a life of luxury compared to what her stubborn pride had brought her. But this was no time to look back and mourn past mistakes. She must look to the future, to the coming of her child.

Each night she vowed that the next day she would go out and find work—anything, as long as it was honest. But the cold and snow, the apathy brought on by hunger, and her advanced pregnancy forced her to remain where she was.

For the time being, she assured herself. *But come spring . . .*

Still, as the days of winter marched on in their frigid procession, Anna Rose found it increasingly difficult to see beyond the hour or even the minute. How foolish she had been!

Why was she still being stubborn? There would be no spring unless she did something. Living here in this awful place would kill her before the winter was out. She might not survive to be delivered of Rory's child, even as close as her time was now.

There was help to be had. She knew that for certain. But although it was only a few blocks from this godforsaken spot to Hugh Sinclair's fine house on Wall Street, it seemed to Anna Rose that the two places lay at opposite ends of the earth. And now her time was drawing so near. This was the first day of March and the baby would arrive within the month. How could she go begging for work or even charity in her condition?

"Please, Anna Rose, you must drink this broth I've made. If not for yourself, for the baby."

Mavis had been out begging again. She had been forced to give up picking rags and selling them now that Anna Rose's time was so near. Mavis dared not leave her friend for more than an hour at a time. Still, today she had managed to procure a bit of fat meat and a few dried beans from a servant woman at one of the new mansions on Broadway. She had put her precious scraps into an old iron pot with some clean snow, and had brewed a weak broth.

Not because she felt her hunger pangs any longer, but because her friend insisted, Anna Rose took a cup of broth in her hands. The hot ironstone felt good between her palms. She brought it to her lips and drank some of the scalding brew.

"Slowly now!" Mavis said. "There's more in the pot."

Anna Rose eyed the girl suspiciously. "Have you had any?"

Mavis avoided the smoky-green eyes focused on her. "I will, just as soon as you've finished yours."

The girl was always like that, going without so that Anna Rose could have more than her share. Anna Rose stared at Mavis, seeing her clearly for the first time in weeks as she thought about her unselfish sacrifices. Her thin flesh, the skin almost transparent, clung to her fragile bones. Her red hair had lost its luster. Her eyes were sunken and dull, rimmed with black smudges of fatigue. The poor child was near starving and it was *her* fault! They could go on like this no longer!

"Mavis, I've come to a decision. I know we had no other choice when we came here, but surely the police have given up searching for us by now. We should leave here, find work. This is no way to live."

"But we've a finer place than most and we only have to share it with a few others. It's far better than I've known here before. Why, we've even got clean sand on the floor!"

Anna Rose looked down at the "clean" sand. Months ago it had been their pride and joy. Among the poor, who lived on dirt floors, it was a sign of position to buy the wares of the sandman, who hauled in his goods from the shore. The man who'd trudged through Five Points with his cart months ago had known Mavis from the old days and had given them enough white sand to cover the dirt floor of the cellar room they shared with half a dozen other unfortunates. They'd spent long, amused hours in the fall, making intricate patterns and borders on their floor. But the white sand was now a dirty gray, and all the pretty patterns had long since disappeared like so many dreams vanished into mist.

"Yes, the sand was nice," Anna Rose admitted. "But we can't eat it or build a fire with it. We need food and warmth. We'll never have enough of either here."

"Then what do you propose?" Mavis asked.

"The first day we have without a snowstorm, we'll go to Wall Street. Captain Sinclair will see that we have work, food, and shelter."

Mavis kept a placid expression, but inside she was reeling with joy. She'd waited all this time, thinking what a fine plan that would be, but knowing that it was not her place to suggest such a move. She'd realized the day of the wedding that Anna Rose was in love with the handsome captain. It was clear in her tearful eyes and in the pain etched on her face. How could she suggest that her friend go to live under the roof of the very woman who had taken her man?

"If you like, Anna Rose, that's exactly what we'll do."

Three more days passed before the storm let up. Then, bundled in every rag they owned, including the bed sheets, the two women trudged through the streets. Their spirits were high, for their journey had come to an end.

"Will we sleep in a cozy attic loft again, do you suppose?" Mavis bubbled with chatter all the way.

Anna Rose was struggling to keep up with her friend, but matched her gay spirit. "I doubt Captain Sinclair will stuff us away in his attic. He probably has real servants' quarters.

"Won't that be grand!" Mavis cried.

The streets were crowded and noisy with jingling sleighs as friends and neighbors hailed one another, enjoying the first snowless day in weeks. All of New York seemed like a party in progress. A dozen ragged children stood at the corners of Broadway and Maiden Lane, pelting each other with snowballs. One barely missed Anna Rose and smashed into Mavis's back.

With a cry of threat and excitement, she scooped up a handful of snow and returned the fire of the young hellion who'd hit her.

"You'd better be careful," Anna Rose cautioned. "You'll soon have us both in the midst of the fray, and as big as I am, I make a fine target."

Mavis sobered at the thought and took Anna Rose's arm, leading her down the street and out of range.

Finally they turned onto Wall Street. Anna Rose's legs ached from the walk and the weight of the precious burden she carried. Her feet, shod only in ragged stockings and thin slippers, were numb with cold. But she felt light all over as she caught sight of Hugh's house.

"We're home," she whispered to herself and her baby.

But a house was all they found—a house shuttered, locked, and unwelcoming.

"Perhaps they've only gone out for a time," Mavis suggested with a hopeful note in her voice. "To the market or for a ride."

Peering through the front window, Anna Rose shook her head. "No. I'm afraid not. All the furniture's covered with dustcloths. It's plain they've left the city for the winter. A prolonged honeymoon trip most likely."

It was hard for Anna Rose to disguise her disappointment. She hadn't realized how keenly she'd anticipated seeing Hugh Sinclair again. That, more than the comfort and security of living in his home, had been what she'd most looked forward to. And now what would they do?

Perhaps it was the long walk or the shock of disappointment, or maybe her natural time had simply come. She remembered suddenly that she and Rory had made use of the *Olympia*'s pantry almost exactly nine months before. Whatever the cause, on the way home, strange twinges in her belly turned to excruciating cramps. By the time they reached their cold cellar room, Anna Rose McShane was in labor.

"You lie down, Anna Rose. I'll run and fetch old Mrs. Penny. She promised she'd come for the birthing." Mavis managed to keep her voice calm, but the wild glare of her frightened eyes was anything but reassuring.

Anna Rose slumped down on the lumpy mattress they'd procured from a burned-out house. She felt dazed and weary. She had no idea how long Mavis was gone. It seemed forever as she drifted in and out of a dreamlike state punctuated by severe pain. At times, she opened her eyes to see figures grouped around her, staring down and shaking their heads. Most of them were faceless, but once she recognized Rory and another time Hugh was there.

Then the faces became only two: Mavis and a wizened old woman with rough hands and a rougher voice.

"Push, damnee! Push like the very devil!"

Anna Rose tried. She strained. She screamed. She twisted until her body seemed to be tearing apart by bits and pieces. Always the midwife's voice was there, not gentle, but scolding, yelling, cursing. Then suddenly, it was over. Anna Rose closed her eyes and gave herself up to the exhaustion that had been her companion for so many hours.

But before she slept, she heard Mrs. Penny's jarring words. " 'Tain't likely she'll make it. Iffen she does, she won't be able to feed the youngun'. Her teats is dried up from not eatin' right."

"But what'll I do?" Mavis sounded near hysteria.

"Get you a bottle, a rag, and some milk. You'll have to learn her to feed that way. Puny thing, though. She probably won't last the week out. 'Twere mine, I'd let it starve. Ain't worth keepin' and it a girl child at that."

The feeble cry of her baby made Anna Rose ache with longing. She tried to rise to take her child in her arms. She would defend it with her last bit of strength. But she found she couldn't move; she was too weak even to open her eyes. Mavis's angry voice, ordering the midwife out of their room, was the last thing she heard before the thin thread of consciousness unraveled and she slipped away.

Even as she crossed over the dark threshold, she tried to tell Mavis of the decision she'd come to when she saw the starving woman with her baby that first night in Five Points. *If it was the only way* . . . But the words refused to come. Soon all was quiet and black and cold.

But Anna Rose need not have worried about her child. Already Mavis was making plans. And if all else failed, she knew what she would have to do. It was not what she wanted, but she realized sadly that it might be the only way to keep both mother and daughter alive.

Hugh and Madelaine Sinclair had not gone far when they left New York. The doctor had advised against a tedious journey even as he told them that Madelaine needed rest, quiet, and around the clock care after her miscarriage. Still, he advised they leave the city for a time. So the Sinclairs had gone only as far as the Townsend summer house on the New Jersey shore, a very quiet spot in the dead of winter.

They were both deeply depressed by the loss of the child. Worse, the doctor had warned them it was highly unlikely that

Madelaine would conceive again, and if she did, the pregnancy might put her own life in jeopardy. It was a gloomy picture the physician painted. Hugh had insisted upon a second opinion, but that prognosis had proved identical to the first.

The Sinclairs desperately wanted children—Hugh to carry on his name and Madelaine because she was born with a mother's instincts. And too, they had both lost parents early. They longed to give their own child the family togetherness they had both missed when they were growing up. But the prospects now looked dismal . . . until a warm spring evening less than a week after their return to the old Dutch house on Wall Street.

Mavis was nearing her wits' end from tending the desperately ill Anna Rose, while trying to keep her month-old daughter alive as well.

The day after the child's birth, Mavis's prayers seemed to have been answered when a full-breasted woman named Naomi, who had heard about the unfortunate situation, presented herself at the door, offering herself as wet nurse.

"It's the least I can do for a fellow human bein'," the pale, lank-haired woman said, bestowing a thin smile on Mavis.

"Oh, bless you!" the girl cried, gladly handing the screaming infant over to the stranger.

But before the woman put the hungry child to her breast, her eyes narrowed and she said, "Of course, you can pay?"

Mavis felt her heart sink. Pay with *what*? she wondered. She had but a few pennies, and she offered Naomi one of her precious coins, hoping that would be enough.

The hard-faced young woman accepted it and pulled her breast free of the dirty rags she was wearing. Mavis breathed a sigh of relief and sank down beside Anna Rose, who was still drifting in and out of consciousness. She watched in silence as the child suckled greedily.

But only hours later, the infant was deathly ill, screaming louder than ever, gasping for breath, and vomiting up Naomi's milk.

Desperate with fear that the baby might die before she found help, Mavis ran to Mrs. Penny's to ask her what to do.

The old woman glared at her and the crying babe. "Still alive is it? Well, it won't be for long with that slut Naomi nursing it."

"What do you mean?" Mavis sobbed.

"Got the milk fever, she has. Her own baby died of it no more'n a week ago. Now she's going around passing off her bad milk as good, sellin' it for whatever she can get. I told you, you

166

want that baby to live, you get yourself a rag and a bottle." She gave the child a contemptuous glance. "I still say it ain't worth keepin'!"

The rag, milk, and bottle arrangement worked for a time. Anna Rose's baby was a greedy little thing, half-starved as she was when she came into the world. But as the weather turned warm, the wild garlic sprang up in the meadows about the city where the milch cows grazed, flavoring the milk they gave. The baby refused the odd-tasting stuff, regurgitating it when Mavis managed to force a few drops into her tiny mouth. Without nourishment, the child became listless and fretful, growing thinner and weaker every day.

Finally, Mavis realized that she had no other choice. The plan she had put off too long was the only route left. She wrapped the naked child in a clean piece of the old sheeting, told Anna Rose—who heard not a word of it—that she would be back soon, and headed out of the Five Points district with the starving child in her arms.

Mavis knew this was not an uncommon occurrence. Almost every day some child from a poor family wound up on a rich couple's doorstep. But her conscience still ached at the thought of giving Anna Rose's daughter to strangers.

She wasn't sure where she was going, but it had to be a better part of town. She thought first of the new townhouses on Broadway, and then it struck her. The perfect place! The perfect people! They could keep the baby just for now, then give her back when Anna Rose was better. Quickly, she headed toward Wall Street. All the way there, she prayed that by now the Sinclairs had returned to the city.

Lights in the windows relieved her dread as she neared the stone house. For a time, she hid in the shadows across the way and watched. She could see that dinner was being served beneath a glittering chandelier. Even where she sat huddled in the darkness she could smell the mouth-watering aromas of roast lamb and potatoes. Her empty stomach ached with hunger.

For a moment or two, Mavis considered knocking at the front door so she could explain the whole situation to the captain himself. Surely he would take them all in and get a doctor to tend Anna Rose. But she quickly dismissed that idea, for Anna Rose would be furious. That would be charity, after all, and Anna Rose had more than her share of pride. Besides, Mavis was certain Anna Rose would not want the man she loved to see her in her current state.

The child squirmed in Mavis's arms. "Hush now!" she

whispered to the whimpering baby. "Maybe I'll never taste a morsel of that good food, but you'll grow up plump and pretty, thinking the whole world eats meat at every meal, you lucky little girl."

Mavis darted across the street when she was sure no one was about. She pounded the brass knocker as hard as she could, deposited the crying infant on the stoop, then dashed back to her hiding place. Her heart was pounding as if she had just stolen someone's purse.

As she watched, the white-haired butler opened the door, saw the child, and turned back toward the hallway, calling out something Mavis couldn't hear. An instant later, the beautiful lady herself appeared, her tall husband beside her. He leaned down to peer at Anna Rose's crying infant.

"A baby? Oh, the poor darling! Hugh, who on earth could have abandoned such a tiny, sweet thing?" Mavis heard Mrs. Sinclair's clear voice distinctly.

"There's no telling, my dear, but it happens all the time in this city. New York has many poor families, many unwed and destitute mothers. Often, I've heard, they leave their children at the doors of wealthy homes, hoping their sons and daughters will be taken in and raised in higher circumstances."

"You mean we can keep it?" Mavis noted that Madelaine Sinclair's voice was filled with as much excitement and wonder as a little girl's, as if she'd just been told by her father that she might keep a foundling kitten.

Hugh Sinclair drew back and stared at his wife. "Madelaine! Think about what you're saying. We know nothing about this infant. It may be seriously ill."

"All the more reason to take it in, Hugh." She reached down and lifted Anna Rose's daughter, cradling her close.

A long silence passed between the couple. Even the baby's crying stopped. Finally the captain shook his head, smiled, and said, "All right, my darling. We'll take the child in for the time being. But you mustn't allow yourself to become attached. The mother may change her mind and show up here, wanting her wee one back. At any rate, we'll have to put an advertisement in the papers. If no one comes to claim the baby within a month's time, then we can assume it has been legally abandoned. After that, we'll discuss what to do with the child."

"Oh, Hugh! I've tried so hard to keep my faith through our recent ordeal. And now here is a baby we can raise as our own!" She unfolded a corner of the blanket, staring down at the naked child. "Hugh darling, we have a daughter! I'd like to name her for my mother, if you don't mind. It's what I'd planned to name our first girl all along."

Mavis noticed that her husband was frowning. "Madelaine, you haven't listened to a word I've said."

She hugged the baby to her breast and smiled up at him. "Hugh dearest, I've heard every word, but it doesn't matter." She reached up to kiss his cheek. "Never mind about her parents. This darling child is ours! Everything is perfect at last. We have each other and now a daughter of our very own."

Mavis lingered a moment longer, tears in her eyes, as she watched the tall, handsome captain smile at his wife, then bend to kiss the infant's forehead. He had relented, and it was obvious that he was as pleased as his wife to have the baby.

Mavis breathed a long sigh of relief as she watched the happy couple take Anna Rose's daughter into their fine home and, she was certain, into their good hearts.

Anna Rose had no way of knowing how long she had drifted in a world between worlds. But when she awoke at last, the sun was shining, the air was warm, and the little room was silent.

"Mavis?" Her throat and mouth were parched, her voice weak.

"Glory be!" The excited cry reached her ears before she saw her friend. Mavis rushed to her and fell on her with happy hugs. "I thought you'd left for good and always. Oh, Anna Rose, I was so scared! I didn't know what to do to help you."

"How long?" Anna Rose managed.

"It's nigh onto a month you've been fevered and talking out of your wits. You never said a sane word the whole time. Oh, thank the good Lord you're back!"

"My baby?" Anna Rose stretched her thin arms out. "Give her to me."

A strange look crossed Mavis's face and struck terror in Anna Rose's heart. The midwife's words came flooding back. Tears filled Anna Rose's eyes.

She struggled to sit up, glancing frantically about the room. "Where's my baby? Mavis, answer me!"

The girl was sobbing now. "Please, Anna Rose, don't hate me! I did the best I knew how."

Anna Rose went silent for a moment, then gasped. "She's not . . . ?"

"No! No!" Realizing with horror that Anna Rose thought her baby was dead, Mavis rushed to her side, pressing her back down. "You mustn't get up yet. The baby's fine. It's just . . ."

"Just what? What have you done with her?"

Mavis's bottom lip trembled and a new rush of tears flooded down her cheeks as she said quickly, "I gave her away."

Mavis's whole story came tumbling out, spilling like the tears from her eyes. She explained about the wet nurse and the garlic-flavored milk and the final decision that she'd had to make alone because Anna Rose was too sick to understand. She ended by saying, "Don't you see? There was nothing else I could do! She would have died!"

For a long time, Anna Rose could only stare in stunned silence. *Her baby . . . Rory's baby!* Granted, she had considered the idea herself, but it seemed unthinkable that Mavis should have done such a thing without her consent. The cry that finally tore from her throat was a tortured, strangled scream: "No-o-o!"

"Anna Rose, please!" Mavis soothed, stroking her matted hair, patting her quaking shoulders, trying as best she could to console her. "Please, listen to me. It's not like I gave her to strangers. That man . . . the captain . . . the one that lives in Wall Street in the lovely house. I left the baby there. And you should have seen the love in his wife's face when she took your wee one in."

Anna Rose's screams died in her throat. She stared dumbly up at Mavis as the truth sank in. It was the final blow. Hugh Sinclair's wife was now mother to her child!

"You gave my baby to *her*?"

"It was the only way. She would have died for sure. Starved to death! Tiny and sweet as she was I couldn't let that happen. I thought you'd be happy that I found a decent home for her. It seemed right that you knew the people." She paused, casting about for anything that might make her friend feel better. "Maybe they'll even give her back now that you're better, Anna Rose."

Mavis went on and on, trying to explain, but Anna Rose heard none of it. She felt numb, almost paralyzed with shock.

Finally, Mavis's words pierced her fog. "It was a sight to bring tears to your eyes, the way that man looked at that baby. All the love you could ever imagine from a real father."

Anna Rose felt calmer suddenly. As reason returned, she began to understand the wisdom of Mavis's actions. This was the only way the girl could have saved them both. And she had chosen the child's parents well. Yet the news was ever so painful. Anna Rose's own thoughts on giving her child away had seemed so reasonable, so logical at the time. This tearing, aching regret came from never having held her child, nor even having seen her face. But she would see her, hold her, love her!

As weary and drained as Anna Rose was, a plan was taking shape in her mind. Her heart would be empty until she had her baby back. But at least her daughter was alive and well, even if she was with Hugh and his wife for the time being. For now, that was the best place for her to . . .

Anna Rose stopped in mid-thought. *She? Her?* "My baby has no name!" she said to Mavis. "What did you call her?"

Mavis looked stricken. "Just 'baby.' It wasn't my place to choose a name."

Anna Rose closed her eyes and thought for a moment. "Heather! I'll name her Heather."

Mavis only nodded. There was no need to point out to her friend that the Sinclairs had undoubtedly chosen their own name for the poor little thing.

As soon as Anna Rose was strong enough, she set out to find work. Eventually, she meant to go to Hugh Sinclair and offer herself as nursemaid to his foundling daughter. Then when the time was right, she would tell him the whole truth and claim her child. But not just yet. She would not present herself to him in rags and tatters. No, she would go as a lady! Perhaps not one of the "topping folk" like Hugh's wife, but at least she would be clean, well-dressed, and respectable.

Once again, Mavis's connections among the inhabitants of Five Points or perhaps her skills at begging provided what Anna Rose needed in the form of a treadbare gown to wear as she plied her trade with scissors and paper.

For weeks, she roamed the streets, snipping away, stuffing her extra money under the old mattress, praying for the day to come when she and Mavis could afford a real home where she could care for her daughter. But food was dear, and neither she nor Mavis was growing wealthy on their meager wages.

One evening as they sat on the floor counting their stacks of coins, Anna Rose sighed wearily. "I'll just have to work harder, that's all. Tomorrow I'll try Battery Park. There should be picnickers there who'll want to buy my silhouettes."

"And I'll hire out evenings to wash dishes," Mavis volunteered. "I make precious little as a cook during the day." She reached out and touched her friend's arm compassionately. "Don't worry, Anna Rose! We'll have a place for your little Heather in no time."

Anna Rose smiled. "Oh, I do hope so!"

It was a warm spring day, a good day for customers. With her basket over her arm and a friendly smile on her thin face, Anna Rose worked her way down Broadway, snipping silhouettes and feeling more change in her purse than it had known in months.

At the corner of Broadway and Wall Streets she paused as a thought struck her. Did she dare? A sudden surge of emotion and motherly longing swept her along. If she went down Wall Street, she might see her daughter. She pulled her straw hat down to cover her face and passed slowly on the opposite side of the street. She could see that the Sinclairs were in residence in the city, but that was all she could see as she passed by the first time. Then, as she made a second excursion along the busy way, her prayers were answered.

The door opened. Hugh came out first, then Mrs. Sinclair, radiant in a peach silk gown, her flaxen hair piled high. They paused on the top step and turned back to the door. Anna Rose watched with an ache in her heart as she saw Madelaine Sinclair's arms go out to accept a pink bundle from a servant.

"Heather," she breathed almost silently.

She continued to watch and to ache as she saw Hugh reach for the baby and kiss her forehead, just below the red-gold curl that reminded her so of Rory's wayward forelock. Then the family climbed into a waiting carriage, which moved away slowly with the tide of traffic. Unconsciously Anna Rose followed.

Had it not been for the Sinclairs and their morning outing, Anna Rose's destiny might have taken a different direction. But as the carriage turned into William Street and continued toward the Battery to South William, Anna Rose followed. And it was there that she saw the sign.

Even before she arrived at the Del-Monicos' Restaurant Français, she realized by the tantalizing aroma of roasting veal that she was very near. She smiled as she thought of the two jovial brothers and their nephew and the way they had befriended her soon after her arrival. Although their meeting had been only months ago, it seemed like years, and she wondered if they would even remember her now.

Anna Rose watched as the throngs filling the streets of the business district hurried in a steady stream toward the restaurant, drawn by the promise of a good, hot lunch served by congenial hosts. Although she had enough money in her purse to pay for a meal and the smells tempted her senses, she dared not enter unescorted. Still, she moved closer.

From the street, she could see the rough pine tables with their spanking white cloths and the long bar where those who couldn't find a seat were served. She spied Lorenzo, his blond head bobbing as he dashed about serving one table and then the next. Then she noticed something else, a small sign in the window: Cashier Needed, Apply Within.

She knew they would never hire a woman for the position. The very idea was scandalous! But it took Anna Rose only a moment to make up her mind that she would apply just the same.

Several men, waiting in line at the door, glared at her as she shouldered her way past them. She was polite in excusing herself, but determined to get through. It took her eyes a moment to adjust to the dim interior after the bright noon sun. Before she saw him, Pietro was at her side.

"Anna Rose, how good to see you again! But Mrs. Tibbs's girl Lena has been here already this morning for her bonbons."

"I'm no longer employed by Mrs. Tibbs, Mr. Del-Monico. In fact, I'm here because of your advertisement. I'd like the position of cashier."

Pietro was expertly maneuvering Anna Rose away from the stares of the men in the restaurant. As they passed through the door to the kitchen, the smells of veal, butter, garlic, and baking bread made Anna Rose's mouth water even as her rumbling stomach reminded her she hadn't eaten since the night before.

"Sit down! Sit down!" Pietro insisted, already dishing up a feast for her. "You'll eat! And we'll talk."

Anna Rose did eat, and the food was delicious, the best she had tasted since she had left her own mother's table. It was no wonder. The Del-Monicos brought all their vegetables fresh from their New Jersey farm. And Lorenzo was at the Fulton and Washington markets each morning at four to buy fish, meat, and fowl.

By the time she had polished off her second plate of veal, at Pietro's insistence, and had sopped up the last drop of gravy with her bread, she had also procured a position as cashier at Delmonico's. After so many months of ill fortune, she could hardly believe her good luck.

Pietro continued a steady stream of talk all the while. "And this young friend of yours that you mentioned, is she presently employed or could she come along with you? We could use a handy girl in the kitchen."

Anna Rose could hardly contain her excitement or her gratitude. "I'm sure Mavis would be delighted to work for you, Mr. Del-Monico."

He covered her hand with his big fingers and squeezed. "Please, Anna Rose, it's Pietro now. It will get far too confusing if you have to call all of us Mr. Del-Monico. When can you begin work?"

"Tomorrow?" she suggested.

"Fine. I'll see you at seven-thirty in the morning."

Pietro opened the kitchen door and called, "Lorenzo, Giovanni, one of you take the sign out of the window. Anna Rose is coming to work for us. We'll start a new trend, hiring the first lady cashier in all of New York City!"

Not only the other two Del-Monicos, but every man in the place cheered. Anna Rose threaded her way through the restaurant, blushing slightly amidst their good wishes and admiring glances.

So, she thought, *here begins my new and better life!*

16

For the first time since Rory's death, Anna Rose's life seemed to be coming together in a proper and pleasing pattern. She was working at something useful and being paid well for her talents. She was mingling with interesting people. Perhaps best of all, because it brought her nearer to her daughter, the Del-Monicos had insisted that she and Mavis move to a room above the restaurant.

"For convenience, since you come to work so early and leave so late," Giovanni had told her, careful at the time to hide his total horror at the thought of the two women living in the notorious Five Points district.

Anna Rose and Mavis moved into the upstairs room that was neatly furnished with two real beds, leaving behind the single mattress stuffed with cattails that they'd shared all winter. They also had a chest of drawers, a washstand, a rocking chair, a desk, and their very own copper bathtub.

"I think I must have starved to death sometime during the winter and gone straight to heaven!" Mavis said delightedly as she took her first, long soak in the tub.

The Del-Monicos had insisted that the women use all the water they needed. "There's always plenty," Pietro told them. "We have the Tea Water Cart deliver from the pump at Baxter and Mulberry Street twice a day. At three cents the load, we've no need to hoard it." He hadn't added at the time that the two women both looked as if they needed a good scrub with lye soap and a boar-bristle brush. And those dreary, cast-off gowns they'd been wearing! Any self-respecting ragpicker would have burned them, to be sure!

174

Their tattered and unwashed conditions had not been by choice, however. Soon, both Mavis and Anna Rose were the height of fastidiousness with their clean hair and their shining faces, and both were delighted with their new Guinea blue uniforms and starched white aprons, also provided by their employers.

Anna Rose put in long hours. Although her job as cashier was a simple enough task, she also spent part of each evening cutting silhouettes to the delight of the customers and the Del-Monicos as well. But there was so much else to do. Mavis gladly welcomed Anna Rose's help in preparing the mountains of vegetables and meats that Lorenzo brought in each morning just after dawn. The Del-Monicos themselves did all the cooking, but it was left to the two women to clean up after them—and clean they did! Scrubbing pots, pans, floors, walls, and washing every dish and piece of cutlery in the place ten dozen times a day, it seemed. The mountains of dirty dishes were proof that business was indeed good.

Another pleasant change had taken place in Anna Rose's life. Michael Flynn was once more a part of it, but his role was very different now, for she no longer depended upon him for anything but his charming company.

She had been at Delmonico's only a few days when he appeared one afternoon during the lull between lunch and dinner.

"Anna Rose! Anna Rose McShane! Is that really you?"

She turned, almost dropping the basket of napkins in her hand when she saw Michael Flynn coming toward her. Her first inclination was to slap his face and call him all the vile names that had crossed her mind during the long months she and Mavis had struggled to survive. He had his nerve turning up now, she thought angrily.

But she knew she couldn't cause a scene with customers looking on. "Mr. Flynn," Anna Rose said quietly. "I thought you must be dead."

He laughed and took her hand, but she removed it from his grasp.

"I was sure you were. Anna Rose! I still can't believe it. I thought I'd searched every nook and cranny of this town. You must have found some hiding place."

"I haven't been hiding at all," she countered coolly. "When you decided to leave us to our own devices and disappeared, Mrs. Vannatta threw us out. Or, more to the point, we were forced to flee to escape arrest. We could hardly afford to broadcast our whereabouts with every constable in New York looking for us."

He shook his head and avoided her direct gaze. "I'm sorry,

Anna Rose. I know it was rough on you. I never meant for anything like that to happen. You see, an old friend of mine in Albany took ill suddenly. I had to go to him. He had no family, no one to take care of him in his final hours. Of course, after he passed, I had to arrange the funeral and then see to his affairs."

Flynn looked at Anna Rose through hooded eyes to see if she bought the tale. But her face remained coldly unemotional. He hurried on, "I arrived at Mrs. Vannatta's too late to bail you out. I tried to find you then. God, I almost went out of my mind searching the city! But it was as if you'd simply vanished."

Flynn paused long enough to offer Anna Rose an appropriately mournful look before he continued. "When I heard that the lady cashier at Delmonico's was named Anna Rose, I had to see for myself. I still can't believe it's really you!"

Anna Rose smiled, but with a decided lack of warmth. Once again the lesson was brought home to her: *Lean not on a man, but depend instead upon your own strength and resources*.

"Well, here's your proof," she said, "Anna Rose McShane in the flesh, back from oblivion to the real world, Mr. Flynn!"

"Where were you all this time?" he asked.

"Five Points," she answered simply.

"My God!" He gasped. "I never even dreamed of looking there! What ever possessed you to go to that den of thieves and cutthroats?"

"We hadn't much choice with the police chasing us. It was Mavis's idea. She said we'd be safe from the law there."

He shook his head, then breathed a sigh of real relief. He'd almost lost her! "I mean to make this up to you. You've been through hell and it's all my fault."

"But I survived," Anna Rose said stoically.

Flynn smiled. "I might have known you would, Anna Rose. Look at all you'd been through even before we met. You have a way about you, a quiet strength that I've never seen in another woman."

She didn't know how to respond. He sounded so sincere, something out of character for him most of the time. And he acted as if he'd genuinely missed her and been concerned for her welfare. Perhaps she had judged him too harshly.

Suddenly, he was scanning her figure, taking in the slim waist beneath the cotton of her gown. Surprise registered in his dark eyes as he said, "You've had the baby!"

She bit her bottom lip, unprepared for this subject that still iced her heart with pain. In response she nodded silently.

"And where is the little scamp? Home with Mavis?"

"Gone." It was the only syllable she could manage. It was enough.

His face showed sympathy, and he reached out to touch her hand. "I'm so sorry."

She couldn't bear to talk about the child any longer. Quickly, she pulled away. "I really must get back to work, Mr. Flynn. It's been nice seeing you again."

He leaned close, pressed her arm, and smiled in a fashion that promised something—she wasn't sure just what. "We'll see each other often from now on. I'm about to become a regular at Delmonico's."

He said good-bye, then sauntered out. But for a few moments he stood on the street watching her at her work, setting the tables.

Anna Rose knew he was staring at her, and that made her a bit nervous. But she would have been far more concerned had she known what Michael Flynn was thinking at that moment.

He still had her redemption papers in his possession. But he had no plans to show them to her just yet. First, he would give himself some time to see how things developed from here. He'd made a good start. She seemed to believe his story of a dying friend.

Now all he had to do was follow through with his newest scheme. He was still bent on getting even with Hugh Sinclair for disrupting his plans. And what better tool to use against the man than the woman he had loved . . . the woman he still talked about when the two of them were alone . . . the woman he was still hoping to find someday.

"Anna Rose Flynn," he muttered under his breath. "Has a nice ring to it."

When he waved good-bye to her that day, Anna Rose waved back and smiled. She still knew nothing of his devious plans for her or the reasoning behind them.

Flynn had not told her the truth about his sudden disappearance a few months back, Anna Rose thought later. But whatever had happened, it seemed to have changed him. He was a quieter, more serious, more likable person than she remembered.

Flynn seemed to be paying honest court to Anna Rose, though she did nothing to encourage him. After all, she had her daughter to think of, and another serious relationship with a man was the last thing she wanted right now. But he refused to be dissuaded from his mission to win her. He dominated her one day and night off each week, squiring her around town to the theater in John Street, to the new Astor House on Broadway for dinner, on picnics to Battery Park, and on coach rides during the season.

However, her favorite outing was an excursion across the narrow causeway at the foot of Manhattan to take in a concert or an opera at the beautiful Castle Garden. The circular building, which had been built originally as a military installation and been called Castle Clinton, was now transformed into a fairyland setting with seats around its circular walls and balconies that would accommodate six thousand while performances took place in the central rotunda.

It was after just such an evening in late summer, with the romantic mood of *Romeo and Juliet* still wrapping them in its bittersweet aura, that Michael Flynn pursued his quest to its limit.

They were walking through Battery Park, its lush grass gleaming with dew in the glow of the illuminating gas lamps. The swish-swish of Anna Rose's rustling taffeta skirt was the only sound between them for a time. But, suddenly, Michael tightened his hold on her arm and said, "Let's sit down for a moment, Anna Rose."

She laughed. "We've been sitting for hours. It feels good to walk."

"I want to talk to you," he said solemnly.

Anna Rose offered no further argument. She let him lead her to the wooden bench in a shadowed part of the park. After they were seated, Flynn was silent for a long time, but all the while his dark eyes were caressing her, making her feel the warmth of his gaze.

Finally, made nervous by his close scrutiny, Anna Rose asked, "Michael, what's troubling you? You've been unusually quiet all evening."

"*You* are!" he answered vehemently.

She only stared.

"Anna Rose, don't you know that I'm in love with you? Can't you tell? When I first saw you at Mrs. Tibbs's place I knew. But things weren't right for us then. You needed time to recover from old hurts. I was waiting, trying to give you that time. Then you vanished and I nearly went crazy. I felt like a part of my heart had been ripped out. You'll never know how hard I searched for you all those months. And now that we've had more time together, I'm sure of it. I want to marry you!"

His words struck her dumb. How could she have been so blind to what was happening? Yes, when she thought back over the past months, Flynn had treated her with a lover's concern. And she did feel differently toward him now. How could she help it? He was always so good and kind to her. So why, when he gazed into her eyes as he was doing this very minute, did her heart not quicken, her breath not come faster, her pulses not pound? Was it because

178

she had never thought of him as a man with hungers and needs, but simply as a friend?

He leaned toward her, clasping her close, covering her lips with his. His mouth moved over hers with a lover's ardor, while his warm hands crept to her bare shoulders.

She felt a certain stirring in her blood, an awakening of something long forgotten. Memories flashed through her emotion-hazed mind—Rory's blue eyes glittering as he leaned down to kiss her by the stream, then again on their wedding night, and one last time as he lay dying in her arms. Those memories brought pleasure, but pain as well. Then, suddenly, there was another phantom in her mind, dark of hair and eye, his mouth caressing, bruising, demanding. Her pulses raced unaccountably. It was Hugh Sinclair, also on her wedding night. But other fainter sensations stirred deeper, stronger memories. She felt feverish suddenly as she remembered strong hands stroking her and a heart beating with savage fierceness against her breast.

She pulled away from Flynn quickly, her head reeling. "No, please!" She pressed the heel of her palm to her forehead and bit her lower lip to stop its trembling.

Flynn smiled, sure that his kiss had sparked her emotion-charged reaction. When Anna Rose reached out, he took her hand and squeezed it tightly in his long, slender fingers.

"I'm sorry, darling. I didn't mean to upset you," he whispered.

"It's not your fault."

He frowned. What was she saying? Of course it was!

She turned toward him, her eyes blurred with a film of tears. "You are a dear friend, Michael Flynn, and an understanding man as well. So I hope you'll understand that I need more time. You've come at me so suddenly with your offer. It's been such a short while since . . ."

"It's been over a year since your husband died, Anna Rose. That's a decent period of mourning under any circumstances." He was working hard to control his anger. He'd been so sure she would agree to his proposal on the spot. "But, of course, I'll give you time. Only please, darling, don't make me wait too long."

Anna Rose forced a smile and nodded.

Anna Rose confided in no one—not even Mavis—about Flynn's proposal of marriage. But over the next few days everyone knew that something was bothering her. She grew absentminded, forgetting regular customers' names or counting out the wrong change when they paid their checks, and there was a faraway look about her that made others wonder if she was taking ill. In truth, although Michael Flynn was much on her mind, there were two others who occupied most of her thoughts—Hugh Sinclair and her daughter Heather.

She still couldn't bring herself to call her baby by her other name, even though Mavis had confided to her that she'd passed the Sinclairs' nursemaid, out with the child in the park recently, and overheard her call the little girl Charity.

Anna Rose had no way of knowing that her daughter now bore the name of Madelaine's long-deceased mother or that the name had been bestowed with great love and respect. To her it simply seemed an insult, as if Hugh and his wife considered her Heather no more than a *charity* case. Well, it wouldn't be so for long! Soon she would have enough money saved that she could go to Hugh, seek a position in his household, then, at the right moment, confront him with the child's true parentage. She would demand that he return Heather to her. If that meant working out her bond for him and an additional seven years' servitude for bearing Heather, then so be it!

For days, Anna Rose had been mentally writing Hugh a letter, trying to make it perfect. Now she thought the wording was right. She determined to sit down with parchment and quill before the day was done. As she worked in the kitchen, Anna Rose rehearsed once more in her mind exactly what she would say:

> Dear Captain Sinclair,
>
> I am now situated nicely, supporting myself by working at Delmonico's Restaurant. Still, I felt inclined to contact you, not to beg charity, but to offer you my services.
>
> I have heard pleasant rumors recently to the effect that you are now a father. My sincerest congratulations to you and your wife!
>
> But on to my special reason for writing to you. I desire an interview with you so that I might apply in person for the position of nursemaid in your home. As you know from having met them at my wedding back in Scotland, I have vast experience in this area, having helped raise my five younger sisters and brothers. I have faith that I can happily manage your small daughter.
>
> I am not at all displeased with my position at Delmonico's, nor they with me, the Del-Monicos say. But I do long for a home and family—even someone else's—at this point in my life.
>
> I thank you most heartily for your time and con-

sideration and I will look forward to your reply. I may be
reached at the restaurant at any time.

My kindest regards to Mrs. Sinclair and to yourself,
Captain . . .

Your willing servant,
Anna Rose Mackintosh McShane

While Anna Rose was composing in her head, she was actually
supposed to be grating cheese for the dinner entrée of filets and
macaroni. Mavis's words brought her back to the here and now.
"Do you plan to cook that cheese with the macaroni or let it melt
in your hand, Anna Rose?"
She stared down. Her fingers, strangling the wedge of soggy
cheese, were poised motionless over the grater and had been for
some time. How long she'd held it, she had no idea. But the
cheese had turned as soft as clabber.
"I've come to a decision, Mavis," she announced without
preamble. "It's time I went to Heather. I can't marry Michael
Flynn."
Mavis's mouth dropped open and her eyes went wide. When
she found her voice, she said, "And whoever thought you might?
The man's a fine enough escort, but he'd make no sort of husband
at all." She leaned closer and whispered, "I know where he
disappeared to last year. In jail he was! For cheating at cards! And
a man who cheats at the gaming table will cheat in the bed right
enough."
Mavis rambled on and on, but Anna Rose wasn't listening. Her
busy mind was whirling with her scheme to regain her lost
daughter.

First things first, Anna Rose decided. That very night she
posted her letter to Hugh Sinclair. Then she tried to break the news
to Michael Flynn as gently as she could. She decided not to tell
him of her plans to go to Hugh Sinclair seeking employment. Nor
did she confide in him that she had a daughter and meant to get her
back. She was afraid that Flynn, out of jealousy, might try to block
her moves. If she refused to marry him, he might go to Hugh and
convince him not to hire her as part of his household staff. She had
no idea what to expect from Flynn when she turned down his
proposal. Anger, probably. Michael Flynn was a man of volatile
emotions, who set out to get what he wanted, refusing to let
anything stop him.
His reaction was totally unexpected. She hardly knew how to
deal with it or with him. When she told him, kindly, that if she

181

were ready to marry right now, he would be her choice, but that she needed more time to recover from all that had happened in the last year, he simply refused to accept that as a rejection.

"I understand," he said. "I'm willing to wait, Anna Rose. You and I have plenty of time. I didn't mean to rush you so, it's just that I'm wildly in love for the first time in my life."

"But, Michael—" she tried to explain.

He sealed off any further objections with a most passionate kiss. Then he left Delmonico's, the last customer to depart that early fall evening.

Anna Rose sighed as she climbed the stairs to her room. She would just have to let things stand as they were. There was no arguing with the man. He had locked onto this idea of their marriage like a bulldog onto a tramp's britches leg.

Mavis was already asleep when Anna Rose tiptoed into the room. She went over and pulled up a light blanket against the slight chill in the air. She smiled down at the girl. How much she had changed over the past months! With proper food and a decent place to live, she was filling out, becoming a real beauty with her long shining hair and smooth, rosy complexion. In no time now, every young man in New York would be turning a longing eye in her direction.

Mavis stirred. "Anna Rose, what time is it?"

"Time we were both asleep, my girl." She sat down beside her friend and took her hand. "But there's something I must tell you before you drift off again. I've written to him."

Mavis blinked and sat up. "To your captain?"

"Not *my* captain!" Anna Rose replied with a shake of her head. "But to Captain Sinclair, yes. I should hear from him very soon, perhaps by tomorrow."

"And what do you suppose he'll say?"

"I expect I'll be hired, one way or another. But what about you, Mavis? Do you want to come with me? I'm sure they could use another maid."

The girl leaned forward and kissed Anna Rose's cheek. "You're a dear to ask, but I like it here. Besides, once you're gone, the restaurant will need a new cashier. We'll see each other often, Anna Rose, don't you worry."

"Of course we will, dear." Anna Rose patted Mavis's bright hair affectionately. "Now you go back to sleep."

The messenger, who had been tipped generously by Anna Rose, wasted no time in seeing that her letter got to the proper house on Wall Street that night. Nor was he willing to give up his valuable missive to the butler.

"The sender said, 'Deliver this into the hands of Captain Hugh Sinclair.' I'll hand it over to none other." The lanky lad in Anna Rose's hire and Hugh's man Chadwick attempted to stare each other down for some moments before the old butler gave way. A moment later, the captain himself appeared at the door.

"Yes, I'm Captain Sinclair," he said gruffly. "What is it?"

The mailboy drew up with importance. "The lady what give me this said I was to deliver it to your hands, personal, Cap'n sir."

Hugh took the folded sheet and stared at it blankly. His name was written across the paper in a neat, precise script. "What lady?" he demanded of the lad.

"I wouldn't be knowin' her name, Cap'n, but mayhap she signed the letter she wrote you."

Hugh, dressed only in a robe hastily pulled on when he'd left his bed, called for Chadwick to tip the lad, then went to his study to read the letter.

Hugh scanned the bottom of the page for the sender's name. *Anna Rose!* He shouldn't have been surprised; he knew from Flynn that she had resurfaced and was working at Delmonico's. But to see this letter, written by her, signed with the name he knew so well . . . He sank down into the nearest chair, breathing hard, fighting for composure.

When he'd first heard from Michael Flynn where she was, Hugh's inclination had been to rush to her, demanding that she surrender herself to his protection. But how would Madelaine have taken that? If he had explained to his wife that this was Rory's widow, that she was alone and homeless, he was sure Madelaine would have welcomed Anna Rose with open arms and taken her right in as part of the family. But how would Anna Rose have taken that? And how would *he* have handled it?

Since they'd been married, Hugh had discovered that Madelaine was too kind and loving for her own good. She would invite any beggar off the streets into their kitchen for a free meal, offer enormous sums of her own money to the most suspect charities, welcome the servants' friends and families into her own parlor for tea and cakes. And, Hugh was sure, if he brought Anna Rose here to live with them, Madelaine would take Rory's widow under her wing and treat her like a sister. If Hugh chose to indulge in a bit of wandering affection and Anna Rose would permit it, Madelaine would simply turn her lovely eyes away, not wanting to cause any discomfort for anyone else. No! The temptation was too great! He had finally convinced himself of that fact and had managed to stay clear of Delmonico's and Anna Rose.

But when he read her letter, his heart thundered with excitement. Imagine! Having Anna Rose always here . . . always with the baby . . . always with *him*! He felt a surge of blood course downward, making him ache with more need than he'd felt in almost a year. What a temptation it was! And hadn't Madelaine mentioned only recently that she thought Charity should have her own nanny?

Suddenly, he crumpled Anna Rose's letter in his fist and slammed it down hard on the arm of the chair.

"Damn you, Sinclair!" he growled. "You'd do that to them both, wouldn't you, and all for your own selfish pleasure?"

He slumped in the chair, feeling miserable, cursing himself.

"Darling, aren't you coming back to bed?"

Hugh's head jerked toward the door. Madelaine, her golden hair loose and cascading about her shoulders, stood smiling at him. Her blue-green eyes were still bright with the passion he had begun to ignite before they were interrupted. The flesh-colored silk of her thin robe—the one he'd ordered from Paris—molded itself to every lush curve of her slender form. She was smiling, inviting him with her eyes, her lips, her whole body. Just looking at her riddled him with guilt for the thoughts he'd been thinking moments before.

"Of course, my dearest. I only had to read this letter that the messenger boy brought." He rose, stuffed the crumpled paper into the pocket of his robe, and went to her, pulling her into his arms and kissing her deeply.

Madelaine nuzzled his chest with her lips when their kiss was over and sighed. "Something important, Hugh? Not business, I hope, at this hour!"

He laughed softly and picked her up in his arms, heading not for the stairs, but the wide sofa close at hand. "Neither business nor important, dear heart. I'll tell you all about it later. But now . . ."

Even as Hugh stripped away her thin night things and pleasured her lavishly—making his wife moan and sigh—his thoughts remained on Anna Rose. And when he entered Madelaine's warm, welcoming flesh, he closed his eyes, imagining that another woman lay beneath him, damning himself for his fantasies.

Hugh Sinclair's reply to Anna Rose's letter was almost a week in coming. She had all but given up hope. Reading his stiff and overcordial words gave her an odd feeling, as if this were a communication to some poor relation or from a businessman to his hireling:

184

September 10, 1835

My dear Mrs. McShane:

Concerning your letter seeking employment, I am not entirely certain that Mrs. Sinclair desires the services of a nursemaid. However, if you wish to come around tomorrow in the morning, I shall do my best to see you.

I hope you realize that your flight from the *Olympia* and your disappearance over the past months have weighed heavily upon a number of persons who were concerned about you. But I suppose you feel that those persons should simply be happy that you have once more chosen to make your whereabouts known to them. Should my wife and I decide to hire a nanny for our Charity, we could not abide such flighty behavior. That will have to be understood at the outset of any agreement.

I will expect you tomorrow before noon. Should you decide not to put in an appearance, please leave word to that effect at Delmonico's.

I must admit, in spite of everything, that I look forward to seeing you again, Anna Rose. It has been a *very* long time!

> Ever respectfully,
> Hugh Sinclair

Back in her room, Anna Rose read the note with many of the same reactions Hugh had felt as he devoured her words. But a coldness lodged in the center of her heart. He had not forgiven her. He probably never would. Still, Hugh aside, it was her daughter she sought, not a lover who was another woman's husband. She had been lucky to have the love of one good man; she could live without the love of another, forever, if need be. But she could not live without her daughter!

Anna Rose went to the clothespress and peered in, trying to decide what to wear the next morning for her meeting with Hugh. It was her day off. She'd explained to Flynn earlier that she had an important errand to take care of so she wouldn't be able to join him on the coach ride up along the old Boston Post Road. He'd wanted to know what errand, but she'd carefully evaded him when he pressed her for an answer. "Something personal," was all she'd told him.

She sank to her bed, feeling drained suddenly as she thought about the day ahead. It was indeed "something personal." She was going to be with her daughter, finally.

For a long time, she lay across the bed, trying to block out a recurring thought that demanded to be recognized. Finally, she spoke it aloud, as if verbalization might chase it from her brain.

"And I'll be seeing Hugh again," she whispered. "Dear Hugh . . ."

17

Anna Rose stood on the back stoop of the old Dutch house, her gloved hand raised to knock, as the bells of Trinity Church struck nine. She had given a great deal of thought whether she should present herself at the front or the back. Finally, she'd decided that this show of humility would make a point in her favor. She wanted Hugh Sinclair to see that she was at last offering herself to serve out her term of bondage, even though she'd been careful not to mention that in her letter. But she owed him. And she would repay her passage in honest labor, if that was what he required of her. Beyond considering Hugh's reaction, she had thought of his wife as well. Mrs. Sinclair would hardly hire someone who had brass enough to come right up to the front door as if she were a proper guest. No, a servant, above all, should know her place!

And a mother should know her daughter, she reminded herself. Above all, that fact must remain uppermost in her mind. She was doing this *for Heather.* Nothing else mattered.

Still, she realized suddenly that she was trembling inside her simple gray wool dress, and it had nothing to do with the September crispness of the morning air. This was the moment she had looked forward to, and the moment she had dreaded for weeks . . . no, months. Over a year, in fact, since the moment she'd fled the *Olympia.*

In a few minutes, she would come face-to-face with the consequences of her entire life up to now—her marriage to Rory, his sudden death, her refusal to accept Hugh's charity in the form of marriage, the daughter she had given birth to but had never seen. Could she withstand all that at once?

"I must!" she murmured. Then squaring her shoulders, she pounded the knocker at the servants' entrance soundly.

An antiquated, white-haired man opened the door almost at once. "Yes, miss?"

"I've come to speak with Captain Sinclair, please."

"Is he expecting you?"

"Yes, I believe he's been expecting me for some time now."

The butler's eyes narrowed in confusion. "Your name?"

"Mrs. Anna Rose McShane."

A flicker of recognition lit the old servant's face, as if he'd been told to watch for her arrival. He opened the kitchen door wider and motioned for Anna Rose to come in. She tiptoed for no reason that she could think of. But the place was so huge, and as silent as a church.

Anna Rose stood alone in the big, empty kitchen for what seemed an exceedingly long time. She let her gaze roam the beamed ceiling, where copper pots hung on nails beside strings of dried peppers, garlic, and herbs. A great black pot sat on a spider over the fire in the vast brick fireplace, bubbling and hissing, sending savory smells into the room.

Suddenly, a door swung open. Anna Rose moved slightly, expecting to see the servant who had let her in. Instead, a hefty woman with a red face and silvery-white hair covered by a spotless mobcap bustled into the room. She stopped short and eyed Anna Rose suspiciously.

"And what might you be doing in my kitchen, missy?" she demanded.

"I'm here to apply for the position of nursemaid to Heath—to Miss Charity."

The cook stepped closer and placed her hands on her wide hips as if to bar Anna Rose's way into the household. "There ain't no such position to be had here! What help Mrs. Sinclair needs, she has aplenty. There's me own self, Katy O'Carlin, to begin with, then the wet nurse, and the upstairs maid who takes wee Charity out for her mornin' and evenin' strolls," the woman said, obviously threatened by the thought that someone else might be hired to take over her tiny charge. "Besides, Mrs. Sinclair ain't posted no notices for help wanted or I'd know."

Faced with such a formidable guardian of the household, Anna Rose felt a moment's uncertainty. Maybe it would be better if she just left before the butler came back and showed her out himself. She started to turn toward the door, then remembered that Hugh himself had invited her to this interview. Suddenly, she heard the gentle music of her daughter's cry somewhere in another part of the house. Her heart melted even as her resolve stiffened. She planted her feet firmly and smiled at the hefty cook.

"I'll wait, if you don't mind, Katy O'Carlin, to hear it from the captain himself."

Katy looked as if she herself were about to remove Anna Rose from the room. But Chadwick returned just in time to stop the cook from using force.

"Captain Sinclair will see you now, Mrs. McShane. Please, follow me to the library."

Anna Rose had the sudden impulse to cast a triumphant glance in the cook's direction. But she curbed her urge since this interview with Hugh Sinclair was no guarantee of the position she sought. Katy O'Carlin might have the last word yet. And if she did get the job, she wanted to work here without animosity lingering in the air between herself and the formidable Irish woman.

Anna Rose thought she had readied herself for this meeting, but she was unprepared for the emotional impact of seeing Hugh again. She entered the large, book-lined room and he rose to greet her, his hand outstretched in a welcoming handshake. Her heart fluttered uncontrollably, and here knees went weak. Her hand felt unaccountably cold against the caressing warmth of his palm.

No! she told herself. *You must not allow the old feelings to surface!*

But there seemed little she could do to keep her emotions in check. The way his gaze seemed to penetrate when he looked at her . . . the touching gentleness of the familiar expression on his weathered face . . . the heat that passed between them even as they stood apart, it was all still there. Hugh Sinclair was still the same desirable man who had cast some sort of seductive spell over her the first time they met, who had inflamed her forever with one passionate kiss.

"Anna Rose, can it really be you after all this time?" He continued holding her hand and sent her senses reeling when he leaned forward to kiss her cheek. She turned her head quickly so that his lips only brushed her hair. He released his grip and she backed away from him, quickly placing herself out of his reach.

"Yes, Captain Sinclair, after all this time." Her words gave no hint of her raging emotions.

A frown chased the smile from his face. "You've taken your cue from my note," he said with a frown. "I'm sorry if it sounded stiff and formal. Your own letter took me quite by surprise, I have to admit. But I've adjusted to the idea now, Anna Rose. And I have to say that it's wonderful to see you again. Please, let's drop the act, both of us. If I remember correctly, you called me Hugh not so very long ago."

She looked away, unable to bear the expression of hurt and confusion in his eyes. "But that was a different time and place, and we were different people then. Now, you are here in your own home and I stand before you as a servant seeking a position." She had meant to add, too, that when they last saw each other they were both free. But she couldn't bring herself to speak of his wife.

Hugh Sinclair was fighting for control. Since the moment he had heard that Anna Rose was working at Delmonico's, he had avoided the place, not even driving down South William Street for fear he might catch a glimpse of her from a distance. He knew all too well what his reaction to the sight of her would be. He had lived these past months with devils eating away at him—dreaming of her, longing for her, needing her more desperately than he needed the air he breathed.

During the months that he and Madelaine had been married, he had learned that he did not love his wife as he should, that he could never truly love any other woman as long as Anna Rose was on the same planet with him.

He had made a mistake, marrying Madelaine. It pained him to admit it to himself and he would never have said such a thing to his wife or to anyone else. He remained as kind, caring, and attentive as he had ever been, as any husband could be. Everyone thought that his marriage to Madelaine was a match made in heaven. But for Hugh Sinclair, this "blissful" state of matrimony had become sheer hell at times. He felt guilty when he made love to his wife, guiltier still when he refrained. It seemed that his entire existence these days was spent cheating, either on his wife or on Anna Rose, the woman he truly loved.

That night when her note arrived, he had vowed that he would ignore it completely. He had waited days before answering it. But in the end, his need to see her, to be near her again, had won out over his better judgment. Feigning none other than husbandly and fatherly concern, he had spoken to Madelaine about Anna Rose, explaining that she was the widow of a friend and that she would make the perfect nanny for their daughter. Madelaine had been delighted with the idea. He had almost managed to convince himself that the only reason he had for wanting to see Anna Rose McShane was so that he could interview her for a position in his household.

But now, as she stood before him—her misty-green eyes wide

with anticipation, the morning sun turning her soft hair to colors of bronze and gold, her full lips pouting ever so slightly—he was forced to admit to himself that he wanted Anna Rose near for far different and much less honorable reasons.

Hugh's long, pensive silence set Anna Rose's nerves on edge. "I've heard that there's a baby in your home now," she prompted, careful to avoid telling him the truth about Heather. She was still uncertain how she would regain her daughter permanently, without creating pain and unhappiness all around.

"Yes, it was a miracle, her coming to us. Some poor wretch left her abandoned on our doorstep." He rushed on excitedly, telling her the full story, unaware of her painful familiarity with the details.

Anna Rose had difficulty understanding her own reaction to the change in Hugh when he spoke of the baby. She felt a mingling of jealousy and compassion, looking at him now. Hugh himself looked more child than adult. As he talked about his "daughter," his gray eyes lit up with something akin to wonder and a broad smile appeared on his craggy face. It was as if fatherhood had shaved years from his age.

She couldn't listen to the love and enthusiasm of his words and keep her eyes dry, so she focused her attention on the leaves of the buttonwood tree outside the tall library window. They tossed and danced in the morning breeze from the harbor, like bright-kilted Highlanders stepping to the skirl of the pipes. Someday she would take her daughter back to Scotland, she vowed, to gather the heather she was named for, and to dance the old jigs and flings of the homeland.

Only when Hugh spoke his wife's name did he draw Anna Rose's attention back. "Madelaine loves that baby as if it were her own. You see, she recently lost the child she was carrying. She'll probably never have another."

Anna Rose, her nerves frayed and her tears ready to flow, was about to tell him that the child had a mother and a name all her own, but then Hugh added, "I have to admit that I, too, love Charity as much as I could ever love a child of my own flesh and blood. I was against taking the infant in that night when we found her. But I think I'd rather give up breathing now than be separated from my sweet daughter. I can't imagine what life was like before she came to us." He laughed softly. "It must have been deadly dull."

The lump grew larger in Anna Rose's throat as she listened to the sea captain's tender confession. How could she tell him that his Charity was hers? That she wanted her daughter back? And what rights would she have at this late date? Granted, the choice to give up the child had not been hers. But had she been able to voice an opinion at the time the decision was made, she would have been forced to agree with Mavis or consign her daughter to an early grave. So she owed Hugh—and his wife—for her baby's life.

Hugh forced a shallow laugh. "You must think I've gone soft, Anna Rose. Away too long from the sea, eh? To think that I, of all people, could be so moved by such a tiny being."

Anna Rose sank down into a chair and stared at her lap, at her fingers worrying a lace-edged handkerchief. "Babies have that effect on people, so I've heard. You needn't be embarrassed."

"Oh, I'm not! I'll tell the whole world I love my daughter, as I love no other woman on earth . . ." His voice drifted off, then he added in a whisper, "Save one, Anna Rose."

She was still looking down or she would have seen the intense gaze he bestowed on her as he spoke those words.

Just then, she felt a powerful need to end this interview, to be done with it and leave. "Captain Sinclair, I don't want to take up too much of your time." She steeled herself against the emotions warring within her and the wild beating of her heart. She was all business now. The very fact that she'd made a sudden decision not to tell Hugh the baby was hers—at least, not right now—only enforced her resolve to serve as Heather's nursemaid. "As I stated before, I'm seeking a new position. Something quieter and more settled than I now have at Delmonico's. I'm good with children. As you know, I have five younger brothers and sisters."

Hugh laughed, remembering the Mackintosh brood, and slapped his knee. "How well I remember that strapping lot! You must miss them all greatly."

"I do," she answered in a quiet tone, still avoiding his eyes. "Perhaps that's why I feel the need to be a part of a family. I'd like the position of nursemaid to your daughter. And since I do owe you some service anyway—"

Hugh was on his feet at once. "Anna Rose, you owe me nothing! Forget those stupid redemption papers. They're gone and forgotten!"

At that moment, Madelaine Sinclair entered the room, carrying the baby in her arms. "Hugh darling, Katy said something about the woman coming for an interview with you." Her gentle blue eyes fell on Anna Rose, seated near the desk. "Oh, this must be she!"

Madelaine, a vision in ruffled silk the same wheat-gold color as

191

her hair, stood cradling the child to her breast as she moved toward Anna Rose and offered her hand. "I'm Mrs. Sinclair."

Anna Rose fixed her eyes on the baby—her baby.

When she made no reply, Hugh added for her, "This is Anna Rose McShane, my dear."

At his words, Madelaine's eyes widened and her smiling face absolutely glowed. "McShane? Why, Hugh! You didn't tell me her last name before. This must be young Rory's wife. You've even told me all about their penny wedding." Madelaine leaned down and brushed Anna Rose's cheek with her lips. "You must forgive me, Anna Rose! I simply didn't make the connection before when Hugh told me about your letter. He said you were an old acquaintance, but I never realized! Well, this is just too great a stroke of luck! Having you here will be like having a member of the family looking after our Charity."

"Madelaine, you don't want to rush into anything," Hugh cautioned. "Shouldn't we talk it over first?"

Anna Rose looked away, with embarrassment. Hugh's words made her feel as if she were being viewed on the auction block.

"My darling, there's nothing to talk over." She beamed at Anna Rose. "You have nice eyes and a mouth that's used to smiling, I can tell. Anyone would know at a glance that you're marvelous with children. It's as if fate led you to our door. I've been thinking for weeks now that I'd speak to my husband about hiring a nursemaid. All the servants adore Charity, but she really needs her own nanny." She turned toward Hugh and offered him a brilliant, persuasive smile. "I do hope my husband will engage your services at once, Anna Rose. You can move right in this very day."

Anna Rose found herself struggling for words, her gaze torn between the bright blue eyes of her tiny daughter and the smiling, lovely face of the child's other "mother." To her utmost surprise, she found that she liked Madelaine Sinclair immediately. She somehow reminded her of Iris. Or rather, Hugh's wife was the sort of person Anna Rose had always wished her sister might be— sweet of temper as well as of face. And so open and honest, the kind of person who would treat a stranger kindly, and never say a word to hurt a soul.

"He hasn't hired me yet, ma'am," Anna Rose managed. "We were still discussing the matter when you came in."

"Oh, Anna Rose, of course you have the job!" Hugh's wife exclaimed. "And do call me Madelaine. We're ever so informal here, and you are almost family, after all."

Hugh's face darkened with concern, his brows shadowing his

almost black eyes. "Madelaine, are you sure you need another servant?"

Anna Rose could tell Hugh was against the idea, but couldn't guess why. Before his wife appeared, he'd seemed so happy to see her; she'd been so confident that he meant to hire her.

Madelaine bestowed such a tender look on her husband that Anna Rose felt as if she were interrupting an intimate exchange between man and wife. "Darling, Charity is six months old now. Before we know it, she'll be walking, running, needing a dozen servants to keep up with her." Her gaze went back to Anna Rose. "Besides, I can tell that I'm going to like this young woman. She has a certain strong look about her, yet there's a softness, a gentleness, too. Yes, Anna Rose will be the perfect influence on our little Charity."

Anna Rose blushed and looked down, while Hugh's thoughts, in spite of himself, went to memories of a different kind of softness Anna Rose possessed. Knowing how he still felt about her, how could he agree to have Anna Rose come and live in the same house with him and his wife? It would be too painful . . . *too dangerous!*

"Madelaine, why don't we think it over for a time, talk about it more, and then I'll notify Mrs. McShane when we come to a decision?"

Madelaine laughed and said, "My dear Captain Sinclair, you are not hiring on a seaman for one of your ships! Anna Rose is to be my first mate and we will not stand on formalities. The matter is all settled as far as I'm concerned."

Anna Rose sat quietly, watching her daughter now, wishing that she could hold her. She didn't see the look of dismay on Hugh's face or the determined expression his wife bestowed on him.

"Hugh, I really must insist!" Madelaine said firmly. "Anna Rose can do the work, and if we don't hire her this instant, someone else will before we have a chance. Charity needs her!"

Hugh shrugged slightly and sighed. It seemed he had no choice in the matter. "Very well, Madelaine. Mrs. McShane, it seems you have the job." *And heaven help us all!* he added in his thoughts.

"Thank you, darling!" Madelaine said as she went to hug him.

A moment later, Anna Rose's new employer placed the sweetsmelling bundle in her arms. "Meet your new nanny, Charity dear. This is Anna Rose."

Anna Rose felt her heart swell with love as she stared down into the most beautiful face she had ever seen, all pink and gold and blue-blue eyes. It was as if she were gazing at a delicate miniature of Rory's face. Her breasts ached to feel her child sucking. Tears filmed her eyes and she made no effort to hold them back this time.

She rocked Charity gently in her arms and hummed a lullaby. It was as if the rest of the world—Hugh and his wife included—had vanished. Only Anna Rose and her baby remained.

"Well, Anna Rose, I can see that you and our daughter are going to get along just fine," Madelaine said brightly.

Anna Rose looked up through her tears and smiled at the woman. "Thank you, Mrs. Sinclair, for everything."

Anna Rose could hardly bear to leave her daughter, but she had to go back to Delmonico's long enough to collect her belongings and to tell Mavis and her former employers the good news.

With tears in her soft eyes, Mavis hugged her friend. "Oh, Anna Rose, I'm so relieved. My conscience has pained me something dreadful these past months for having given your baby away."

"You hush that now, Mavis!" Anna Rose scolded gently. "You saved Heather's life and mine, too. I'll be grateful to you forevermore."

The two women were upstairs in their room, Mavis sitting on the bed while Anna Rose quickly packed.

"What are they like, the captain and his wife?" Mavis asked cautiously. It still bothered her that Anna Rose loved the man. Could she be happy living with the couple, seeing them together every day—every night?

Anna Rose gave Mavis a knowing glance. "Captain Sinclair is gruff, hardheaded, outspoken. But he turns to jelly whenever he speaks of the baby. Heather has him twisted twice around her little finger already."

"And Mrs. Sinclair?" Mavis prompted.

Anna Rose gazed up at the ceiling, trying to form the right words. "Madeline Sinclair is difficult to figure out. She treated me as if I were some long-lost family member, returned to the fold. Hugh had told her all about Rory and about being at our wedding."

Mavis raised her brow when Anna Rose called the captain by his Christian name.

"On first meeting, Mrs. Sinclair seems almost flighty," Anna Rose continued. "But it took me only a moment to see that she rules the roost. I'd be without the job if she hadn't insisted. Hugh wanted to take time to consider, talk it over, make me wait. I don't think he wanted me there."

"Why ever not? I thought he still held redemption papers on you, and had been waiting for you to reappear so he could press you into service."

Anna Rose shrugged as she stuffed her last petticoat into a carpetbag. "I have no idea what was going through his mind. He did tell me to forget the redemption papers, which I'm only too happy to do. But I don't understand him. At first, he seemed glad to see me. He even apologized for writing such a stiff and formal note. He seemed a bit tense, but he had started to relax before his wife came in." Anna Rose swung around to face Mavis, a look of realization glowing on her face. "That's it! He seemed to go absolutely rigid when his wife came in. And that's when he began backing off from hiring me."

"Oh-h-h, Anna Rose!" Mavis moaned softly. "That doesn't sound good!"

"What do you mean?"

"You loved the captain, didn't you?"

Anna Rose's mouth dropped open, then snapped quickly shut. "I never said such a thing!"

Mavis chuckled softly. "Some things need no words for the telling, my friend. I had only to look at your face the first time you saw them together. And did he love you, too?"

"What a thing to ask!" Anna Rose felt her face growing warm, and the collar of her dress seemed to be choking her.

"And what's your answer?"

She looked away so that Mavis couldn't read anything else on her face, in her eyes. "He never declared himself, if that's what you mean. He did offer to marry me, but only because he felt honor-bound. I'll have no husband that way."

"And so when you turned him away, he married his Madelaine on the rebound."

Anna Rose stared hard at Mavis's wise, young face, letting her words sink in. "That can't be! Hugh's not that sort of man."

"Any man, once he's set his sights on taking a bride, will head for the altar like a starving horse to the feed bag! I've seen it happen often enough. Why, there were some poor fellows, jilted and forlorn, who'd even come to the ladies at Mrs. Tibbs's and swear undying love, begging the ladies to marry them. And these were upstanding gentlemen! Not sailors and drifters and the like. It's in a man's blood, when the time comes: marry or die! And if one's not available, he'll take the next to come his way."

Anna Rose forced a thin laugh. "Well, I don't think Hugh Sinclair ever loved me!"

"Can you be so sure?"

Anna Rose thought for a long time. She hadn't realized that she loved Hugh until it was too late. With Rory things had been different. They had both been so young and full of hope and plans. Love had seemed to come so naturally to them. But Hugh was a more complicated man than her husband had been. He was not one to use flowery phrases or to declare himself before he was really, truly sure.

"Perhaps he did love me." She said the words more to herself than to Mavis.

"And perhaps he still does!" Mavis answered.

Later, after bidding a tearful farewell to Mavis, Anna Rose walked back to the house in Wall Street, mulling everything over in her mind. If what Mavis suspected was true, she would have to be on her guard every moment that she was under Hugh's roof. She was fond of his wife already, and she had no intention of coming between them. She didn't want any sort of trouble. Her sole purpose in taking this position was to be with her daughter. What she had felt in the past or continued to feel for Hugh Sinclair must play no part in her life from here on.

Yes, Mavis was very wise for her tender years!

Anna Rose started up the stairs of the Sinclair house at the stroke of high noon. The knob turned in her hand and the door was opened for her. Hugh Sinclair stood in the entrance, his face grim. But his dark eyes seemed to soften when they alit on her, sending a curious shiver down Anna Rose's spine.

"What took you so long, Anna Rose?" he demanded. "I was worried that you might have changed your mind, that you might not come back."

"I'm sorry. But I've been gone only an hour."

She tried to pass him, but he seemed to be blocking her way intentionally.

"Please, I'd like to go up to my room now."

"Of course. Locking her eyes with his smoky gaze, he added in a husky whisper, "I'm glad you're back, Anna Rose."

She moved past him to the stairs, feeling her heart pound in her breast. All the things Mavis had said came rushing back to her. Oh, Lord! How was she going to deal with this? She couldn't let herself feel anything for him—she mustn't!

But how could she force herself to stop loving him?

18

Anna Rose felt at once proud of her mothering instincts and ashamed of her cowardice as she sat in the bright sun of the back garden, watching her daughter nap in her pram. She had been in the Sinclair household for three months now and still she was regarded simply as "Charity's nanny." She wanted to shout to the world that this was her daughter! But she couldn't bring herself to reveal her secret to Hugh, proud father that he was. And mentioning anything of the sort to Madelaine was most definitely out of the question. Hugh's wife had been unaccountably kind to Anna Rose, treating her more like a member of the family than a paid servant. It was almost as if the Sinclairs had adopted both daughter and mother.

Anna Rose sighed and tucked the blanket more securely around the sleeping baby. "Oh, Heather," she whispered. "What am I to do?" But when her daughter only napped on, Anna Rose's mind went back to the problem.

When she'd realized she couldn't bring herself to tell them the truth, she had thought briefly of stealing her child away in the middle of the night. That seemed the simplest and easiest solution. But two things stopped her. First, the Sinclairs had been too decent to her and her daughter for her to repay their kindness with such treachery. Second, and more difficult for her to accept, she was finding it harder every day to imagine life without Hugh, even if she was constantly aware that the man she loved was happily married to a woman she liked and respected deeply.

So far, nothing untoward had passed between Hugh and herself since she had evaded his kiss that very first day. But Anna Rose could feel something building. Emotional pressure? Growing desire? She couldn't quite put a name to it, but she knew that Hugh was fighting some sort of inner battle and losing ground all the time. That unsettling knowledge raised her own level of awareness. Quite often lately she'd turned to catch him staring at her with a faraway, longing gaze in his troubled dark eyes. She remembered that look well. It thrilled and frightened her now, as it had the very first time he'd looked at her that way.

However, what disturbed her the most was that every day she looked forward to whatever might transpire between them. Anna Rose knew she must refuse him, but, when the time actually came, would she have the willpower to deny her own desires?

She leaned back against the trunk of the buttonwood tree, smoothing her gloved hands over the soft folds of the sky-blue cashmere cape that the Sinclairs had insisted she buy. She closed her eyes. "What am I to do?" she repeated with another long sigh. "What indeed?"

Hugh Sinclair sat alone in his library, brooding over his plight. He had been lucky so far; no one knew what was going on inside his mind and his heart. Madelaine took his long silences and his reluctance to make love to her as worry over business. He let her believe that, for it was far simpler than trying to explain the truth to his wife. The servants avoided him, sensing that his temper might erupt at any moment. Only Anna Rose seemed oblivious to his gray moods.

She was so wrapped up in her young charge that she had little time or inclination to notice anyone else around her. Even Madelaine had voiced her amazement at the woman's total devotion to Charity.

Not an hour before, his wife had commented to him, "Hugh, it's as if some divine hand chose Anna Rose to come to us. Why, she's like a second mother to our Charity!"

At his wife's statement, Hugh had retreated to his library—a dark, solitary place to hide, to sort out his feelings, and to lick his wounds.

"Divine hand, indeed!" he growled, sweeping his arm in an angry arc that cleared his desk, but did little to clear his thoughts. "It's the devil's own handiwork, damnit!"

He let his head drop forward into his hands, and ran his fingers through his dark hair. He tugged hard, wanting to feel some form of physical pain, in the hopes it would relieve the mental anguish he'd lived with every minute of these past months. But it was no use. He sighed heavily and let his fists drop back to the desk top.

He was more tormented than ever now that Michael Flynn was escorting Anna Rose about town. At first, Hugh had welcomed the eager fellow's courting mission, thinking that would make it easier for him to abandon his emotional attraction to Anna Rose. But it had taken only one night of anguish, while Anna Rose was at the theater with the other man, for Hugh to realize that his jealousy was totally uncontrollable. He had waited up for them like an anxious father, and he had been less than civil to Flynn when he finally brought her home. Although Anna Rose had said nothing about the episode, Hugh was sure she was furious. She had every right to be! But Hugh simply couldn't help the way he felt about her.

The wine-colored velvet drapes were closed. Even though it was a bright, crisp December noon, to Hugh Sinclair it seemed like the deadest hour of a dreary, black night. Last evening had only capped off his frustrations. He'd come so close to actually entering Anna Rose's room and confronting her with the truth of his situation. He'd stood outside her door, poised to knock, for nearly half an hour. One more brandy and . . . He refused to let himself think of what might have happened.

He leaned back in his leather chair and closed his eyes, conjuring up Anna Rose's face and form without even trying. She lived there now, just behind his eyelids, always ready to present her heart-rending image at the least opportune moment.

"Last night . . ." he murmured. "Damn me to hell for what I almost did to both Anna Rose and Madelaine!"

He stood up abruptly and jerked the curtains wide, allowing sunlight to flood the room, hoping that light would also flood his soul. But, as his eyes adjusted to the brightness, pain stabbed through his heart. He uttered a low curse.

There she was, his beautiful, innocent tormentor, leaning against the tree with the warm sun on her face—caressing her, kissing her, making her smile with the pleasure of its warm intimacies. He tried to turn away from the sight of her, but it was no use. As he stood staring at the woman he desired more than life itself, Hugh Sinclair knew that whatever was going to happen would happen soon. He was only human, after all!

A few nights later, Hugh came home hoping for a quiet evening and early bed. He'd had a long, wearying day at the Townsend Wine Company. Recently, he had taken on more responsibility from his wife's father, hoping to escape the house and the torture he experienced every minute that he was under the same roof with the two women. Old Phinias had quickly agreed to the arrangement. He had grand plans for Hugh, for the aging merchant wanted to retire soon and turn the whole operation over to his son-in-law. Hugh had not bargained for taking over such a giant task in the beginning. Still, he was glad of the heavy work load now. It was a relief to concentrate on something other than his painful personal dilemma.

However, things were anything but quiet in the Sinclair household when he arrived home from the office. The women were in an unusually high state of excitement.

"Darling!" Madelaine greeted him, her blue-green eyes glittering as she brushed his cheek with a kiss. "Wait until you see the surprise we have for you."

With tired eyes, he glanced at his wife's new gown—a fetching bronze Turkish satin. Weary as he was, he smiled his approval. "It's lovely, my dear. But do I have to see everything you bought today?"

Hugh knew that Captain Constantine's *North Star* had docked recently with a shipment of the latest fashions, straight from Paris. Madelaine had been bubbling with the news the night before and with her plans to go shopping today. Obviously, her expedition had been an unqualified success.

Madelaine laughed softly at her husband's worried expression. "No, darling, I won't subject you to a parade of gowns tonight. But I do have a surprise for you. Michael is taking Anna Rose to the ballet tonight."

"Wonderful!" he muttered under his breath, feeling the jealousy twist through him like a serpent once more.

Madelaine paid no attention as she hurried on enthusiastically. "I decided that Anna Rose needed something fashionable to wear for the occasion and so . . ."

Hugh's wife continued her excited discourse, but he heard no more. At that moment, Anna Rose entered the room and his heart all but stopped at the sight of her. After a moment of stunned silence, he quickly pulled himself together. Already, Madelaine was looking at him oddly, sensing, he was sure, that he had drawn away from her both physically and emotionally. His wife was no fool, and sooner or later, she would realize what was happening.

"Good evening, Captain," Anna Rose said almost shyly. He could feel the caress of her quiet voice, like a lover's ardent embrace, making him weak and strong in the same instant.

Her smoky-green eyes locked with Hugh's intense gaze. Why was he looking at her that way, now, right in front of his wife? She felt uncomfortable enough already, dressed as she was, and at his expense. She hadn't wanted to go shopping and she certainly hadn't wanted this extravagant gown. But Hugh's wife had insisted. And once Madelaine Sinclair set her mind to something, there was no changing it.

"Darling," Madelaine said, interrupting the long silence, "Anna Rose said good-evening!"

He nodded, trying to find his voice, trying to find his breath. Only after an extension of the lengthy silence did he manage to speak her name, returning the brief but emotional greeting.

Madelaine was bubbling on and on about their shopping

excursion, but her husband wasn't listening. All of his senses were consumed by the woman standing before him—Anna Rose in changeable pearl silk that mirrored the warm hue of her slightly flushed throat, of her breasts that peeked tantalizingly at him from beneath the creamy lace of her low-cut gown. But he had only to close his eyes to remember their smooth texture and fullness and the cool feel of them against his palms.

With a huge effort, he forced such thoughts away. It was madness to relive those nights on the ship, nights when she had been deathly ill and in his care. He'd taken no liberties except in his mind. He'd sponged her burning body to bring down her fever, that was all. But the sight and the scent and the feel of her lived on in his consciousness, another sort of fever. And seeing her now—gowned and perfumed, her shining hair piled in elegant style—only served to make his pulses race, imagining, remembering, what lay beneath her fashionable facade and how desperately he wanted her—how totally he needed her.

Anna Rose was well aware of Hugh's discomfort, and she too was troubled. He shouldn't gaze at her that way—as if he were stripping the clothes from her, layer by layer—especially in front of his wife. Still, his look made her feel pleasantly strange. She felt warm all over, as if Hugh were holding her, kissing her without ever touching her physically. She grew dizzy with longing.

Someone was knocking loudly at the front door, making Anna Rose jump.

"Oh, that will be Michael!" Madelaine cried excitedly. "I can hardly wait until he sees you, Anna Rose. Won't he be delighted! You'll be the handsomest couple at the ballet."

Flynn was indeed impressed with his lady's appearance. Hugh noted that he clung to her arm and hurried her out as if he couldn't wait to get her alone. The jealousy boiled inside him, ugly and rampant. He acted the distrusting father in every way, finally warning Flynn to have Anna Rose home before midnight.

After the couple left, Madelaine scolded him mildly. "My dear, whatever's come over you? You were really rather rude to Michael. He's not some callow youth, after all, and Anna Rose is quite old enough to do as she pleases on her night off."

Hugh stifled a groan at his wife's words. How well he knew that!

After dinner, Madelaine went to bed early, pleading fatigue from her shopping trip. But Hugh remained in his library, watching the hands of the clock on the mantel move slowly as he waited for Anna Rose to return.

All through the evening Michael Flynn treated Anna Rose with the tenderest consideration. He was always polite and amusing when they were together, but tonight he acted with special gallantry, as if she were royalty. It was enough to turn any woman's head.

After the ballet, Michael took her to a quiet but fashionable café where they could be alone in a curtained booth in the midst of the crowd. As they sipped champagne, Flynn gently covered her hand with his.

She lifted her questioning gaze to his, finding his dark eyes sparked with desire.

"My darling, I hadn't meant to rush you," he said, "but, by God, I feel like I can't wait another minute. The way you look tonight is almost more than I can bear." He brought her fingers to his lips and kissed them thoroughly. "I love you so!" he whispered.

Anna Rose felt a blush heating her cheeks. She hadn't forgotten Michael's proposal, but lately, she had put off making any important decisions—including this one—wanting things simply to go on as they were. Still, she knew that was unfair. He deserved an answer. She hadn't meant to lead him on. She'd tried time and again, as gently as possible, to reject his offer. But the man turned a deaf ear to her refusals.

"Anna Rose, have you nothing to say to me?" he asked in a pleading voice.

"I'm sorry. I was thinking."

"Then you haven't made up your mind yet. But why not, my darling? Surely, you must know your own heart by now."

She felt like crying as she realized she must make him understand that she could never marry him. But the tears were for Hugh and the hopelessness of her love for him. "I do know my heart, Michael. That's why this is so difficult for me. If only I had someone to talk to."

He slid closer to her and slipped his arm about her bare shoulders, squeezing gently. "My dearest, you have the best listener in the world here holding you. And I'll understand, whatever you have to tell me. At least, I'll try to."

He seemed so warm and open with her suddenly, like a very dear old friend. Perhaps he would understand. She decided to tell him all that she was feeling. And so she did, beginning at the very start of it, with her marriage to Rory and Hugh's strange affect on her that day.

"Hugh's always been a ladies' man, my dear. I'm not surprised that you found him unsettling, even on your wedding day. But it was dastardly of him to take liberties that very night when you were so disheartened and vulnerable."

Anna Rose was quick to blame herself and to defend Hugh, of course. She felt Flynn grow tense beside her.

Still trying to explain her feelings, she went on to tell him of the horror of her husband's death and the weeks following when she was so ill and Hugh had cared for her. Finally, she confided in him about her daughter, wondering why he looked at her so oddly when she mentioned how tragic it was that Rory had not lived to see his child and that now the baby belonged to Hugh and Madelaine.

"That would seem the appropriate place for her." His brusque comment left her confused.

At length, she got around to speaking of Flynn's proposal. "You see, Michael, I'm afraid I do know my own heart. All too well! I'm very fond of you. You've been so good and kind to me all these months. I wish I could return your love." She lowered her lashes, fearing the hurt she might see in his eyes. "But it wouldn't be right of me to accept your proposal, still caring for Hugh as I do. I'm afraid I'd make you totally miserable."

Flynn leaned down and kissed her bare shoulder, whispering against her cool flesh, "Oh, darling, you could never make me miserable! Don't you see? My love is great enough for both of us. And once we are man and wife, your affections will turn to me, I'm sure of it."

In the curtained booth where no one could see, Flynn allowed himself the liberty of kissing her with unreined passion while one hand crept up to cup her breast tenderly. Anna Rose tried to pull away at first, but her body was starved for a man's touch. She gloried for a moment in his gentle fondling. However, the glow faded quickly, for Michael Flynn's was not the touch she craved.

"Please, Michael, it's late. Take me home now."

He drew away and stared into her eyes, his handsome face solemn. "I refuse to accept what you've told me tonight as a final rejection. I want you to think about what I've said, darling. At least consider it carefully before you throw your life away. Hugh Sinclair is a happily married man. Don't waste away pining for what you can never have. Give me the chance to make you happy, my dearest. I'm offering you all the love you could ever desire, enough to last till the end of time and beyond."

Flynn could see that Anna Rose was deeply moved by his words, exactly as he had planned. She was a stubborn woman, not easily manipulated. But he'd felt her respond to him when he kissed her and touched her breast. She was a passionate woman who had been without a man too long. By refusing to allow her to reject him verbally, he was setting the stage with great care for his planned seduction. He meant to have her, one way or another. And now that he was sure Hugh Sinclair had lied to him about keeping his distance while she was ill, his own determination doubled. Who did Anna Rose think she was kidding, saying the child was by her husband? He'd almost laughed out loud at that statement. He wondered if Sinclair knew. If not, the information was of even greater value to him.

Flynn continued his amorous but solicitous pose all the way home, only taking the mildest liberties as they rode through the streets of New York in a closed carriage. *Just enough to stir her, but not enough to satisfy her,* he cautioned himself. *A few kisses, a fondling caress now and then. Soon I'll have her begging me to marry her so that she can have it all!*

Anna Rose felt more confused than ever when Michael left her that night. Was it the champagne or the man himself? The way he'd kissed her in the carriage on the ride home had left her with a strange feeling of heaviness. And when his hands had brushed her breasts—not by accident, she was sure—she had felt her body respond, her flesh warming, her nipples tightening. Now an unaccountable lethargy had settled over her, and an unrelenting ache centered low in her body. She longed for bed, for sleep to put an end to these uneasy stirrings.

Hoping not to wake the family since it was quite late, she slipped into the house and closed the door softly behind her. The entranceway was in shadows although a lamp flickered on the stairs to light her way up. She headed down the hall, bent on bed and oblivion.

She was passing the parlor when a dark shadow loomed in the library door across the hall. A quiet cry of alarm escaped her.

"You're late!" Hugh's slightly slurred voice accused.

He came toward her, a tumbler of brandy in his hand. He was in his dressing gown, the gray velvet his wife had given him for his birthday last month. Anna Rose herself had stitched the gold monogram upon the lapel. Now the flourished *S* gleamed dully at her, reminding her of the sensuous feel of that soft fabric against her own skin. The robe was only loosely belted and Anna Rose had difficulty keeping her eyes from the opening above his waist. Hugh wore no shirt and the sight of the dark hair on his chest was disconcerting.

"I'm sorry I woke you," she said in an uncertain voice.

"You didn't. I waited up for you." He was coming nearer with every word he spoke.

"Well, I'm home safely. You can join your wife now."

He stood directly before her, one hand on his hip and a strange smile curving his lips. Slowly, he brought the brandy glass to his mouth and drained it before he spoke. "I don't think my wife would appreciate my joining her just now. She doesn't like having her slumber disturbed. Besides, you and I have some unfinished business to discuss, *Mrs. McShane*"

He wasn't drunk, Anna Rose could tell. But suddenly she was as afraid of him as if he had been dangerously inebriated. His very stance held a threat, and the way he said her name . . .

"Hugh, please," she began, backing away from him into the parlor.

"Please what?" he demanded, following her step for step, his smile gone. "Please leave you alone? Please stop thinking about you? Please stop loving you, Anna Rose? I'm afraid I can't do any of those things, God help me! God help us both!"

The words sounded like a whispered prayer as Anna Rose realized that the confrontation she had longed for and dreaded was finally here.

She continued backing away, not even conscious that she was moving. Hugh followed her into the room, closing the door behind him. The click of the lock made her jump.

"Leave that door open!" she ordered.

He ignored her words and smiled once more. But his expression was in no way comforting. In three long strides, he covered the distance separating them. She trembled as he reached for her and dug his hard fingers into the bare flesh of her shoulders, his touch burning her like a hot curl of flame.

"Hugh, you're hurting me! Please!"

He released her so quickly that she stumbled slightly. For a long time, he stood only a half pace away, scorching her with hot, angry eyes.

"Why did you come back here, Anna Rose?" His low, even voice was more frightening than if he had yelled at her.

"I had to. That's all. I just had to, Hugh."

"Did you know that I was very upset with you for coming back when you did? Damnit, Anna Rose, Madelaine and I had worked things out. We were actually quite happy together. But now . . ."

If he was trying to make her feel guilty, he was succeeding. She'd never been more ashamed in her life. Tears brimmed in her eyes for an instant, but then her own anger flared to match his. He had no right to censure her this way. She had done nothing to lead him on. If there was a problem, it was of his making.

His voice interrupted her thoughts. "If you hadn't come, we'd be—"

"Stop it, Hugh! I've heard enough!" she cried. "I've done nothing to come between you and your wife. I never meant to. If it will make you feel any easier, I may wed soon myself." She was stunned by her own words.

Hugh flinched as if she had hit him. His face lost all expression for an instant, then contorted in something akin to pain. He looked shocked by her statement. "You can't mean that!"

"But I do!" She was grasping at anything, trying to dissuade him from his obvious course. "Michael Flynn asked me some time ago. Tonight he pressed me for an answer."

"You didn't give him one?" Hugh's voice had softened. "Oh, Anna Rose, you couldn't have!"

She looked away, pained by the hurt in his eyes. "No," she answered softly, unable to wound him further. "I've told him nothing yet."

"Thank God!" He came to her, slowly now, as if he feared she might flee. His hands on her were gentle this time. He cradled her against his bare chest and whispered her name over and over.

Anna Rose knew she should reject his embrace. But she had dreamed of having his arms about her for too long. She found herself powerless to refuse his tenderness.

"Darling, don't ever do that to me again." His breath touched her forehead like the lightest kiss as he spoke. "Forget about Michael Flynn. He'll never marry anyone. I don't know what games he's playing with you, but you must believe me. He won't marry you. Besides, you don't love him."

Anna Rose didn't want to talk about Flynn. She didn't want to talk at all. She clung to Hugh, damning herself for the adulteress she was, but knowing that she could do nothing to stop what was happening between them. She could feel the heat rising. It was as if everything that had kept them apart had been preordained to make this moment as sweet, as achingly wonderful as it could be.

When his arms tightened around her and his mouth came down hard on her lips, the last fragile barrier of her resistance gave way. It was as if they were on the deck of the *Olympia* again. But there was no wine to fog her senses, no sleeping husband to prick her conscience. She had no way of knowing how long he kissed her. It lasted forever and only a moment. But it was not enough for either of them.

The rush of pain came only when he released her. She was crying, but silently, guilt and fear and longing forcing the tears from her eyes. What they were doing wasn't right. But how could she stop an avalanche after the first boulder had already been dislodged? What would become of the two of them? They had no future together. Only pain and unhappiness could come of such an affair. But it would be far more painful to let go now. No! She couldn't stand the empty hurt a moment longer!

Hugh read her embattled expression. His own faced looked strained and serious. His breath caressed her eyelids as he whispered, "Anna Rose, tell me honestly, this very instant, that you want no more and I swear I will release you. I'll never touch you again!"

He was offering her an out. One final chance to keep her honor intact. Why wouldn't her words come? She tried and tried, but she had no voice. The honesty he demanded stayed her reply.

When only her silence greeted him, Hugh lifted her gently in his arms and took her to the brocade couch, leaning her back against satin pillows. He brushed her lips lightly this time before his mouth moved hungrily down her throat. As he teased at the pulse there with the hard tip of his tongue, his hands strayed to her bodice. But the silk beneath his fingers did not satisfy. Soon he had slipped the gown from her shoulders. His eyes, heavy-lidded with desire, devoured the sight of her naked breasts, causing their crests to strain for his touch.

"Oh, my darling," he moaned against one hardening nipple. "You have no idea how long I've dreamed of holding you this way."

She gasped softly when his mouth found her, suckling until her breasts ached and her veins filled with liquid fire. Her fingers twined through the hair at the nape of his neck, holding him to the tender spot.

"Hugh, oh, my dearest!" she moaned, feeling her desire rising until she could stand no more.

Attuned to her needs, Hugh rose and expertly stripped away her grown and underthings. She lay before him in the dim light of one guttering lamp, naked but unashamed.

She ached so with wanting him that she could hardly breathe. *Perhaps,* she thought, *I was born for this one ecstatic moment!*

Although she was more than ready, Hugh loved her slowly, carefully, paying homage to each part of her body with his eyes, his hands, his mouth. She writhed beneath his touch, praying the end of the world would not come until he had possessed her totally. After that . . . *nothing else mattered!*

All the while that he tortured her so lovingly, still withholding what she longed for most, Hugh murmured softly to her, a litany of love words. Suddenly, his quiet tone changed. Her name rasped from his throat again and again. She understood and cried, "Oh, yes, darling, now!"

His first thrust was deep and fierce, as if he had held back too long. Anna Rose gripped the corded muscles of his shoulders, clinging to him as if to life itself. She felt every move of his body, every heartbeat, every breath he took. They were no longer two people, but one wild and fiery being, bent on loving to the exclusion of all else.

The ultimate sensation began slowly, building and building until Anna Rose thought she would die from it. All her senses seemed expanded. Her tender breasts throbbed, her thigh muscles clenched, her womb cradled him in its liquid heat as it would a much-wanted unborn child.

When the final earth-moving plunge came, Anna Rose was ready. She opened herself to receive and he gave her his all. At the same instant, they both cried out, smothering their sounds of ecstasy in a deep, prolonged kiss.

Near dawn, when Anna Rose finally crept to her room, some of the magic had deserted her. She was gripped by remorse. She loved Hugh and he had made it plain that he returned her affection in the fullest measure. Tonight had been wonderful . . . *too wonderful!* She couldn't allow it to go on. But how could she stay under the same roof with him, see him every day, and keep her distance? The answer was all too clear: she couldn't. As much as it tore her heart to think of leaving, she must.

She lay in her bed, sobbing into her pillow after she had reached the decision. Without Hugh, it seemed that nothing mattered any longer.

A sudden cry from the next room made her realize that one thing did matter. She hurried through the door to the adjoining nursery and took up her little daughter. Charity clung to her natural mother as if she understood the secret of their special bond.

"Hush, darling," Anna Rose soothed. "Don't cry, my baby. It was only a bad dream."

She sat down with Charity clutched tightly to her breast and rocked her, crying softly as she hummed the child's favorite tune. Soon the golden-haired baby drifted off again. But Anna Rose held her still, kissing the sweet, fluttery eyelids, memorizing the softly bowed mouth and up-tilted nose. A new rush of tears flooded.

How could she leave her own child? Now that she had found her and grown to love her, how could she give her up? She couldn't! She realized, when she left, she would have to take Heather with her.

Anna Rose continued rocking her baby, thinking back over the past months of her life, the life she was about to give up forever.

Had it not been for the tension between Hugh and herself, Anna Rose would have known complete joy here with her daughter.

Every day, Charity provided some new miracle as she grew and learned. And this wasn't simply in her mother's prideful eye. Everyone who saw Charity Sinclair, with her china blue eyes and sun-bright curls, commented on what an extraordinary child she was.

Madelaine, too, had become Anna Rose's treasured friend. She could understand now why Hugh had married her. The woman was goodness and sunshine through and through. Anna Rose would miss their close companionship—their strolls in the park, their shopping excursions, their shared dreams for the child who was a daughter to them both. They had come to be almost like sisters. But now her own transgressions had changed all that. She was no longer worthy to call Madelaine Sinclair her friend.

Anna Rose let her mind wander back to the time she had just shared with Hugh—time stolen from another woman who loved him, too—and her very soul seemed to shudder with anguish. Why did she have to love Hugh Sinclair so desperately? And why had she passed up her chance to become his wife! *If only* . . .

Anna Rose stood up and put her sleeping daughter back to bed. Then, with her decision made and a definite purpose in mind, she went back to her room and sat down at her writing table. She wrote:

Dear Captain & Mrs. Sinclair:

By the time you read this, you will know that I have taken my daughter away, for I am Charity's natural mother. Her real name is Heather, and she was left at your doorstep when I was desperately ill shortly after her birth. I knew nothing of her fate until I recovered. I had hoped, when the time came, to explain all this to you, face-to-face. I detest having to take the coward's way out. But for reasons that shall remain unspoken, I can no longer stay here. I know that you love this sweet child as much as I do. For this reason, I hope that you

will consider her happiness and allow us to go our own
way together.

My heartfelt thanks to both of you for all that you
have done. Surely my daughter would have died had it
not been for your kindness in taking her in.

Ever gratefully,
Anna Rose McShane

She read the note over carefully, then folded it and tucked it
away until the proper time. Tomorrow she would take her savings
and purchase tickets on a southbound stage for herself and Mavis.
She was sure the girl, who was still working at Delmonico's,
would agree to accompany her. That way, no eyebrows would be
raised at a woman traveling alone with her child. And, too, Hugh
and Madelaine would be searching for one woman, not two. On
their departure date, she would simply take Charity out for a stroll
in her pram and never return. By the time darkness set in and the
Sinclairs began searching, she and her daughter would be out of
the city. They would find her note when they searched her room.

It was a simple, but painful, plan. Nevertheless, it was the only
way.

19

Anna Rose wasted no time, for the next morning she was out
early. Her first stop was at Delmonico's to see Mavis.

"La, don't you look like one of the toppin' folk in that fine blue
cape and bombazine gown, Mistress McShane!" Mavis hugged
her friend, then went back to scrubbing potatoes at the kitchen
sink. She wasn't in the least surprised to see Anna Rose, who
often stopped in for a chat. But today Anna Rose seemed nervous
and on edge. "Help yourself to a cup of tea," said Mavis, "while
you tell me what brings you out so early on an icy morning like
this."

Anna Rose, shivering from the cold, accepted the hot tea
gratefully. But she got right to the point. "Mavis," she began in a
quiet voice. "It's happened—exactly what you warned me
about!"

The younger woman, noting the anguished tone in her friend's voice, wiped her hands on her long apron and came to sit down at the table.

"I'm not sure what you're talking about, Anna Rose."

"Hugh and me." She looked down guiltily, unable to meet Mavis's inquiring gaze. "Last night, he told me he loves me."

Mavis caught her breath and gasped, "Lord, Anna Rose! What'll you do now?"

"I have to leave, of course. If I stay, it will ruin everything . . . all our lives."

Seeing that her friend was fighting tears, Mavis covered Anna Rose's trembling hand with her own. "There, there! It can't be all that bad. But what about Heather? How can you bear to let her go? I know you'll be miserable without that precious baby."

Anna Rose swallowed hard, trying to control her emotions. "I'm taking her with me, Mavis. I have to!"

"They'll let you?"

"They won't know. I have it all planned, but I need your help." Anna Rose looked directly at Mavis. "Will you come with us? I'm heading south. But it will look suspicious if I'm traveling all alone. I need you with me, Mavis. Please, will you help me?"

Mavis leaned back and touched her forehead as if she felt a migraine coming on. "Oh, Anna Rose, you've come at me with so much all at once! And yet you've told me nearly nothing. When? How? And where do you plan to go from here other than 'south'?"

Anna Rose quickly explained her plan to leave as soon as possible. She had money saved to buy their tickets on a stage and she hoped to get to Georgia, her original destination when she had left Scotland. By the time Anna Rose left Delmonico's, Mavis had agreed to help her.

Before noon Anna Rose had secured the necessary tickets on a southbound stage, which would leave at the end of the week. She had three days to wait before their departure. But that would give her time to make sure everything was in order. She only hoped that Hugh would keep his distance until that time. She knew she would have to keep herself carefully in check, act as if everything were perfectly normal—at least, as normal as they could be after the night before.

She opened the back door and hurried through, slamming it quickly against December's wintry blast. Bright sun flooded the scrubbed wood floor and a cheery fire blazed beneath a bubbling pot of pea soup. The whole atmosphere in the kitchen was wonderfully deceptively cozy, she mused.

Anna Rose was just hanging her blue cape on one of the pegs beside the door when she heard Chadwick's voice, raised in distress. "Captain Sinclair! Come quick!"

Hugh and Anna Rose coverged in the hallway at the same moment. The sight that greeted them froze the blood in Anna Rose's veins and turned Hugh as pale as stone.

"Madelaine!" he gasped.

His wife lay sprawled on the floor of the hallway, her eyes closed and her face pasty white. Hugh slipped his arms under her and lifted her gently.

"Get her up to her bed quickly," Anna Rose advised. "What happened, Chadwick?"

The old butler looked shaken. "I don't know. She was coming down the hallway, about to show me a spot on the couch in the parlor that needed cleaning, when all of a sudden, she swayed, then dropped down to the floor. Fainted dead away!"

The other servants had gathered. "Get the smelling salts, Katy," Anna Rose ordered. "Bring them upstairs. And hurry! Chadwick, send someone for the doctor."

For the moment, Anna Rose forgot all about her own problems, totally concerned about Madelaine Sinclair. She waited with Hugh in his wife's bedroom. Madelaine had come around, but she still looked deathly pale.

"Really, my dears," Madelaine said in a weak voice, "I'm fine. A lady is allowed an occasional swoon, after all. Now, if you'll just help me up."

She reached out her hand to Hugh. He clasped it in both of his, but refused to allow her out of bed.

"Not until after Dr. Whitehead has had a look at you, my darling."

Anna Rose glanced at Hugh. His face was a mask of concern. She was worried, too. And for some unaccountable reason, she felt uneasy about her own plans now. Then she chided herself mentally. The doctor would be here soon. Madelaine would be fine. She, Mavis, and Heather would leave at the end of the week on schedule. What could go wrong?

When Dr. Whitehead had finished his examination of Madelaine, he called Hugh and Anna Rose back into the bedroom. Hugh was still shaken, and although Anna Rose had taken things in hand only a short while before, she was feeling none too steady on her feet now.

"Well, Mrs. Sinclair, other than scaring the wits out of your entire household, I'd say you've done no real damage."

"What's wrong with her, Doctor?" Hugh asked anxiously.

The thin old physician and his patient exchanged secret smiles.

"Nothing she won't be cured of in about six months' time," the doctor answered cryptically. "Congratulations, Captain Sinclair. You're about to become a father. I can't say that I'm pleased about it, as delicate as Mrs. Sinclair is, but your wife declares she's delighted."

Hugh expelled a heavy sigh and sank into a chair beside the bed, his head bowing as if in prayer. Anna Rose, with a twinge of conscience and envy, watched as Madelaine reached out and stroked his thick black hair with tender affection. Hugh took her fingers in his and placed a kiss in her palm.

"The doctor warned us, dear. How could we have let this happen?" Hugh asked anxiously.

Madelaine gave him a cheery smile. "Oh, come now, darling! Admit it! You're as pleased as I am. I'm perfectly all right. After all, pregnant women are expected to faint occasionally. It happens all the time."

Anna Rose frowned. She'd never fainted. A bit of light-headedness from time to time, but she'd never passed out on her feet.

"Doctor?" Hugh asked, suspicious of his wife's answer.

"She's in no danger yet. But after the miscarriage, I think it's wise that she stay in bed for the rest of her time. She isn't as strong as most. It's only a precaution, but it's for the good of your wife and the baby, Captain Sinclair."

"Of course!" Hugh replied. "She'll be waited on hand and foot."

The physician turned to Anna Rose then. "Young woman, Mrs. Sinclair has told me how good you are with little Charity. She's also requested that you nurse her through her term. She assures me you won't hesitate to take on this added responsibility. I hope her faith in you is not misplaced. She'll need very careful tending."

Madelaine did not allow Anna Rose time to answer before she pleaded, "I know it's an imposition, dear, but I'll feel more comfortable with you taking care of me than if I have some stranger always hovering about. Everything will turn out fine, believe me."

Anna Rose was torn. She hated to lie to Madelaine, but what else could she do? She certainly couldn't tell her she'd be leaving at the end of the week. Yet she didn't want to upset her further by insisting that they hire some outsider as a nurse. Without looking at Hugh, Anna Rose nodded her assent to his pregnant wife.

"There! It's all settled then," Madelaine said, beaming with pleasure. "We shall simply spend a cozy winter together while we await the arrival of this darling baby."

Actually, the entire episode proved a relief to Anna Rose in the next days. Hugh was constantly at his wife's side. So although she saw much of him, Madelaine was always there as well. There was no opportunity for a repeat performance of the night in the parlor. The situation proved painful, but safe.

Anna Rose would remember the date until the day she died, as if December 16, 1835, had been burned into her heart with a flaming brand.

That morning—two days after Madelaine's fainting spell and the day before Anna Rose's planned escape—began with bitter cold that offered no hope of letting up. A gale wind blew through the city, rattling panes and howling down chimneys, only adding to her uneasiness.

The past few days had been trying. Charity was suffering from a mild case of the croup, and Madelaine, at first the perfect patient, had unexpectedly grown restless and nervous. As her time of departure drew nearer, Anna Rose's own anxiety increased.

To add to her problems, Hugh was in an especially foul humor. He snapped at the servants, was rude to the doctor, and finally, late that afternoon, ordered Anna Rose to his library.

She went, but with great trepidation. Surely, Hugh couldn't mean to take advantage of his wife's bedridden state to reenact their disgraceful performance of the other night. Granted, their time together lived in Anna Rose's heart and mind every minute of every day, but she refused to allow it to happen again. It was wrong! Still, what else could he want?

"Yes, what is it?" he snapped, not looking up from his work, as she entered the library that afternoon.

"I haven't any idea!" she replied, matching his surly tone. "You ordered me here."

"Oh, it's you, Anna Rose." His voice was still harsh, but less intimidating. "I thought you were one of the other servants."

His words stung, and she flinched in spite of herself.

"It's about tonight," he continued. "I insist you cancel your plans."

Anna Rose could hardly believe what she was hearing. She would have been the first one to call off her plans to attend the theater with Michael Flynn, if she dared. But a refusal at this late date would appear peculiar. Everything she did in these last hours before she fled New York must seem perfectly normal in order to allay suspicion tomorrow. She needed as much time as possible to lapse between the hour she left with Heather and the moment when the Sinclairs realized they must instigate a search.

"I'm afraid I can't do that," she replied.

"Madelaine needs you."

She eyed him closely, but he avoided meeting her gaze. He was not telling her the true reason behind his demand.

"Your wife will be perfectly fine, Hugh. By the time Michael arrives for me, she will be fed and fast asleep. If she should wake before I return, Katy is more than capable of looking after her. Besides, Madelaine has insisted that I not change my plans on her account. If I do, she'll be upset needlessly."

Hugh's frown deepened. "Weren't you listening to me the other night? I told you he'll never marry you, no matter how often he's proposed."

Anna Rose was forced to suppress a smile. *So*, she thought, *the truth comes out!*

"If it will ease your mind, I'll confess that I've given up any notion of considering his offer, although I don't agree with you. I think he is totally sincere. But I could never marry him now. Not after what's happened." Anna Rose looked down, suddenly shy at having mentioned their lovemaking, no matter how obliquely.

"You feel bad about what happened, don't you?" Hugh said, a brusque tenderness in his voice.

She nodded, unable to speak.

A deep, masculine sigh filled the silence between them before he said quietly, "I know, Anna Rose. I feel the same way. It's even worse for me. You see, I'm probably responsible for Madelaine's fainting spell the next morning. I'm afraid I wasn't too gentle with her after I left you."

Anna Rose's head shot up. "You don't mean you went to her after we . . . after you and I . . . Oh, Hugh!" she stammered.

Suddenly she understood the depth of Hugh's jealousy of Michael Flynn. She knew, of course, that Hugh slept with his wife. What firmer proof could she possibly have than Madelaine's present state? But all these months, she had forced herself not to dwell on their private relationship. To have him state these intimate facts to her so bluntly—to realize that moments after his arms had held her, his lips had kissed hers, Madelaine had experienced the same proof of his passionate nature—was almost more than Anna Rose could bear. Her heart ached and she felt sick with her own envy.

Hugh was on his feet, coming toward her. "Anna Rose, for the love of God, don't look at me that way! I'm not a monster!" he groaned, misunderstanding the reasons behind her stricken expression. "I shouldn't have said anything to you, but I feel so guilty about the way I treated her. It's eating away at me. I can't say my conscience is exactly easy where you are concerned either."

She tried to move away, but she wasn't quick enough. He caught her shoulders in his firm grasp and drew her to him, burying his face against her hair.

His words were muffled, but no less moving. "Why is life so complicated? Why does love have to hurt so?"

With a great effort, both physically and emotionally, Anna Rose pulled away from his embrace. "Hugh, wiser men than you have asked those questions from the beginning of time, but found no answers."

He straightened, the weakness she had witnessed a moment earlier gone now. "You're right, of course, Anna Rose. 'Why' is probably the most foolish and useless word in the English language."

"I agree," she whispered, suddenly sorry that his control had returned so quickly, for comforting him had taken away some of her own uncertainty.

"Anna Rose, I've noticed your nervousness for the past few days. I know its cause."

She caught her breath. Had he discovered her note in its hiding place?

"I realize," he continued, "that it's a great strain, being the third party here in this house and wondering at what moment I might corner you and take advantage again. You have my promise that I won't. I hope that brings you some measure of comfort."

She was so relieved that she could think of no reply. She stood rooted to the spot, not bothering to fend him off when he embraced her once more.

"Darling, I will keep my promise. I swear it! But give me one more moment. The other night meant everything to me. I want you to understand that I love you now and I always will, even though we can't be together."

When his mouth came down on hers, hot and searching, Anna Rose felt her defenses crumbling. Tears flooded her eyes. She had never wanted him more than she did at this very moment. But this would be their final confrontation, their final kiss. After tomorrow, Hugh Sinclair would live only in her memory. Perhaps sometime in the distant future, she would find the strength to let go, to ease this man she loved so desperately to the darkest corner of her heart. But for now, he filled her soul and her heart with such love and longing that she never wanted to forget him.

"You'd better go," he said gently. "Forget what I said about Flynn, darling. You have your own life to lead and it's hardly my place to dictate to you. I have no right. But I hope you'll remember that I love you, Anna Rose. I'll *always* love you."

She answered in the same words, even though her moving lips produced no sound. Their eyes met and lingered in a painful farewell, then she turned and fled the room.

Hugh managed to be almost cordial to Flynn when he called for Anna Rose that evening, albeit in a rather stiff manner. Still, it was a relief to Anna Rose when they left the house and she was able to escape the oppressive atmosphere within. Madelaine and Charity were both still fretful, and a certain depressing heaviness seemed to hang in the air that evening like a shroud. She hoped the theater would lift her spirits and calm her nerves.

She might have guessed, though, that Michael Flynn would choose this night of all others to demand an answer from her. She knew what she must tell him, but how much easier it would be simply to slip away tomorrow without having to face this final trial.

On the way to the theater, he turned in the closed carriage and stared at her questioningly for several moments, smiling his appreciation of her burgundy taffeta gown with its form-fitting bodice and enticingly low neckline.

"I'd almost forgotten what a lovely creature you are, Anna Rose. Or could it be that you grow more beautiful every day?"

Flynn had been away from the city for several weeks, speculating in cotton in the southern states. This was only the second time he'd seen Anna Rose since his return. But he hadn't given up on his mission to marry her in order to spite Hugh Sinclair. While he was away, several casual women had flitted in and out of his life like so many passionate butterflies. In fact, there was a certain dark-haired, almond-eyed beauty he'd met in Savannah who'd promised to wait for him. But, of course, she was far from the marrying kind. His pursuit of Anna Rose was still uppermost in his mind.

Smiling into her eyes, he reached for her hand and brought it to his lips. "How much longer do you plan to keep me danglin', darling? Can't you see I'm a starved man?" he asked, nibbling at her fingertips.

"You want me to be sure, don't you, Michael?" she said firmly, removing her hand from his grasp.

He straightened in his seat. "Is Sinclair still a problem?" he demanded. "If so, you're being foolish, Anna Rose. He's a married man. It seems after all you've been through that you'd realize life does not always work out the way one plans. One takes what one has and makes of it what one can. In a way, it's very like those silhouettes I've seen you fashion from bits of paper. Somewhere in each shapeless scrap lurks a hidden image. But the task is left to you to give it form and substance."

His analogy intrigued her, but it was not altogether clear. "I don't understand what you mean, Michael."

"It's like this, my darling. At present, your life is still a shapeless mass. You've left your family, lost your husband, given up your child, and the man you're convinced has sole claim on your heart is married to someone else. Where does that leave you?"

Anna Rose looked down at Flynn's hand stroking hers and murmured, "Nowhere very pleasant, I'm afraid."

"But you're so wrong, my love!" He gripped her shoulders and turned her to face him. "Here I am, the answer to your prayers! Michael Flynn—handsome, clever, gentle, understanding Michael, who loves you. Why won't you marry me and allow me to give you the happiness you deserve? Don't let your life remain a dark, shapeless mass. Give it form and substance. Marry me, Anna Rose!"

Without allowing her a chance to reply, he drew her into his arms, parting her lips with an expert thrust of his tongue as his hand found her full breast.

Anna Rose tried to pull away, but he held her fast, kissing her deeply and expertly. Here was her proof, if she'd needed any. When Hugh had kissed her this way, the earth had moved beneath her feet. But with Michael . . . *nothing*. At last their carriage drew up in front of the John Street Theater and, to her great relief, he released her.

"Think about it, darling," he whispered close to her ear. "You and I would be perfect together. I'm convinced of it. I'll even give you a bit more time—until the end of the evening."

All during the performance—a farce that Anna Rose could barely follow because of her quandary—Michael acted like a lovesick youth, holding her hand, nibbling her fingertips, and whispering until the people sitting close by shushed him angrily.

The words he whispered made an odd sort of sense. After they were married, he wanted to take her south, to Savannah. He had a land deal brewing there, and she would love the old city with its moss-draped oaks and flowering azaleas, he told her.

Whatever am I thinking? she asked herself suddenly. It made no sense at all! Her plans were set. She would leave early the next morning and after that she'd no longer have to worry about any problems here in New York, including Michael Flynn.

"Please, Michael, let me watch the show," she said as he whispered more endearments to her. "I promise we'll talk afterward."

Flynn settled back, secure in the thought that he would have her answer before the end of the evening.

But the performance was not over yet when the first bells began to ring. The audience rustled in their seats, knowing what the clanging meant: fire! Several people rose and rushed out, anxious for their homes or businesses.

"Damn cold night for a fire!" Michael whispered.

"What difference does it make?"

"The water will freeze in the hoses and these high winds will whip the flames."

The bells kept ringing, sounding from new quarters. More and more theatergoers hurried out. Anna Rose felt a prickling fear along her spine.

"Michael, can you tell which section the fire's in?"

He cocked his head and listened. To Anna Rose the clanging of the bells seemed to be coming from everywhere now.

"Sounds like the business district. Wall Street or William."

Her blood froze. "Please. Let's go!"

"There's nothing to worry about, Anna Rose."

"How can you say that? I have this awful feeling!" She knew she sounded hysterical, but she couldn't help it.

Outside the theater, the street was a mob scene. Fire wagons tried in vain to forge through as the horses screamed in panic and reared dangerously. People were yelling, crying, running everywhere. Glowing ashes swirled all about them like fiery snowflakes. Thick clouds of black smoke billowed through the air, burning Anna Rose's eyes, choking her.

She steeled herself against the biting cold of the wind and turned toward the Battery, dreading what she would see. The night sky glowed blood red in that direction. The Wall Street district was ablaze as if hell had come to earth. She struck out on foot, but Flynn caught her arm.

"Anna Rose, stop! Are you crazy? You'll freeze before you reach the house."

"But your carriage will never get through. The traffic is snarled all the way."

He refused to listen to her panicked words, but shoved her into the vehicle. It seemed to take hours as they crept south toward

Wall Street, the inferno, and the Sinclair house. The heat was so intense that Anna Rose could feel it on her tear-streaked cheeks.

Was this the end of the world? she wondered. Surely, it was the end of hers. Hugh and Heather were in the house!

"Let me out, Michael! I have to go help them. Madelaine and my daughter are both sick in bed."

"Anna Rose, don't!"

But his protests died in the hot, freezing gale when the carriage door flew open and she bounded into the awful night.

Struggling through the snow and the tangle of useless fire hoses, Anna Rose made her way to the corner of Broad and Wall streets. A fireman stopped her.

"You can't go beyond this point, ma'am."

"But my baby!" she screamed, trying to shove past him.

He shook his head, holding her back in a firm grasp. "Sorry. It's too dangerous."

Leaning around the man, she could see Hugh's house. The walls were still standing, but the roof was ablaze. Inside, the windows were lit with flames. Screams of pain and terror filled the night, all of them seeming to Anna Rose to come from that one house.

A sob tore from her throat. Although the closest flames were a block away, they seemed to be reaching out to her, beckoning for her to join her loved ones in death. She screamed her daughter's name. Then she staggered and went limp with shock and pain. A strong arm reached out to steady her.

"Please, mister," the fireman said to Flynn. "Get her out of here before she gets hurt. She says her baby's in one of those houses, but there ain't nothing we can do for any of them people. Poor bastards! Caught 'em in their beds sound asleep."

"Jesus!" Flynn breathed, the word frosting the air about his flame-lit face.

"You best hurry, mister," the fireman persisted. "Captain Mix is gone in a boat over to the Brooklyn Navy Yard to fetch gunpowder. He'll be back soon to start blowing up part of this block. Might slow the fire down. Otherwise, we'll all be burnt out by morning."

The fireman was wrong. The blaze was still eating away at New York the following morning and the one after that. The high winds spread blazing embers throughout the entire city, burning in all nearly a thousand buildings, the very heart of New York. The dynamite, when it finally arrived, put a stop to the conflagration on the third day. But Anna Rose knew none of this.

When she collapsed into Flynn's arms after seeing the ruins of Hugh's house, she knew only blessed oblivion for hours. When she came out of her deep, nightmare-induced sleep, she was far south of the burning city.

"There was nothing we could do," Flynn told her. "If we'd stayed, we'd have lost our lives, too."

He held her close, letting her weep against his shoulder as they bumped along in the stage bound for Philadelphia and points south. He felt sorry for her. But, hell! He'd saved her life. Still, it hadn't been his name she'd sobbed repeatedly while she was out of her head. It had been Hugh Sinclair she'd called for. So now he knew what her answer to his marriage proposal would have been.

Well, that was fine! He didn't intend to give her another chance to turn him down. He didn't need a woman who spent all her time grieving for a dead man. He'd stay with her awhile, he decided. But he wouldn't marry her. Half the point of making her his wife had been to get Sinclair's goat. Now that he was dead, what was the use?

He touched his breast pocket and smiled. He still had her redemption papers. And now he knew what he'd do with them as soon as he'd had his fill of her.

For the first time in her life, fate, it seemed, had beaten Anna Rose to her knees. She knew she was drifting in a deep black pool of grief that threatened to suck the very life from her. But try as she might to fight her way back to the surface, the effort proved too great.

Over and over she asked herself, "When have I sinned so to bring this hell-on-earth upon myself and those I love?"

The answer, of course, lay plainly before her, tearing at her already bleeding heart. *She and Hugh—adulterers both!* He had paid with his life. But she would be called upon to pay far more . . . until the day she too died. She had lost everyone she loved.

She closed her eyes, feeling nothing except emptiness. All gone! All gone! the wagon wheels seemed to be whispering.

Hugh, Heather, Madelaine and her unborn baby, all gone, forever.

Anna Rose bit her lip until blood seeped into her mouth. She let her nails pierce her palms. The blessed balm of physical pain. *All gone!*

She would see those flames for the rest of her life. How she wished she had been in the burning house, too.

A sob escaped her and her shoulders quaked with renewed grief. Suddenly, she felt a rough hand touch hers. She opened her

221

eyes to see the rugged, gray-haired man on the opposite seat gazing at her with genuine sympathy. She had no idea who he was, but she knew he had not been with them all the way.

"Is there anything I can do to help, ma'am?" he asked gently.

She shook her head, feeling strangely soothed by the Highland lilt in his voice. He reminded her, she realized, of her own father.

"I'm afraid there's nothing anyone can do," she answered at length. "But you're kind to offer, sir."

"Well, if you think of something, dear lady, you call on Angus Campbell. I'll be here."

Anna Rose managed a weak smile and a nod for the soft-voiced stranger. There was still some good in the world, she realized with a fleeting spark of hope.

20

It was not a happy Christmas Day in New York City.

A solitary figure stood gazing at the charred and crumbled wreckage of the Wall Street house, trying to fathom the loss. There was no need for a funeral. After the fire, there was nothing left to bury from the ruins of the old Dutch dwelling.

Gone! All gone! the man thought with a silent shake of his head.

Four days after the fire had burned itself out, Hugh Sinclair, his hands bandaged and the gash in his forehead swathed with gauze, stood numbly staring at the pile of blackened rubble that had been his home such a short time before.

He knew how it had happened—the explosion of a gas main at the corner of Hanover and Pearl streets. But why? Why had it been such a bitterly cold night that the water froze in the firemen's hoses? Why had the wind blown so wildly, spreading the burning embers far and wide? And why had he had to leave the house when he did . . . leaving Madelaine bedridden and helpless?

He closed his eyes, going over the horror in his mind. He saw himself again on the stairs, taking them two at a time to answer his wife's frantic summons.

"Hugh, please hurry!"

An uneasiness in his mind quickened his steps as much as

Madelaine's cry. Hugh had been sure all evening that something was about to happen. It was in the very air. This feeling of dread he'd been harboring all day was part of the reason he'd wanted Anna Rose to stay home instead of going to the theater. He'd sensed that Madelaine might need her help.

But when he entered the bedroom, his wife was sitting up, looking amazingly fit, her eyes bright and her cheeks glowing with health. Still, the frown on her face told him that something was amiss.

"Oh, darling, I'm so worried!" she cried at the sight of him.

He went to her and took her trembling hands in his. "Madelaine, whatever's wrong? Why aren't you sleeping?"

She gripped his hands tightly. "It's Charity. I can hear her coughing all the way from the nursery. She's much worse, Hugh, I can tell. I'm so frightened. I wish Anna Rose were here."

"Katy's with her," he answered, trying to soothe her fears. "I'm sure she'll do anything that's necessary, darling."

"Hugh, I know you'll think I'm only being foolish, but I'd feel so much better if Dr. Whitehead could have a look at her."

Hugh frowned at her, remembering her unreasonable fears when she was pregnant before. "Madelaine, I'm sure you're worrying needlessly. Besides, it's very late and it's freezing outside. You can't expect the doctor to come out on a night like this."

Madelaine burst into tears at his words and clung to him as if to life itself. "Please, Hugh! Oh, please! I'm so frightened! If anything happened to that baby, I don't know what I'd do."

Hugh kissed her forehead in understanding, his mind already made up that he must go fetch the doctor, if not for Charity's well-being, for Madelaine's peace of mind.

At that moment, Katy appeared at the door, a grave look on her ruddy face. "Pardon me, Captain, but it's the wee babe. She's burning with fever and likely to strangle with that cough unless something's done. I've exhausted me own knowledge of remedies. We'll be needin' a doctor or a priest before this night's done."

Katy's dire prediction took its toll on Hugh. Suddenly, Madelaine's fears became very real to him. Grabbing his coat, he called, "I'll be back as soon as I can." Then he dashed out into the freezing night.

Luckily, Dr. Whitehead's home was nearby. Hugh pulled his collar up around his ears—stinging with cold after only moments—and bent his large frame into the gusty blasts. His footing was less than sure on the icy street, but he hurried as best he could.

Not a light showed at the physician's windows. He banged repeatedly on the door before he heard muffled stirring inside.

"I'm coming!" the old doctor yelled grumpily. "Never mind beating my door down!"

While he waited, Hugh stamped his feet and hugged his coat closer in a vain attempt to keep warm. The night was as cold and bitter as the icy North Atlantic in the dead of winter, he mused. And any ship caught in a wind like this would have her sails ripped to shreds.

Finally, the door creaked open.

"Yes, what is it?" the old man growled.

"Hugh Sinclair, Dr. Whitehead. It's my daughter. She's very ill."

"Keep her warm. Give her a dose of castor oil," he instructed abruptly. "I'll drop by first thing in the morning. Good night now!"

Hugh caught the edge of the door as the doctor tried to close it. He shoved it open and strode into the hallway.

"See here, Whitehead, the child's suffering! She needs you now!"

Old Dr. Whitehead, who's snowy pate matched his name, squinted at Hugh through thick spectacles. "You can't expect me to go out in this cold! Besides, it's almost midnight, man! I told you, I'll stop first thing in the morning."

Hugh was past trying to reason or be polite. He grabbed Whitehead by the lapels of his robe and gave him a shake. "My daughter is dying, Doctor! You will see her tonight! Now haul on your trousers and get your medical bag or I swear by all that's holy, I'll drag you through the streets all the way to my doorstep as you are!"

A few minutes later, Hugh and the grumbling physician were making their way back toward Wall Street.

They were only a short distance from Hugh's house when the first alarm sounded. The church bells clanged urgently through the cold air. Leaving Dr. Whitehead in his wake, Hugh charged toward home. But even as he rounded the corner, he could see that he was too late. Tongues of flame leaped through the roof to illuminate the night sky with an eerie, bloody glow.

He dashed for the burning house, up the stairs, and into the smoke-filled entranceway. Only one thought possessed him: He had to save his family.

Without pause, ignoring the flames overhead and the smoke

filling his eyes and lungs, he ran to the nursery, the closest room at the head of the stairs. He bundled Charity in a blanket to protect her from the thick clouds of black smoke.

Total confusion reigned in the house, the servants dashing this way and that, trying to save what they could. Catching Katy O'Carlin on the fly as he dashed toward the stairs, he thrust the crying child into her arms and ordered her out of the house.

"But Miss Madelaine!" she cried.

"I'm going back for her now. You and the others get out of here. Fast! Take Charity to Dr. Whitehead's house. You should all be safe there."

The heat was so intense by the time he went back up the stairs that he could feel his eyebrows and the hair on his arms singeing. The smoke was thicker now, and he choked on the acrid fumes.

"Madelaine!" he called out. "Madelaine, are you all right?"

Only the sound of flames consuming wood greeted his question.

His heart thundering, he raced down the hall, vowing to die himself rather than let the fire have her. A crackling, orange ball seemed to be chasing him, engulfing him. He could hear the ceiling beams overhead straining and groaning, trying to stay in place even as the intense heat ate them away.

He was almost there. Maybe he'd make it after all. He could see the open doorway. He had only to dash in, scoop her into his arms, and race back down the stairs.

"Madelaine, hang on! I'm coming, darling!"

Those had been his last words and their utterance his last memory as the groaning of the beams overhead gave way to a terrible roar. An instant after that, all was black, blazing hell.

It was only later, when he came to on the couch in Dr. Whitehead's living room, that he learned of the valiant fireman who had risked his life to drag Hugh out of the burning house after the beam crashed down on him. As for Madelaine, they all assured him, sadly, she was probably dead already when he made his futile attempt to save her. There was nothing he could have done.

Now, standing in the icy, blackened, litter-strewn street, Hugh Sinclair reviewed the past days as if he were reliving a nightmare, a hell-come-to-earth.

Of course Madelaine's death weighed heavily upon him. But it was not the only burden he carried. Anna Rose's whereabouts were still unknown. So his loss was doubled, with the uncertainty almost harder to bear than the painful reality of death.

Slowly, he walked up the front steps, marveling at the familiar feel of the worn stone beneath his boots. How often had he made this climb? But never before under such sad circumstances.

He stood at the top, looking out over the charred remains of his home. The ugly black skeleton seemed foreign and frightening to him. Still, until the debris could be cleared away, this hideous shrine would be the only headstone marking the final resting place of his wife and his unborn child.

He bowed his head for a moment, then bent to place a spray of holly and Christmas roses on the stair. Somewhere down the street, a group of carolers were strolling, singing joyous songs. The incongruity of the sound in such a place brought tears to his eyes.

He meant to leave then, to escape the pain. But something perverse in his nature forced him to linger. He wandered through the ruins, some still smoldering, and identified as best he could the rooms he had known so well. He kicked aside broken dishes in the pantry, located all that remained of his desk in the library, but he could find nothing that had been untouched by the inferno.

Shoulders sagging in despair, he turned to leave. Then, suddenly, his tear-blurred vision focused on an object at his feet. He stooped to pick it up. The book, amazingly, had not been burned. Somehow it had remained intact in the midst of the holocaust, like the fine old sycamore at the corner of Beaver and William streets that still stood without a scar upon it, although destruction lay to every side.

He opened the cover and read, "This Bible belongs to Anna Rose Mackintosh McShane. Given to her on her wedding day by her loving mother, Margaret Grant Mackintosh."

The words seemed to glow on the page, and once more he felt a stirring of hope. Perhaps the Bible was an omen. Maybe Anna Rose had somehow lived through the flaming terror of that night.

He had no idea where Anna Rose was now. Alive or dead . . . safe or injured. He'd made inquiries everywhere he went these past few days, even going to Flynn's empty rooms, but there was no word from her. Still, that was understandable. The city was in chaos and would be for some time yet. Many families continued to search for loved ones who remained unaccounted for. The few public buildings in the city that remained standing had become registry points. Survivors, separated from their loved ones, went to those places to sign their names on lists. He had read every list in the city. Anna Rose's name was not on any of them.

But still, Hugh had a feeling—perhaps it was only hope—that Anna Rose was safe somewhere. The John Street Theater had escaped the blaze, which had burned everything in its path from Wall Street at William, east to the river. All that remained of the old Dutch village, the town that had been called New Amsterdam, was gone. But perhaps Flynn had gotten her out of the burning city. They might have escaped across the river or to the north. He could only hope. After all that had happened—so tragically, so needlessly—prayers were beyond him.

He looked out over the ruined street. The loss of the major portion of the city and the entire financial district had brought destruction to most of the great fortunes of New York's wealthiest men, his own included. The insurance companies, faced with such incalculable losses, had declared bankruptcy. No claims would be honored.

So there it was! Hugh Sinclair was a man set adrift, the same as if he had been caught in a wild storm at sea. His ship, his *life*, had literally been burned to the waterline.

What did he have left? The clothes on his back, a small motherless daughter, a neglected parcel of land in Georgia, his ship's master's papers and, he realized suddenly, a vast determination to make a new life for himself, somewhere, somehow.

He would go back to the sea, let the wind, sun, and salt heal his wounds. With his pay from one more voyage, he could retire to The Highlands, the plantation in Georgia that his father had deserted so long ago. He would put all the pain of his past life behind him. With his little daughter Charity, he would start over anew.

Hugh turned once more toward the place where Madelaine slept and bid her a final, silent farewell. At the same time, he finally managed a prayer that Anna Rose was safe and that someday he would find her again.

Even as Hugh Sinclair was making his plans for the future, another hand was directing Anna Rose McShane's destiny. After what seemed an endless day of weak-timbered bridges and corduroy roads, the stagecoach finally stopped for the night at an inn outside Baltimore.

"At last!" the friendly Angus Campbell sighed. "I'm afraid these old bones wouldn't have stood much more of that bouncing about tonight. May I help you, Mrs. McShane? It's quite a step down."

Anna Rose, exhausted from their long days of travel and still numb with shock and grief—knowing that Hugh and Heather were dead yet refusing to allow herself to accept it—offered her fellow passenger a weak smile. "Thank you, Mr. Campbell. It seems my traveling companion has decoached without me."

Campbell gave Anna Rose a hearty chuckle as he offered his hand to help her down from the high coach. "Don't be too hard on him, ma'am. No doubt he's headed to the tavern for a sip of something fortifying to ease his aches and pains. A first rate idea! I can't blame your Mr. Flynn at all!"

Without thinking, Anna Rose said quickly, "He's not my Mr. Flynn!"

Angus Campbell's face flushed to a ruddy hue. "Oh, I beg your pardon, ma'am. I meant nothing out of order by my comment."

"It's I who should apologize, sir," Anna Rose was quick to add, feeling bad that she might have hurt the man's feelings. He had been so kind to her the whole trip, while Michael had remained sullen and bad-tempered all the way. It would certainly be a relief to be out of Flynn's company, if only for the night.

"Will you be taking supper downstairs with the others, Mrs. McShane?"

She felt empty; she'd eaten nothing all day. But the very thought of food sickened her. Too weary even to consider eating, she shook her head. "No, Mr. Campbell. I'm too tired. I only want my bed."

He led her to the desk where a hard-faced, skinny woman eyed them curiously and demanded, "Your daughter or your wife, mister?"

Angus coughed in embarrassment. "Neither, I'm afraid, madam! This is Mrs. McShane. She's traveling with—"

"I'm traveling alone," Anna Rose broke in.

The woman gave Angus a cold stare. "Don't matter to me none anyways. What you do elsewhere's your own business, but here I got my rules! No fornicatin' under my roof! She'll sleep with the women, same as any other female guest, married or no." Then she turned to Anna Rose. "Follow me! I'll show you up. And just in case you decide to come back down, there's no ladies allowed in the taproom."

The surly woman poked her head into a cold, crowded room already occupied by several other females and a few noisy children.

"The big room's all full up," she grumbled. "Have to give you a room to your own self."

Anna Rose breathed a sigh of relief until she saw the cramped cubicle that was to be hers. Still, it contained a bed. And she'd slept in far worse places. At any rate, she was oblivious to her hard mattress and tattered blanket as sleep claimed her the instant her head touched the lumpy pillow.

Downstairs, Michael Flynn, too, had refused the innkeeper's greasy dinner, but not in favor of sleep. He stood at the rough bar, pulling long and hard at the rum bottle. He was wide awake and primed for action.

The more he thought about Anna Rose and the more he drank, the more determined he became to lay his claim on her tonight. She wouldn't be with him much longer. His funds were running alarmingly low. His attempts at enlarging his stakes at the card tables of the inns along the route had proved disastrous. Now his purse had barely a jingle to it, and he still had many miles to cover before he reached Savannah. In fact, he already knew that there would be boat fare for only one by the time they arrived in Charleston. Anna Rose, with her sullen gaze and quiet mourning, had been a burden to him all the way. He was sick and tired of her, but not quite ready to ditch her yet—not until he got what he wanted from her.

So, he decided, *it's tonight or never!* And *never* was out of the question when it came to Flynn and females!

He watched closely until the sour-faced, sharp-toned woman left the desk, then he hurried up the stairs. As with any inn of the day, this place was strictly divided into male and female sections, even for married couples. They could neither eat nor sleep together. He knew that if he was caught going near the women's floor, he'd be tossed out and forced to sleep in the coach tonight. So he eased his way down the hall, opening one door after another until he found the room where Anna Rose was sleeping.

Michael Flynn had not spent all his years as an upstanding businessman. Tonight his experience as a professional thief came in handy as he tiptoed soundlessly into Anna Rose's room.

He lit the candle beside her bed and stood gazing down at her. She was still wearing the burgundy gown she'd had on the night of the fire, but it was soiled, rumpled, and ripped at one sleeve now. Still, she was a delicious-looking woman. Yes, he'd waited as long as he intended to.

Anna Rose's sleep had been troubled by terrifying dreams of Rory's death, Heather's birth, and flames—flames and smoke everywhere, burning everything and everyone in sight. When the smell of the lighted candle reached her, her eyes flickered open. She cried out, seeing in her first waking vision fire consuming Michael Flynn's face. When she tried to scream, Flynn sat down beside her quickly and covered her mouth with his hand.

"It's all right, Anna Rose. You were having a nightmare."

The sudden relief flooding through her made her weak. She fell back against the pillows, covering her eyes with the back of her hand.

"Oh, Michael, I certainly was! I'm glad you woke me." She sat up and stared at him. "It can't be time for the coach to leave already. It seems as if I just came to bed."

Smiling, using all his charm, Flynn reached out and caressed her tired, lined face. "No, darling. We have all night yet."

Before she could say another word, he leaned down and kissed her, first gently, but then with demanding intensity. Anna Rose tried to fight him off, but he had her firmly pinned beneath him.

When he finally raised himself from her, he was still smiling. "You do have a way of making things interesting, you little minx! I might have known you were the type to lead a man on and then try to withhold the ultimate pleasure. But it won't work with me, Anna Rose. I've been thinking about this for a long, long time. And you can't fool me. I know you want a man. You want me."

She pulled away from him, more frightened than she had been by her nightmares. Although she was huddled in the corner against the rough board walls, she was still within his reach.

"I don't know what you're talking about, Flynn."

He laughed. "Of course you do! Why do you think I brought you along on this trip?"

Anna Rose thought for a moment, struggling for an answer. She'd given little thought to why she was with Flynn or where they were headed. Most of the trip she'd been dazed and confused, her only thoughts centered on the two people she had loved and lost. Finally, she ventured, "To save my life . . . to marry me?"

Now he really laughed. "Women, oh, women! No, Anna Rose, you've missed your chance of becoming Mrs. Flynn. I no longer have any intentions of marrying you. As for saving your life, that was merely coincidental to my plans for you."

"What plans?" He reached toward her and suddenly she knew exactly what he had in mind. "No, stay away!" she cried.

Once again, he clamped one hand over her mouth to keep her quiet while struggling at the fastenings of her gown with the other. She fought desperately until he released her without warning.

"Don't scream, Anna Rose!" His voice was hard now, threatening. "I have something here that I think will change your mind and make you far more cooperative."

Reaching into his breast pocket, he pulled out a sheaf of papers and waved them before her face.

"You see, you have no rights at all in this matter. I *own* you for the next seven years. But, if you please me tonight, I'll make it pleasant for you in the years to come. If not, I swear to you, I'll go down below and sell these papers. Sell *you*, Anna Rose, to the highest bidder!"

Anna Rose gasped as the realization sank in.

Seeing the shocked expression on her face, Flynn smiled and nodded. "That's right, Anna Rose. Before he died in the fire, Hugh Sinclair *sold* you to me."

"I don't believe you!" she said with a sob that came from the deepest part of her heart."

"See for yourself." He spread the redemption papers before her. Hugh had never bothered to write his signature in the owner's space. Now the name "Michael Flynn" occupied that spot.

A million thoughts spun round in Anna Rose's head as she stared at the papers through tear-blurred eyes. Suddenly, her whole life and all the miserable things that had happened to her began to make some sort of cockeyed sense. She'd heard of an old man back home once who went through his whole life with a dark cloud over his head, meeting only ill luck at every turn. Everyone said he was cursed while still in his mother's womb. Maybe she was like him, doomed from the day she was born to have nothing go right until she reached the cradle of the tomb. Well, if that was it, so be it! But she was damned if she would submit to Michael Flynn after he had courted her, tricked her into thinking he loved her, and was now demanding that she accept him, laughing at her all the while. Nor would she be sold to some stranger.

Flynn's hand was on her breast. But now she saw that the papers were lying right there before her for the taking. She could grab them and tear them to shreds while Flynn was preoccupied with fondling her. But what good would that do? He would only leave her here stranded, without a penny to her name, no friends, no family, and no place to go. Her decision came quickly. If it was her lot to be some man's servant, she could at least choose her own master. One who was kind and decent and honest!

She snatched up the redemption papers, shoved Flynn to the floor, and dashed into the hallway and down the stairs. Flynn came after her, shouting her name and cursing, but she had spied her new master already.

Angus Campbell sat in the taproom with his boots propped up before the fire, enjoying a tankard of ale with some of the other male customers before going off to bed.

As Anna Rose ran through the main room, the sour-tempered woman at the front desk grabbed her arm. "Here, now! You can't go in the taproom! I told you already—"

But Anna Rose refused to be stopped. She shoved the woman aside and all but flung herself at the surprised Angus Campbell.

Her words came tumbling out. "Please, sir, I beg you to buy me from Michael Flynn. I thought he meant to marry me—I had no idea he had my redemption papers. Now he says if I don't allow him to bed me, he'll sell me to the highest bidder and that could be anyone here. Please, you're my only hope!"

Campbell jumped to his feet. "Mrs. McShane, whatever's happened? Slowly, dear lady. I can't make heads nor tails of what you're saying."

"Never mind what she's saying!" Flynn's angry voice boomed from across the room. "She's out of her head, that one. An imbecile, hadn't you guessed already? All that moaning and babbling in the coach. The woman suffers from delusions. I never mentioned marriage. She's a servant! I own her—body and soul!"

Anna Rose, trembling with fright, looked up at Angus Campbell with a wide, pleading gaze. His shaggy gray brows were twitching and his eyes were narrowed in rage. When he spoke, his quiet voice was far more threatening than Flynn's shouts. "I've yet to meet the man who owns another's soul. As for any other claim you might have on this young woman, that is about to come to an end. Let me see those papers, my dear," he said gently.

Anna Rose handed over the documents, being careful to stay as close as possible to Angus Campbell's protective form. Flynn stood a short distance away, scowling at the two of them.

While Angus read over the papers, Flynn taunted, "He doesn't need you, Anna Rose. The man's a slave owner. What would he do with another servant? And a poor one at that!"

Campbell shot Flynn a fierce glance. "Aye," he said. "I have over three hundred *involuntary servants* in my care. And my house woman, Dahlia, is as good as they come, like family really. But there's always room at Rosedhu Plantation for a woman who'll give me an honest day's work."

"Or an honest night's!" Flynn muttered under his breath.

The Scottish gentleman with his shock of white hair, yet still a youthful twinkle in his blue-gray eyes, laughed heartily. "At my age? What decent woman would have me? Still, it's a tempting thought, Mr. Flynn. But I'd take no woman against her will. I'm not a braggart, mind you, but I've never had to force any woman as it seems you must."

Anna Rose almost smiled as she heard the other men in the room chuckle at Campbell's remark and saw the color drain from Flynn's face.

Anna Rose watched Flynn's expression change suddenly. He was smiling again, but the expression failed to reach his dark eyes. He was up to something, but what now?

Campbell, too, noted the change, but pretended to be still

engrossed in the papers. Flynn began talking calmly, but Campbell was not listening to a word of it. Instead, he was watching Flynn's facial expressions, trying to figure out what this rascally Irishman had up his sleeve. If they had been facing each other across a gaming table, Campbell would have bet his last acre of rice swamp that the man had an ace tucked up the frayed ruffle of his cuff.

Flynn finally blurted out, "All right, Campbell. The truth is that I've run out of funds and I have to sell her papers. You seem like a kind, generous fellow. I'll allow you to make an offer."

"Done!" Angus Campbell agreed, pulling out his purse. "The price here is fifty dollars. That seems fair enough."

But as he started counting out the bills, Flynn stopped him. "Plus her expenses," he said. "That will come to five hundred even."

Angus Campbell was a man of peace. But Flynn's words both angered and disgusted him. He felt like smashing a fist into his grinning face. He'd bargained over slaves often enough at the markets in Charleston, Savannah, and New Orleans. But this was a Scotswoman Flynn was selling. And his haggling inflamed the Highlander's temper. He grabbed Flynn's collar in one big, hard fist and drew the man up to eye level.

"I'll give ye the fifty and not a copper more! And you, my *fine gentleman* will use part of it to buy a nag as sorry as yourself and be on your way this very night! I won't put a name to what I think of a man who would sell a woman who's trusted him with her very life."

"Well, I suppose fifty will do," Flynn answered nervously. "After all, she's costing me more every day that I have to pay her way."

Campbell was upon Flynn now, a towering pillar of rage. He shook the other man until he begged for release, then tossed him against the far wall, scattering tables, chairs, tankards, and astonished customers. Campbell threw the bills in Flynn's face, and he scrambled about on his hands and knees collecting them.

"Damn ye! Get your horse and be gone now!" Campbell yelled. "And if I ever lay eyes on ye again, it'll be the death of ye!"

Angus Campbell, feeling younger than he had in years, gave Michael Flynn the toe of his boot to speed him on his way. The tavern crowd cheered and Campbell smiled all around, giving an especially fond look to Anna Rose. She returned his warm gaze, and suddenly Angus felt years younger than his fifty-nine summers. He hadn't experienced any such pounding of heart and

233

coursing of blood since before his wife Clara died fifteen years back.

He felt almost as if he had just bought himself a bride!

When everything calmed down in the taproom and Flynn was long gone, Angus turned to Anna Rose. He was holding her redemption papers up before him for her, for everyone, to see. Slowly, he tore them in two, then again and again until there was nothing left but tiny shreds, which he tossed into the fire.

"Mr. Campbell!" Anna Rose cried, surprise mingling with gratitude in her tone.

"You're no one's servant any longer, my dear. You're a free woman!"

Anna Rose felt as if Angus Campbell had miraculously relieved her of some heavy burden. She managed a whispered "Thank you!" But now what would she do, where would she go?

Angus came to her and took her hand in his. He smiled and his blue-gray eyes danced merrily. "Will you still come to my plantation with me, Anna Rose McShane? You're not the sort of woman to accept charity, I can tell by the looks of you. So you'll be the housekeeper at Rosedhu. It's a good life there in the rice country. You'll find Darien a pleasing place to live."

Anna Rose stared at the man, struggling to find her voice. "You own a rice plantation, in Darien?"

"That I do, and a handsome place it is! But it'll be all the handsomer with you gracing the premises, young lady. What do you say?"

What could she say, but yes! She'd make a good housekeeper, and it was a position she would enjoy. Angus Campbell was a kind man. In time, she was sure they would become good friends. And, too, for better or for worse, she would finally reach her destination in America. Granted she had lost so much during her long journey—Rory, Heather, Hugh. She would be a long time mourning them, to her grave and beyond. But now, thanks to Angus Campbell, she had some hope for the future. She would make a good, new life for herself in Georgia. She would work hard and save her money. And soon, she prayed, she would have her family with her again. Maybe the dark cloud hovering over her had rained its last!

She lifted her eyes and stared at him steadily. "Very well, Mr. Campbell. I'll go with you to your plantation—the place you call Black Rose."

He raised her hand to his lips, smiled warmly into her misty-green eyes, and kissed her fingertips. "I promise you I'll never make you sorry for that decision, Anna Rose McShane."

21

On the evening Anna Rose and Angus Campbell arrived in Darien, the early winter twilight was already painting the South Georgia forests of oak, pine, and cypress in shades of indigo and dusky purple. The winter-dry marsh grass swayed in the wind, whispering its secrets to the river. And the water answered back with a soothing lap of its waves. Anna Rose took it all in breathlessly as their small steamer docked, after a long day's sail from Savannah.

The very name "Darien" was magic to her. She had been through hell and back since leaving her home in Scotland. But this sleepy, tree-sheltered town at the broad river's edge was like a balm, soothing all the hurt away, offering new hope for a brighter, happier future.

Tears came to her eyes as she told Angus, "My father always dreamed of coming here. He could never remember the name, though. He called it New Inverness."

She'd been wondering about her family a good deal on this trip. Before the stage left Baltimore, she had written to them, telling about the terrible fire in New York and her long journey southward. She'd also hinted that she might soon find a way to bring them to America. With Angus Campbell's help, she could realize that dream at last. He had promised his assistance as soon as she told him about the misfortune that had befallen her father and her family's hopes of joining her someday.

She had told Angus much about herself during their travels. He knew of her marriage and the heroic circumstances of Rory's death, her early hardships in New York and the better times as well. Still unable to deal with her most recent losses, she had explained only briefly that the fire had taken the lives of her baby daughter and the man she loved. Angus hadn't pressed her for details, but instead he'd tried to divert her sorrow by telling her about his plantation.

Already, Anna Rose had learned that Angus was a businessman, first and last, who shared none of Michael Flynn's dilettante ways. That was reassuring!

During the trip south, Angus had spent long hours explaining to her the details of his rice plantation's operation. She understood now how the coastal rivers, such as the broad Altamaha on which Rosedhu was situated, were essential to the rice cultivation of the area. These waterways transported fertile topsoil from the upper regions of the state to the floodplain, thus providing a perpetual system of fertilization for the coastal plantations. The same rivers, affected by the tidal flow of the Atlantic, furnished an easy and efficient means of both drainage and irrigation.

The profitable operation of Rosedhu, Angus had told her, required the labor of several hundred slaves to work its eight thousand acres of land, most of which was rice swamps divided into twenty-acre fields.

Angus further explained that a local planter had journeyed to Holland to study their dike system. When he returned, he had shared his findings with the other planters of the region, who then adapted the principle to their own use. Slaves had been set to work immediately building dikes all along the edge of the river. The cultivation of rice required the flooding of the fields with fresh water at various stages of the crop's development. This was easily accomplished by the opening of the trunks or floodgates in the dikes at high tide. The drainage procedure was accomplished in a like manner on the ebb flow.

"The rice season," Angus said, "runs from spring to autumn. I alone decide when to plant, after careful consideration when the moon is full, but always before the high spring tides."

Anna Rose had followed his every word, fascinated by the entire process. "I can hardly wait to see the first harvest!" she exclaimed, thinking back to the excitement of harvest time on the Mackintosh croft.

"That'll be in late August or early September," Angus answered. "But I'm afraid you won't get to see the process."

"Why not?" her disappointment had been plain in her voice.

"We'll be at The Ridge, a few miles from Darien, during that time, at my summer house. The plantation's not a healthy place during the hot months. All the planters and their families move in early spring and stay until after the first black frost." When she frowned at the unfamiliar term, Angus had explained, "Three white frosts bring the black frost, when all the potato vines shrivel and the leaves turn sooty. We know then that all the dangers from the swamp miasmas have passed. You'll like the cottage at The Ridge, I'm sure. It's not as large as Rosedhu, but very comfortable. Life there is decidedly more casual."

"And your slaves?" she'd inquired.

"It's different with them. They're immune to the dangerous illnesses we suffer. Maybe it's the dark pigment of their skin or the fact that their race originated in Africa's hot climate. At any rate, they can safely stay on the island to work the crops. But we must go."

By the time they sailed into Darien, Anna Rose felt she knew all there was to know about a rice plantation. But she was in for a few surprises.

Angus had sent word ahead by messenger from Savannah, where they'd stayed the night before, that one of his plantation boats should meet them in Darien. They'd been on the dock only long enough to have their baggage unloaded when a great cheer rose from up the river.

"That'll be my man Pride and the crew," Angus told her.

Anna Rose strained her eyes against the gathering darkness to see the brightly painted boat pulling alongside the quay. Pride, she guessed correctly, was the figure standing in the stern at the tiller.

Anna Rose would soon learn that Pride was descended from Ashanti warriors, and was as tough as the hollowed-out cypress-trunk canoe he commanded. He towered a full head over Angus Campbell. At first glance, the slave seemed as black and mysterious as the southern night to Anna Rose. She drew back closer to Angus as the huge man approached them.

Pride offered his white master a bow and, much to Anna Rose's surprise, said in a cultured tone, "Welcome back, Major Campbell. I trust you had a comfortable and profitable trip."

"Thank you, Pride, but I'm afraid it was neither. It will be good to get home. This is Mrs. McShane. She'll be the new housekeeper at Rosedhu, assisted by Dahlia, of course."

Anna Rose felt discomfitted by the introduction, not sure what she was supposed to do. Surely she shouldn't curtsy or offer her hand. Finally, she simply nodded and said, "I'm pleased to meet you, Pride."

In turn, the tall slave bowed formally. But he offered no smile of welcome with his greeting.

"How have things been since I left, Pride? Any further trouble with the new overseer?"

In silent answer, Pride darted a meaningful glance toward the eight oarsmen in the boat, then looked back at their master.

"You're right, of course. This is not the place to discuss it," Angus replied. "We'll talk when we get home."

Although puzzled by all this, Anna Rose could hardly ask questions. Even if she'd felt it her place to pry, she was too weary to press Angus for answers. It was enough to sit in the boat and feel the gentle sway of the water while the oarsmen chanted a wild, sweet song to the rhythm of each stroke they made with their paddles. She was further lulled by the sounds of night birds in the thick forests near the riverbank. The air had a brisk chill to it, but none of the harsh edge of winter she had experienced in New York or in Scotland.

After a quarter hour or so, the forest disappeared. The moon had risen, and Anna Rose could see no land in any direction, only silvery stubble breaking through the calm surface of the water on both sides of the boat.

"This is my property—the main canal through the rice fields," Angus explained. "Watch just ahead. You'll see Rosedhu soon beyond the trees."

What trees? Anna Rose wondered. She could see nothing beyond the watery expanse. Then they rounded a bend in the narrow channel and the great sentinels came into view. She had no name yet to call the magnolias, but she marveled at their wide-spreading branches and their broad, flat leaves, frosted by the moon's glow. And, as Angus had promised, just beyond these two giant guardians she spied the lighted windows of the plantation house. The very size of the place awed her.

"All this is yours?" she asked a bit breathlessly.

Angus nodded silently, his eyes gleaming with pleasure at her reaction.

Pride blew a shrill signal on a conch shell to announce their arrival at the plantation landing. The lonely sound reminded Anna Rose of her father's tales of ancient Highland clansmen summoned to the fray in the same manner. But no battle lines were drawn up when they reached the dock, only a dancing lot of servants, called out into the night by the blast to welcome the master home.

Anna Rose shrank back from the mob of sooty faces peering at her, from the dark hands reaching out to touch her. Their strange guttural words mingled and melded into a confusing, unintelligible chatter.

"It's all right, Anna Rose," Angus whispered, placing a reassuring hand on her arm. "They won't harm you. You're the first white woman some of them have ever seen. As I told you, my wife died many years ago. I haven't entertained much since that time. And few of them ever leave the isolated confines of Rosedhu. They are only trying to show you their respect. Smile at them and say hello. Then they'll be satisfied."

She did as Angus instructed, speaking softly to his people and smiling all the while. They reacted with ecstatic pleasure, gratitude, and applause.

"Listen to me, all of you!" The master's voice boomed through the night. "This is Mrs. McShane. She will live at Rosedhu from now on and you will take orders from her as you would from me. If you please Mrs. McShane, you will also please me."

A chorus of agreement followed his speech. Then, taking Anna Rose's arm, Angus led her up the shell-lined path, between the magnolias, to the front piazza of the mansion. Their welcoming committee dispersed, leaving only Pride to accompany them.

At the front steps, the man turned away, starting around to the back entrance. Campbell stopped him. "Come in the front. We have business to discuss, and it's late already."

Pride glanced right and left, checking to make sure none of the others saw him, then nodded and followed them in the front door.

Anna Rose took all this in, silently wondering what was going on. The relationship between the master of Rosedhu and this particular slave seemed different from the others. Also, while she had hardly been able to understand the words of the other slaves, Pride spoke flawless, cultured English. She decided not to ask any questions just yet. Maybe she could listen and learn.

A tall, strongly built woman, who shared Pride's bold Ashanti features, waited just inside to greet them. It was impossible to guess her age, but the silver in her hair told Anna Rose that she was older than she looked. "Welcome home, Major Campbell," she said softly.

"Dahlia, this is Mrs. McShane, my new housekeeper. You will assist her in any way you can, I'm sure."

Dahlia inclined her head. "Yessir, Major Campbell. We're pleased to have you here, ma'am." Although Dahlia did not smile as she spoke, Anna Rose felt no hostility from the woman, only a cool reserve.

"Is Mr. LaFarge about?" Angus asked the woman.

For the first time, Anna Rose noted a change in Dahlia's expression, but she couldn't detect its meaning. "He in the office, Major," she answered.

"Have him come to my study immediately, please."

Anna Rose saw a flicker of something between anger and fear cross Dahlia's face. But when she answered, her voice was calm. "Yes, Major Campbell."

Then Angus turned to Anna Rose. "I know you're tired. If you would like, I'll have Dahlia show you to your room immediately and carry your supper up. But this shouldn't take long. And I've grown rather fond of your company at mealtimes."

"May I come with you, Angus?"

His face clouded with indecision. "It might not be pleasant. I think I'll probably have to fire my overseer. But I suppose there's no need trying to shelter you from the darker side of plantation life. You might as well start learning right now."

She nodded her understanding, then followed him down the hall to his study. Pride was there already, holding the door wide for them. No one spoke until he closed it again.

"All right, Pride, what do you have to tell me before he gets here?"

"It was as we both suspected, Major. The minute you left, he took to the whip. Three of our best workers ran—Plato, Floyd, and Big Jim."

"And?" Campbell prompted, a deep frown on his face.

"We found Floyd dead in the swamp. A rattler got him. The hounds treed Plato. LaFarge whipped him senseless. He's in isolation now with old Sheba looking after him."

"Will he make it?"

"I doubt he wants to," Pride answered with a shrug. "Once LaFarge gets it in for you, it's only a matter of time."

"What about Big Jim?"

"Nobody's seen him. He could be dead in the swamp or drowned in the river. He took a boat. Maybe he got away. LaFarge posted notices in Darien, Savannah, and Saint Simons. If he's still in the area, he'll be found."

"Damn!" Campbell cursed. "Big Jim was the best man on the place. And he never caused any trouble. What happened?"

"Why don't you ask me what happened, Major Campbell, instead of this lying nigger?" The drawled question was spoken in a tone of such cold contempt that Anna Rose felt the words chill her through.

She had been listening tensely to the conversation between Angus and Pride with fear and distaste. Now she turned quickly to see the overseer, LaFarge, for the first time. The man was tall, burly, and as dark as some of the lighter slaves. Long black hair fell straight to his open collar, and small, colorless eyes squinted out from his whiskey-bloated face. The man so reeked of liquor that Anna Rose turned slightly away.

"I hear there's been some trouble while I was up North," Angus said.

"No more than usual." LaFarge's chilly eyes strayed to Anna Rose and lingered. "I took care of it. As for Big Jim, he'll come back, dead or alive. Count on it!"

"A hell of a lot of good he is to me dead!" Angus roared. "What happened?"

"All three of those lazy bastards refused to work once you left. None of them finished their tasks for three days running. Testing me, that's what they was up to. Well, they found out who they was dealing with all right! Yancy LaFarge don't take sass from no nigger!"

Anna Rose knew of the task system practiced at Rosedhu. Angus had explained it to her on the trip. Each slave was assigned a certain amount of labor to be accomplished during the working hours, sunup to sundown. Once that work was completed, the hours left over were free time. The more industrious workers spent their leisure tending their own gardens or making wooden pails, tables, or boats to sell in Darien. Those who did not finish their tasks were reported to the overseer by their black "driver," and he in turn reported them to the plantation owner, who allotted whatever punishment he deemed necessary to encourage the erring slave to work harder. Angus had told her also that only the master could dole out lashes and that he personally never resorted to the whip.

This, Anna Rose surmised, was the cause of the present conflict between Angus and his overseer. She could tell by the color rising in Angus's usually placid face that this man LaFarge had pushed his employer's patience to the limit by far overstepping his authority.

"Damn you, LaFarge!" Angus raged. "I left strict orders against the whip! You knew the rules here before you hired on. How many lashes did you give them to make them run?"

The overseer's eyes narrowed and a nerve jumped at his temple as he answered, "I don't know what your double-headed nigger here's been telling you, Major." His eyes cut to Pride and Anna Rose read a veiled threat. "I had Driver give Floyd and Plato thirty each. Less than the black devils deserved by a long shot. But I didn't lay a finger to Big Jim a-tall."

Pride made an angry sound—something between a cough and a snarl.

"Then why did Jim run?" Angus demanded.

"Nothing I done," LaFarge snapped. "He did it his own self. I know that nigger's alligator hide don't feel a thing. So instead of having him whipped, I made him deal out his woman's punishment."

Angus was out of his chair, starting toward Yancy LaFarge with a murderous gleam in his eyes. "You had Fancy beaten? My God, man, and her with child?"

Anna Rose felt sick. She wanted to flee the room. But to do so she'd have to pass LaFarge. She had no desire to be any closer to this detestable man. She breathed deeply, trying to calm herself, trying not to hear any more of what was being said. She had thought this place was heaven. Now, suddenly, the veil had been yanked rudely from her eyes.

"She wasn't pregnant no more," LaFarge stated angrily. "Dropped her sucker three days after you left, but she was still lazing around the sick house, claiming she was too weak to work. I just had her man touch her up a bit to put some life back in her."

"Big Jim wouldn't have whipped his own wife. He'd have died first." Anna Rose had never heard such a cold tone from Angus Campbell. He glared at LaFarge and demanded, "How'd you make him do it?"

Yancy LaFarge, still lounging against the doorframe, just smiled. But his expression sent a shiver along Anna Rose's spine.

It was Pride who answered Angus's question. "He took the baby—Big Jim's firstborn son—and threatened to bash that poor squalling child's brains out against the barn wall if Big Jim didn't whip Fancy. She begged Jim to do it to save little Jimbo."

Except for a stifled cry from Anna Rose, the room went suddenly, deadly silent. No one moved. It was as if the horrible reality of what had happened had frozen them all into cold marble. Anna Rose felt her stomach churning. She had to force herself to breathe. Thoughts of her own child, threatened in such a hideous fashion, flashed through her mind, making her feel weak and ill.

Angus Campbell broke the harsh silence, his voice hard and deadly calm. "LaFarge, I want you off my property before sunup."

The overseer offered his employer a slow, lazy grin. "Oh, I don't think so, Major. You see, you and me, we got us a contract."

Angus jerked open a desk drawer and pulled out two items: a pistol and LaFarge's contract. He held the gun on the overseer and motioned to Anna Rose. She approached Angus uncertainly.

"Be so good as to tear this worthless paper to shreds for me, won't you?" Angus said the words in a cordial, but icy tone.

When the paper was in a dozen scraps, Anna Rose let the pieces fall from her trembling hands.

"There!" Angus said, still holding the pistol with deadly aim. "So much for our contract, LaFarge. Now, before I have more time to think all this through and get really angry, I think you would be well-advised to remove yourself from my home and my island. In fact, should I ever again see your face anywhere, I can't promise you that I won't shoot you on the spot."

LaFarge stood his ground for only a moment more, long enough to give each of the other three people in the room a hard, evil stare. Then he turned and stormed out, slamming the door after him.

Anna Rose sagged down into a chair, exhausted from the experience. Angus went to her immediately.

"Are you all right, Anna Rose? I'm so sorry! I had no idea things would get this ugly. I would never have let you be a witness to such a scene."

Anna Rose got up and squared her shoulders. Yes, it had been ugly, she thought, but so had a lot of other things in her life. It was time she faced the fact that this place was no better or worse than the rest of the world. There would always be a stinging thistle hiding in the sweetest meadow.

"I'm fine, Angus," she replied, even managing a weak smile for him. "But I certainly am glad you got rid of that man and I hope I never see his face again either."

"Don't worry, my dear. He's gone for good."

As they left the room, Anna Rose noticed that Pride remained, a worried frown on his dark face.

Angus and Anna Rose shared a late supper in strained silence. Although she had been famished when they had arrived, she found she could eat little. The scenes conjured up by the discussion before dinner still constricted her throat and made her stomach churn with anguish. She was trying to fight the discomfort, but the whole episode was still too vivid in her mind.

Finally, when Dahlia brought coffee, Angus cleared his throat and spoke. "Again let me say how sorry I am, Anna Rose. I had no idea how bad things were. I should have spoken with Pride first."

"Is it always so unpleasant?" she managed.

"No," he answered firmly. "But it's an unnatural and unholy state: slavery. There are those on both sides who take unfair advantage. Yancy LaFarge, unfortunately, is one of them."

"You'll have to find a new man now?"

"Yes, but it may take a while. And there's no guarantee that the next overseer will be any better than LaFarge. Most of them are drifters and misfits." He shook his head as if he still had trouble grasping what had happened. "I really thought LaFarge would work out. My son, Weyman, suggested him. Seems they met in Louisiana sometime back. LaFarge comes of a good New Orleans family. He's had some schooling. But the man's got a mean streak as wide as the Altamaha."

Anna Rose knew her question sounded impertinent, but she had to ask. "Why do you own slaves, Angus, if you don't approve of the system and it presents such constant problems?"

Campbell stared at Anna Rose for a moment, trying to form a suitable answer. Finally, he shook his head and answered, "I'm afraid I have little choice. I was born to this land and into this way of life. My great-grandfather was among the clansmen forced to forfeit their lands and hide out in the wildest parts of Scotland following the Jacobite rebellion in 1715. Twenty years later, he sailed out of Inverness on Captain Dunbar's *Prince of Wales* for the New World, with the promise of freedom and a grant of five hundred acres when he reached this place. That original land grant is part of Rosedhu today. More acreage was added when my grandfather helped General Oglethorpe chase the Spaniards off at Bloody Marsh in 1742. I inherited everything here when my father died. I only hope that my own son will be up to the task when my time of rest comes."

Anna Rose understood about inherited land and the responsibility that came with it. Her own father, with his inherited croft, had been faced with a similiar situation, albeit on a much smaller scale. But there the similarity ended. The Mackintosh clan had worked their farm from generation to generation. When extra hands were needed, they were hired, not purchased as livestock.

"As for slavery," Angus continued patiently, "the Scotsmen hereabouts tried to avoid the institution. For many years, slaves were not allowed in Georgia. Back in 1739, the citizens of Savannah petitioned General Oglethorpe to change the law, but the farmers of New Inverness and the good Germans at Ebenezer township refused to sign it, recognizing the evils of the institution. The battle, for or against, was hard fought for many years. But in 1749, greed won out over good sense. The law was changed to allow Georgia planters the same *advantage* of slavery as their Carolina neighbors. The sanction of the law and the natural craving for wealth finally induced the local planters—my grandfather among them—to accept the system. Huge fortunes were invested in slaves to create the rice plantations. Now, even greater fortunes would collapse without slave labor. We are caught in a web of evil of our own spinning, I'm afraid. If I were to sell my people, families would be broken up, something I have never done. Were I to free them, I would be ruined. The unpaid laborer is the very backbone of the rice economy. And the land I own, except for a few hundred acres of timber, is fit for no other crops. As it is, I run on credit the year round. And, if a hurricane or a flood comes and I lose a harvest, I plunge into debt for a time. The economy is as fragile as the rice swamps themselves."

Angus shook his head with weary resignation as he finished.

"I still can't get over LaFarge," Anna Rose stated. "I knew the moment I saw him that the man was a devil!"

Angus laughed softly and nodded. "You are a better judge of human nature than I am, my dear, and I hired the man. But do I take from your statement that you don't hate me for what's happened tonight?"

"Hate you?" Anna Rose was shocked. "You are obviously trying to make the best of a horrible situation where your people are concerned. And I will do all I can to help. Starting tomorrow. As for tonight . . ." She put a hand to her mouth to stifle a yawn.

"Indeed!" Angus nodded. "It's well past bedtime. I'll have Dahlia show you to your room."

Dahlia led Anna Rose up the stairs to the second floor. Rosedhu had wide halls with floors of sand-scrubbed heart pine. Delicately tinted wallpaper brightened most of the rooms. And windows at each end of the upstairs hall, from floor to high ceiling, could be opened to catch the breeze in hot weather. But tonight those windows were shuttered and fires glowed in the bedroom grates to ward off the chill. The master bedroom was at the front of the house. Dahlia led Anna Rose to a smaller guest room at the back. Outside in the hallway, a permanent ladder led up into the attic.

"Why are the stairs to the attic down, Dahlia?" Anna Rose asked, hoping to break the uncomfortable silence between them.

"Rice families is most always on the move, ma'am. It's easier to have the attic stairs down and in place so we can get to things in a hurry."

"Do you go to The Ridge with Major Campbell in the summer?"

"Yes, ma'am. All the house servants go."

"Pride, too?" Anna Rose had yet to figure out exactly what position he held on Rosedhu's staff.

"My boy goes where the Major goes," Dahlia answered with the first smile she had exhibited. "The Major, he say, 'That Pride's my right hand!' "

"You mean Pride is your son? Why, I should have guessed! There's a strong family resemblance."

"Pride's my baby and the only double-headed man on the whole plantation."

" 'Double-headed'? I don't understand, Dahlia." She had heard the same odd term from LaFarge, but then it had seemed an insult from his smirking lips.

Dahlia moved closer to Anna Rose and whispered her next words. "He can read and write and cipher. Major Campbell taught him even though he could get in a heap of trouble for doing it. But the Major say to me, 'This boy is smart! And a brain wasted is a sin against the Almighty.' He took to teaching my Pride real quiet like. Only problem is he got to be real careful around other folks, especially that Mr. LaFarge. He don't hold with smart niggers."

Now a few things were coming clear in Anna Rose's mind. Angus's treatment of and close association with Pride was unique. It was understandable that the white overseer would feel hostile toward the man. And Yancy LaFarge obviously knew Pride's secret. She only hoped the disgruntled overseer wouldn't make trouble now that Angus had dismissed him. Already she felt like a part of Rosedhu and one of its people—proud of their accomplishments, worried about their problems.

"This is your room, Miz McShane," Dahlia said. "Major Campbell picked it for you. It was young Master Campbell's room before he took off. Mr. Weyman, he up and left home a few years back. He and his daddy wasn't seeing eye to eye on most things. So he left."

"Where is he now? Does he ever come to visit?"

"Oh, now and again he turns up, usually wanting money from his daddy. It's just beyond me how such a good man could raise up such a worthless pup as that boy!" Suddenly, Dahlia drew back, a look of nervousness on her face. " 'Scuse me, ma'am. I'm speaking out of turn. That's my main sin, I reckon, a big mouth. But I wet-nursed that boy. And was he mine, I'd skin the hide off him now and again just to set him right. But his mama, God rest her, was always one to spare the rod. A kind, sweet lady, Miz Clara was. I loved her like she was my own ma. It grieves my heart to think how her own son took advantage of her. But that's all over now."

Dahlia hurried into the bedroom, poked up the fire, and turned down the bed. Someone else had already unpacked Anna Rose's steamer trunk, putting away all the new clothes Angus had insisted upon purchasing for her while they were in Savannah.

"There's hot water in the tub in the bath closet, ma'am. Can I get you anything else?"

"No, thank you, Dahlia. Everything is perfect. What time does Major Campbell rise for breakfast?"

"Oh, ma'am, he's up 'fore the sun. The conch blows about four, but the Major's already awake by then."

"Would you call me, please, so that I can breakfast with him?" Dahlia frowned slightly at the thought of a lady rising so early.

"Major Campbell should not have to take his meals alone now that I'm here," Anna Rose insisted. "And I want to get an early start learning my new job."

Dahlia smiled. "You're a fine lady, Miz McShane. The Major, he's been needing somebody like you on the place. He's been powerful lonesome these past years. Maybe his luck done changed. Lord, I hope so. I'll wake you, ma'am, I will."

Anna Rose slept that night, but not deeply. Her mind was too filled with the new sights, sounds, and faces of Rosedhu. Mixed and mingled with those were snatches of other times and places. Hugh, Heather, her parents, Rory, they all put in unsettling appearances during the night. Even Yancy LaFarge was there.

Still, though some of her dreams were troubled, she felt as if she had finally come home, to stay.

22

An answer to the letter Anna Rose had mailed to her family from Baltimore eight months earlier finally arrived from a surprising source: her sister Iris. It was a week after the rice fields were flooded for the harvest that Pride came from the mail boat in Darien with Iris Mackintosh Kilgore's letter.

Over a year had passed since she'd last heard from home. Whatever letters her family might have sent to Hugh Sinclair's Wall Street address had not arrived; she had left no forwarding address that horrible night.

Standing in the cozy parlor of Angus Campbell's summer cottage, Anna Rose's hands trembled as she worked at the wax seal. Finally, the paper fell open and she read:

Inverness, Scotland
May 17, 1836

My dear Sister,
  You will no doubt be surprised to hear from me after the ill blood that passed between us shortly before your departure. But I wish you to know that I harbor no

247

lingering malice toward you for the wrong you did me in marrying Rory McShane. I must admit that I did hate you for some time. For you to go as you did—even if it was Mother's idea—and leave the full responsibility of the family on my shoulders was an act of selfishness on your part. I never could have neglected our family so!

Anna Rose frowned at the paper and reread the beginning of the letter. For someone who held no malice, Iris had a strange way of showing it, trying to inflict guilt from every possible source. And hadn't Rory and then her mother told her that Iris hoped to come to America as soon as possible? Certainly, her staying on was not by choice. What had kept her at home all this time? Anna Rose had difficulty believing that Iris remained out of some deep sense of family obligation.

She read on:

You know, of course, that I was married. I have since had a child, a sickly, worrisome infant since birth. But somehow my son and my marriage seem unconnected since the lad never saw his father, indeed, the man died before I ever knew him well. Please, no tears on my account! It was a mistake from start to finish. As for poor Jaimie, he was a nice enough man, I suppose, but not the type of husband I will choose when next I marry. I fancy I should like someone a bit older and more settled like your Angus Campbell, for instance. Your report of the man absolutely glowed with promise of another wedding in your future!

Anna Rose stared at the words, aghast. The thought of marrying Angus had never entered her mind. And she certainly hadn't meant to write anything to her family that would give them such an impression. As for Iris's widowhood, that came as a terrible shock. But even more shocking was her sister's curt dismissal of the whole tragic matter. She hadn't bothered even to divulge when, where, or how the poor man had died. The one bright note in the paragraph was news of Iris's son, but she'd failed to mention his name or even the date of his birth.

I am presently considering a proposal myself. The man is not young, but he is wealthy. I will accept only if he promises to bring me to America and to set me up in a fine house with at least as many slaves as your Major Campbell owns.

248

As for the rest of the family, they are the same. Father goes down steadily and Mother grows old and gray before her time. She really did need your help, Anna Rose. You should never have left.

I will let you know my plans as soon as they are made. While you are enjoying all the pleasures and luxuries of the grand plantation mistress, think now and again of your poor relations—your sick father, your ailing mother, your little sisters and brothers who have barely enough to eat. I only hope your promised help comes soon enough to save them!

Your sister,
Iris Kilgore

Anna Rose was miserable and in tears, still staring down at Iris's letter, when Angus walked in.

"My dear, whatever's wrong?" He hurried to her and led her to a chair.

In silent answer, Anna Rose held out the letter to him.

"Oh, I'm so sorry!" Angus murmured. "Bad news from home?"

"Read it," Anna Rose whispered.

Silence reigned in the sunny parlor until Angus had finished. Then he uttered an oath. "What's the girl trying to do to you? How could she write such things, and you so far away?"

Anna Rose shook her head and wiped at her tears. "She's right, you know. I should never have left them. She may have tried to hurt me in stating things so bluntly, but every word of it is true, Angus."

His heart, pounding frantically already from reading that Anna Rose had written of him to her family in such glowing terms, raced even faster. Yes, he decided, the time had come!

"Anna Rose, dry your tears!"

She looked up at him, surprised by his bright tone and even more shocked by the broad smile on his face.

"We're sending for them—your whole family, including this sharp-tongued sister of yours. I'll have a bank draft drawn up this very day and we'll send it on the next boat. They'll be here before you know it. Now, show me a smile!"

Anna Rose did better than that. "Oh, Angus!" she cried, and flung herself into his arms, hugging him soundly. "How can I thank you?"

Angus had waited months for this, the feel of her close to him, the warmth of her breasts pressing against his hard chest. He closed his eyes, smiled, and sighed. "Anna Rose, my dear, your pleasure is quite thanks enough!"

The next day, they went to the bank in Darien, drew out the funds, mailed the letter, then waited.

A full year after her arrival at Angus Campbell's Altamaha River rice plantation, they were still waiting. But Anna Rose's days sped quickly past. Each day she learned new things about her position as housekeeper and her whole new way of life. This was indeed a curious world she had come to. Every hour brought its own fresh surprises—some wonderful, like the fiery sunsets that turned the might Altamaha to liquid bronze and gold; some designed to fill the heart with dread, like the poisonous snakes that slithered out of the marshes in the summer heat, and the constant, though groundless, Angus declared, rumors that a slave uprising could erupt at any time.

Still, whatever came to pass, Anna Rose knew she belonged here. She felt a part of this land and the unique relationships fostered by plantation life. Little by little, the hurts of the past were fading to dim memories. If there was one difficult area, it was her feelings about slavery. But she had learned to tell herself, as Angus had, that in this place slavery was a necessary evil. In spite of that ever-nagging guilt, she loved the South—the people, the land, the water, the house itself, which had come to be her home as much as Angus Campbell's.

The main house at Rosedhu was set on a slight rise overlooking the rice fields to the north and south. For miles and miles in all directions, the land was flat, with lawn yielding to water and the water to marsh grass or broad expanses of rice swamp. Far away in the distance, the water finally reached the horizon, but it was impossible to guess exactly where sea met sky. The broad view gave Anna Rose a sense of freedom and a feeling of oneness with nature.

Rosedhu's site, Angus explained, had been chosen by his ancestor because of the unusual elevation of that spot—an old Indian mound or kitchen midden, where for centuries the coastal natives of the Guale tribe had feasted, discarding their oyster shells until the debris heap actually formed a hill. The rest of the land within the slave-built dikes was actually below the water level.

Beyond the immediate yard of the big house were four settlements, called by everyone on the island simply "the villages." These were the slave quarters, rows of small dwellings facing each other across a wide central street. Anna Rose spent many hours of her early days at Rosedhu in the villages, teaching Angus's people the basics of hygiene, and suggesting to the men repairs that would make their houses more comfortable. This, she learned, was actually the job of the planter's wife. But since Angus had been a widower for many years, Clara's wise teachings had been sadly neglected and all but forgotten.

Once she learned the ropes, Anna Rose's life fell into a regular routine. She rose each morning in time to have breakfast with Angus. Over steaming coffee, fresh eggs, fried bacon, the corn mush locally called "grits," and huge biscuits filled with butter and dewberry jam or orange marmalade made from fruit on the plantation, they talked over their plans for the day. They became as comfortable with each other as any husband and wife discussing domestic matters. When Angus left to make his morning rounds, Anna Rose's work began in earnest.

Her first job was to go to the kitchen, a separate house out back, to give Hagar, the cook, the day's menu. Once that was done and the supplies doled out from the smokehouse and the storeroom, she assigned the tasks for each of the household staff. From that point, Dahlia took over to see that everyone completed his or her work and did a proper job of it.

At first, this had seemed a monumental task to Anna Rose. There were more than a dozen house servants. She had trouble keeping them all straight and remembering who should do what when. She felt lucky to have been a part of Madelaine Sinclair's household staff. Not only had Hugh's wife schooled her in the etiquette of the upper classes, she had also taught her a great deal concerning the management of servants and the running of a large house.

Angus helped too. He did everything in his power to make her job easier—explaining things, gently correcting her occasional mistakes, and maintaining his temper and his patience when she faltered. He also provided her with a leather-bound ledger and told her how to go about keeping a schedule of household duties. Finally, he gave Anna Rose her own tiny servant, a seven-year-old named Bitsy, who walked at her heels carrying a basket containing the vast assortment of keys to the various storerooms, pantry, sugar chest, and smokehouse.

Usually, the rest of her morning was spent visiting the "sick house," as the slaves called the infirmary, and the "baby house," where the children under twelve, who were not yet old enough to be sent to the fields, tended the infants while their mothers worked. One of the sitters' responsibilities was to carry the nursing babies out to the fields to be suckled by their mothers at feeding time. Anna Rose was appalled that the new mothers were sent back to the rice swamps only two weeks after they had given birth. But Angus and Dahlia both assured her that this was common practice and that neither mother nor child suffered for it. Still, Anna Rose had her doubts.

At three in the afternoon, Angus joined her back at the house for their big meal of the day, usually ham, mutton, venison, or a duck shot in the marshes and roasted to perfection on a spit in the huge fireplace of the cookhouse. Rice was served with almost every meal. Hagar, the cook, took great pride in her kitchen skills and in showing Anna Rose how to prepare rice properly.

"That gray goo they serves most places and calls rice ain't nowhere near the real thing," she explained cheerfully as she and one of her assistants pounded the husks from the rice with a huge wooden pestle in a mortar made of a hollowed-out tree trunk. "Here, Ditto," she said to one of the boys lounging near the kitchen door. "Go out and fan this here rice for the master's dinner."

Ditto and his twin brother Dot obeyed immediately, scampering through the door with their flat-bottomed baskets called fanners filled with rice. They held the baskets high, then let them drop. The wind blew the husks away, leaving perfectly clean kernels.

"Up Charleston way," Hagar continued, "I hear they boils their rice for a whole hour! That ain't no way to cook rice, Miz McShane. I wouldn't trust nobody who cooks rice a whole hour. You puts it in a good pot of water—cold or boiling, it don't matter—and you lets it roll for fifteen minutes. Not fourteen and a half, not sixteen, but fifteen per'xactly. Then you grabs it off the fire and you steams it for a hour."

Having seen the tender, pearly grains on her plate—each one separate, plump, and perfect—at meal after meal, Anna Rose had to admit that Hagar's method worked.

The time between the afternoon and evening meals was Anna Rose's favorite part of the day. This was when she had a few hours to do as she pleased. When Angus was free, he would take her riding, carefully educating her to the ladylike posture required for a sidesaddle. The sleek horses in the Rosedhu stables were a far cry from the sturdy ponies she had ridden as a child. And until now, riding astride was all she had known of the equestrian art. But she had no fear and she was a fast learner. Angus's profuse praise never failed to bring a warm blush of satisfaction to her cheeks.

When Angus was tied up with plantation matters, Bitsy and her older brother Tom-Tom usually accompanied Anna Rose on her afternoon jaunts. They taught her how to catch the delicious bream fish and perch from the Altamaha. They named foreign plants for her. They showed her the best places along the dike to watch for the ships coming into Darien from the sea.

Both children were bright and attentive. When Anna Rose decided to teach them the alphabet, they learned quickly and eagerly, copying to perfection the letters she traced with a stick in the sand. But she made them swear to tell no one, not even their parents, that they were learning to read. She was taking a risk and she knew it. Still, they hungered for knowledge. Someone had to teach them.

It came as a frightening shock the day Angus, his face stern, caught her in the upstairs hallway late one afternoon. "Anna Rose," he said, " I have to speak with you. Come down to the library, at once."

She followed silently, not certain what to expect, but sure that Angus was displeased about something. When they entered the book-lined room, he closed the door.

"We have a thief in our midst," he announced without preamble.

Anna Rose only stared, not knowing if she was being accused or merely warned.

"A small thief, I believe," he added with a glimmer of amusement in his blue-gray eyes.

"I don't understand." She really didn't—his words or his expression. Theft was a very serious crime on the plantation. "What's been taken, Angus?"

He strode to the far corner of the library and leaned down toward a bottom shelf, indicating an empty spot where four or five volumes had been.

"A few very old, but not very rare books. Tomes of the most elemental level. Do you know anything about this?"

Anna Rose was mystified. "Why, no! How could I?"

Suddenly, Angus's face broke into a broad smile. "I assumed that some of your 'students' might be behind this plot to denude my library, book by book."

"You know?" she asked quietly.

He nodded. "Not much goes on at Rosedhu that escapes me, Anna Rose. Tom-Tom would have died for you before he'd have told. But Bitsy's worst sin is that of pride. She simply had to show off for me the other morning when she was helping clear the breakfast dishes. I'd lingered over coffee and my newspaper, as usual. She happened to spot a few words she recognized and would have burst, I'm sure, if she hadn't read them aloud. When I

253

questioned her about this amazing ability, the truth of her great reading skills and how she came by them tumbled out."

"I'm sorry, Angus. I know it's forbidden."

"Aye," he said with a sigh. "It is that, foolish as it seems. And were either you or I caught at our endeavors, I would be forced to forfeit a huge fine. But, between us, Anna Rose, I'm pleased by what you're doing. Confine your efforts to Tom-Tom and Bitsy for now, and be discrete. As isolated as we are here, we should have no problems." He smiled at her then, and added, "Please tell Bitsy that if she needs more books to have you help her choose anytime she likes. She may find the Greek grammar she pilfered a bit beyond her expertise at the present."

Anna Rose felt a deep sense of relief. She had imagined all sorts of terrible things. She had even thought that the two children she'd tutored might be beaten because of her efforts to teach them. But she should have known better. Angus Campbell was too good, too kind to dole out punishment unjustly. And he was too generous a man to let a hunger for knowledge go unsatisfied in even the smallest black servant.

The master of Rosedhu stood across the room from his housekeeper, watching the worry lines leave her face. He was sorry that he'd approached her on this matter in such a way. He should merely have told her that he both knew and approved of what she was teaching her two favorite companions. What right had he to add to the woes life had dealt her already? He vowed silently never again to upset her, if he could avoid it.

To Angus Campbell, Anna Rose McShane was not only the dearest, but the loveliest woman he had ever set eyes on. Even the shadow of sadness in her gray-green eyes added a haunting poignancy to her beauty. But that beauty was more than a surface thing. He had seen her with his people—her calm assurance, her even justice, and the way they all adored her. When she stood, still and silent, on the piazza at sunset, staring out over the river, her expression was that of almost religious reverence. She loved this land almost as much as he did. As for loving him, perhaps not. But she possessed a kind and generous spirit, and beyond that her youthful enthusiasm made him feel young again. Yet, because of all she had been forced to endure, she had a maturity and understanding far beyond her years.

She had come to Rosedhu barely a year before, a beaten down and desolate girl. He had wondered at the time if he was doing the right thing, to cast her into such an unfamiliar setting. He'd even considered paying her passage back to Scotland so that the deep wounds in her heart might heal in the bosom of her family. But he had discarded that idea quickly. Pure selfishness had forced him to bring her here. Still, no matter the motivation, his instincts had been correct. Rosedhu had provided a healing balm to her spirit. She had taken charge, and now she was as much a part of the place as he was himself. Only one barrier still separated them.

"Anna Rose?" His manner was hesitant as he stood across the library from her, measuring her with his eyes.

"Yes, Angus?"

"I have to be away for a few days. I've had a letter from one of the absentee planters hereabouts who plans to return to his holdings soon. He wants me to see if his house is in order since he'll be bringing his daughter to live here with him. There's a Cherokee woman who supposedly cleans occasionally, and of course he has an overseer. But I promised him I'd look in to make sure the house is ready before his arrival." He stared at her oddly then and shook his head. "I feel my age at this time."

"Is the journey that long, Angus?"

"No. His land borders mine on the far side. I knew him well once. But the last time I saw him, he was beardless youth and his father was master of The Highlands. Now, after so many years, he's finally coming to take possession of his inheritance. A man grown! It's hard to imagine."

"How long will you be gone?" Anna Rose knew there was more on Angus's mind than his trip. He'd been away before, but he'd never seemed concerned about leaving.

"Before I go, I have something to ask you, Anna Rose. I hope I'll be gone long enough for you to make a decision."

Anna Rose, confused at his words, moved closer to Angus, as if to hear him better.

He closed the distance between them and reached for her hand, holding it between his own large fingers and stroking it gently. "My dear, I know this may come as a surprise to you, but in the year you've been at Rosedhu I've grown uncommonly fond of you. Each day since you arrived has been precious to me. *You* are precious to me, Anna Rose." He paused and took a deep, steadying breath. "I'm asking you to be my wife."

She stood, staring at him, her shock complete. She had never considered marrying again. She'd known the love of two good men. That was enough for one lifetime, she'd told herself, carefully locking her deepest emotions away to keep herself safe from further pain.

Anna Rose's first reaction was to let him down gently. But even as she tried to form the right words to reject his offer, somewhere

255

deep inside she felt a subtle change taking place. This was not some offhand, compulsive offer made by a love-struck suitor. This was an honest plea from a man who knew his mind and his heart, a man who had worked his whole life to build his fortune. And now he was pleading with her to share all that he possessed. He was offering her a chance to live a full life at his side, as his well-loved wife.

"Don't try to answer now. I know this is sudden. I want you to think about it while I'm away." He turned from her, staring out the window at the sun dropping toward the marsh. "It's a beautiful afternoon. Why don't we go for a ride?"

Anna Rose nodded, still unable to find her voice.

They rode side by side along the narrow dike. The last glow of sunset colored the western horizon and already winter stars twinkled in the darkening eastern sky. But the air was gentle for February, seasoned with fresh smells and a tang of salt.

Angus raised his head as if he caught some scent on the breeze. "It won't be long till planting time. How quickly the seasons, the years, pass!"

"Yes," Anna Rose answered. "I'd hoped my family would be here by spring. Each passing day seems to take me farther away from where I began, from all I knew before."

She silently added that soon, she sensed, she would begin yet another season of her life. Suddenly, it seemed clear and right that she should accept Angus's proposal. He was good and kind and gentle—not just with her, but with the smallest child or the toughest field hand. Perhaps as Angus's wife she wouldn't experience the mystical romance she'd known with Rory, or the deep, soul-shattering passion her love for Hugh had brought, but she'd never be alone again. She and Angus were comfortable together, tenderly so. She glanced at him. His eyes were alight with the wonder of the sun setting over his world. She was about to confess her thoughts to him when his words interrupted her.

"You've been thinking often lately of your family, haven't you, Anna Rose?"

"I never stop thinking of them," she admitted.

"You should hear soon. Ships come to Darien every day. A letter's sure to arrive before long. In fact, I've been meaning to speak to you about that. I want you to write to your mother again tonight. Urge her to speed the family's departure. Perhaps your father is well enough to travel by now. The sea air should be good for him."

Anna Rose turned to look at Angus once more, but his face was only a dark silhouette in the fading light. "You really want them here, don't you?"

"I want whatever will make you happy, my dear. Besides, there's plenty of room at Rosedhu and it will seem good to have guests . . . family . . . filling the halls again."

Anna Rose's heart was racing. Was she really hearing this or only dreaming? But maybe he mentioned her family at this moment only as a bribe.

"Don't you want to wait until I've made my decision before you bring them here?"

"Certainly not! If you won't marry me, you'll need your family all the more. You've been alone too long, my dear."

Tears came to Anna Rose's eyes. Suddenly, she felt an overwhelming affection for this man. He was not one to make deals and flimsy promises. He really cared what happened to her.

"Oh, Angus, how can I thank you?" she whispered.

"By being happy, Anna Rose." He reached over and patted her hand. "Simply by being happy."

They rode home silently, uninterrupted by any of the slaves, who usually ran out to greet them. Supper was waiting when they returned to the house. After eating quickly, Angus saw Anna Rose to her room. They stood for a moment outside her door, staring at each other as if they'd never really taken the time before to see clearly. Anna Rose could feel Angus's loving gaze. It brought a blush to her cheeks even as it warmed her heart. She tried to work up the courage to tell him her decision. But somehow the timing seemed wrong. She decided to wait until his return as he had requested. Angus was a wise man. Perhaps he sensed that she needed the days ahead to think everything through carefully.

"I'll be leaving early in the morning." He reached up and brushed a stray wisp of thick chestnut hair back from her forehead. "I'd like to kiss you once before I go."

Anna Rose had often wondered what his kiss would be like. Now she nodded, tilted her face up to his, and closed her eyes. His lips were warm and gentle, filling her with a great sense of peace and belonging. His arms closed round her in an embrace, and she felt his body against hers for the first time. He was surprisingly hard and muscular, and there was no denying his arousal. Her pulses quickened and she experienced a feeling of longing she had nearly forgotten. The impact came as a shock, the moment when he released her an even greater one.

"I love you, Anna Rose."

His voice trembled as he spoke the words. She looked up at him to see his eyes misty with tears. Before she could answer, he turned her gently toward her room, saying, "Now, go write to your mother, my darling. I'll be back in two or three days. By then, I hope you'll be ready with your answer."

Rosedhu Plantation
February 10, 1837

Dear Mother and Father,

I have the grandest news to tell you. I am still here at Rosedhu, working for Angus Campbell. We get on quite well as you have probably surmised from my letters. This very night, that dear man requested that I write to you and beg that you hurry your plans to come to America. He is the kindest of men. He took me in when I was penniless and forsaken, and now he wants to add to our happiness by having you all here. My joy will be complete as soon as I see you again.

There is another reason for my delight this evening. Angus has asked me to marry him. He did not press me for an answer, but asked me to think about it. I have thought. And I have decided. I could look the whole world over and not find another to match him. I thought when Rory died that my world had ended. Then when our daughter was lost in that dreadful fire, I was sure I would feel nothing but pain ever again. How resilient is the human heart! I will always miss Rory and my dear little Heather. But with Angus at my side, I will have someone to share my pain and my joy. I know you will love Angus as much as I do!

Anna Rose stared at the words she'd written, oddly surprised that she had admitted her true feelings to her family before confessing them to herself. Yes, she realized, she did love Angus. Earlier she had thought only that she was willing to marry him, but nothing of *love* had crossed her mind. She could wait no longer to tell him her decision. Shoving the letter aside and pulling on a wrapper, she hurried out of the room.

She knocked at Angus's door. "Yes, who is it?" came his muffled answer.

"Anna Rose, Angus." She was trembling with excitement. "I need to speak with you."

He had retired already, she could tell by the creaking of bed ropes and rustling of covers. When he opened the door, he was wearing a dark robe, hastily donned.

He peered out at her, frowning. "Anna Rose, what's wrong?"

She laughed. "Oh, Angus, nothing is wrong! Everything is right for the first time in so long." She paused and gave him a glowing smile. "Yes!" she announced.

"Yes?" He gazed at her, puzzled.

"Yes, I'll marry you!"

For a moment, his frown remained. Then slowly she watched his eyes light up with something akin to wonder. His lips parted, but no sound came. Then he laughed. He threw back his head and gave a great hardy howl of joy. The next instant, she was in his arms as he danced a jig about the room, sweeping her along with him. When they tripped on the braided rug and fell atop the covers of the great mahogany bed that was carved with sheaths of rice, he kissed her. It was a lingering, searching kiss, that fanned them both with its fire. At length, Angus put her away from him and sat staring into her bright eyes.

"I have had a great deal of happiness in my life," he said solemnly. "Almost as much happiness as sadness. But never, ever, have I felt this way before. I'll confess to you, Anna Rose, that until the night that Flynn sold you to me, I considered my life drawing rapidly to its conclusion. My only thought was to live out my remaining days here at Rosedhu in comparative peace and comfort. But that night, when I beat the blackguard and booted him out of the inn, I felt a new spark. And when you agreed to come with me, the spark burst into flame. At this moment, I feel a veritable inferno of blazing emotion."

"Oh, Angus," she whispered, touching his glowing face with gentle fingertips. "You are a dear, dear man!"

"Did you really mean it, Anna Rose?" he asked quietly. "That you might love me?"

She shook her head. "No. Not that I might love you, Angus. I do love you."

Weary now with spent emotions, she leaned her head against his broad chest. He stroked her hair and sighed.

"Have you written your letter, my darling?"

"Yes. I told my family to hurry. I also told them that we were to be married."

He smiled down at her and kissed her forehead with great tenderness. "Shall we plan the wedding for after their arrival, then?"

"No, Angus." Anna Rose lifted her face to look up into his warm eyes. "I don't want to wait that long. By the time my family arrives, I hope I'll be carrying our first child."

He looked shocked at first. He'd never considered the possibility of becoming a father again. Then he grinned down at her and laughed aloud happily. "Of course, my darling! Whatever you wish. We'll have a child, a dozen, if you like! When shall we set the date?"

"Perhaps just before spring planting?"

"The perfect time."

They shared one final, quiet kiss before Anna Rose said good night and went back to her room.

She finished her letter quickly, then sat at her window, gazing out at the stars and wondering how any woman alive could deserve such happiness.

23

Only a few days after her eldest daughter's letter arrived, bringing the glad tidings, Margaret Mackintosh's spirits dived from the heights of ectasy to the depths of despair. She felt that her life had reached its lowest ebb. Thin from years of tending her invalid husband and trying to run the croft herself, weak with weariness and grief, and dressed in stiff black garb, she stood with her brood in the little kirkyard near Inverness. The cold wind whipped the stark landscape, seeming to freeze the tears on Meg's cheeks as she heard the moan of the coffin ropes and watched the plain box containing her Johnnie's mortal remains lowered into the muddy hole.

It had been almost three years since John's accident. But that had been a soft, warm spring—a time of hope and promise. How harsh the world had become since then!

The only sounds in the stillness were the parson's thin voice, the wailing wind, and the whimpering of Iris's sickly son. Poor little Shane, who had been born prematurely, had been a fretful child from the first. Perhaps he'd inherited his unfortunate temperament from his mother, a perpetually miserable being.

Margaret glanced at her daughter. What a mess she had made of her life! She realized Iris had a right to be bitter, widowed at barely sixteen when poor Jaimie caught a fever at sea, leaving her with a son to raise all alone. But most women would have shouldered such a burden with acceptance and become stronger and better for it. Not Iris! She had fought the fates with a vengeance and was still battling against the laws of nature, man, and God.

Jaimie had hardly known his wife, had never seen his son. He'd shipped out only a few days after their marriage and had not come home again. Iris had suffered an uncomfortable pregnancy and a terrible delivery. The doctor had said it was a wonder that either mother or son survived the ordeal.

As for Iris's maternal instincts, Margaret had seen staghound bitches that showered more love and care on their pups. Iris was one of those unfortunate women who simply had no business being a mother. And little Shane suffered constantly because of it. Margaret had come to feel that he was more her child than Iris's. That seemed to suit Iris to a tee.

Shane let out a high-pitched shriek when Iris pinched his thin arm to end his squirming. Margaret, forgetting the parson's funeral oration, hurried to take the child from her daughter. She gave Iris a reproving look, but was met with only a superior glare from her cold gray eyes. Iris gladly handed over her burden to her mother.

Shane snuggled close to his grandmother's warm, safe bosom, hiccuping softly as his sobs subsided. Soon he was fast asleep with his thumb in his mouth. Margaret hugged him closer and smiled down at the little love. But her smile turned to a grimace as she noted the angry blue mark forming on his arm where his mother had pinched him. She prayed that Iris would never have any other children to torment. She was sure that her daughter shared that hope.

Margaret glanced at the younger boys and girls beside her. It was hard to believe how they were growing. Shane was her only baby now. Cullen, Ewan, Laurel, and Fern seemed so grown-up. In no time at all, they would be seeking their own fortunes in the world. But how much better it would be for them to set out on their own in America. She would tell them the news as soon as their father was decently buried. Once they returned to the cottage and their friends and neighbors had left, she would explain her plans in detail, plans prompted by John's death and Anna Rose's recent letter.

The peat fire inside the cottage was warm, thawing Margaret Mackintosh's body as well as her soul. The amenities had been observed and now the last of the neighbors were filing out into the night. When they were gone, she knew the house would seem empty. John was not in the next room. John was gone, forever. Now she must pick up the pieces and direct all their lives in the best manner she could. She sent up a silent prayer to her husband, asking for his guidance.

"Thank goodness all those nosy people are finally gone!" Iris said. "They don't care about us. They only came here to stare. I'm going to bed now. Shane has worn me out this evening."

Meg glanced over at her grandchild, sleeping in the cradle where she had put him after she had fed him and changed his clothes. All the while, the boy's mother had been busy charming the young men who had come to pay their respects, showing no remorse whatsoever over her recent broken engagement to Mr. Sloane, a widower three times her age. No doubt she planned to slip out later to meet one of her young admirers as she so often did—had done even during her brief, ill-fated engagement—thinking that her mother knew nothing of her late-night liaisons.

"You'll stay here just a bit, Iris," Margaret commanded. "I have something to say to all of you."

"I'm sure it can wait till morning, Mother."

"It cannot! Sit down!"

Her children quickly formed a circle around her. Margaret glanced from one face to the next. They all looked tired, drained, emotionally spent. It was exactly the way she felt. But she forced herself on, determined to give her children some hope to dream on this very night.

"A letter from Anna Rose has come. With all that's happened, I've had no time to share it with you until now." She forced a smile as she continued. "It's good news. Very good news. Your sister is about to be married again."

A general murmur of excitement passed through the room.

"The man who will be her husband—Major Angus Campbell— has sent the fare for us to go to America, as you know. And now he urges us, Anna Rose says, to make haste with our journey. Soon now, we'll go to live on his rice plantation near Darien, Georgia. It's what your father dreamed of for all of us. And now that he's gone . . ." Her voice trailed off as tears caught in her throat.

The younger children were on their feet now, dancing about and firing questions at her. Only Iris remained still and silent, a scheming light dawning in her eyes.

"Please, children! Listen to me," Margaret said, raising her hands to get their attention. "You have to give me time to work things out. It may take weeks or months to find a buyer for the croft. And we'll have to visit all our relatives to say good-bye before we sail. There'll be supplies to buy for the trip. It won't be an easy journey. We must all prepare carefully."

Iris rose, her face sour again. "I don't know why you wanted

262

me to hear this. I'm sure I'm not included in Anna Rose's grand plans."

Margaret was shocked. "Of course you're included, Iris! Why would you ever think otherwise?"

"Because Anna Rose always despised me. I suppose I gave her good cause. There was never any love lost between us. And now that she's lost her baby, but I have Shane . . ."

Margaret narrowed her eyes in warning. She guessed what Iris was about to say and it was not fit for the younger children's ears. The girl's confession to her mother at the time of Shane's birth still shocked Margaret when she thought of it. She was still not convinced that Iris was telling the truth, though why anyone would make up such a tale, she had no inkling.

"Anna Rose adores children, Iris. She always has. She will love Shane. As for her harboring any ill feelings toward you, I'm certain that's all in the past. You're family as much as any one of us, and sisters always grow closer as they get older."

Iris only shrugged, trying to hide her delight at the prospect of going to America. Anna Rose seemed to have it all now. Well, Iris vowed, she would have her own fair share and more! Thank goodness, sickly old Ezra Sloane had canceled their plans to wed. Now she would be free to marry the rich Georgia planter of her choice. Perhaps even Anna Rose's Major Campbell would strike her fancy. She smiled slightly at the thought. Yes, that would be interesting!

"I'm going to bed now, if you're finished, Mother."

Margaret was too annoyed with Iris to want her to stay any longer. She would not have this moment ruined for the rest of them.

"Good night, then. I'll see to Shane if he needs anything."

The last went without saying. Iris never rose from her bed at night to tend her son. As far as she was concerned, her mother could have Shane and be welcomed to him!

Long after the last of her children had gone to sleep, Margaret sat staring into the fire. Her lips moved soundlessly as she explained to John—wherever he was—that they would soon be leaving. That was the hardest part, to think of deserting the home where she had been so happily married and of leaving her husband alone on that cold, windy hill where they had laid him to rest today.

But by the time the pale light of dawn streaked the windows, Margaret Mackintosh had cried all her tears and said all her farewells. When the time for leaving came, she would be ready to face her new life.

Anna Rose felt almost as lighthearted as she had the first time she had married. The kiss of spring was on the land and her wedding day promised to be lovely.

"I couldn't have asked for better had I ordered it myself," Anna Rose told Dahlia as the servant helped her dress.

"It's a good sign all right, Miss Anna Rose," Dahlia agreed. "You and the Major gonna have a fine life together. And by this time next year, we'll be turning this old room of yours into a nursery again."

Anna Rose blushed slightly and looked away. She was unutterably nervous about her wedding night. She so wanted everything to go well. But she had so little experience. How was she to know what Angus expected of her?

Dahlia seemed to be reading her mind. "Don't you worry none about tonight, Miss Anna Rose. The Major, he worships the ground you walks on. He won't do nothin' to hurt his darlin'. You just act sweet and lovin' like you always do and it'll be just fine."

Anna Rose squeezed her hand. "Thank you, Dahlia. I'll try. I do so want to make him happy."

"You will. You already have. And won't nothin' make that man happier than having a baby in this house again. That young Mr. Weyman ain't never been a proper son to his daddy. He just bring him grief and more grief."

Dahlia's words bothered Anna Rose. She had yet to meet Weyman Campbell. But Angus had asked her permission to invite his son to the wedding. Of course, she had agreed. They had heard nothing after Angus wrote to his last known address in Charleston, telling his son of their coming marriage. Still, from what Anna Rose had heard of Weyman, he might turn up unannounced.

Angus seemed reluctant to talk about his son. But Dahlia had filled in the whole story for Anna Rose. Weyman Campbell had been his mother's darling from the time of his birth, when she was told by her doctor that he would be her one and only child. He was kept in the very same room with Angus and Clara until he was almost ten years old. Clara refused to allow him to sleep alone in the nursery down the hall, even with a servant always in attendance.

But this showering of love and attention, this overprotection of the boy, seemed to do more harm than good as he grew up. He became arrogant, abusive, and impossible to discipline. By the time he was sixteen, every girl slave on the plantation feared him. The seed of the master's demanding son explained the numerous lighter-skinned slaves at Rosedhu.

When the time came, Weyman was sent away to the university. He lasted only weeks at Franklin College in Athens before being expelled for misconduct. Other institutions, other expulsions, had followed in rapid succession. Finally, in frustration, Angus gave up. Clara had died; there was no need to force Weyman to return to Rosedhu, and they had run out of universities. Angus gave his misfit son a small stake and wished him well before turning him out upon the world. Since that time, Weyman had drifted from city to city, in and out of trouble, always needing money. At last, Angus had cut him off completely. No communication had passed between father and son for two years before Angus sent the wedding invitation. It was clear to Anna Rose that Angus had been deeply wounded when Weyman sent no reply.

Anna Rose sighed, dreading the thought of Weyman Campbell's showing up for the wedding. She wanted the day to be perfect. But surely it would not be if this man came. Later, she could welcome her stepson with more confidence. But the wedding and the wedding night seemed all she could handle right now. She needed no unannounced guests to further set her nerves on edge.

Dahlia had left her alone for a moment. Anna Rose stood before the tall mirror, gazing at the gown Angus had insisted she have made for the wedding. They'd made a special trip to Savannah to visit the finest mantua-maker in the city. The tiny Frenchwoman had fashioned a simple but beautiful linen costume of saffron—the ancient shade that distinguished Gaelic grandees—with low neck, tight waist, and long full sleeves laced in gold and silver as was traditional. The finishing touch, a length of the red and green tartan of Clan Mackintosh, was draped about Anna Rose's shoulder, falling in front to the hem of her gown. A cairngorm brooch, her wedding gift from the groom, fastened the plaid shawl at her breast. The silver pin, exquisitely handwrought and set with a pair of smoky quartz stones, took the shape of a thistle for Scotland and a Cherokee rose for Georgia.

Anna Rose knew that in ancient days, such a fine piece of jewelry would have been worn by some Highland warrior into battle so that if he fell, a stranger might trade the heavy cairngorm brooch for the price of a decent burial for the hapless soldier. But this piece held a much more sentimental meaning for the bride. It served to remind her that although she was far from her home, a part of Scotland would live on with her for as long as she was Angus Campbell's wife.

Dahlia had styled her mistress's spice-colored hair into a cascade of curls down her back with smooth swoops at each side and beau-catcher curls framing her face. Anna Rose could hardly believe the image in her mirror was her own. She was more used to seeing her hair tossed freely by the coastal winds into a tumble of unruly curls, and she dressed simply for daily life at Rosedhu in a cotton frock, white apron, and sensible shoes. No, this had to be some stranger staring back at her.

"Tom-Tom done got back from the errand I sent him on," Dahlia called from the door, rousing Anna Rose from her musings. "Look here."

The tall servant, her dark eyes gleaming with delight, held out a crown of orange blossoms fresh with dew for Anna Rose to wear in her hair.

"They're the first of the year. I was 'fraid they might not open in time. But I should of knowed they would. Seems like everything's gone right since you came here, Miss Anna Rose."

Dahlia placed the delicate crown on Anna Rose's head. The waxy, white blossoms perfumed the whole room and nodded gently as she turned to view the effect in the mirror.

"These came from the orange trees along the dike?" For the past days, Anna Rose had watched the buds grow plumper every day. But she'd never thought of putting them to this use.

"That's right! Tom-Tom says he picked 'em at the place y'all go fishing all the time."

Any further discussion was cut off when Anna Rose's little helper, Bitsy, dressed in her Sunday best, scurried up to the door. "Y'all best hurry, Miss Anna Rose. All the people are here and the parson, too. And Master Angus," she paused to giggle, "he's wearin' his fine skirt and getting powerful nervous."

"Has Master Angus's son arrived?" Anna Rose asked.

Bitsy shook her head. "Ain't seen hide nor hair of him."

Anna Rose said a silent prayer of thanks before she started downstairs, unaware that another surprise awaited her below.

Angus had mentioned to Anna Rose that the owner of The Highlands and his daughter would be arriving any day, he hoped in time for the wedding. There was no reason for him to keep the name of their neighbor from her; it had simply never occurred to him to mention it. And she hadn't thought to ask.

As it was, she didn't spy him until after she and Angus had spoken their vows before the flower-bedecked fireplace in the parlor. All of Anna Rose's attention during the ceremony focused on Angus, dressed in the "skirt" that had so amused Bitsy, his kilt of the dark green and black Campbell plaid, and looking remarkably happy and youthful.

The final part of the ceremony touched Anna Rose deeply. After the parson had pronounced them man and wife, and Anna Rose had accepted her husband's first kiss, Angus, with slightly trembling hands, unfastened the cairngorm brooch. Then he slipped the Mackintosh tartan from her shoulders, replacing it with his own clan's plaid.

"Now you are truly a Campbell, my dear," he whispered to her.

"Now I am truly your wife," she replied softly.

Then came the rush of well-wishers—planters and their wives from nearby islands, townsfolk from Darien and Midway. Their newly arrived neighbor was almost the last, and that was good. Had Hugh Sinclair been among the first to come forward, Anna Rose would have had no voice left to speak to the other guests.

"Ah, Captain Sinclair," Angus called out warmly. "So, you arrived in time. I hardly recognized you. But then it's been a few years, eh?"

Anna Rose, at her new husband's side, had been chatting with a neighbor. Hearing Angus speak the name Sinclair, she broke off in mid-sentence and stared at the man coming toward them. She could actually feel the blood draining from her face while the rest of her went numb. How could it be?

"My dear, I'd like you to meet our new neighbor," Angus said happily.

Anna Rose tried to return her husband's smile, but her face felt paralyzed, her whole body refused to move. She felt a sense of vast relief that Hugh was alive, mingled with confused feelings of panic, regret, and hopelessness that the sight of him could still arouse such a bittersweet ache in her heart even as she clung to her new husband's arm. She wanted him alive and well, but she did not want him back in her life, not now!

She fought against her blacker thoughts. This was her wedding day to Angus Campbell. Already she was his wife in name, and before many hours passed she would be his by deed as well. The fact that Hugh Sinclair stood here before her had nothing to do with that.

Anna Rose watched as Hugh came slowly toward her, joy and pain in his eyes. He looked older, weary from all that fate had heaped upon him. He reached for her trembling hand and brought it to his lips. "Mrs. Campbell," he said in a voice husky with emotion. "It seems I'm always turning up unexpectedly at your weddings."

"Hugh . . ." Her voice failed her when there was so much she wanted to say.

"You two know each other?" Angus asked, looking from his

wife to his neighbor, then back again to Anna Rose's pale countenance.

"We do," Hugh answered. "I first met the lady in Scotland, and I captained the ship that brought her to America. Then, for a brief time, she cared for my daughter."

Anna Rose, still unable to find her voice, was thankful that Hugh was able to explain their association so simply and casually to her husband. She knew she could not have managed it. Then she thought with grim irony how Hugh might have added that he'd tended her intimately in the crossing, that he'd asked her to marry him, and that he had made beautiful love to her once on a brocade couch.

"Well, this is a pleasant surprise!" Angus enthused. "Imagine you two happening upon each other this way! I'm sure we're both delighted to have you back here at The Highlands, Captain. And where is your little daughter?"

Suddenly, Angus's words chased all else from Anna Rose's mind. *Charity . . . Heather! She was alive!* In that instant of realization, Anna Rose could not hold back the tears. They brimmed in her eyes, then slipped silently down her cheeks. She wanted to hug Hugh to let him know how happy she was, but she forced herself to remain calm.

"Charity is well," Hugh answered simply, speaking directly to Anna Rose, "and as bright and lovely as ever. Although, there's a touch of sadness about her pretty mouth now, from losing her mother and her nurse in the same night."

"I'm sorry, Hugh," Anna Rose said softly. "Poor Madelaine. The fire?"

He nodded silently.

The painful moment was interrrupted when Pride entered to announce that the wedding dinner was served. There was no chance for further conversation during the meal, since Hugh was seated at the opposite end of the long dining table from the bridal couple.

Anna Rose had regained a measure of her composure. She ate the she-crab bisque, the seasoned rice with tiny pink shrimp, the roasted goose, the jellies and ices, but she tasted nothing. She smiled and nodded as guests conversed with her, responding politely and appropriately. She acted the perfect hostess, the glowing bride. She fooled almost everyone. No one, not even her husband, noticed the stormy hue of her eyes or the way her gaze slipped time and again to linger on the weathered face of the man at the far end of the table.

Only Hugh Sinclair noticed her uneasiness. He'd seen that

glazed, dark look in her eyes before. The night Rory fell to his death, the day she slipped away to lose herself in the streets of New York, the morning she came back to him, and another less pleasant day when she told him she meant to marry Michael Flynn. The troubled gaze she kept casting his way only served to intensify the ache he felt inside.

Damn! Hugh thought. Why had he come back to The Highlands? He should have stayed at sea. But then what would have become of Charity? She had survived well enough with Madelaine's aunt for a year. But Hugh had missed her terribly. Here on the plantation, the girl would grow strong and fine. His Indian housekeeper, Willow-in-the-Wind, was a lovely, gentle woman, who would be the next best thing to a mother. Madelaine would have approved. Madelaine would even have been pleased that Anna Rose was here. After all, in spite of his deception where his wife was concerned, the two women had been close friends.

Hugh glanced up and caught Anna Rose staring at him. He smiled at her; she quickly looked away, a faint flicker of pain touching her features. This was his fault, too. Had he been on time, he might have stopped the wedding. He could have stood when the parson asked if anyone could show just cause. But would he have had the courage to speak out? Would Anna Rose have wanted him to?

With the silver fork in his left hand he shoved a naked-pink shrimp around his plate, chastising himself silently for daring to think such thoughts. Angus Campbell was a good man. Anna Rose could hardly have done better in choosing a husband. Certainly her tastes had improved since she married Rory McShane, then considered a match with Michael Flynn. He smiled grimly, thinking that Angus Campbell was a far-sight better choice than Hugh Sinclair was as well!

The fact that Hugh himself still loved her was neither here nor there. Had she ever truly loved him? He doubted it. He had been the pursuer all along. Perhaps they were both better off now that she was safely married again. He knew Anna Rose well enough to realize that she would not betray her husband with another man as he had betrayed poor sweet Madelaine.

At that moment, Hugh Sinclair came to a decision. No, more than that, he made a vow: Never would he be anything other than a good and loyal friend to both Anna Rose and Angus Campbell.

The thought brought with it both pain and relief.

"Champagne, sir?" The servant at his elbow offered a tall goblet of bubbling wine.

"Yes, thank you."

Hugh took the frosty, long-stemmed glass in his hand, raised it toward Anna Rose in salute, then drained the glass.

The bride saw his gesture and blushed appropriately, remembering another bottle of champagne, another wedding night.

This wedding was so very different from her first. There was none of the wild elation or the giddy anticipation of the unknown that Anna Rose had experienced on the day she became Mrs. Rory McShane. No pipes played, no dancers whirled. After the rather staid wedding supper, the guests paid their final respects, invited the newlyweds to visit, and then took their leave of Rosedhu.

The early spring twilight was fast approaching, and purplish-gray storm clouds had gathered out over the river. Hurriedly, in order to reach their homes before the rain started falling, the planters and their families boarded their brightly painted plantation boats and sped away. Angus and Anna Rose stood on the front piazza waving until the last of the canoes snaked out of sight, following the narrow cut through the marshes.

Angus put an arm about his bride's shoulders and drew her close to him. "Ah, my darling, it's been quite a day!" He sighed happily.

"That it has," she replied, thinking of more than the wedding alone.

"You must be exhausted. Why don't you go up to our room and relax for a time? I've had Dahlia draw a bath for you."

"What about you, Angus? Your day has been every bit as long and tiring as mine—happily so, of course."

He hugged her and smiled. "Yes, I'm happy indeed! And I'll admit to a touch of weariness. I'll follow you up soon. But first there's some business I must attend to."

Anna Rose drew away from her husband and stared up at him, frowning. "Business? On our wedding night?"

Realizing that the words made her sound overly anxious, she flushed deeply. But Angus smiled at her embarrassed expression, delighted to the core by what she'd said.

"Ah, my dear wife, what a gem I've plucked in you! I won't be long. I promise you. But I must take care of this first. It would hardly be neighborly of me to send Captain Sinclair all the way back to The Highlands without answering his questions about the state of his plantation. He has much work to do, and there's no need for him to come all this way again in a few days' time. You do understand, don't you, my darling?"

Anna Rose hadn't realized that Hugh was still there. Although she hadn't seen him leave, she had assumed that he'd departed with the other guests, slipping away without saying good-bye, so that he might spare them both further discomfort. But when she glanced around, he was there, standing just inside the doorway.

"Of course I understand, Angus," Anna Rose answered softly so that Hugh wouldn't hear. "But, if neither of you objects, I'd like to join you. Much has happened since the night of the fire in New York. I'd like to find out what transpired after I fled the city."

"Certainly, Anna Rose. I'm sure Captain Sinclair will welcome your company as much as I will. I'd only thought to spare you the dull details of plantation talk." Angus turned toward the other man. "Sinclair, you don't object to my wife's company, do you?"

A crooked smile played over Hugh's lips. What a provoking way Angus Campbell had of putting things. He replied in like fashion, "Why, Major Campbell, I *long* for your beautiful bride's company!"

Anna Rose felt Hugh's words deep down inside her, but she fought against the warmth his tone aroused. Taking her husband's arm, she said, "Come, Angus, let's go back inside. The wind brings a chill with it this late in the day."

Soon the three of them were settled in the library—the two men with brandies and Anna Rose with a cup of tea. She sipped slowly, listening only halfheartedly as Angus reviewed lists of figures from a long sheet. Rainfall tables, hurricane charts, crop figures, and slave prices. He also provided Hugh a complete rundown of the condition of the fields, forests, and outbuildings at The Highlands.

When he finished with his full and efficient report, Hugh gave a low whistle and shook his head. "I don't know how I can thank you, Angus. You've thought of everything. I'd have been months, digging out all that information for myself. And until I had it, I'd have felt like a stranger on my own land."

"Ah, don't mention it, Hugh." Angus beamed with pleasure as he spoke. "You'd have done the same for me were our roles reversed."

"Aye!" Hugh answered, offering his hand. "And should you ever need *anything* done that I can accomplish in your stead, you have only to say the word, my friend."

Anna Rose happened to be looking at Hugh as he spoke, and she saw the expression on his face change from open warmth to carefully guarded desire. At that moment, she realized she and Hugh were sharing some of the same feelings, and the same regrets. That knowledge pained her all the more. She looked down

271

at her teacup, hiding her brimming eyes from her husband and her former lover.

Angus slammed a thick ledger shut, making her jump.

"Well, Hugh, shall we quit with business now and spend a bit of time with my bride?"

"It will be my pleasure, sir."

The two men moved away from the high plantation desk to the cozy inglenook beside the fire. Angus sat next to Anna Rose on the sofa and Hugh took a chair across from them. The arrangement was so civilized that Anna Rose wanted to laugh and cry at the same time. They all sat there, silent for a time.

At last, Angus broke the ice. "I read all about the fire. It must have been dreadful. You lost everything, Hugh?"

Once more he cast a guarded look toward Anna Rose as he replied, "Not as much as I'd thought."

"The house?" Anna Rose whispered.

Hugh nodded, his dark eyes bleak suddenly. "And my wife and unborn child with it."

Anna Rose felt a new stab of pain. She should never have left that night. She might have saved Madelaine.

As if reading her thoughts, Hugh said gently, "No one could have saved Madelaine. The firemen assured me she died in her sleep from the smoke, never knowing what happened. I tried to reach her and almost lost my own life in the attempt. At least I was able to save Charity."

"And she's well, you say?" Anna Rose asked again, knowing she wouldn't believe the words until she could actually see her daughter for herself.

"As bright as a freshly minted Birmingham copper!" Hugh answered.

Anna Rose wondered if Hugh had any idea how close he had come to the mark, comparing the child with a counterfeit coin. She had hoped someday to confess to him that Charity was really her daughter. She had even dreamed, in impulsive moments, of a time when the two of them might share the duties of parenting. But that would remain only a dream now. And she could see no advantage to telling Heather's adoptive father the real truth.

"I suppose Delmonico's was burned," she said.

"To the ground!" Then Hugh smiled and added, "But you know the indomitable Del-Monicos as well as anyone. Already, they've built a fine new restaurant at the corner of William and Beaver streets."

"And Mavis?" Anna Rose had often wondered about her young friend.

"Still at Del's and being courted extravagantly by the young fireman who risked his life to save hers. He's a fine lad and they seem to be very much in love. I expect they'll be married very soon."

"Oh!" she sighed, brushing a tear from the corner of her eye. "I'm so happy for her. She's a sweet girl and deserves a good life."

They chatted on for some time, Anna Rose asking questions, Hugh providing polite answers, and all the while, Angus seeming content to listen and to gaze lovingly at his animated bride. Already he realized that these two young people had been much closer than they'd admitted to him. But he could tell, too, that both of them were fighting to keep any former relationship where it now belonged, in the past. He felt no jealousy, only gratitude that fate had given him a full and happy life again.

Suddenly, lightning flashed through the sky, lighting up the windows in a savage display, then deep rumbling thunder rattled the panes.

"Time I was on my way," Hugh said, rising quickly.

"You can't leave in this storm," Angus protested. "We always have the guest rooms ready. You'll stay here with us for the night."

Hugh smiled cordially at his host, but shook his head. "My daughter is spending her first night in a strange place. The storm's likely to add to her anxiety. I must go home. But thank you."

His excuse was legitimate, but his reasons ran deeper, like a wound cut through flesh to the bare bone. He had spent one of Anna Rose's wedding nights in close proximity. He could not endure that sort of hell again!

He promised to bring Charity to Rosedhu for a visit and extended an invitation for the Campbells to come to The Highlands for a weekend sometime soon. Then he was gone—a lone figure, hunched against the driving rain—leaving the bride and groom to consummate their vows.

The master's great "rice bed," as the servants called it, seemed even larger to Anna Rose now that she lay beneath its canopy. The mattress was deep and soft, stuffed with dried moss from the plantation trees. The sheets were fine linen and held a scent of spicy bay.

It occurred to her just then that she had never before made love in a real bed. The closest she had come was when she and Rory . . . She cut the thought off before it was finished. The last person she wanted to think about right now was Hugh Sinclair, the last place on earth, his shipboard bunk.

Anna Rose lay alone in the big bed, waiting for Angus to come to her. She closed her eyes and put all other thoughts from her mind. He was her husband now, and soon they would be man and wife in the deepest, most lasting sense of the words, which made her very happy. Angus was a dear man who truly cared for her. He would sooner die than hurt her in any way. That thought brought a surge of loyalty and honest devotion to her breast.

"Anna Rose?"

Angus's voice was deep and soft. His tred had been even softer. She didn't realize he was in the room until he was standing beside her.

He reached out and touched her cheek with cool fingertips. She clutched his hand and brought his palm to her lips, tasting the salt of his flesh and feeling her blood course through her. Her husband slid into bed beside her, sharing his warmth and his strength.

Anna Rose turned to him and stared, unblinking, as she said, "I love you, Angus. Truly I do!"

He gathered her close without a word, kissing her forehead, her eyelids, her cheeks until every nerve seemed to stir back to life after a long sleep. His strong hands kneaded her back and buttocks, firing her senses and sending spasms of desire through her body.

"Ah, love," he sighed, "it's been so long for me. You may have to guide me along the path."

But his knowing hands and lips belied his words as he sought out, caressed, fondled, and stroked every sensitive part of his bride's tender flesh, uncovering the best kept of her body's secrets. Long before Angus made any move to take her, Anna Rose was writhing in his arms, pressed fast to his strong, tough nakedness.

As he finally laid her back against the pillows and rose above her, Angus whispered, "I dreamed of its being this way, but I never really believed it until now, my darling."

"Angus, please!" Anna Rose choked out, gripping his arms and trying to bring him down to her at last.

Then she felt the pressure, the full penetration. She gasped softly at this powerful sensation. They were one, and Anna Rose, her eyes wide open in wonder at the pleasure and the heat and the rightness of their first coupling, held her husband fast, murmuring his name over and over until she fell silent in her ecstasy.

After Angus shifted his weight from her body, Anna Rose was still aware of his hands stroking her face. The candle continued to flicker beside the bed. She looked up at him and smiled a weary, happy smile. He bent and kissed her tenderly.

"Sleep now, my darling wife," he whispered. "I'll try not to disturb you. I only want to fill my eyes with your wonder for a while longer."

Anna Rose drifted off, satisfied that becoming Mrs. Angus Campbell had been the right choice.

Satisfied . . . satisfied . . . satisfied . . .

24

The note read simply: "In my haste, I brought no gift to your wedding. I hope you will accept this, even though it belongs to you already."

There was no signature, but none was needed once Anna Rose stripped away the tissue paper and saw the gift. For several moments, she stared, unbelieving. Then she clutched it to her breast, murmuring her gratitude to whatever divine power had saved it from burning.

"What is it, darling?"

Angus had been working at his desk, too busy with his maps and early crop reports to concern himself with yet another wedding gift. They had been arriving for days, delivered by slave couriers, and the novelty had worn off for him. But, glancing up to see the expression of delight and wonder on his wife's face, his curiosity was piqued. She looked especially lovely today, he noted. The bright blush of her cheeks matched the warm rose glow of her silk gown. She looked, her husband thought, like a rosebud at its fullest, about to burst into riotous bloom.

"My Bible!" she exclaimed. "I left it in New York. I was sure it must have been burned along with all my other things. But somehow Hugh saved it. And, look, Angus! It's not even scorched."

She hurried over to the desk and placed the book before her husband for his inspection. As he thumbed through it, several black silhouettes fell out.

"What's this?" he asked.

Anna Rose gave an excited cry. "My family! I cut all their

likenesses before I left home." She spread them out for Angus to see, careful not to display the two of Rory and Hugh.

"Well, this is indeed a happy discovery for you, my dear. Why don't we have them framed to hang with the other family portraits on the stairs?"

Anna Rose thought of Angus's imposing ancestors who always seemed to be glaring at her from within their gilt frames. Somehow she couldn't see John and Margaret Mackintosh fitting in with the Scottish nobility that graced Rosedhu's walls.

"No, Angus. I'd like to keep them here in my Bible. They aren't for sharing, and they're really not very good. I was a mere child when I cut these."

"A very talented child!" he said, smiling up at her with pride. *Dear, dear Anna Rose,* he thought. *How can I break the news to you?*

It had been wise of Margaret Mackintosh to write to him instead of directly to her daughter, for the death of Anna Rose's father was sure to upset her terribly. For so long now, she had dreamed aloud to Angus of her whole family's coming here to be together again.

"Angus, I think I'll go out for a stroll along the dike while you finish your work."

She was once more clutching the Bible to her breast. Angus knew she wanted to be alone—to think, to remember, to plan the future.

"A fine idea, darling. It's a lovely afternoon. I wish I could go with you, but . . ." He made a wide gesture with his arms, indicating the ledgers spread out before him.

Anna Rose came to him, smiled, and kissed his cheek. "Don't work too hard, darling."

Once she was gone, Angus made no further attempt to mask his grim mood. The letter from Margaret Mackintosh had arrived in Darien by steamer the night before. Pride had delivered it to him this morning with the rest of the mail. He opened the envelope and reread the somber message.

April 20, 1837
Inverness, Scotland

My dear Major Campbell,

I cannot tell you how pleased I was with my daughter's news of her upcoming marriage to you. I pray by now you are happily man and wife. Treat her gently and lovingly and you will want for no amount of returned affection, I assure you.

I must thank you again for the passage money you

sent and for your kind invitation to join you and my daughter as soon as possible. I am sure Anna Rose has told you how this entire family has longed to come to America. It has been a family dream for so long. It was my poor John's fondest wish.

But, alas, I must convey sad news. Not all of the family will be coming. My dear husband departed this world on Thursday last, peacefully, I thank God, while he slept. No finer man nor dearer mate ever walked the face of the earth. But he had suffered long by the time he was called from us, so that his release came as a blessing.

I am writing to you, Major Campbell, hoping that you will find a way to soften the blow for our dear Anna Rose. She was her father's favorite. After she left us, he spoke of her so often, and always as if she were still in our midst. I know that she has suffered a great deal since her departure from us. I hate to spoil her happiness now. So I count on your maturity and wisdom to make her see that this was God's will.

As for our travel plans, I am afraid we have none at present. There is so much to do here before we leave. And, too, my little grandson Shane has taken ill. The doctor says a sea voyage at this time would be dangerous for him. But we shall come! That I promise you! I will let you know the moment our plans are decided.

My dearest love and best wishes to you and your sweet bride.

> With fondest regards,
> Margaret Mackintosh

With a heavy sigh, Angus slumped back in his deep leather chair. As much as he would prefer to put it off indefinitely, his decision was made. He must tell Anna Rose immediately, then allow her time to mourn. But it would be one of the most difficult tasks he had ever undertaken.

The island was at its loveliest in late May. Already the seed rice had been planted in trenches and the fields flooded for six days, then drained. The rice was sprouting, new and green. In fact, the entire vista looked as if it had been given a coat of fresh green paint. The marshes, which had been dead-brown all winter, now glowed with life. Bees hummed in the wild honeysuckle that blossomed yellow and white over fence posts and hedges. The Indian azaleas were a riot of bright pink in the woods. And tiny red and white flowers starred the lacy cypress vines that climbed the oaks.

Anna Rose dreaded the thought of leaving Rosedhu in a few days. How could Angus bear to desert Campbell Island when it was at its most beautiful? Still, the cottage at The Ridge had been delightful last summer. It would be even nicer this year. As Angus's wife, she would be the true mistress. She knew, too, that soon the misty morning haze would turn to a poisonous miasma that would cling to the land, the water, and the marshes, threatening to strike down any white person it found. And now, more than ever, she must guard her health.

She hadn't told Angus yet; she wanted to be certain before she said anything. But she was almost sure she was carrying his child. All the signs pointed to it. Every day that passed she became more convinced. The sheer joy she experienced each waking hour and even in her dreams seemed proof positive that a new life was quickening within her body. What a miracle! What a gift! And soon her whole family would be here to share her joy.

Anna Rose, smiling at her secret, wandered on along the narrow pathway atop the dike. The river was placid today, as if it too were in a pleasant frame of mind. The orange trees shading the walk still gave off the heady perfume that would forevermore remind her of her wedding day. But most of the blossoms were gone now, leaving tiny green nubs in their places. Soon these would grow large and ripen to gold as the trees bore their fruit. She stopped to touch one of the embryonic oranges, feeling a surge of empathy for the mother tree.

"Hallo!" The man's voice carried across the water to her.

She shaded her eyes against the afternoon glare of the sun and spied a canoe drawing along toward the landing. It was brightly painted, yellow and green, but she didn't recognize it. Some traveler, perhaps, from a distant plantation upriver. She waved back in welcome. Angus had taught her that Rosedhu was a refuge for all river traffic. Both friend and passing stranger were to be accorded their full measure of Campbell hospitality.

As she stood watching the boat draw nearer, she saw that it carried two passengers, but no boatmen. The man who had called out to her was rowing it himself. The person with him was much smaller and almost hidden beneath a wide-brimmed straw hat. His wife, Anna Rose assumed. But as she hurried to the dock, she saw that the long golden hair belonged not to a woman, but to a child. And the man was none other than Hugh Sinclair.

Anna Rose stopped in her tracks. Her heart fluttered with excitement. "Heather!" she murmured.

She watched as Hugh tossed the line to one of the dockhands, then scooped up the tiny girl and leaped to the platform with her clinging to his neck. Heather turned toward Anna Rose, smiled, and waved. Soon, Anna Rose was running to greet them.

Heather, although she was only two, seemed to remember her former nurse. Anna Rose smiled, thinking that Hugh must have refreshed her daughter's memory. Heather went into her arms without hesitation, babbling on and on with childish prattle. Anna Rose couldn't stop hugging and kissing her.

Hugh stood by, watching the two of them, and laughing. "She wouldn't give me a moment's rest until I rowed her over to see you, Anna Rose. Once I told her you were here, I knew no peace."

Still cuddling her daughter, Anna Rose said, "You should have brought her with you the last time you came, Hugh."

"To a wedding? That would have been frowned upon by some of your guests. Besides, I had no idea you were to be the bride. I only came because Angus has done so much for me and I wanted to wish him well." A shadow crossed his features suddenly. "To be honest, had I known in advance that he was marrying you, Anna Rose, I'm not sure I would have had the heart to come."

Anna Rose turned from him quickly and started toward the house, carrying Heather. It hurt to hear such words. There was nothing between them any longer; there couldn't be. Their love had been wrong from the start. Now it was finished! Hugh must realize that. *She* must realize that!

"Come along!" she called back over her shoulder. "Angus will be anxious to see you and to meet Hea—Charity." She must remember not to make that slip again. She would have to force herself once more into thinking as well as speaking of her daughter by her other name.

She smiled down into the little girl's pretty face. More than ever, Charity looked like Rory, with her gentian blue eyes and her open, innocent expression. Her cheeks were round and rosy, and the rebellious lock of corn-colored hair she'd inherited from her father refused to stay tucked up beneath its pink ribbon. Anna Rose kissed her nose and Charity giggled and gave her an openmouthed smack in return.

"My little love!" Anna Rose said squeezing her with delight.

"Well, what have we here?" Angus, finished with his work, stood on the front piazza watching Anna Rose and their guests approach. He had a wide welcoming smile on his tanned face.

"This is Hugh's daughter, Charity," she said. "Isn't she a beauty, Angus? And she's as bright as she is pretty."

Angus knelt down and stretched out his arms to the child. When Anna Rose set her on her feet, she ran to Angus as if he were her long-lost grandfather. He scooped her up and swung her in a wide arc over his head. Anna Rose started toward them, concerned that Angus might frighten the child. But when Charity squealed with glee, Anna Rose stood back, watching the two of them and thinking what a fine father her husband would be.

"Hello, Angus!" Hugh called. "I see you've met my daughter already."

"Met her and claimed her!" Angus replied. "But I doubt she's yours."

Anna Rose stiffened at the words.

"If she is, your wife must have been a beauty of the highest order, Hugh Sinclair. For no sea-bitten Galloway man ever produced such an exquisite jewel as Charity."

Both men laughed. Charity giggled and tugged at Angus's sleeve, begging to be tossed over his head again. Anna Rose breathed a sigh of relief, still shaken by her husband's innocent remark.

Hugh explained that Charity and he could stay for only a brief visit. They were on their way to Darien to do some shopping and to check stage schedules to Savannah. While having lemonade in the parlor, Hugh told the Campbells of his growing concern over the coming fever season.

"You'd never know it to look at her now, but Charity was ill a good bit last winter. I don't want her staying at The Highlands during the hot months. I thought we'd travel up to Savannah. I'm sure I can find a small house for my daughter and Willow."

"Willow?" Anna Rose asked.

"My Indian housekeeper. I hate to think how I'll manage without her, but Charity needs her more."

"You don't mean you're planning to stay on at the plantation through the summer, man?" Angus's shock was clear in his tone.

"I've little choice. The place needs more care after years of neglect than I can give it unless I'm there. I'm remodeling entirely. But you needn't worry about me. Believe me, Angus, in my travels I've had a touch of every fever known to man. I believe I'm as immune as the slaves that work the rice swamps. I'll be fine."

Anna Rose cast a cautious look toward her husband. Dared she propose aloud what she was thinking?

"But Savannah's so far," Angus protested. "And your little girl's without her mother. She shouldn't have to be exiled from her father as well. Especially after you've been apart for the year you were at sea. Why don't you find a place at The Ridge? Then when you have a few free hours, you could come visit her."

"Charity could stay with us." Anna Rose allowed the words to rush out, afraid she might lose her courage if she spoke too slowly.

The two men were staring at her when she looked up. As she watched, her husband smiled and nodded. But Hugh's suntanned face wore a deep frown.

"What a fine idea!" Angus agreed. "It will be a joy to have a child in my house again."

Hugh looked down at his hands and shook his head. "I couldn't impose any more than I have already."

"Anna Rose?" Angus said. "Would you feel it an imposition to have little Charity with us?"

"A joy, as you said, Angus!" she replied softly. "I feel almost as if she's my own child." She stopped herself, afraid to say more.

Hugh turned to his daughter, who had been eyeing a plate of cookies longingly. He held out his arms to her and took her on his lap. "Charity, how would you like to have Anna Rose take care of you again?"

The little girl's eyes sparkled and she nodded so vigorously that her blond curls danced about her face.

Hugh looked up, smiling. "Well, I suppose it's all settled, then, if you're sure. I can't tell you what a weight this takes off my mind. I hadn't fancied the idea of Charity's being way off in Savannah all summer and fall."

Anna Rose was fighting tears. The thought of having her daughter all summer long was almost more than she could bear. Nothing, nothing in the world could spoil this glorious day!

Angus waited until they were alone in their bedroom to speak with Anna Rose. He hated to spoil her special mood; he'd even pondered putting off his duty until after he had loved her tenderly and thoroughly. But that would be unfair. The sooner she knew the truth, the better for everyone. The next few days would be difficult at best, with the move to the cottage and everything in turmoil. She needed these final few days at Rosedhu to deal with the news. Then when they reached the summer house, he hoped that she would feel she had left the sadness behind. Having Hugh's little daughter with them would help, he was sure.

He stood at a window, gazing out over the broad lawn that stretched to the canal. The twin magnolias glowed with huge, waxy-white blossoms. The moon was an enormous silver disk hanging low over the river. It had been a hot day, but the night air was balmy. The scent of early summer flowers wafted in through the open windows.

"Anna Rose," he said softly, "you aren't asleep, are you?"

"No, Angus. I'm too excited to sleep. Think of it! A whole summer to have Charity with us! We'll have such a grand time!"

"I'm sure we will, my dear."

Anna Rose, suddenly attuned to her husband's somber mood, sat up in bed and stared at his back. "Angus, is anything wrong? You sound so strange. You aren't having second thoughts about keeping Charity, are you?"

"Of course not, dear!" He turned slowly and went to sit beside her on the bed. Tenderly, he bent to kiss her lips, then he smoothed the bright tendrils of hair back from her forehead.

"Anna Rose, you have made my life complete. I'll never be able to thank you or repay you for what you've done for me. When we met, I was an old man, seeing no future before me and very little in my past to recommend it. You changed all that, my dearest. There is nothing in this world I wouldn't do for you. But there are things I can't do, hurts that I can't bear for you."

"Angus, you're frightening me. What are you talking about?"

"A season for all things," he said quietly. "A time to live and a time to die."

"Oh, Angus!" she cried, throwing her arms around his neck and clinging to him. "You aren't ill?"

"No, love," he answered softly, "only sick at heart that I must give you bad news. It's your father."

"Papa?" Anna Rose's small voice sounded like a child's.

"He passed away some weeks ago. Your mother wrote to me, hoping I could soften the blow when I told you. But how does one lessen such a loss?"

She sobbed softly against his chest for some time, then looked up at him through tear-starred lashes. "Did he suffer?"

"Not at the end. Your mother wrote that he went peacefully in his sleep."

"Thank God for that!"

For hours, Anna Rose lay in her husband's arms, crying softly, going back over her life as if she were turning pages in a well-loved book. Her father was there in every chapter—big, strong, laughing John Mackintosh. But her book ended all too abruptly, on her wedding day to Rory.

I should never have left! she thought miserably.

If only she had been there, she was convinced she might have made his last days and hours easier. Then she chided herself silently for such thoughts. Her mother, she was sure, had done everything she could to make his final days pleasant and to ease her husband's passing. They had all known that the end was in sight. Now, at least, the bad times were behind them, and her father would know no more pain.

"Angus?" she said at length.

"Yes, my darling?"

"I'm all right now, I think. I loved my father dearly, but I can accept his death. It will take me some time to adjust to the idea of his being gone. But, as you said, there is a season for all things. A time to live and a time to die. One passes on and another is born to take his place." She seemed to be talking to herself more than to him. "Angus?"

"What, my darling?"

This seemed the time to Anna Rose, the very time to soften sorrow with hope. "When our son is born, may I name him John after my father? It would please me so. And I know it would make my mother happy."

Angus stared at her. She was almost smiling, although tears still glowed damply on her face. "Anna Rose, are you telling me . . . ?"

"Yes, love, yes! I'm carrying your child. Our child."

"Anna Rose, my dearest, dearest heart!" He buried his face in her hair and wept with her.

The black night sky had turned to the pearl gray of dawn before they finally slept, still clinging to each other, but dreaming of future happiness, not pondering past woes.

25

Anna Rose and Angus Campbell were the talk of the Ridge society that summer. As yet, no one could tell by looking that Anna Rose was with child, and it would have been unseemly for Angus to go about bragging of his own prowess in bed. But they knew. They all knew! The women, as they sipped lemonade on their shaded piazzas, whispered about it behind their palmetto fans, and the men, over cards, made coarse jokes about "Angus, that damned old stallion—too ancient to race, but still a frisky enough stud when it came time to mount his mare."

The word spread like wildfire thanks to the servants' grapevine.

Of course, Dahlia was one of the first to know her mistress's secret. She in turn whispered it to Hagar, the cook, who told an upstairs maid, who confided in a cousin over at Butler Plantation. And so the tendrils of the grapevine reached and stretched and wound themselves throughout all the rice plantations of the low country. Soon the owners and their wives were plucking the ripe, juicy fruit from the summer's fastest growing vine and savoring its delicious novelty.

The word spread all the way to Charleston by a roundabout route. A planter from South Carolina's upcountry had been down in Florida, visiting his ailing brother. On the way home, late in July, he stopped off at Saint Simons Island to spend a few days with the King family at Retreat Plantation. The news had reached that place, via a slave from Darien who had married one of the Retreat women. The South Carolina planter heard the tale while riding over the island with his host.

The South Carolinian found the story most amusing. A rather elderly gentleman himself—not at all looking forward to turning sixty in the fall—the planter decided to retell the tale in Charleston to a pretty prostitute, claiming that he himself was the great stud, but also mentioning that the same thing had happened to the master of Rosedhu Plantation, and wasn't that a coincidence!

His lady of the evening respun the yarn for the amusement of her sisters in sin, who had a good laugh over such wild happenings. They decided that it must be something in the swamp miasmas the rice people feared so. And they all agreed that were they wives of aging rice planters, they too would fear such an infection.

The owner of this house of ill repute happened upon their laughter and demanded to know what he'd missed. When one girl told her boss the whole tale, the tall man frowned and fixed a hard gaze on the woman as he demanded, "You're certain the man said *Rosedhu* Plantation?"

"Aye, that it was! A rice swamp down in Georgia, named for a bloomin' black rose!" The woman howled anew, curling her carmine-tinted lips.

It took Weyman Campbell the rest of the day to set the affairs of his Charleston establishment in order. But by the following morning he was on a steamer bound for Savannah, then on to Darien.

During the whole trip, his mind was churning with anger. So, his father had finally done as he'd threatened to do for so many years. Angus had warned his son that if he refused to settle down and take his rightful place in the family, which included dull plantation duties, he might lose his position as sole heir to the

Campbell fortune. Weyman had scoffed at the old man's words. Angus Campbell was well past the age to marry, much less father more children, or so his son had imagined.

Weyman had received the wedding invitation some months before, flipping it aside with hardly a glance. A Scottish woman, by her name. No doubt some wealthy widow who would double the fortune due him one day soon. He'd wished the old man a good, short life and celebrated that night by getting royally drunk with one of the girls.

But if this rumor of a child was true, the whole complexion of his future had changed. He leaned over the railing of the boat, watching the golden isles slip past in the distance. The scene was familiar, but brought no tug of sentimentality to his heart. He hated the plantation—the dank smell of the mud flats, the isolation, the mosquitoes, the sameness of everything. And now, most of all, he hated his father—for making good his threat to produce another heir and so forcing his firstborn to return home.

The Ridge was a charming settlement, three miles distance from the bustling little town of Darien. Set on a bluff overlooking the salt marshes, the summer cottages neatly lined either side of a wide shell-paved road, shaded by huge moss-hung oaks. The houses, with their broad piazzas and high-ceilinged rooms, caught the cool salt breezes from the sea, but kept their owners safe from the deadly miasmas that breathed fever over the lower lands in hot weather.

Angus Campbell's "Rosebud" was one of the larger homes, almost too spacious to be called a cottage. Made of the native tabby, with walls twelve inches thick for insulation and the roof cedar-shingled to let hot air escape, the house was always cool and pleasant. The rooms were smaller than those at Rosedhu, but still very comfortable. There were four bedrooms upstairs and a parlor, a dining room, and Angus's study downstairs. Wide, central halls ran through both floors, front to back. These dogtrots, as they were called, allowed the sea breezes to waft through the house, cooling and freshening as they passed. The furnishings were lighter and less formal than those at Rosedhu, with bright chintz upholstery and light, lacy curtains that fluttered prettily at the open windows in the constant breeze.

Anna Rose's favorite spot was the back piazza. The wide porch was large enough for summer dances and barbecues, but most of the time it was where the mistress received afternoon guests or sat in the shade and entertained little Charity with games and stories. The piazza was completely overhung by an ancient wisteria vine thick with fragrant purple clusters. Bees hummed among the blossoms, adding their soothing song to the hot, lazy afternoons.

It was there on just such a day in August that Anna Rose first met her stepson, Weyman Campbell. Dahlia had carried Charity upstairs for her nap only a few moments before. Since the day was so hot and humid, none of Anna Rose's neighbors had bestirred themselves this afternoon to go visiting. She didn't mind the solitude at all. In fact, she rather enjoyed the absence of her neighbors' never-ceasing gossip.

"You ought to be upstairs, taking a rest under your net, 'stead of settin' out here in the heat just temptin' any ole skeeter that comes along, Miz Anna Rose." Dahlia had given her a thorough scolding before carrying Charity upstairs. Anna Rose had really meant to follow the servant's advice. But leaning back in her big white wicker chair, and rocking slowly in time to the drone of the bees, she had almost nodded off where she was. Only when she heard the faint crunch of boots on the drive did her eyes open.

"Angus," she said, delighted, thinking that he had returned early from Rosedhu. But instead, she saw a stranger approaching. He was tall and slender, not powerfully built so far as she could see from the loose-fitting, white linen suit he wore. A wide-brimmed hat shaded his face, but she could see even from a distance that his hair—the tawny-brown color of marsh grass in winter—was long and straight, brushing his open collar. As he strode nearer, she saw his face. He was clean-shaven and almost as beautiful as a girl. Only the iciness of his pale blue eyes marred the perfection.

"Afternoon, ma'am." He spoke with what Anna Rose had come to recognize as a "Geechee drawl," an affectation normal among gentlemen from Savannah or coastal South Carolina.

Anna Rose sat up and shaded her eyes. He had not yet reached the piazza and the bright afternoon sun on his white suit was all but blinding.

"Hello," she answered. She was somewhat at a loss, unused to gentlemen callers presenting themselves unannounced. Should she invite him up for refreshment? She wasn't certain. Just then the door opened behind her and the ever-watchful Dahlia came onto the porch, taking up her silent post behind her mistress's chair.

"Won't you come up for a glass of lemonade?" she asked, made bold now by the other woman's presence.

"Thank you, ma'am. That's kind of you. It's been a mighty dry walk from the docks."

Anna Rose glanced back at Dahlia, who suddenly wore a disapproving frown.

"You walked all the way from Darien?" Anna Rose said incredulously. "Dahlia, bring another tumbler, quickly please."

The housekeeper was truly scowling now. "Miz Anna Rose, I don't think . . ."

"Now, Dahlia!" she commanded, annoyed by the woman's balking. "You can see for yourself the young man is hot and thirsty. What would Major Campbell say if we kept a guest waiting?"

Dahlia turned to obey, but not without a few words of disapproval muttered under her breath. Anna Rose couldn't figure the woman's reaction.

"Won't you come up and have a seat?" she invited. "My husband should be home anytime now."

The man drew nearer, removed his hat, and stood staring at her almost too appraisingly, his pale eyes aglitter with something akin to amusement. Anna Rose grew uncomfortable under his gaze. Such open evaluation of a woman—especially one obviously with child—was not befitting a gentleman. To distract him, she once more mentioned Angus.

He laughed softly. "Angus Campbell is your husband, ma'am?"

"Yes, he is. I assumed you knew that."

He was still chuckling as he drawled, "Then I s'pose I ought to call you 'Mother.'"

Anna Rose's fingers flew to her lips to stifle a cry of surprise and dismay. For months now, she had planned so carefully for her first meeting with Angus's son, should that day ever come. She had assumed that he would write ahead before he came for a visit. She would plan a dinner party to reintroduce him to their friends, at which time she would act the gracious and matronly hostess. A fitting mate for her worldly and far more mature husband.

But this was all wrong! Here she was, collapsed in a chair after playing with Charity, her slippers kicked off, and her plain cotton frock covered up by an even plainer white apron, identical to the ones the servants wore while doing chores. Her hair was loose about her shoulders, and curls, damp from the humidity, fringed her face. All in all, she surmised, she must look a mess.

"You're Weyman?" she gasped, sitting up straighter, patting her hair in place, and trying to regain some of her composure.

"I am indeed!" He bowed slightly to her. "The prodigal son, ma'am, come home at last."

"Do sit down, won't you? Oh, your father will be so surprised and pleased!"

Again he laughed, but the sound was humorless. "Surprised?

Most certainly, ma'am. But pleased? Somehow, I have difficulty picturing that, little Mother."

Anna Rose blushed when he called her that. Did he really mean to address her as *mother*? Or was he referring to her present state—something no gentleman should do? In either case, it made her highly uncomfortable. And it was ridiculous besides, since he was obviously several years her senior. She made some quick calculations in her head. She was nineteen now, and Weyman Campbell would soon turn thirty. Yes, there was quite an age difference! Far too much for him to be addressing her in such a fashion.

Weyman was sitting across from her now, his long legs stretched out between them, boots crossed at the ankles. He dangled the hat from one finger as he continued staring at her with a bemused smirk on his face.

"I received the wedding invitation."

Anna Rose avoided his unsettling gaze. "We'd hoped you'd come."

"I doubt that!"

She shot him a warning look, angered by his attitude. "Your father wanted you here. He really did! You should have come for his sake."

He sat up straighter, acknowledging her chastisement. "A thousand pardons, Mother dear!"

"Don't call me that!" she snapped. "My name is Anna Rose, and since I'm so much younger than you, your calling me mother is a silly notion."

"No sillier than the fact that you are my legal stepmother," he hurled back at her. "Why on earth did you marry him? For his money? Surely, you could have found a younger man with equal wealth."

Anna Rose was beginning to understand why Angus had such difficulty with his son. Weyman Campbell was smug, conceited, devious, and insulting. An all-around unpleasant person.

"Not that it's any of your concern, sir, but I married your father for love!"

Weyman threw back his head and laughed long and hard. "Oh, come now!" he managed at length. "A pretty young thing like you? In love with a man who's so close to death that he's already had himself fitted for his coffin?"

"What a terrible thing to say about your own father!" she gasped. "And it's not true!"

"Dahlia, tell her!"

Anna Rose was so upset that she hadn't heard the woman when she returned to the porch.

"Go ahead, tell her," Weyman prompted.

Anna Rose turned and stared at the servant, her gaze demanding an answer, until Dahlia finally nodded her head.

"You see! It is true! He had himself measured for it years ago, shortly after Mother died. Then one winter he had the grippe, and being the tightfisted old scoundrel he is, not wanting anyone else to choose the materials for his box because they might spend too much, he had his coffin made to his own specifications. He carries it with him every year. From Rosedhu to the cottage in spring, then back to the plantation attic in the fall. Just in case. Why do you think the attic stairs are always kept down?"

"Here's your lemonade, sir!"

Dahlia slapped the tumbler on the table in front of him with such force that some of the drink sloshed onto his dusty trouser leg. He leveled a furious glare at her which she returned in kind.

"You worthless idiot! See what you've done. I ought to have you tied and whipped!"

"Stop that!" Anna Rose cried. "I won't have anyone threatening one of my servants!"

Weyman smiled his slow unpleasant smile and raised his glass to Anna Rose. "Sorry, ma'am," he drawled. "I forgot my place for a moment. I also forgot how loose and easy my daddy is with his niggers, especially the womenfolk. Course you know all about him and Dahlia here?"

Anna Rose sipped her drink silently, refusing to rise to his bait. But that failed to stop him.

"After I was born, you see, the doctor told Daddy that he better leave off pesterin' my mother. Well, that must have come as quite a blow to him. By looking at you," his gaze strayed to the rise beneath Anna Rose's apron, "anyone can tell that you know what he's like, even now that he's old. Imagine how, as a young man, he must have taken the news that he would no longer be permitted in his own wife's bed. But there was Dahlia—fine and musky with wantin' it, and not yet dropped a sucker. Yes, sir, she was ripe and ready and my daddy went right to the scent like a hog in rutting season!"

He paused, holding up his glass and staring at it, smiling, as if he could see the whole horrible scene he was describing.

Suddenly, his gaze darted to Dahlia and his smile broadened to a leering grin. "And how's my half brother Pride these days? Still Daddy's favorite boy?"

Anna Rose gasped aloud. From behind her, she heard Dahlia make a strangled sound of denial.

Just then, Angus rode up the drive with Pride beside him. They dismounted, and Pride led the horses away toward the stable.

289

"Hallo!" Angus called. "Company, I see."

Her husband was in a grand mood, Anna Rose could tell. She had to warn him. Quickly, she got up and ran down the walk to meet him.

"Darling, you shouldn't be out in this hot sun," he fussed good-heartedly.

She was clinging to his arm, trying to slow his progress until she could speak with him.

"I've missed you, Angus!" Her tone sounded as desperate as she felt.

He laughed and brushed her warm forehead with his lips. "But I've been gone only a few hours, darling. Still, it's nice to hear. Who's our guest?" Weyman's back was to them and he was partially hidden by one of the columns supporting the roof.

"Angus, please! Listen to me." She pulled at his arm so determinedly that he finally stopped to hear her out. "It's Weyman!"

First he frowned, then smiled. "Well, bless me! He's finally come home. I couldn't be more pleased."

"He's come back to start trouble, Angus." Anna Rose's voice was trembling as she spoke the words. "You've got to send him away!"

Her husband patted her hand and smiled down at her. "Now, darling, let's give the boy a chance. Perhaps he's changed. He probably came to meet you and, I would hope, to mend a few fences. Let's don't jump to any dire conclusions before we know the truth of the matter. Come along now. It's been years since I laid eyes on the lad."

Anna Rose felt limp, deflated, and helpless. If Angus refused to listen to her, then he would be meeting his armed opponent defenseless. But there was nothing more she could do.

The meeting went worse than she had anticipated. By the time they reached the piazza, Weyman Campbell was a changed man. Gone were his vicious leer and his hurtful, sarcastic words. He embraced his father, then faced him with tearful eyes, saying, "Can you ever forgive me? I was almost afraid to come home after all the pain I've caused you over the years."

By the look on her husband's face, Anna Rose could tell that these were the words Angus had prayed to hear for ever so long. He actually believed his son! Anna Rose knew that Angus was anything but a fool. But even the wisest man could be duped by as clever a trickster as Weyman Campbell. She sat by, seething silently, as father and son talked at length. It was obvious that Weyman knew what was expected of him and had come here to play out his charade to perfection. Anna Rose let him talk on and on, thinking that he had undone himself by behaving so badly before Angus arrived. Once she and her husband were alone, she would tell him all that had happened earlier. Angus would not be fooled for long!

But later, when they were in their bedroom dressing for supper and Anna Rose took the opportunity to warn Angus about his son's dual character, he dismissed her concern.

"Darling, he didn't mean to be impolite to you. Weyman is often misunderstood because he speaks bluntly. Why, he told me after you came upstairs how delighted he is that I've married you! He even said he'd suggested calling you Mother, but that you flew into a mild rage at the idea." Angus paused and chuckled. "It seems to me that you and Weyman simply got off on the wrong footing, my dear. He's grown into a fine, steady man. Give yourself time to get to know him before you make any judgments against him. That's all I ask."

"But, Angus, you don't understand!" Anna Rose was frantic, seeing how her husband had been hoodwinked by his son. "He said terrible things about you!"

"Such as?" Angus's smile had faded. He was obviously concerned about what she had to say.

"Have you had your coffin made?"

He laughed. "Oh, that! Yes, my darling, I must admit to that bit of morbid folly. You see, after Clara died, I was beside myself with grief. I really had no desire to continue life without her. Then I fell ill, and well, you can understand, can't you?"

She hung her head. He made it sound like a natural thing to do. And indeed, it was the sort of thing that would have shocked a son who had just suffered the loss of one parent.

But what about Weyman's tale about Angus and Dahlia? *No!* she decided. She could not bring herself to talk about that. Perhaps there had been something between them long ago, but not any longer. At any rate, she didn't want to know.

Still, there was the way Weyman had looked at her, measuring her as if she were some slave girl on the block.

"Is there anything else bothering you, my dear?" Angus sounded so gentle, so concerned.

"I don't like the way he looks at me," she admitted quietly.

Angus pulled her into his arms and hugged her. "Darling, I don't like the way any other man looks at you, but there's little I can do about it short of calling each and every one of them out for pistols at dawn. We must both face the fact that you are a most beautiful and fascinating woman. I can't blame my son for finding

291

you attractive. Were you free, he'd no doubt pay court to you himself."

So, with easy answers, Angus dismissed all of his wife's misgivings concerning her stepson. Over supper, Angus seemed oblivious to the way Weyman kept staring at her, sending private messages with his cold blue eyes.

In the weeks that followed, Anna Rose suffered silently. Only she and Dahlia were allowed to see that dark side Weyman Campbell possessed. When he was with his father, he seemed to be everything that Angus had ever dreamed his son might be. Angus was overjoyed that finally his boy had come to see the light. There was no talking to him, Anna Rose discovered. From the mildest complaint to the most serious charge, Angus simply refused to hear any unfavorable comments about his son.

Finally, in mid-September, Anna Rose breathed with relief when Weyman announced that business called him back to Charleston. He had been very vague about exactly what his business was—something to do with real estate, he'd hinted. He'd mentioned owning several houses.

On the bright fall morning that he was to depart, Weyman rose early to bid farewell to his father over breakfast. Angus was needed at Rosedhu that day. Father and son had planned to ride as far as Darien together, but Weyman found some excuse at the last moment to keep him at the cottage.

Anna Rose awoke to a great feeling of release.

"He's gone!" were her first words as she yawned and stretched, feeling deliciously free of a heavy burden.

The knock at her door came right on cue—Dahlia with her tea, she supposed, and called, "Come in."

"Ah, little Mother, how fresh and tempting you look first thing in the morning!"

Anna Rose gasped and clutched the sheet to her breast. "What are you doing here? I thought you'd left already. Get out!"

Weyman came toward the bed, smiling, his eyes busy with the sight of her. He sat down beside her and reached out to cup her warm cheek. Anna Rose drew away, but he only laughed and leaned closer.

"I'll scream," she choked out.

"No, you won't." His voice was quiet, deadly. "If you should do anything so foolish, I'll have any servants who come to your aid whipped soundly before I leave. Then I'll stop over at Rosedhu and explain to *dear Father* that there's been some

292

trouble . . . that when you called me to your room to say good-bye, I went in all innocence, but that you . . ."

"You wouldn't!" she cried, knowing full well that he would.

"And which of us do you think he would believe? After all, I'm his son, your stepson, and I've told him how much I respect you. On the other hand, he thinks that you feel nothing but jealousy toward me, that you are convinced I've come back here to claim my share of his fortune and to make trouble between the two of you."

"And haven't you?"

"Ah, you and I know that, but father is as ignorant of the fact as an innocent babe. I promise you, *my darling mother,* that your husband will not take kindly to any words you say against me."

Anna Rose felt her blood turning to ice. He spoke the awful truth. The child she carried would never be as dear to Angus as this terrible first son. Angus's sole heir had won his father's approval completely in these past weeks. She was totally at his mercy now.

She stiffened as the hand touching her cheek crept up, the fingers twisting in her hair, forcing her head back.

"Please, no," she gasped, but his lips were on her throat, his teeth nipping the soft flesh beneath her jaw.

She lashed out with clenched fists, trying to beat him off. But he caught her wrists in a bruising grip and shoved her farther back into the pillows. She could do nothing to ward off his advances.

After it was over and he had gone at last, Anna Rose lay aching, inside and out. She felt dirtied from his touch, his kisses. Still, she was thankful and amazed that he hadn't raped her. She shuddered and moaned into her pillow, remembering his promise, his threat: "I hate to leave you unsated, *Mother,* but I find the idea of coupling with a pregnant woman most repulsive. However, our time will come. I'll be back, say in the spring. You'll be yourself again by then, and I promise you, the next child you carry will be mine!"

All day she stayed in bed, too weak and drained to move. Dahlia hovered about, sponging her fevered brow, urging tea and broth, fussing and worrying over her. She wanted to call the doctor from Darien, but Anna Rose would not allow it.

"I'll be all right, Dahlia, really. I'm just tired today."

It was a lame excuse, but the servant accepted it and let her be. When Angus returned that evening, he was all concern, alarmed that the baby might come too early. But finally, he brightened, saying, "I know your trouble, darling. It's Weyman, isn't it?"

Anna Rose felt the blood drain from her face at his words. She went weak all over.

"You're just feeling depressed and let down because he's gone. I know exactly what you're experiencing. I've felt the same way all day. It was such a pleasure having him here. We'll both miss him, but he'll be back, my dear."

Anna Rose sighed, and buried her face against Angus's chest, trying to stop her trembling. "Yes, my darling. I'm sure the way I feel is because of your son."

26

Hugh Sinclair stood at the upstairs bedroom window of The Highlands, watching a late-September storm sweep over the island to drench the land and whip the river to a fury. For the most part, he could see nothing outside in the darkness, only fat raindrops splatting on the glass and his own grim reflection by the light of the lamp on the table. But from time to time, great sheets of lightning lit the sky, turning the landscape below—the gnarled oaks, the wind-twisted cedars, the endless black marshes—into a nightmare setting. The scene and the storm suited his mood. The thunder that followed rattled the windows and seemed to shake the very foundations of the house, matching the dull thud of his heart.

"Damn this godforsaken place!" he cried, slamming his heavy tumbler of whiskey down on the table.

He fell down on the rumpled bed. He'd tried to sleep. For hours, he'd tried. He needed rest. He'd ridden miles today, from before sunup until long after dark, checking fences and dikes, marking timber to be cut for the sawmill in Darien, inspecting repairs to the slave cabins that he'd ordered weeks before. Every day was as busy and as exhausting as the one before it; he saw to that. If he didn't actually have work to do, he manufactured tasks, for at present, idleness could prove his ruin.

He pounded his pillows into shape, reached again for his glass, and refilled it with more amber liquid. Then he stared at the drink, smiled, and sighed. "Ah, my good and faithful friend! What would I do without you?" He tossed the whiskey off in a single long swallow.

A welcome sting bit into his throat and gut. But after the fire died, the pain and emptiness remained. Hugh Sinclair was a man beset by devils—demons of his own making, but nonetheless real to him.

Hugh closed his eyes and let his thoughts drift—a dangerous proposition. Before long his mental ship had sailed to warm, familiar waters. "Anna Rose!" He sighed the name. It tasted good on his tongue, far better than the whiskey he'd been drinking.

All summer, since the day he'd delivered Charity into Anna Rose's keeping at the cottage, he had forced himself to stay away, sending messages often, but always pleading too much work to visit. He had missed his daughter, but he had missed Anna Rose far more. Convinced she was dead, he had almost managed to conquer his grief. But finding her again—alive, but wed to Angus Campbell—had brought a new kind of pain, a unique brand of torture. So he was living like a cloistered monk at The Highlands these long, hot months, hoping to rid his thoughts of her by keeping his distance. It hadn't worked. Now it was almost time to go collect his daughter, and he both looked forward to and dreaded the prospect.

This wasn't the first time that Hugh felt as if he had crossed some invisible line from one life into the next. Gone was the pitching deck beneath his feet, the woman he had married, his comfortable home in New York, everything that was familiar to him. Now, he was in a strange land, a place of rice swamps and fevers and suspicious black faces, his only comfort being the woman he could never have. He might have adjusted smoothly to this new life, if he had not rediscovered her here. He tried not to think of what life might have been like had he found her in time for them to have a second chance. But boredom and loneliness bred fantasies. There was no way he could control his thoughts, his desires.

Now, weakened by weariness and compelled by too much drink, Hugh allowed himself the luxury to think the thoughts he had been fighting. He closed his eyes and let his memory drift back, first to the ship. It seemed so long ago, but how well he remembered a younger, more innocent Anna Rose. What dreams he had spun as he nursed her back to health after Rory's death! While she was ill, she had been so dependent upon him, so vulnerable, so trusting. He had never imagined that there would be any difficulty in persuading her to marry him.

When Hugh's memory reached the morning of their arrival in New York and Anna Rose's disappearance, he frowned and muttered, thrashed about the bed, then calmed himself again. There were better, happier times to remember.

The parlor of his house . . . the brocade couch . . . and Anna Rose, refusing him at first, then admitting her own love and need, accepting him willingly, eagerly. He could still see her proud breasts, straining for his touch, still feel her warm, pliant body beneath his. Even now her urgent pleas rang in his ears: "Hugh darling, I can't help myself. I want you so . . . I love you!"

Hugh's pleasant visions were shattered by a new crash of thunder and a brilliant bolt of lightening that filled the night sky. He shot up in bed, cursing at the throbbing pain in his groin. He got up. He paced. He poured himself another drink.

The first white frost came unexpectedly in October. Then warm weather returned for a few weeks, causing the rice planters to cast fearful glances toward the southern skies. They muttered beneath their breaths about the storm seasons not being over yet. It had been twelve years since the last killer hurricane. But the span of time, rather than making the planters complacent, only served as a warning that the Georgia coast was due anytime for another fierce tropical storm that would flood the rice fields with salt water and ruin the crops and the economy of the whole area. Each day of October was filled with worry, until at last, November and the second white frost arrived, signaling the advent of the long-awaited black frost and the end of the storm and fever seasons.

The inhabitants of Rosebud cottage were astir with preparations for the move back home on that bright November morning when Hugh Sinclair arrived to fetch his daughter back to The Highlands. He had sent word ahead that he would be coming, in order to give Anna Rose notice in case she wished to be away when he arrived. Now, as he rode up the drive, he damned himself for sending the note. He wanted to see her! God, how he wanted to see her!

But as he rode up the drive to Rosebud cottage, the first person he saw was Charity. She flew out the door, arms wide, crying, "Daddy, Daddy, you're here!"

He dismounted and swept the bright child up into his arms. She was all pink and white and gold with long curls dancing above her frock and pinafore. He held her close and kissed her warm cheek, inhaling her scents of rose soap and rice powder.

"Ah, baby, how you've grown!"

"Don't call me baby, Daddy! Anna Rose says I'm a big girl now." Every word she uttered came out with breathless excitement. She wiggled and squirmed in her father's arms, gesturing toward the house, urging him to enter.

As Hugh mounted the steps, Anna Rose appeared at the door.

For the briefest instant, he caught her in an unguarded moment, watching a look of longing, then pain cross her face. Or had he only imagined what he wanted to see? A moment later, she had full control of herself, smiling an invitation for Hugh to enter as if he were just any guest arriving for a visit.

He smiled back, warmly, admiring the high color of her cheeks and the sparkle of her misty-green eyes, realizing that both were accentuated by impending motherhood. The full, blue gingham gown she wore could no longer conceal the fact that her time was drawing near. Still, Hugh had always considered a woman with child the most beautiful being in God's creation. And in Anna Rose's case, this was especially true.

She was fully aware of his appreciative gaze. In spite of herself, the look he gave her warmed her through, sending little tingles of pleasure along her flesh. Would she ever be able to react normally when Hugh was near her? she wondered.

"You look well, Anna Rose," he said in greeting, pressing her hand.

She laughed. "I look large, my dear friend! No need plying me with compliments at this stage of things."

"Would it be indecent for me to ask how much longer?" Yes, it was indecent for a man to refer to her condition in any way; he knew that. But they had made their way into the parlor, and were alone except for Charity. And, as Anna Rose had said, they were simply "dear friends."

She glanced down shyly and laced her fingers over her apron. "About three more months."

Charity had been standing between them, holding Hugh's leg and Anna Rose's skirts. "I'm going to help with baby Johnnie," she said importantly. "Anna Rose says I can. And it's going to be just like if I had my very own baby brother!"

Hugh laughed and ruffled his daughter's silky hair. "Oh? Is that so, young lady? And just who decided that this will be a boy and that he'll be named Johnnie?"

"Anna Rose says so!" the child announced, grinning with pleasure.

Once again, Anna Rose looked embarrassed, but the blush became her, Hugh thought.

She shrugged and said, "Charity and I make up games together. We got tired of calling the baby 'it,' so we decided he would be a boy. We've a fifty-fifty chance of being right after all. And Angus and I have decided to call a boy John, after my father."

"Then you're hoping for a son?" he asked.

"A healthy baby—boy or girl." Her eyes misted as her gaze lit on her daughter. She touched the child's face lovingly. "One that will never know hunger or loneliness." She said the words softly, almost to herself, recalling with deep pain her first infant's starving wails.

Hugh detected her mood of sudden melancholy. "No child of yours could ever be lonely, Anna Rose," he replied.

Dahlia appeared at the door just then. "'Scuse me, ma'am, but it's time this child changed clothes for her trip home with her daddy. Come with me, Miss Charity."

The little girl still clung to Anna Rose, staring up at her as if she could never get enough of being with this kindly, loving woman. Anna Rose laughed softly and pried Charity's hands from her skirt. "Go along now, sweetheart. You don't want to keep your father waiting."

"I want to stay here, Anna Rose, with you," the child whined.

"But I'll be leaving too, very soon," Anna Rose reasoned gently. "And besides, we'll see each other often once we get home. Your father can bring you to Rosedhu, or perhaps Angus and I can visit The Highlands after Johnnie's born."

"Promise?" Charity asked with sudden elation, a delighted smile lighting her face.

"Yes, I promise! Now run along with Dahlia, dear."

Charity skipped out of the room, leaving Anna Rose alone with Hugh. A long silence passed, seeming to separate them for a time. Finally, Hugh cleared his throat, and asked, "Where's Angus?"

"He's gone ahead to Rosedhu in the big boat. He wanted to make sure everything was in order by the time I arrived. Angus is so afraid I'll overdo."

"He's a wise man, your husband," Hugh agreed. "You shouldn't have to go through a strenuous move in your condition."

She laughed. "I'm not made of china, after all. I'm strong and healthy and there's not the slightest need for everyone to fuss over me so. Why, look at the slave women! They have their babies, sometimes right there in the fields, then immediately go back to their work."

Hugh frowned. "You're not like them, Anna Rose. You mustn't take your condition so lightly. Remember how it was with Madelaine? How she had to stay in bed?"

Anna Rose, without thinking, reached out to him and touched his hand. "Hugh, please don't! It's too painful to think back on all that."

"It would be much more painful if I lost you, too!" he said

without thinking. His deepest feelings came pouring out before he could stop them. "I won't let anything happen to you!"

Anna Rose looked down, embarrassed. She moved slightly away from him. She couldn't allow it to make any difference in the way she felt, but she knew for certain that Hugh's concern for her had nothing to do with promises he'd made to her first husband, or his friendship with the second man she'd married. Hugh Sinclair simply, deeply cared for her. She also knew that with all her might she must try to ignore that reality and the way it tugged at her heart.

"I'm sorry," he whispered. "I never meant . . ." Then suddenly his voice turned hard, almost bitter. "Damnit all, I did mean it, Anna Rose! I just didn't mean to say anything to trouble you."

She didn't answer. She couldn't look at him. All she could do was stand there, wishing she hadn't heard, begging her heart not to listen. How could she love her husband and still love Hugh at the same time? What was she going to do?

After another long silence, Hugh said, "I'll wait on the piazza until Charity's ready to go."

When Anna Rose only nodded, he turned and strode out.

Anna Rose slumped to a chair as soon as he was gone. She brushed furiously at her tears, not wanting the servants or Charity to see that she'd been crying. But she couldn't stop. Seeing Hugh again, hearing the words he spoke so fervently, had released a wellspring of suppressed emotions.

Why did everything have to change? The past months had seemed an enchanted time, having her daughter with her and the new baby on the way. Occasionally, she had allowed herself to think of Hugh and feel the familiar flutter of her heart. But those times had been only pleasant, fleeting moments in her full and happy existence. Angus—dear, loving Angus—had always been there, her anchor to reality. And Charity had given her little time to think of anyone else all these months.

Only now did she realize what a dream world she'd been living in. Charity was leaving. And Angus, who beamed with pride and adoration every time he looked at her, was not the man who owned her heart. Nor would he ever have the sole possession of it that a husband deserved. Not as long as Hugh Sinclair lived and breathed and walked the earth.

She battled with her feelings as she sat staring blankly out the window. Part of her rejoiced in the knowledge that Hugh still cared. But another part of her mourned for Angus. What kind of wife could she be to him, if Hugh could always claim her heart?

The baby kicked. She sat back, giving him more room, and clasped her hands over her rounded belly. "Sh-h-h, love," she whispered. "Calm yourself, my little darling. It will be all right. We have each other, you and I."

After a time, her unborn child, seemingly soothed by her words, was still once more. Anna Rose, too, felt a certain calm descend over her. She rose and walked out to the piazza. She wanted to see Charity off, and she couldn't let Hugh leave thinking he had offended her.

When she appeared, Hugh looked at her expectantly, but said nothing. Anna Rose hated the lines of concern that she saw etched in his face. She had put them there; she must smooth them away before she let him go.

"Hugh, I want to thank you," she said in a gentle voice.

"You thank me? Whatever for?"

"For allowing me to have Charity all summer long. I love her so. I always have. She's like my own daughter." It was as close as she could come to telling him the truth.

"You'll be a wonderful mother, Anna Rose. But I'm the one who should be thanking you, and Angus. It isn't every man his age who'd be willing to take on another's small child." He bit his lower lip, wanting to call back the words. Under the circumstances, his remark about her husband's age seemed almost spiteful.

"It's all right," Anna Rose soothed. "Angus would be the first to admit that he is more grandfather than new father material. He jokes about it all the time."

"He would," Hugh replied, smiling. "He's that way. A good man!"

"Yes, he is." She let her eyes meet his, wanting desperately for him to understand the meaning of her next words. "I would never do *anything* to hurt him, Hugh."

"I know that, Anna Rose." He understood—completely, painfully—and he longed to reassure her. "Neither would I, intentionally."

"I'm glad to hear it," she answered softly. "Then we can be friends . . . dear friends, as I said earlier?"

"If that's all we can be." It seemed to Anna Rose that Hugh's eyes held all the sadness of the ages as he spoke those words. Her heart ached for him, and for herself.

"It is," Anna Rose stated softly, but firmly.

Just then, Charity came racing out onto the piazza. Anna Rose

300

caught her hand. "Gently, my dear, like a lady! Ladies don't race about and they don't shout and . . ."

Staring down at her slippers, thoroughly chastised, Charity continued the string of admonishments she'd heard all summer from Anna Rose and Dahlia. "And they don't climb fences and rip their stockings or get their frocks dirty or play with rough boys. I know, Anna Rose."

"You won't forget?"

Charity solemnly stared up at Anna Rose and shook her head. "I won't forget. Not never!"

"Not ever, darling," Anna Rose corrected gently, reaching out to caress her soft cheek.

Anna Rose felt her heart breaking as her daughter hugged her and kissed her and told her good-bye. They had shared such a perfect summer. They would be together again. Yes! But when would they ever again be so close, so happy, so much like mother and daughter?

It was difficult to let Hugh go, too, because it seemed as if Anna Rose herself were sending him away. Not just for today, but for always. They would see each other again. But the words he had let slip earlier would stand between them, like a threatening barrier, forcing them to keep their distance and guard their tongues.

Anna Rose stood for a long time, watching them ride down the road. Charity turned and waved several times before they rode out of sight around a bend. When they were gone, it seemed to Anna Rose that she was left with only a deep, empty well where her heart had been.

Her spirits brightened as Anna Rose sat in the fancifully painted plantation boat, listening to the singsong chants of the oarsmen. They sped over the calm water, through the crisp November afternoon. The marshes, turned golden by the frost, waved gently in the breeze, and white gulls wheeled overhead, swooping and diving to catch their dinner. She glanced up, shading her eyes against the bright sky. Sailing along directly overhead in a perfect V-formation, a flock of brown pelicans seemed to point the way to Rosedhu. She laughed and motioned to Pride to look.

The tall slave nodded and grinned. "Good sign, Miss Anna Rose. Lucky! We'll be home safe and sound before you know it."

Anna Rose settled back in her seat to think over the events of the long, hot, busy summer. She was sure Rosedhu would seem especially isolated and quiet after the steady stream of neighbors dropping in at the cottage almost every afternoon or evening, the never-ending calls she and Angus had paid in return, and the countless parties they'd attended.

Still, Anna Rose doubted she would miss all the activity once she returned to Rosedhu. She realized that she was looking forward to the quiet routine of plantation life. It would be good to sit in the parlor before the fire and knit while she awaited the arrival of her baby.

"There's home!" cried one of the boatmen, raising his great conch shell to signal their arrival.

Anna Rose looked up to see Rosedhu gleaming brilliant white through the trees. Her heart gave a little skip of joy. "Home!" she breathed. "My home!"

Angus waited at the landing to greet his wife, helping her from the boat, telling her to watch her step, asking if the trip had bothered her.

"I'm fine, Angus," she assured him. "The water was smooth as could be and I found the cool, fresh air exhilarating."

"Well, come along then, darling. Cook has a light supper ready for us. Then you must rest."

Twilight came quickly in the southern skies, and lingered only for a brief time before night fell. By the time Anna Rose and Angus reached the house, lamps were burning and fires had been lit to ward off the night's chill.

Everything, Anna Rose noted, looked perfectly in order. The place had not suffered by her absence. More than the look of the house, the feel of it was right. This was, indeed, her home now—hers and her husband's. And soon their child would be born here. Yes, all was right and proper and comfortable.

Angus had some work to do before going upstairs. The rice harvest had been good in September, he informed her proudly. After the grain had been cut and stacked by the slaves, then flailed and winnowed at Rosedhu, the clean rice had been shipped up to the mill at Savannah for fine polishing. Reports on the sale of the year's crop were just now coming in from Angus's rice factor in the city.

"I'm anxious to look over the latest figures, darling. You go on up. I won't be long." Angus kissed his wife's forehead and smiled, anxious to be done with his work so that he could join her.

Anna Rose found her bath waiting. She soaked in her tub for a long time, letting the hot water sooth the travel aches from her body. Then Dahlia helped her into a soft linen gown and she climbed between the sheets of the great rice bed, realizing suddenly that she was far more exhausted than she had thought. She fell asleep in minutes.

The howl of the wind outside woke her. A nor'easter was moving in from the coast. The room was dark when she opened her eyes. The fire had burned low, casting only a faint glow on the hearth. Sleepily, she reached over to touch her husband. But the place beside her was cold. Angus had not come to bed yet, and she judged that it must be well past midnight. But then, Angus often got so caught up in his work that he lost all sense of time.

Anna Rose got up and pulled on a thick robe, then went out into the hallway. The house was quiet, but lamps still flickered to light the way for the master to his bed. By the tall-case clock at the head of the stairs, Anna Rose saw that it was almost two.

"That man!" she sighed in soft dismay. "He'll work himself to death!"

She moved carefully down the stairs. The house was so quiet that it made her shiver. It was almost as if she were there all alone. Not a servant was about. But then, it was well past their bedtime, too, and Angus would not have required anyone to stay up just because he chose to lose sleep.

The door to the study was closed. Anna Rose knocked softly, but received no reply. She called. Still no answer. Finally, she turned the knob and opened the door. The lamps burned brightly inside. Angus was still at his desk, as she had thought he would be. But he was turned with his back toward her, staring out the windows at the storm.

"Darling, I hate to disturb you, but it is quite late."

Angus didn't answer, didn't move.

Anna Rose smiled. He did have a way of losing himself in thought. Or maybe he had fallen asleep. His head was tilted back against the soft leather.

"Angus, please come to bed."

Anna Rose moved toward him and reached out to touch his shoulder. At the slight pressure of her hand, he fell to one side. She screamed, then clutched at him. His eyes were still closed, his face ashen. She cried out again, this time hysterically.

"He's dead! My God, he's dead!"

She was unaware of the hurrying feet, the supporting hands, the excited voices. Somehow, she was taken back to her bed. Someone was soothing her, giving her a calming potion to drink, assuring her that all would be well.

But even in her fogged state, she didn't believe it.

Angus Campbell was, indeed, a very sick man, the doctor said. But he was a very lucky one, too. He had suffered a mild heart seizure—not uncommon for a man his age, especially one who worked as hard as he did, the physician admonished. Angus would be confined to bed until the doctor said otherwise. He would be allowed no tobacco, no alcohol, no exertion, no excitement. And, if he followed orders, he would, in all likelihood, recover. If he did not follow orders, the doctor pronounced solemnly, he refused to be held responsible.

As for Anna Rose, she had suffered a serious shock and should stay as quiet as possible until her time came to deliver.

So the next few weeks, until Christmas, passed with a sickroom atmosphere pervading Rosedhu, both patients occupying the great rice bed.

Anna Rose thought of sending a message to Weyman in Charleston, telling him of Angus's illness. But, even though his father was ill, she couldn't bring herself to summon the younger Campbell. After all, the doctor had advised her to remain calm, too, and Weyman Campbell's presence would be anything but a calming influence. Besides, Angus seemed to be gradually improving.

The week before Christmas, Angus summoned Dahlia and Pride to the bedside. "I've called you here because I want to make sure preparations for the holiday go ahead as usual. I won't have my people denied their merrymaking simply because I can't enjoy it this year."

Anna Rose really hadn't thought much about Christmas. Back in Scotland it had been just another day to see that the cow was milked, the chickens fed, and the farm and house work done. Her first Christmas in America had slipped by unnoticed by the inhabitants of Five Points. And the year after that, she'd been somewhere between New York and Georgia on a stage with Michael Flynn. But Angus's words brought back to her all the joy and excitement of the previous holiday season at Rosedhu. How could she have forgotten? Her mind had obviously been preoccupied with her ailing husband and the coming of their child.

Christmas at Rosedhu was a grand time, with preparations beginning back in the summer with the melon harvest. When the first watermelons had been picked, some were packed away in cotton seeds to preserve them until the holidays. The slaves would get two full days off—Christmas Eve and Christmas Day. Angus always ordered several cattle slaughtered and a few pigs for the big barbecue. Then there would be fiddle playing, singing and dancing, and general merrymaking about the place.

The most fun of all, as Anna Rose remembered from the year before, were the gifts for the "Got you's". On Christmas morning all the house servants crept about trying to be the first to wish pleasant tidings of the season to each other and to the master and the mistress. They would spring out of hiding to cry "Merry

Christmas! Got you!'' and then claim a present. It was a wonderful custom, Anna Rose discovered.

"Now you don't worry yourself none, Major Campbell," Dahlia replied, eyes shining. "There's plenty of time for everything to get done. I'll send Pride out to the woods with some men to catch the hogs. And me and Hagar will get together and plan what else needs doin'. The fruitcakes have been seasonin' in cheesecloth soaked in bourbon for weeks now already. And I put little ones out gathering pecans back in September. Yessir, we'll have us a big Christmas this year!"

The holiday preparations soon brought the plantation back to life, and tantalizing aromas drifted up to the bedroom, where the two invalids remained.

For the first time in weeks, Anna Rose saw a genuine smile of pleasure on her husband's face. He squeezed her hand and said, "Ah, darling, it's going to be all right! Christmas is coming, and I'm going to live to see our baby born. I haven't been so sure until now."

"Oh, Angus!" Anna Rose buried her head against his shoulder and wept with relief. "Angus, you frightened me so!"

He kissed her gently. "I promise never to do it again, my darling. We have years and years of happiness in store for us yet."

For a long time, Anna Rose clung to Angus, listening to his heart beat stronger than it had since the attack. The sound was the sweetest music she had ever heard.

She was so filled with relief that she failed to notice the look of sadness and distress deep in her husband's eyes. She knew nothing of the private discussion Angus had had with his doctor only that morning.

27

It was the last day of January in 1838—one of those clear, cold days, when the wind through the pine trees made the needles rattle, dead leaves underfoot crunched with the crispness of an overnight freeze, and sunlight spangled the water with pale gold. All the rain barrels were covered with a thin layer of ice, and woodsmoke drifted up to the big house from the cabins. At

Rosedhu, the crackle of roaring fires and the smell of hot, spiced cider gave the place an added homey touch.

Anna Rose lay abed, sipping tea as she read a letter from home Pride had brought that morning from Darien.

November 2, 1837

My Dears,

How happy I was to hear your glad tidings! And to think that if you have a son, he will be named for my dear Johnnie! I wept when I read the news. By the time you receive this, I may be a grandmother once again. Oh, how I wish I could be there for the big event!

But, alas, our plans move slowly. I have yet to find a buyer for the croft, Shane remains in poor condition, and of course, there is always Iris to contend with. Although your sister claims to be most anxious to leave for America, she seems to thrive on trying what little patience I have left.

Last month, she went to Inverness with the butter and eggs as usual. But she never returned, not by nightfall of the second day. You can imagine my anguish, and, I must admit, my anger! I still have no full answer as to where she was. But, when she came home at last, she was wearing a scarlet satin gown, bought with the butter-and-egg money! She said she purchased it to wear at the first social we attend when we reach your home. Somehow, I hardly think that such shocking apparel would be suitable for Iris to wear when meeting your friends!

Enough of my problems! I promise that we will join you soon. One prospective buyer presented himself to me only yesterday. I pray that he will be suitable. Also, the doctor says that Shane is improving and may soon be well enough to travel. Now, if there were only some way I could control Iris's scandalous actions until I can get her on the boat!

My fondest love to you both and to little Johnnie when he arrives. God bless you all!

With deepest affection,
Margaret Mackintosh

Anna Rose smiled as she finished reading. Perhaps her mother would make it in time for the birth. Johnnie certainly seemed to be taking his own good time about coming. Still, the doctor had said it might be several weeks yet. . . .

Suddenly, Anna Rose clutched her belly and bent forward, crying out for Dahlia. "No, I don't suppose Mother will make it after all!" she murmured. Her words were followed by several deep breaths as she tried her best to control the pain.

"The perfect day for this . . . it feels right to me. . . ." Anna Rose gasped to Dahlia between contractions.

"You just lie easy, ma'am. That doctor will be here before you know it!"

Leaving one of the maids with her charge, Dahlia ran back downstairs to see if the doctor's boat had pulled in from Darien yet. She didn't feel as calm as she looked. In her time, Dahlia had birthed her fair share of babies among her own kind, but the master's child was a different matter. And this baby, she was sure, was early by several weeks.

She hurried out onto the front veranda to see if she could spot the physician coming in aboard one of the plantation boats. There was no sign of him yet, but the gathering at the front steps inflamed her. Every slave on the place was there, including the field workers, and old Zimba, the witchwoman. The crazy old fortune-teller squatted in the dirt, casting her chicken bones to foretell the mistress's fate and the baby's sex and future.

"Shoo now, y'all!" Dahlia shouted at them, flapping her apron. "This ain't no barbecue! It's a birthin'. Now git on outta here, I tell you!"

The crowd, mumbling in protest, dispersed. Dahlia held her place, hands on hips, until everyone had gone before she hurried back inside.

"Dahlia, how is she?" Angus Campbell came out of the library. He had been allowed out of bed only two weeks before, and he still tired easily. Right now he looked rumpled, gray, and old beyond his years with worry.

"You just calm yourself, Major!" Dahlia ordered. "When that doctor gets here, he's gonna have his hands full without you having another spell too!"

"Don't worry about me, Dahlia. I'll be fine. But how's my wife?"

Dahlia smiled at him and touched his hand reassuringly. "She a fine strong lady, sir. No need to worry. But you shouldn't be all by yourself now. I got to go back upstairs and tend to her till that doctor gets here."

"I won't be alone long. I've sent word over to Hugh Sinclair at The Highlands. He'll be here directly to keep the vigil with me."

"That's good, Major." Dahlia started up the stairs, then turned back and pointed a finger at her master. "But you stay away from that brandy and out of those cigars! You hear me?"

Angus chuckled at her commanding tone. Feeling somewhat relieved that Dahlia had the situation well in hand, he nodded his promise to behave himself.

Upstairs, Dahlia found her mistress far more advanced in her labor than she would have liked.

"No doctor?" Anna Rose moaned.

Dahlia shook her head. "By the looks of things, it's going to be just me and you and that child, Miz Anna Rose. I know what to do, and nature will show that little one the way, but I don't know about you, ma'am. That appears to be one big baby you're fixin' to birth. I sure would feel easier in my mind if this wasn't your first."

Anna Rose stared hard at the other woman, considering. She had had to confide in the doctor that she had given birth before. He had suspected anyway. There were certain signs left by the first pregnancy that were unmistakable to his trained eye. Now, Anna Rose made a quick decision—one that she feared she might live to regret in future years. But she had to trust Dahlia with her secret.

"This isn't my first child. I've had one other."

The servant's eyes showed only a momentary flicker of surprise, then she nodded in calm acceptance. What white folks did was their own business. She wondered, though, if her mistress had ever told the Major.

"Well, that's good to hear," Dahlia answered. "Then you know what a job of work we got ahead of us, ma'am."

Anna Rose nodded, at the same time clutching her stomach as new contractions sent waves of agony through her.

The two islands that comprised Rosedhu and The Highlands lay adjacent to each other, with only a wide creek separating them. In the past months, Hugh and Angus had had small shelters built on either shore to stable horses, post messengers, and house their rowboats. So it had taken Campbell's message little over an hour to reach Sinclair.

Angus, in his excitement, had not bothered to explain the situation at Rosedhu in his hasty note to his friend. He'd said only for Hugh to hurry, that the matter was desperate.

Hugh did not even let his boat reach the other shore before he leaped out, sloshing through the shallows, and running for the stables. A horse was saddled and waiting. All he had to do was mount up and put spurs to horseflesh. Taking a shortcut, he soared over fences and across winter fields, his heart in his throat, wondering what had happened. Had Angus had another seizure? Was Anna Rose ill? He had no idea. But something was terribly wrong at Rosedhu!

He jerked the reins so cruelly when he reached the house that his horse reared, nearly unseating him.

"Whoa, boy, whoa!" he gentled, feeling guilty suddenly when he realized how hard he'd ridden the animal.

Tom-Tom stood in the drive, waiting to take the reins when Hugh dismounted. He tossed them to the boy and told him to rub the horse down good and give him some oats. Then Hugh hurried up the stairs, taking them two at a time.

He didn't bother to knock, but burst into the house, and called for his friend. "Angus? Angus, what's wrong?"

The master of Rosedhu rushed into the hall, waving his arms. "Quiet, man! For the love of God!" He gave his friend a broad smile and slapped him on the shoulder then.

"Angus, you're all right!" The relief was as plain in Hugh's voice as it was on his face. Then he frowned. "But what's so urgent? I nearly killed my horse and came close to breaking my own neck racing over here. Your note sounded desperate."

Angus's smile grew and he shook his head. He extended an arm to usher his friend into the study. "I'm sorry if I upset you, Sinclair. But it's not every day that a man becomes a father."

Hugh's mouth dropped open. Then he clapped it shut and grinned back. "A father! Well, I'll be damned!"

"And at my age!" Angus continued. "Why, it's like a miracle!"

"Is Anna Rose all right?" Suddenly, Hugh wasn't smiling any longer. He had dreaded this day for months, fearing for the woman he loved.

Angus shrugged. "Dahlia won't let me up there. She sent me away hours ago, when the labor first started."

"Dahlia?" Hugh cried. "Where the hell's the doctor?"

"I haven't any idea." Angus looked worried as he answered. "I sent Pride over to fetch him a good while ago. But they haven't returned. I'm afraid he won't make it in time."

Hugh paced, staring at the floor and shaking his head. After several minutes of this, he stopped and looked toward Angus. "What can I do? Do you want me to row over to town? Maybe I could locate him?"

The father-to-be took a seat before the fire and gestured for his guest to join him. "Pride will find him. You can keep me company. Have a drink and talk to me so I don't have to think about what's happening upstairs. A man could lose his mind waiting."

Angus didn't have to tell him that! Hugh went to the decanter on the sideboard. "I wish I could do more. How about you, Angus? A brandy?"

"I'd love one, but, no."

"I forgot. Doctor's orders?"

Angus chuckled. "More serious than that, my friend. Dahlia's orders!"

The two men sat there for hours, discussing everything and nothing. Though the conversation never stopped, it did slow from time to time as they'd glance upward at the sound of a muffled cry from Anna Rose. At those moments, infrequent though they were, they would both grow silent for long moments.

After one of these pauses, Angus finally resumed the conversation, but his proud smile had vanished. He looked old and weary again. Very quietly, he said, "I shouldn't have put you through this, my friend."

"Nonsense! I'm only too glad to be here with you. A man shouldn't be alone at a time like this."

"Don't lie to me, Sinclair. You may be glad to be here—for all that it pains you—but it's not for my sake. You need to be close to Anna Rose right now every bit as much as I do."

Hugh was struck dumb by the man's words. What was Campbell getting at?

"You needn't look so shocked, my young friend. They say wisdom comes with age. Well, if that's so, I should be a very wise man by now, I think you'll agree. And it doesn't take much wisdom, at any rate, to see the way you feel about my wife. It's plain on your face every time you look at her."

Hugh experienced a sinking feeling. Had he been that transparent? "See here, Campbell, if you're suggesting that Anna Rose and I—"

Angus cut him off sharply. "I'm not suggesting that you and my wife have been anything but proper friends since our marriage. What you were to each other before that time, I can only guess. Anna Rose has never spoken of your relationship and I've never felt it my place to ask. But I know a man in love when I see one. And there's certainly no doubting it in your case."

Hugh hung his head for a moment, not sure how to reply to Angus Campbell's accusation. He could deny it, but what good would that do? Obviously, Anna Rose's husband was more observant than most. Before he could reply, Angus was speaking again.

"I should thank you, actually. It's a great compliment to a man my age to have his wife so adored by a younger, handsomer man. Especially since she remains faithful to me through it all."

"She does!" Hugh assured him vehemently. "You must believe that, Angus! Neither Anna Rose nor I would ever betray you. We may have made one dreadful mistake in the past—before she met you—but we've learned our lesson from that episode." He got up and strode to the windows, staring out. "God, how many times have I prayed that I could make the guilt go away! Never, ever, would I put Anna Rose through that sort of thing again! I . . ." His voice trailed off.

"You love her *too* much," Angus finished for him. "Is that what you were about to say?"

Hugh answered quietly. "Would it help if I denied it?"

"It might, for the moment." Then Angus shook his head tiredly. "Until the next time I saw you gazing at her. That would bring the whole truth back to me in a flash."

"So, what are you suggesting? That I leave here now and never darken your door again?" Hugh paused, staring steadily at Angus. "I wouldn't blame you, and I'll go, if you ask."

Angus waved a hand of dismissal in the air. "No, no! That's not what I want. I value your friendship, Sinclair. You must know that."

"Then what?" Hugh insisted. "You can't mean to let the situation go on like this."

Angus's head jerked up and he squinted hard at the younger man. "Like *what*? I thought you just vowed to me that nothing had happened between you."

"Nothing has. I swear that to you. And nothing will!" Hugh paused to catch his breath. His head was spinning from the conversation. God, how he hated this! "Nothing will happen in the future either because Anna Rose would never allow it. At the cottage, when I went to get Charity, I almost overstepped my bounds. Your wife stopped me cold. Whatever feelings she may have had for me once have been replaced by her respect and . . . and, yes, her love for you, Angus."

"I thank you for that, Sinclair."

Angus rose and offered his hand in confirmation of their friendship. Hugh took it with only a moment's hesitation.

"And now that we have that settled, I can go on to the true reason I brought all this up in the first place." Angus turned away from Hugh, staring out the window, unable to face the other man

311

as he asked his bold favor. "I had a distressing discussion with my doctor shortly before Christmas. It has left me in quite a quandary. While Anna Rose was so close to her time, no problem presented itself. But eventually, she will begin to wonder why I have put aside my husbandly duties." He paused and Hugh saw his shoulders heave with a heavy sigh before he continued. "I love her too much, Sinclair, to consign her to such a lonely fate. I need your help."

Before either of them could say another word, one of the maids came rushing into the room, her eyes wide and a joyful grin splitting her face. "It's a boy, Major Campbell! A fine, big boy with all his fingers and his toes and a little ole worm of a—" She broke off just in time and clapped a hand over her mouth, giggling.

Both men stared at her for an instant, then laughed heartily.

"And how's my wife?" Angus asked.

The servant grinned again. "She fine, Major. Just fine!"

"Fine" fell a long way short of how Anna Rose Campbell felt at the moment. Unlike Charity, who had strained her mother's body and soul to the limits, little Johnnie had rushed her through labor as if he could hardly wait to be part of the world. Now as she held her lusty son at her breast, she thanked God that he was well and that she would never have to hand him over to others to raise.

When Angus came into the room, Anna Rose smiled at him brightly in spite of how weary the birth had left her.

"We have a son, my darling," she whispered. "A beautiful strapping lad with lungs strong enough already to blow your Highland pipes."

Angus sat down beside her and gazed at the child, who was nursing hungrily while flailing his tiny, balled fists. Angus touched his child's head with trembling fingers and then leaned over to kiss his wife.

"You've done a wondrous job of it, my dearest. He's as beautiful as you said. A bonny, bonny lad, indeed!"

Anna Rose accepted another kiss from the proud new father, feeling tears of joy well up as she gazed into his happy face. What more could a woman ask than to present a healthy child to her husband? Now she knew why her own mother had borne so many sons and daughters over the years. The pain and effort were all worth this one moment alone. The feeling moved her to tears.

A downstairs maid knocked at the open door and waited for permission to speak.

"Yes? What is it?" Angus asked.

"It's Captain Sinclair, sir. He wants to know if he can come up and pay his respects."

Johnnie had had his fill and was sleeping now. Dahlia quickly adjusted Anna Rose's gown, mumbling, "Ain't fittin' that the mistress do her own nursin'. I'll go fetch Maum Venus from the quarter. She can feed her own sucker and little master here easy as pie."

"No!" Anna Rose said firmly, rising from her pillows. After being unable to nurture her daughter, she would refuse to let anyone else nurse this precious son. "I won't have it, Dahlia! I intend to take care of Johnnie myself."

"Hush, darling," Angus soothed. "Of course you'll nurse Johnnie, if you like. Dahlia was only trying to help."

"What about Captain Sinclair?" the maid asked again.

"Do you feel up to seeing him?" Angus asked.

Anna Rose smiled. "Of course. But how did he find out so quickly?"

"I sent for him earlier. He's been here all the while. And as worried as I was, too!"

The look deep in Anna Rose's eyes—a sharpening from soft maternal love to intense melancholy longing—tore at Angus's heart. He believed that his wife loved him. But, whether she admitted it to herself or not, she still loved Hugh Sinclair as well. The thought pained him, even as he realized it would help his plan along.

"Send him up," Angus told the maid.

Angus had looked weary to the bone when he entered the room. But to Anna Rose, Hugh Sinclair appeared to be in much worse condition. His eyes were dark-rimmed and lines of worry etched the long planes of his face. He seemed almost afraid to ask how she was, as if to ask would be to hear the worst possible news. He came into the room, but stood beside the door, making no move to draw near her.

Anna Rose smiled and stretched out a hand to him. "Hugh, how good of you to come! I can't think of anyone I'd rather have meet my son in his first hour."

Hugh came toward her stiffly, took her hand and brushed her fingers with his lips. He was still unsmiling, unsure of himself.

"You're all right, then?" His voice was husky with concern.

"I couldn't be better!" she assured him. Then holding the baby up for his inspection, she said, "Meet John McIntosh Campbell. I've decided to change the middle name to the way it's spelt hereabouts."

"A fine name for a fine lad! Angus, you and your wife are to be

313

congratulated." Hugh turned toward where Angus had been standing, but he was gone. So were Dahlia and the maid.

Hugh started for the door. The last thing he wanted was to be alone with Anna Rose right now, after his most recent discussion with her husband. Sheer panic possessed him for a moment, but then he allowed reason to return. He wasn't being tested; this was Angus's way of letting him know that he trusted him as a friend. There was no need for him to feel self-conscious, alone with Anna Rose.

He smiled, finally, and said, "It's a relief, I'll confess, to see you looking fit, Anna Rose. Angus and I agreed that we were both equally concerned about you. We both value you very highly. Above all others!"

Anna Rose could hardly believe what she was hearing. Hugh spoke the words with such assurance, yet without an ounce of guilt or fear that they might be overheard.

"That's kind of you to say, Hugh. And my husband knows of this deep concern of yours?"

Hugh nodded. "He does! I think he understands that if there is ever anything I can do for him or for you, I am to be called on. Of course, that extends now to young John here as well."

"Thank you, Hugh. I don't know what to say."

Hugh forced his gaze from her face back to the sleeping infant. "He's really a wonderful baby, Anna Rose. If I were a father, he's the sort of child I'd want, with a mother just like you." His smile faded suddenly. "But I don't suppose I'll ever . . ."

His words stabbed at her heart, and she caught his hand and held it tightly. "Hugh, there's something you need to know. I should have told you before now. Rory and I . . ." She broke off for a moment, not daring to tell him the truth that would bring him even closer to her. How could she?

"What, Anna Rose? What about Rory?"

She looked down, not wanting to meet his gaze. "Only that Rory and I had hoped for a baby, too. You sounded so dejected just now. As if you think you'll never father a child. Rory lost that dream in death. But, Hugh, you still have a chance, and you have Charity besides."

"You're right, Anna Rose. I'm only feeling sorry for myself. It's unbecoming, I know. I should thank my stars that Charity is my daughter. I wonder who her poor, unfortunate parents were. They are the ones who deserve my pity. They never got to know her."

Anna Rose smoothed the soft blanket with her fingers, staring at her hands as if their work were of the utmost importance.

"Somehow," she said, "I think her mother knows she's well and happy. Perhaps Charity's father knows, too. At least she's far luckier than most. Did you know, Hugh, that the destitute in New York city's poorest sections often put newborns out to die because they can't afford to feed them? Especially girl children."

"I do know," he said. "It could have happened to Charity."

Anna Rose, still not looking at him, shook her head slowly. "No, never! I think Charity's mother must have realized she was a special child, who must survive. That's why she was left on your doorstep."

"I'll never forget that night," Hugh said in a wistful tone.

Nor would Anna Rose, but she dared not admit it.

A short time later, Hugh's visit ended. He had extended an invitation for the Campbell clan to visit him at The Highlands as soon as mother and son were able to travel. Anna Rose was delighted by the prospect of seeing her daughter again and introducing sister and brother to each other.

After she heard Hugh saying his farewells to Angus below, Anna Rose, with Johnnie nursing once more, settled down for a well-deserved rest. It had been a busy day, a happy day. Perhaps the best day of her whole life. She felt fulfilled and contented now as she never had before.

But a few troubling thoughts kept tumbling through her head. She'd wanted so to tell Hugh that Charity was her daughter, and that the child had been fathered by Rory McShane. Maybe a time would come when she was free to divulge the truth. But she had sensed that this was not the proper moment for such extravagant confessions.

Angus entered the room quietly and took a seat beside the bed. He thought she was sleeping, so he didn't disturb her. And Anna Rose, weary beyond words now, soon drifted off into a pleasant world made of dreams for her son's future.

Her husband watched over her all night. He thought, too, of their son's future. But more of his time was spent pondering his wife's fate. He'd come so close to speaking his mind to Hugh Sinclair that afternoon. His son's birth had interrupted the conversation, and Angus had found it impossible to pick up later where he'd left off. But he must do it.

"I *must*, for your sake, darling," he murmured.

Anna Rose roused from her sleep and blinked at him. "Angus? It's late, my dearest. Come to bed."

He did, and held his wife tenderly until they both drifted off.

28

At any other time of her life, Anna Rose would have hated the weather that raged throughout the month of February. Gale winds whipped the trees shading the house, strewing the grounds with limbs and moss, and driving frothy whitecaps from the river up onto the shore for day after weary, wet day.

But to the young mother, her infant son nestled close to her, her husband always nearby to provide pleasant company, the stormy days passed quickly and happily. By the time she and young Johnnie were ready to leave their bed and venture forth in the world, February's wrath had given way to the first warm, fragrant stirrings of spring.

Once again, the plantation was alive with the chatter and chirp of birds. Jays, cardinals, brown thrashers, and mockingbirds sang their gladness that the cold winds had blown away. The sun warmed the land, bringing forth tender green shoots from tree and shrub, turning the redbuds into drifts of pink and the dogwoods to mounds of spring snow.

On the morning that the Campbells set out for their visit to The Highlands, the world seemed especially bright and deceptively calm. Fluffy clouds hung lazily in the perfect blue of the sky, the water looked like glass, and the marsh had shed its dull winter-brown mantle for the lively green livery of spring. It was a perfect day for John McIntosh Campbell's first boat ride.

"Careful now, darling," Angus cautioned, lending a hand to his wife as she climbed into the plantation dugout.

"I'm perfectly fine, Angus!" she assured him in a cheerfully scolding tone. "You really don't have to keep treating me as if I'm an invalid. The weeks I've been a prisoner in my bed have more than restored me."

Angus winced. "Darling, I never meant for you to feel like a prisoner. I would have let you get up to be about the house, if you'd asked."

"Dahlia wouldn't! I did ask!" She laughed gaily. "But never mind that now. I'm a free woman again and I mean to enjoy every minute of this day and this visit."

Angus beamed at his wife. She was glowing with good health. And the cut of her soft cashmere dress—the same mist-green color as her eyes—showed that motherhood had only enhanced her girlish figure. He tugged her plaid shawl more snugly about her shoulders. The water was not yet warm, so the air about the boat was much cooler than on land. When he was satisfied that his wife was settled, he took Johnnie from Dahlia's arms and handed him over to his mother.

"I think we'll all have a pleasant sojourn at The Highlands, my dear," Angus said with a smile. "It will be interesting to see the place again. In the old days, that plantation rang with gaiety. It was the very social center of the county. But then came the sad times and the Sinclairs went away. I very much doubted that I would ever see any of that clan again."

Angus had his wife's full attention. She had often wondered about Hugh's family. He never spoke of his relations. She'd heard him mention Galloway, but nothing of any life here in America.

"Tell me about the Sinclairs, Angus. Please. I'd like to know."

He looked off down the river as if searching for a starting point. "Hugh's grandfather Lachlan first settled here and built the place. He was a stern old Scotsman with a wild mane of snowy hair and a temper, they say, that could shake The Highlands to its very foundations. But his heart was as huge as his holdings. He'd throw his home open to any and all. I can still remember hearing the skriegh of his pipes on a quiet evening. The sweet, mournful wail would float across the marshes to Rosedhu, reminding me so of my Highland home that tears would spring to my eyes."

Angus paused and shook his head a bit sadly.

"Do go on, dear," Anna Rose urged. "What happened to Lachlan Sinclair?"

'When his soul passed from time to eternity, it was from a broken heart, I fear. He outlived four wives and fathered eleven children. But at the end, he was all alone. The children died—all but one, Hugh's father. Some took the fever, one drowned in the river, another was killed by an alligator while swimming in the Altamaha. His two daughters both died in childbirth and their babes with them. Only the youngest, the meanest, the wiliest survived. Trad Sinclair, his name was. After a terrible argument, he left the poor old man all alone and returned to Scotland, swearing he would never set foot in his father's home again. He kept that promise, never returning until Lachlan Sinclair was dead and the land belonged to him. But that was many years later. According to the tales I've heard, Trad roamed the world for some time. Something of a soldier of fortune, he was. Then a woman stole his heart—a lady of high birth.

"There was only one problem: she had a husband already. But Trad convinced the lady to run away with him. Of course, divorce was out of the question, so they left England and came here to The Highlands. I knew her . . ." Angus paused and frowned in concentration for a time. "Diana, her name was. Lady Diana Marlboro. She was a beautiful woman. No wonder Trad fell in love with her. And high-spirited! I never saw a lady ride so— jumping fences, racing with the stable boys. Why, she was the talk of the county! But a nice woman, too, a gentle person, it seemed. Everything a wife should be, although, of course, she could never marry the man she loved."

Anna Rose gasped in sudden realization. "Then Hugh is . . ."

"Exactly, my dear." Angus nodded. "Born on the wrong side of the blanket, as the servants would say. But loved none the less for it by his parents. The birth of his son turned Trad Sinclair into a new man. His surly, quarrelsome manner vanished. He became totally devoted to fatherhood. His love for Lady Diana seemed to grow a thousandfold after their child was born. But then came the disaster, the thing that changed all their lives and the lives of this whole plantation community."

Anna Rose had been smiling, seeing herself in the role of Lady Diana and the child in her arms as her much-adored son, Hugh. But Angus's grave tone sobered her.

"What happened?" she asked, almost dreading to hear.

"I suppose it was when Hugh was five or six years old. Everyone here had come to accept the peculiar family relationship of the Sinclairs, and of course, Hugh's birth seemed to legitimize things. After all, common law marriage is still acknowledged in this state. We chose simply to ignore the fact that Lady Diana was still legally another man's wife. We liked her; we liked them all. Young Hugh was the brightest lad you ever saw. Quick and polite and smart as a whip."

"He's still all those things, don't you think, Angus?"

Angus looked at his wife, trying to read her eyes and the feelings behind her words. "Aye, he is the same to this day! But what he must have lived through to survive!

"His mother, you see, was a great fashion plate hereabouts. Twice a year, without fail, she went up to Savannah to have a new wardrobe made. Clothes and her 'boys,' as she called Hugh and his father, were her two weaknesses. She was the first to admit it. But it was that former weakness that finally brought an end to her.

You see, Savannah had been ravaged by yellow fever that last summer of her life. By late fall, when she went up to visit her dressmaker, everyone said it was safe. But hardly a household existed that had not been visited by the awful sickness, and most by the grim reaper as well. Lady Diana's dressmaker had lost her little daughter early in the epidemic. And that's what did it. What killed the child lingered on in the air, the very walls, of the dress shop. Lady Diana stayed a week, came home with a trunk full of beautiful new gowns, and died before she could ever wear a one of them. The fever took her quickly, mercilessly."

"Oh, how dreadful for Hugh and his father!"

"It was indeed! Trad took to the bottle, remaining perfectly whiskified for weeks. He near drank himself to death. Meanwhile, young Hugh ran wild, like a frightened little animal left to his own devices to survive. The worst of it was that Trad refused to allow his wife to be buried. He sat alone in that big stone house, day after day, drinking rotgut whiskey and talking to her decaying corpse."

"Oh, how horrible! Angus, please, no more!"

He patted her hand, sorry that he had said so much already, but too caught up in his story not to tell the rest. "At any rate, something had to be done. A friend of Trad's, a sea captain, arrived in Darien, asking around for Sinclair. When he heard the awful tale, he went straightaway to The Highlands, saw to the burying, found young Hugh, and loaded both father and son on his ship bound for Liverpool. That was the last anyone heard of the Sinclairs until Hugh began thinking of coming back. I suppose he remembered me because I'd fed him a time or two, during that sad period after his mother's death. At any rate, he contacted me several times during recent years, and finally wrote, sending a large bank draft and asking me to set things in order for him. I was happy to do it. We had become great friends over the years through our letters."

They had spoken in low tones so as not to disturb the eight oarsmen, who were in their best voice today, singing the praises, as they stroked, of the "new young master and his lily-white mother." For a time, Anna Rose and Angus sat in silence and listened, watching the prow of the boat slice through the deep water to send gentle waves out to either shore. The marsh grass at the river's edge undulated with the motion. The whole scene proved mesmerizing.

Finally, Anna Rose pulled herself free from nature's spell. "Angus, when exactly did Hugh write you that he planned to come back here, for certain?"

He pulled at his chin and gazed skyward. "Oh, dear, I'm no good at remembering dates. But he wrote from Inverness first, on the very eve of his departure, saying he might be sending down a young couple to manage the place for him."

Anna Rose nodded, thinking that that would have been herself and Rory.

"The next I heard was from New York. He advised me his plans had changed, that, most sadly, the young man had died in the crossing. He said he planned to bring the poor fellow's widow to live here and that he, too, would be taking up permanent residence at The Highlands. He said he had had his fill of the sea, at least for the time being, that he wanted a home, a wife, and children to carry on his name."

"But he didn't come then." Anna Rose's words were spoken as much to herself as to her husband.

"No. The next letter arrived with surprising news. No mention of the young widow, but a wedding day drawing near."

"And he was happy at last?"

"Hm-m-m, not deliriously so," Angus answered, a frown marring his brow. "The tone of that letter gave me considerable pause. He went on at such great length explaining himself to me. He said she was a good woman, a lovely woman, that she would be a wonderful mother to their children. But there was none of the usual delirium one hears from a friend who is about to wed his true love."

"Perhaps because he was older, too mature for flowery, romantic phrases?"

Angus shook his head. "I just don't know. But, at any rate, all talk of coming south was silenced for the time being. He said there was something he must do in New York before he could even consider moving down to The Highlands. But then the tragedy struck, and I don't suppose he could face remaining there with his wife dead and his fortune in ruins. It's good that he's come here. He'll have a new start."

"Yes." Anna Rose nodded. "I couldn't agree more."

"Look there, just ahead!" Angus cried suddenly.

Anna Rose gazed toward the direction in which her husband was pointing. They had turned a bend in the canal, and perhaps a mile ahead over the flat marshes, she spied a monumental structure all made of gray stone.

"The Highlands," Angus informed her. "An oddity here-abouts, as you can see. Old Lachlan wanted a part of his mother country here in America. So he bought his own ship to bring him over and filled its hold with ballast stones from the very heart of the Highlands. It's more Roman castle than planter's cottage. But it seems to suit the Sinclair clan somehow."

Just then, their tillerman blew his conch to announce their approach to the landing. From beyond the next bend, an answering call returned to them like an echo.

"The people will be turned out in force to see little Johnnie," Angus said with a laugh. "Hugh says they've spoilt his Charity terribly already."

Anna Rose steeled herself against the rush of adoring, groping servants, just as she had upon her arrival at Rosedhu. But as they approached the dock, she saw only Hugh and a tall woman dressed in a buckskin skirt and jerkin standing next to him. Although a smile of welcome lit Hugh's face, the young woman looked solemn, almost frightened. Before the boat reached the dock, she turned and retreated to the house.

"Hello there!" Hugh hailed. "You made good time."

"With weather like this," Angus returned, "what else could we do?"

For a moment, Hugh's gaze lit on Anna Rose. He offered her a different sort of smile—one that she knew from their very first meeting. Shyly, she looked away.

An avenue of huge oak trees, their moss-hung branches touching the ground in places, led up to the entrance of The Highlands. As they traversed this shadowed lane, Anna Rose felt a shiver pass through her. All sunlight was blotted out by the wide spread of the ancient oaks. Had she believed in ghosts, she surely would have felt that old Lachlan, his son Trad, and the restless soul of Lady Diana inhabited this place. She tightened her grip on her son.

"I must apologize for Charity," Hugh said. "Poor child, she'll be distraught when she wakes from her nap to find that she missed your arrival. She was up hours before dawn this morning, watching the water and listening for the sound of the conch, then running back to the house to report to me that, 'Anna Rose and the baby aren't coming yet, Papa. But soon!' She quite wore herself out."

"Ah, I feel neglected!" Angus blustered. "After all those pony rides to Darien to buy her candy last summer, and she's forgotten me already!"

Hugh laughed. "I'm afraid we menfolk don't count for much with little girls when there's a fair lady arriving with a new baby to meet. Already, Charity has changed her favorite doll's name to Johnnie and cut off the poor creature's hair to make it into a boy. But you just wait, Angus, until John here is running about. He'll

321

hound our every step, begging us to take him fishing, hunting, swimming in the river."

Anna Rose started to object, remembering the son of Lachlan Sinclair who had been killed by an alligator. But she caught herself in time. When Johnnie was older, then she would make the rules for him—hard and fast rules that would keep him from all senseless danger, in spite of these two careless men.

Hugh apologized for the state of his home. He was in the midst of remodeling. Anna Rose could see why. She highly approved of the idea. The interior of the mansion was as gloomy and forbidding as the cold stone facade, with the windows shrouded in heavy velvet drapes, badly moth- and mouse-eaten over the years, and ponderous pieces of mahogany furniture, upholstered in equally somber tones. As at Rosedhu, the walls were adorned with massive portraits of scowling ancestors. The place was a mausoleum, a graveyard of memories of past Sinclairs. The shadowy darkness of the place did not at all mirror Hugh Sinclair's personality.

As if reading Anna Rose's thoughts, Hugh said with a shudder, "I'd almost as soon entomb myself in some ancient crypt as live in this place the way my grandfather decorated it. A few rooms are finished already. So I hope you'll enjoy a brighter stay than I had the first few months. I've closed off the part of the house that's being worked on now. That's the wing my parents used."

That bit of information came as a relief to Anna Rose. She'd dreaded the thought of wandering, unaware, into the chamber where Lady Diana's body had lain in moldering state.

The aching of Anna Rose's breasts signaled her most urgent plight at the moment. She must feed her baby soon.

"You'll want to freshen up before dinner," Hugh said. "I'll show you to your suite."

With great relief, Anna Rose followed their host up the broad staircase to a lovely apartment on the sunny side of the house. The quarters consisted of a large bedroom, bath closet, sitting room, and a tiny dressing room that contained a cradle and a rocking chair. Hugh had thought of everything.

When Anna Rose was settled in the snug alcove with Johnnie at her breast, Angus peeked in and said, "I'm going on down, darling. Is there anything you need?"

She smiled at his thoughtfulness. "Nothing more than a brief spell of quiet with our son, my dear."

"Then I'll see you shortly."

Anna Rose settled herself more comfortably, relaxing totally in the warmth of the sunlit room. The only sound marring the perfect silence was the quiet suckling of her infant. She smiled down at him, thinking what a wonder he was. He was, by far, her most treasured possession.

Charity, alerted by her father that their guests had arrived, tiptoed into the guest suite. Papa had warned her not to disturb Anna Rose. But she was so anxious to see her friend. She couldn't possibly wait another moment.

However, when she entered the bedroom and spied Anna Rose—a look of immeasurable love on her face for the fat, greedy little thing at her breast—Charity felt an overwhelming jealousy, although, of course, she had no way of knowing at her tender age what to call the gnawing ache at the pit of her stomach.

The child checked her appearance—smoothing the ruffled skirt of her yellow dress, touching her golden curls, and tugging her stockings up—before she approached Anna Rose. Her friend would be pleased to know that Charity remembered all the lessons she'd been taught the past summer.

But to Charity's great disappointment, she stood for a long time at the door to the little room unnoticed. Anna Rose was totally engrossed in the baby. Finally, Charity walked up to the chair and placed a chubby hand on Anna Rose's knee.

Anna Rose jumped, as if she'd just been awakened from a dream. "Why, darling! I didn't hear you come in."

Charity said nothing. She only stood there, eyeing the infant unsmilingly.

"This is Johnnie, Charity."

"Awful little," the child observed with a pout.

"Babies are, darling. You were this tiny once."

Charity shook her head until her golden curls danced.

"Oh, yes! Even smaller. But now you're a big girl. And I hope you and Johnnie will be like sister and brother. You'll have to help me teach him everything, just as I taught you."

Charity remained unsmiling. With wide blue eyes brimming with hurt tears, she searched Anna Rose's face.

"What's wrong, dearest? I thought you were happy that we have a baby now."

"You love him more!" Charity accused. "You're his real mommy! You won't love me anymore!"

Still holding the baby, who had finished eating and was now fast asleep, Anna Rose put her arm around Charity and drew the weeping child up on her lap too.

"Charity, how can you think such things? You know I love you! A person can love more than one at a time."

Charity stared up, her crying stopped, but her face still pinched with childish grief. "You mean, like you love Uncle Angus and Papa?"

Anna Rose's breath caught in her throat. Out of the mouths of babes . . . If Charity recognized this in her, then wouldn't everyone else know? Probably not, she decided. Children were far more observant than most adults, and they seemed to see things with a clearer vision.

"I love many people, Charity," Anna Rose responded evenly.

"Then you still love me?"

"I do, and I always will. I promise you, Heather!"

Anna Rose spoke the name without even realizing what she'd done. She could have bitten her tongue off for it, but Charity only looked at her quizzically and asked, "Why did you call me that?"

"It just slipped out. You see, I've always thought that if I had a daughter, I'd name her Heather. And I think of you as my daughter."

In a moment of childish affection, Charity reached up and hugged Anna Rose tightly about the neck. "Will you call me Heather, Anna Rose, please? When nobody's listening, so it can be a secret?"

Anna Rose smiled through the tears in her eyes. "All right, Heather darling, it will be our secret."

The young mother, with her two children cuddled close to her heart, sat for a long, happy time. Anna Rose had dreamed of using her daughter's real name someday, but never had she imagined that that day would ever come to pass. Perhaps at some future date she could tell Heather the real truth of her birth.

She closed her eyes and rocked the children gently, humming them an ancient Scottish lullaby.

The days at The Highlands slipped past in a warm haze of pleasure. Hugh was the perfect host. Only occasionally did Anna Rose feel discomfort under his intense gaze. Although she tried to tell herself that his periodic intimate looks embarrassed her, in truth those private glances, which spoke silent volumes, warmed her through and through. But she had to put herself on closer guard, after what she'd heard from Charity.

She'd been sorely tempted to ride out with Hugh to view his vast holdings. Often Angus tried to press her into going. Although the warm weather seemed to have brought about a marked improvement in her husband's health, he still felt unsure of himself when on horseback. Still, Anna Rose politely refused all of Hugh's offers that would force them to be alone together. Such a situation would have been foolhardy at best.

The one thorn in Anna Rose's side during the visit was Hugh's Indian housekeeper, Willow. The lovely young woman obviously resented her being there, but Anna Rose couldn't figure out why. Seeing the copper-skinned maiden always hovering near Hugh, casting her own intimate gazes when he wasn't looking, made Anna Rose wonder about the nature of their relationship. After all, Hugh Sinclair was a virile man in his prime. There was not another available woman for miles, and she could never imagine Hugh going to the slave cabins for solace. But Willow, with her nubile form temptingly displayed by her soft doeskin costume, and her long sleek hair and large black eyes, was entirely another matter. Anna Rose began having her own pangs of jealousy.

One evening at a supper of rich oyster stew, swamp salad, and a huge roasted trout that had slept in the Atlantic only hours before, Hugh himself brought up the subject that had caused Anna Rose so much curiosity.

"Angus, I haven't thanked you properly for finding Willow for me. She's a wonder! However did you come upon her?"

Anna Rose stared at her husband. She had no idea that Willow had been brought here by his hand.

Angus chuckled and shot Hugh a knowing glance. "I thought you might find her more comfortable, shall we say, than a slave housekeeper. I knew from your letters that you were unused to the condition of slavery, at least in your own household."

Hugh gave a firm nod. "I could never see buying human beings to serve me in New York when there were so many free men in desperate search of employment."

"But of course, the situation is far different down here," Angus pointed out quickly. "If you tried to put white workers into the rice fields, the mortality rate would be staggering."

"I'm learning to live with being a master, though I'll never be quite comfortable with the institution," Hugh added. "But where did you find Willow? I thought all the Indians were gone from these parts long ago."

"Most have moved to other locations. But Willow's family has lived in one part of my swamp for as far back as anyone knows. One of her ancestors was the great *mico,* Tomochichi."

"She's Creek?" Hugh asked.

"Yes, but actually, the Indians from this area were called 'Guale,' though they are, in fact, part of the Creek Confederacy. They once inhabited forty villages up and down the coast, with their main settlement on Guale Island, which, as you probably know, is now called Saint Catherine's. And there are still a few Indians scattered in settlements hereabouts."

"And Willow?" Hugh asked. "How did you manage to lure her to civilization?"

Angus laughed. "It was totally unexpected, my friend. Her people were still living in bark huts when I discovered them. They still smeared themselves with bear grease as protection from the sun and insect bites, and they let their fingernails grow long for eating and fighting. The men of the family all wore loincloths and the women, including Willow, felt perfectly garbed in nothing more than a skirt of woven moss draped about their waists and shells at their wrists and ankles."

Anna Rose contained her shock, thinking to herself that the Indian maid wore little more than that to this day.

"I used to go into the swamp when times were hard and take corn or rice or whatever I had. They would pay me in shells or dried fish. I really had no intentions of trading with them. I only wanted to help out. But being the proud people they are, they would have refused my charity. Finally, a few years back, I arrived at their camp one day to find things in a terrible state. Measles had somehow invaded their swamp stronghold. They were dropping like flies. Willow's father had nothing to trade for the rice I'd brought. Their hunters were all ill or dead. The poor sick chief begged me to take his daughter in exchange for the supplies. So I accepted Willow in barter, hoping to save her from the measles epidemic. She came down with a light case, but with a doctor's help she was saved. I taught her to speak English and to wear more than a moss skirt."

"Not much more!" Hugh added. "But you were extremely generous to send her to me. I'm surprised you didn't keep her at Rosedhu."

Angus was frowning now. "I sent her here to protect her, actually. My son took a liking to her, unfortunately. And she was far too young, I felt, to be subjected to the sort of attention he was paying. About that time, I received your first letter, Hugh, saying that you might soon return. Having Willow live here seemed the sanest measure all around."

"Well, I can't say I blame your son, Angus! Willow is a very beautiful and caring young woman." Anna Rose winced at Hugh's reply. But she barely had time to recover before her husband dealt her another blow.

"That reminds me, Hugh," Angus said. "When Pride brought the mail over today, he had a letter from my son. Weyman plans to arrive in a few days to meet his new brother. So, I'm afraid we'll have to cut our visit with you short."

Hugh cast a quick glance in Anna Rose's direction. He mistook her look of dread for one of disappointment and insisted, "Nonsense, Angus! I've plenty of room here. Weyman can come stay at The Highlands." Then remembering the younger Campbell's penchant for his housekeeper, he added, "I've taught Willow a few things that will help her fend off any untoward advances from your son."

Anna Rose slumped slightly in her chair, her delicious trout cold and forgotten. A slender, long-nailed hand slipped past her shoulder to whisk the china plate away. Turning, Anna Rose's gaze met the dark, defiant stare of Hugh's Indian woman, chilling her to the core.

Suddenly, she wanted desperately to object to Hugh's offer, but it was too late.

"That's very hospitable of you, Hugh," Angus was saying. "It will be a regular house party, like in your grandfather's day. On behalf of my wife and my two sons, I accept wholeheartedly. It will be a grand treat, having our entire family here. Don't you agree, Anna Rose?"

She could only nod and swallow her misery at the very thought of seeing Weyman Campbell once again.

29

Sojourns at coastal plantations were renowned for their lengthy durations in the mid-1800s, but Anna Rose missed her own home, and often joked with Angus that young Johnnie might be ready to enter Franklin College before she saw Rosedhu again. Granted, Hugh was the perfect host and their stay at The Highlands had been delightful. However, when March gave way to April and planting time approached, but still there was no sign of Weyman Campbell, she determined that they should return to Rosedhu, regardless.

"My mother always told me, Angus, that there are two things that begin to smell bad when kept overlong: fish and house-guests!"

Angus laughed heartily, but scolded, "My dear, what an unladylike thing to say! Shame on you, and on your dear mother!"

The Campbells were getting ready to retire for the night. Anna

Rose had checked on Johnnie, who was sleeping soundly. Now, gowned for bed, she sat at the vanity, brushing her long russet hair.

Angus lounged in a nearby chair, his eyes a twinkle as he watched her. Oh, how he ached tonight to hold her, to love her! He sighed. Instead, he would have to content himself with merely touching her, feeling the silk of her long hair against his palms.

"May I do that for you?" he asked.

Anna Rose nodded, smiling at him in the mirror. "If you don't mind, dearest. It's too long for me to manage now, and I hate calling a maid in at this hour."

"No need for a maid," Angus replied, and took the silver brush from her hand. "I love doing it. I love doing everything for you, my darling. I must have done something very good sometime during my early years to deserve such happiness in the twilight of my life."

Anna Rose reached up and caught his hand. "Please don't talk that way, Angus!"

"I'm sorry, dear," he said gently. "I know you hate for me to mention the difference in our ages. But it's God's own truth that you'll be here for many years after I'm gone. I don't want you to be alone. I've tried bringing up this discussion before, but you've always stopped me. I intend to have my say tonight. I want your promise that you'll marry as soon as possible after . . ."

"Angus, please!"

He was talking this way more and more of late, and it distressed her deeply. The doctor had told her after his attack that there would be some lingering weakness. But he had also said that Angus could live an almost normal life for years to come, provided he was careful and sensible.

"Just promise me, Anna Rose." He was not to be silenced tonight.

Anna Rose rested her forehead in her open palm, closed her eyes, and nodded resignedly. "Very well, Angus, I promise. Now, you answer my question. When can we go home?"

"In a few days, darling. I do want to give Weyman time to get here. I'm most anxious to see him, and I know he'd enjoy The Highlands."

This was the only time that Angus had lied to his wife, for it mattered little to him whether his son came to The Highlands or to Rosedhu. What did matter was the fact that he had yet to accomplish his goal. And now he was more determined than ever.

Only two nights before, against doctor's orders, Angus had tried to "exert himself." He felt better and stronger than he had in months. Perhaps the diagnosis was wrong; perhaps there was no need to ask for Hugh Sinclair's aid. These had been his hopes as he joined his wife in their bed.

Anna Rose had been most agreeable to his kisses and his fondling. It had been long enough since Johnnie's birth so that Angus felt he could do her no harm. He needed her desperately and she seemed to match his longing with her own. But even as she came into his arms willingly and passionately, he had discovered, to his total horror and degradation, that the doctor had spoken the truth. He could no longer make love to his wife!

Anna Rose had petted him and whispered her love words, trying to console him. But her forbearance had only made him feel worse. It was one thing to be told that you were less than a man, quite another to find out for certain.

Even though the very thought tore his heart with pain, he could stall his plans no longer. Now that he had the hard-won promise from her that she would not remain a widow after his death, he meant to make sure she had the same amount of happiness for as long as he had left to live.

He knew why Anna Rose had been avoiding Hugh, why she refused to go riding with him or even to be left alone in the same room with him. Well, all that was about to change. Angus planned to see to it. A man would have to be blind not to recognize the deep affection between Hugh and Anna Rose. But he must make sure that their feelings solidified before he would know any peace. When his time came to pass over to the other side, he wanted no doubt as to who Anna Rose's next husband would be. And between now and then, he wanted his wife to receive her full measure of physical affection. Something he could no longer give her.

It was comforting to know, too, that after he was gone and Anna Rose accepted Hugh, their marriage would combine two great plantations, forming the largest single tract on the coast. It was a dream he had cherished for decades.

Angus was thinking, also, of young Johnnie. Weyman would never come back to the land. But John McIntosh Campbell could be raised to the life of a rice planter and from there his fortunes would know no limits. With a toss of the bones, Old Zimba, the witchwoman, had foretold a shining star in Johnnie's future. Angus was not a superstitious man, except where Zimba was concerned. He had seen too many of her predictions come true . . . too many of her conjurings work for good or evil. Although Angus himself would not live to see it, he firmly believed that someday his son John would be a great man.

He closed his eyes and shook his head wearily, feeling his age and infirmity suddenly. All his plans, all his dreams . . . what was the point? Being honest with himself for the first time, he admitted silently that all these excuses for what he planned to do were only ways of masking his pain at the very thought of his wife in another man's arms.

"Darling, come to bed."

Angus had been far away, in a world all his own. He hadn't realized that Anna Rose had retired. Now he rose, tired and dejected, and joined her.

Oh, how he longed to make love to her just once more! He tried not to think about it. He simply kissed her good night, then drew away to his side of the bed. If the situation was hard on him, he knew that it was even more painful for Anna Rose. Well, if his plan worked . . .

Anna Rose lay perfectly still, feigning sleep. It was the only way she could contain her disappointment and frustration. Many months had passed since she'd known physical love from her husband. First, there had been his illness, then Johnnie's birth to keep them apart. But all that was past now. No pain lingered from her labor, and her bleeding had ceased. There was no reason why she should abstain any longer. Two nights before, her heart and her body had filled with warmth as Angus set about the tender preliminaries she knew so well. But then, something had happened. She'd tried not to show her disappointment. He'd been so embarrassed by his inability to perform. Now she feared that he would keep his distance rather than run the risk of another failure. What was she going to do? She longed so for love.

She ached for Angus to turn to her again instead of away. The memory of his tenderness was fading to a blurred shadow in her mind. How she needed for him to take her in his arms once more, to restore her with the passion he had held so long in reserve! Surely, the other night had been only an isolated occurrence. She prayed so!

It worried her, too, that in the absense of any physical love from her husband, dreams of the past were returning to haunt her sleep each night. How often of late had she awakened in a frenzy, her body burning for the ecstasy she had shared with Hugh Sinclair. In the darkest part of the night, she relived their intimacies all too vividly. At those times, she would reach out to Angus. But his waking responses did little to relieve her anguish. Each time, he would say, "Go back to sleep, darling," or "You need your rest, Anna Rose," or "Quiet, dear, you'll wake the baby."

To Anna Rose it almost seemed as if he was deliberately pushing her away, toward Hugh Sinclair. But, of course, she thought, that was ridiculous!

Angus Campbell's plan worked, to his relief and his sorrow. Over breakfast the next morning, he suggested to Hugh that the three of them take a ride around The Highlands to view the pre-planting preparations.

"I'm feeling quite stronger, certainly fit to ride. And, Anna Rose, the fresh air will do you a world of good," Angus said. "I know you'll enjoy seeing the wildlife and all the flowers just coming into bloom."

She smiled and nodded, thinking that exercise would work off last night's frustrations. And as long as Angus felt up to coming along everything would be all right. She quickly agreed.

"A splendid idea!" Hugh said. "I'll have Willow pack us a basket lunch. We can spread it under the pride-of-India trees at the River House. It's one of my favorite places, especially beautiful this time of year with the trees in full bloom."

Anxious to be off, the three hurried through breakfast and went up to change.

Anna Rose had a new Prussian blue riding habit that Angus had bought in Savannah to surprise her. Already she had regained her trim figure after Johnnie's birth, so the close-fitting waist and flared skirt were most becoming. The lead shot sewn into the hem for modesty's sake made the material swirl gracefully about her shapely ankles with each step she took. The pert glengarry bonnet that completed her ensemble sported not only the traditional eagle feathers worn by Scottish warriors, but also sprigs of red whortleberry and sweet gale, the badges of Clans Mackintosh and Campbell.

"Aye, yer a braw lass, Anna Rose! Ye look weel wi' thet glengarry bannet cockit jest so." Angus spoke to his wife in the lusty lilt of the Highlands, the old twinkle once more in his eye. "Would thet I weer a wee bit less auld!"

She gave him a playful rap with her riding crop and tilted one brow at him. "Angus Campbell, I ne'er heard such! And ye wi' yer ain wee bairn abed theer in the cradle! Ye make yerself out to be as auld as the ancient monster of Loch Ness—all scaly and barnacled and covered with slimy green. I winna listen to sech claverin', d'ye hear?"

Only when the two were alone and in high spirits did their bantering voices take on the thick accent of their homeland. At the moment, they were in such fine fettle that their brogues could have been spread on a scone. Anna Rose was feeling so exhilarated at the thought of a brisk ride with Angus and Hugh that she failed to notice her husband's gaiety was forced to match her own.

It was a fine spring day, with the sun bright, but not too hot. No April showers threatened the unblemished azure sky. The wind was no more than a zephyr, and it brought with it a tang of crisp salt from the sea. As she and Angus strode toward the stable, Anna Rose noticed all this and rejoiced in it.

"What a perfect day for a ride!" she said to her husband. "You couldn't have hit upon a better idea, my darling."

"I thought you'd enjoy it, dearest," Angus replied. "I'm anxious to see Hugh's restoration of the old River House." He raised a hand to guard his whisper as he added, "They say when old Lachlan felt especially amorous, he'd lure his wife—whichever one of the four—down to the place for a day or so. Gossip has it that each time he went, his wife bore a child exactly nine months later."

"Angus!" Anna Rose found herself blushing. Whatever had gotten into her staid, gentlemanly husband these past few days? He said the most outrageous things! She only wished his actions were as bold as his words.

Hugh watched them coming toward the stable and his heart began to beat faster. Anna Rose, in her rich blue habit and perky bonnet, had never looked lovelier. *Not even the night that she wore the pearl satin gown and we . . .* He banished the thought abruptly, with a soft oath under his breath. She was a feast for the senses this morning, he thought.

Her husband, on the other hand, had aged beyond his years in the past weeks. Or maybe now that Angus had confided the doctor's diagnosis to him, Hugh only imagined him growing older and wearier each day. A wasting palsy, the doctor had pronounced ominously. Angus had further confided in Hugh that Anna Rose knew nothing of this. She assumed that he was recovering normally from his heart spell. Hugh wasn't sure that was fair of Angus. How much worse it would be for her if her husband were to die suddenly than if she were advised of the situation and could prepare herself for the worst. But that was none of Hugh's affair. Angus had done what he felt was best for his young wife, even to the point of trying to find her a lover. He had turned the older man down flat, of course, Hugh reminded himself with a slight grimace. He quickly forgot his distaste for the idea as Anna Rose neared.

"Hello, you two!" he hailed. "Ready for a smart gallop?"

"I'll leave the galloping to you young folks," Angus answered. "I'm afraid a gentle canter is more my speed these days."

As they rode along the top of the dike, it was easy to see that the rice fields were ready for planting. Following the autumn harvest, the slaves had burned the stubble left from the crop. Then, with hand hoes, they had turned the soil, using what was left of the plants to help fertilize the next crop. During the winter, dikes and floodgates had been repaired. Last month, the trunks had been opened, lightly flooding the fields for twenty days. Now it only remained for the moon to reach the proper phase before the slaves would return to the fields to plant the rice seeds in the already prepared trenches.

"We're in for a prime crop this year," Angus said to Hugh. "I can smell it in the air already."

"Let's hope so!" Hugh replied. "I'm afraid I'm land-poor. I need a good crop to lay in some ready cash. After losing everything in New York, I'm hocked to the hilt."

Anna Rose frowned, worried by this news, but her husband only laughed. "My dear man, don't feel that you're the only one. We all live on credit from harvest to harvest. Rice planting is an expensive proposition. It takes three times the cash, three times the labor, and three times the land of a cotton plantation to make a decent crop. Sometimes it takes three times the toll on the planter, too. And after last year's panic, I wonder that any of us have survived."

"Is it really that bad, Angus?" Anna Rose's question was spoken in a worried tone, causing the two men to exchange cautious glances.

"It is, but we manage, my dear. Prices are sure to rise again soon. At any rate, I certainly didn't mean to wipe the lovely smile from your face." Angus spurred his mount to a slightly faster pace. "Come along now, you two! I didn't suggest this outing so that we could discuss business affairs. Instead, let's search for Bartram's lost Gordonia!"

"What?" Anna Rose called after him.

Hugh rode up beside her and explained. "It's a beautiful, flowering tree—*franklinia alatamaha*. Back in 1765, John Bartram spotted a specimen a few miles northwest of Darien. Later, his son classified and named the plant. It had never been found before growing in the wild. But then, mysteriously, the tree disappeared and has not been seen in this area in over thirty years. I'll show you sketches back at the house, if you like."

Anna Rose listened to the first part of Hugh's discourse with

333

great interest. But soon, something in his eyes distracted her. She felt a warmth creeping through her blood as they rode along together. Though the subject of his lecture was botany, the husky tone of his voice held an intimacy that touched some chord deep inside her.

Suddenly, Hugh's hand was on hers, its warmth sending forbidden thrills to her heart. "Anna Rose, are you feeling unwell? Your face is so flushed."

For a moment, she could find no voice. When she could reassure him at last, the words came out in a strained whisper. Frantically, she looked ahead, up the trail, meaning to urge her horse to more speed so that she could ride in the safety of her husband's company. But they had left the dike for a woodland trail and Angus was no longer in sight. She was on the verge of panic.

Seeming to sense her uneasiness, Hugh said softly, "Anna Rose, you needn't be worried. I'd never take advantage. But I won't lie to you either. You know I still love you . . . still want you."

"Please, Hugh, I don't want to hear this!"

She was the one who was lying. She longed to hear exactly what he was telling her. His words filled her with such lightness that she felt as if she might float right out of her sidesaddle at any moment. For the past weeks, she had felt like an empty shell of a woman. She had never thought of herself as having a passionate nature, but now she wondered. Without the love she craved, she seemed to be shriveling, dying inside.

She had known the love of three men in her life: Rory, Hugh, and Angus. Next to what she felt for the man riding beside her now, her affection for the other two paled in comparison. She damned herself for feeling this way, but it was true. She had loved Rory and she loved Angus. But what she felt for Hugh Sinclair went far beyond the simplest meaning of love.

"You don't have to say anything, Anna Rose." Hugh's voice broke into her troubling thoughts. "There's no need. It's written very plainly on your face, my darling."

He leaned in his saddle, as if he meant to kiss her. Anna Rose tapped her horse's flank with her crop. She was out of his reach instantly, her emotions battling, but her conscience demanding the honorable action of her.

Just ahead, she spied a clearing and a house at the river's edge. Angus stood beneath a cluster of lacy-leafed trees with tall, slender trunks and clusters of lavender flowers in their branches. Her husband waved and shouted, "What took you two so long?"

Anna Rose's heart shrank, fearing she might have to offer an explanation to him. But he asked for none. She sighed with relief as he helped her dismount. Soon Hugh came into the clearing. Lunch was spread, and Anna Rose regained her emotional equilibrium as their conversation moved on to safe ground once more.

Anna Rose might not have calmed so easily had she known that they were being watched. Weyman Campbell stood some distance away, carefully concealed in a fragrant copse of bay trees. He'd gone to the house first and talked to "Sinclair's woman," as he thought of Willow-in-the-Wind. It was beyond the comprehension of a man of his low character that anyone could have such a voluptuous female under his roof and not be helping himself to the full measure of her charms. Since she was a servant and since he had wanted her for a long time, he thought it only his due to sample her wares briefly this morning—just enough, however, to prime himself for more strenuous sport with fairer game.

Now, as he gazed at Anna Rose, his thin lips curled into a grin. His father had chosen well, indeed! How convenient to have this lovely, young creature so handy whenever he came for a visit. And after what he'd learned last week from that drunken customer at his bawdy house, he was even more interested in his stepmother.

The fellow—Flynn, by name, and well in his cups—had brought his whoring business to the house in Charleston specifically because he'd heard that the owner was the son of Angus Campbell.

"Know your father quite well, I do!" Michael Flynn had told him. "And his wife even better!"

Flynn, encouraged by drink, had gone on to tell Weyman how he'd rescued Anna Rose from a similar house in New York City. Weyman had been surprised, but not displeased, to find out that his stepmother was a retired prostitute and that his father had no idea of her past vocation. How much easier that would make everything! Anna Rose would yield most willingly, Weyman was sure, to keep this information from her husband.

But then had come the real shocker. "I sold her myself to your father," said Flynn. "He begged and pleaded with me to have her. Of course, I'd never have done such a thing had I not been in dire straits at the time and your father so besotted with her. Still, as much as he wanted her, he'd only pay fifty dollars to have her. Tight old bastard!"

Weyman had been forced to nod his agreement to this last statement. But he couldn't deny the grim satisfaction of knowing that his father had had to buy a wife.

It had been difficult to contain his excitement at gaining all this information from a total stranger. He had wondered at the time why a man who would sell a woman hadn't tried as well to sell such damaging secrets. Then the truth came out. Michael Flynn, down on his luck as usual, was bent on blackmail. Thinking young Campbell would be horror-stricken by his tale and anxious to keep his father from disgrace, he meant to extort funds from the brothel keeper to hold his peace on the matter. Obviously, he was unfamiliar with his victim's already questionable reputation.

Weyman Campbell had pretended to go along with Flynn, offering him a sizable sum to keep his mouth shut. He'd promised to pay the very next day, as soon as he could gather the funds. In the meantime, Campbell had offered Flynn the best room in the house, adorned by one of the establishment's most charming and talented ladies. And, of course, all the spirits he could drink. Flynn had been quick to accept Campbell's hospitality.

Weyman had chosen Flynn's female companion well, a woman he trusted to do his bidding and keep her mouth shut. He had also chosen the wine carefully, a heavy, sweet vintage that would cover the bitter taste of the fast-acting poison.

By morning, the would-be blackmailer was already stiff with death, and Campbell himself had fallen heir to the extortion scheme. There had been no problems with the authorities about the corpse once Campbell explained that the man, a self-proclaimed drifter, had come from Savannah, and that he had exhibited definite symptoms of yellow fever during the night. A dead wagon had been sent quickly and the body disposed of in a lime-filled grave outside of town.

So ended the scheming of Michael Flynn and so began the plotting of Weyman Campbell.

After lunch, Anna Rose found that she was having a great deal of trouble keeping her eyes open. The afternoon was warm, with a lacy pattern of sunlight filtering down through the leaves of the pride-of-India trees. The men had once more turned to talk of crops, markets, and business in general, in spite of all their promises to keep the outing strictly pleasure. Her mind wandered and her lids drooped.

"My dear, wouldn't you like to go in and lie down for a spell?" Angus asked. "You've had more than your share of exercise and fresh air today."

She yawned in spite of herself. "That would be nice, Angus."

"We'll miss your company, but we will excuse you," Hugh put in.

Hugh offered a hand to help her to her feet. "Stay, where you are!" he commanded Angus when he started to rise as well. "I'll show her to the house."

Anna Rose, despite her vow to never be alone with Hugh, went with him to the house. She glanced back over her shoulder to see Angus, propped against the trunk of one of the smooth-barked trees, staring out over the calm river. He looked so happy and well. It was reassuring to her.

The River House was actually a hunting lodge, with rustic furniture of cypress, and stone walls inside and out. It was a comfortable place with many windows and a huge fireplace.

Hugh showed her to the daybed in an alcove off the main room. "You'll have a nice view of the river from the window. And should you prefer to read rather than nap, help yourself to the bookcase."

"Thank you, Hugh." She lay down on the narrow bed and stretched her arms over her head. She smiled up at him.

"You shouldn't do that!" he said, his voice husky once again.

"What? Thank you?"

"You know that's not what I mean, Anna Rose. You shouldn't look so inviting while I'm still in the room with you. I have more than enough ideas of my own without your giving me more."

Their eyes met for a moment and held, sharing things their lips dared not say. Finally, Anna Rose broke the extended silence, saying quietly, "Then you had better leave, Hugh."

He did, but not before pausing a moment longer to caress her with a longing gaze.

Anna Rose hadn't expected to nap. But before many minutes had passed, she was sound asleep.

Outside, Hugh rejoined Angus, who had taken a cane fishing pole from a shed outside the house and already had a fat perch on his line.

"Fine fishing!" the older man called. "You'd better wet a hook, Hugh."

For a long time they sat side by side on the bank, feeling a tug on the line just often enough to keep them from drowsing off in the sun. Finally, Angus said, "Well, I suppose I'd better be starting back. The doctor said I shouldn't overdo." The words seemed to carry a double connotation.

"Shall I wake Anna Rose?" Hugh asked.

"No, no! You two stay on. It's early yet. I don't want to spoil your afternoon."

"But, Angus," Hugh said uneasily. Under normal circumstances, Angus's plea of fatigue and his desire to return to the house would have seemed perfectly natural. But there was certainly nothing natural about a man setting up a woodland rendezvous for his wife and a lover.

Angus would hear no objections, however. "Anna Rose needs this time away from the house and her duties with young John. As a matter of fact, you both need some time off for a bit of relaxation. See that she enjoys herself! Take your time getting back." Angus looked hard at Hugh, as if he meant to make sure that the other man had taken his meaning. "I'll see you sometime this evening."

Hugh tried to protest. But Anna Rose's husband refused to listen. Angus turned his back, squared his shoulders, and strode away with a forced dignity that belied the pain in his heart, the tears in his eyes. In another moment, he had mounted up and ridden away into the woods.

Hugh sat for a long time on the bank, fighting demons that he knew, in the end, must win out over honor and reason. Still, he held on for nearly an hour before he rose and started toward the house. Even then, his resolve was not firm.

Angus Campbell had certainly managed to make things difficult for him. Perhaps the man was more clever than any of them had ever suspected. Angus might have achieved the results he desired—a healthy lover to satisfy his wife—by simply warning Hugh Sinclair to stay away from Anna Rose or else. That would have pushed Hugh to his very limits. He was not a man to take threats lightly. Under those circumstances, he would have found a way to declare himself to Anna Rose and to follow through with his desires.

He stopped a few paces from the house and shook his head, suddenly struck with another thought. What if Angus Campbell, sensing Hugh's perverse nature, cooked up this whole tale of the doctor's warnings and his desire to have his wife loved properly, guessing that such a request might be the only way to keep them apart? It was a sobering thought!

If that was the truth of the matter, Angus Campbell's scheme had backfired. Now that Hugh was on his way to her, he discovered that there could be no turning back. He had waited too long for this moment, hungered too strongly, ached too deeply. He might have been shocked at Campbell's unusual proposal in the beginning, but now stronger passions drove him.

She was having the loveliest dream. Actually, it was rather shocking. She was lying naked in a meadow of red clover, but she wasn't in the least embarrassed by her unclothed state. It seemed

338

right. It seemed good. Someone—she couldn't quite see his face—was plaiting wildflowers into her hair. She could feel his strong fingers playing through her tresses. Birds sang all about, and bees hummed as they gathered nectar from the blossoms. Every once in a while, her lover would toss a flower on her breast, laughing and saying, "Here's a kiss for you, my love, and another."

The velvety petals did feel as light and tingling as kisses when they brushed her flesh. She kept reaching out to the man—wanting him, needing to love him—but he was just out of her grasp. Still, she knew that soon he would come to her. And that knowledge brought with it peace, calm, and an enfolding warmth.

"Anna Rose." The whisper came not from her dream, but from the real world. She opened her eyes; she saw his face at last. He wasn't smiling, but there was a gentle understanding in his face that made her realize he knew her needs and had come to satisfy them.

"Hugh?" His name on her lips was equally tender. "What are you doing here?"

"Don't you know, my love?"

He leaned down and brushed her lips with his. The kiss made her tremble down deep inside. She pressed her palms against his chest, gently forcing him away.

"Where's Angus?"

He paused a long time trying to think of the right way to tell her. Should he explain that Angus had left them to themselves so that he could give her what her husband was no longer able to? Would she believe him? Probably not. At any rate, he had no desire to make love to Anna Rose simply to fill a void in her life. She had to want him too for the act to mean anything to either one of them. While he was still trying to think what to say, Anna Rose answered her own question.

"He's left us here together, hasn't he? He did it on purpose."

Without even realizing what he was doing, Hugh had been caressing her cheek with one finger. Now suddenly, he saw how her color had risen with his touch.

"You know then?" he asked.

"I've known something was not right with him. He hasn't stopped loving me, but he hasn't loved me either. Till now I could only guess why he kept prolonging our stay with you. He was planning this all the while, wasn't he? Oh, Hugh, what are we going to do?" Her voice was filled with pain and desperation.

"This, darling."

He bent down to taste her lips again, but this time his kiss was

339

far more persuasive. At his hunger, Anna Rose felt her long-denied passions rising, boiling up inside her like a dam about to break. She answered his kiss eagerly, and made no attempt to stay his fondling, searching hands. Soon she lay upon the bed as naked and as unashamed as she had been only a short time before in the clover field of her fantasy. In the very places where the dream flowers had kissed her body, Hugh's lips now tasted her flesh.

When he came to her at last, there were no barriers of guilt or shame between them. Anna Rose accepted Hugh Sinclair's love totally, gratefully, adoringly. There was no place left on earth except his arms, no love left in the universe except their love for each other.

Afterward, they held each other tenderly and talked in quiet voices. So much had gone unsaid for so long.

"He hasn't told you how serious his illness really is," Hugh confessed.

"I guessed as much. Only last night, he made me promise that I'll wed as soon as possible after he's gone. I knew something was troubling him."

Hugh was still holding her, still stroking her as he filled his gaze with her wondrous body. "And now he's chosen your next husband. Rory would have approved."

"Rory?"

"On your wedding day, he made me promise that I'd take care of you if anything happened to him. I wanted to. Oh, how I wanted to, Anna Rose! If only you'd given me half a chance!"

She snuggled closer to his chest, sighing and breathing in his male musk. The very scent of him made her weak with renewed longing.

"I'm glad you told me, Hugh. About Angus and about Rory. Now I won't go blundering about as I have in the past." She sat up suddenly and stilled his busy hands, her face set in serious lines. "Hugh, there's something I must tell you. I should have before now, but I've been afraid to."

"What is it, darling?"

"It's Charity. She's *my* daughter."

He stared at her for a long time, trying to make sense of the words. "I don't understand, Anna Rose."

Before giving herself time to lose her nerve, she told him the story of her move to Five Points and that dreadful winter of her daughter's birth. The expression in his eyes told her that he both believed and accepted the fact. He held her and soothed her and dried her tears. At last the pain of that time was purged from her heart.

They still had much to talk about, but it was growing late. When Anna Rose was calm again, they dressed and prepared to leave the River House, neither of them realizing that all of their lovemaking had been seen, all of their secrets heard.

Weyman Campbell, pleased beyond words with his afternoon's discoveries, followed them at some distance as they headed back to the manse. How delightful to find out that Anna Rose still plied her old trade!

It was not until a few nights later that Weyman Campbell made his move. Everyone at The Highlands had welcomed him, his father with an embrace, and Anna Rose with as much civility as she could muster. She had managed to keep herself very busy and out of his way since his arrival.

But on this night the moon was full and the other men had gone with some of the slaves on a coon hunt. Anna Rose thought that Weyman had gone with them. She fell asleep, feeling secure in the knowledge that he was no threat to her.

When she awoke sometime after midnight to find a tall shadow looming over her bed, she gave a soft cry.

"Get out of my room!" she commanded.

He sauntered over to the bed and sat down beside her, letting his hand stroke her bare arm. "In a while, Anna Rose. First, I have some things to tell you, and you would be wise to listen carefully." The hard tone of his voice alarmed her further.

"I can't think of anything you could possibly say that would interest me!"

"Oh, come now! We both know my father is dying. Soon you and I and that baby of yours will be the heirs to his fortune. To my way of thinking, that's at least one heir too many. I am his firstborn of his first marriage. I think you should persuade him to tear up that new will he's made. After all, you'll be well taken care of." He leaned down close to her face and whispered, "You see, I know all about you and Sinclair. I was at the River House the other afternoon."

Anna Rose gasped and struggled away from him. "I won't let you steal what belongs to Johnnie!"

"I see it the other way around. You are the thief!"

Anna Rose was shivering, her heart pounding. She wanted more than anything to be away from this man. How could such a kind father sire such a detestable son?

Summoning all her courage, she said, "I will not even try to persuade Angus to change his will. And it won't do you any good to threaten me. He knows all about Hugh and . . ."

When she floundered momentarily, Weyman seized upon his chance. "Ah, but there's more! A late friend of yours told me all about you, your past and how my father came to marry you."

Anna Rose stared through the darkness, not comprehending.

"The gentleman's name was Flynn, and the address he mentioned was a certain house in Cherry Street, near the East Side docks. He referred to the place as a 'sailors' heaven!' He also told me my father *bought* his soiled dove for a mere fifty dollars. I will, of course, return your price to you when I come into my inheritance. For now, I thought you might like to make your first payment for my silence in trade."

Anna Rose was numb with shock. She could find no words to deny his accusations, no strength to scream for help when he grabbed her. A moment later, it was too late as his mouth bore down on hers, bruising and demanding.

Had the heavens not opened up to force the hunters home in a drenching downpour, Weyman Campbell might have accomplished his goal. As it was, Angus entered the room in the nick of time.

His eyes flashing and his voice thundering, Angus hauled his son from atop his wife and beat him nearly unconscious.

Anna Rose could only cower on the bed, sobbing, as she watched. When it was done, and Weyman Campbell had been sent on his way in the stormy night, Angus collapsed on the bed beside his weeping wife.

"Oh, Angus, I'm so sorry!" she cried.

"Anna Rose, this is not your doing. I know that. I only wish I hadn't been such an old fool. I should have realized sooner that this change in him was all an act. But I'm done with him now. I told him that from this night forward I have only one son—our son."

The weariness in Angus's voice frightened Anna Rose. "Angus, are you all right? It isn't your heart?"

He reached out and took her hand, bringing it gently to his lips. "Oh, my dear, it is my heart, and it's breaking right now for what I've done to you. Come lie close to me. Let me hold you for a while."

The terrible night ended in a quiet, tremulous peace as Anna Rose lay encircled by her husband's arms, feeling the faintly erratic beat of his heart against her breasts.

30

To Anna Rose it seemed that Angus was never the same after that awful night. When he was forced to send his firstborn son away, something died within him. Each day he seemed to grow weaker. Anna Rose tried her best to cheer him. But it was as if Angus Campbell had already given up and consigned himself to the grave. She remembered with horror the story of how he'd had himself fitted for his coffin after his first wife's death.

Indeed, their whole world had changed. The panic of 1837, which had blighted the rest of the country's economy the year before, reached the South, weighing heavily upon the rice planters. Markets were scarce and prices well below standard in 1838. Shipping came to a virtual standstill, a marked blow to the thriving town of Darien. Merchandise ran low in the shops and some stores closed altogether. Even the summer months at the cottage on The Ridge were different. The lavish socials of the past season gave way to quiet suppers or picnics on the bluff. No one felt in the mood to entertain. No one had the funds. "Economy" became the watchword of their lives.

The two bright spots in Anna Rose's life these days were her growing children and her recaptured love for Hugh Sinclair. Although their busy lives and the distance separating their two plantations prevented any frequency of their meeting, the times they did share—usually at Hugh's River House—fostered a new found closeness between them.

The summer months had proved extremely difficult, with Anna Rose at the cottage and Hugh at The Highlands. On several occasions when Angus knew Hugh was coming for a visit, he made up an excuse to be away. But Anna Rose could never bring herself to submit to her passions under her husband's roof. So what should have been bright days, when Hugh was at the cottage to see his daughter, were darkened by the frustrating distance separating the two lovers.

The move back to Rosedhu held a special kind of excitement for Anna Rose that fall. No sooner were they comfortably situated at home than she received the long-awaited message, asking her to come to the River House the next afternoon. She slept little the night before her rendezvous, counting the hours until she would be in Hugh's arms once more. On the appointed day, she went about her duties automatically, hoping to pass the morning quickly.

When Angus joined her for dinner at three, they exchanged the usual casual conversation about plantation duties. Anna Rose could not eat, and only toyed with her food. When dessert was placed before them, Anna Rose was still trying to work up the courage to tell Angus she would be away most of the afternoon and early evening. He never questioned her, for he both understood and approved of her destination when she went "for a ride." Still, there was that pained look deep in his eyes when he knew she would be with Hugh. He had every right to disapprove, though he had instigated this whole affair.

Anna Rose poked at the whipped cream atop her pecan pie, trying to force the words out.

"What are your plans for the rest of the day, my dear?"

Angus's question made her jump nearly out of her skin. But she controlled her voice carefully as she answered, "It's such a fine day that I thought I might take a long ride."

An uncomfortable silence followed. Finally, Angus said with forced affability, "You should! You've been cooped up here too much since our return. And you've suffered through a long, hot summer." He pushed his chair back from the table abruptly and rose. "Enjoy yourself, my dear."

Anna Rose cringed within as her husband bent stiffly to brush her cheek with dry lips. This was the only show of affection he offered these days, something less than would be afforded a well-loved daughter. It wounded her deeply that he no longer shared her bed, sleeping on a daybed in his office. But he had set the rules. She was only a pawn in this strange game of love.

She sighed and left the table, willing her conscience to leave her be.

Hugh was waiting at the River House when she arrived. He looked wonderful! The summer sun had bronzed his skin, and his dark hair was windswept from his ride. His full-sleeved linen shirt was open at the neck, and tight buckskin britches clung to his form like a second skin. He ran toward her and, never giving her a chance to dismount, swept her out of the saddle and into his strong arms.

Without a word of greeting, his lips took hers prisoner. She felt dizzy with her rush of release and longing. She clung to him tightly, returning his passion with a frenzied display of her own.

When he reached the door, Hugh finally broke away and stared down into her face. "It's been so long, my darling!"

"Too long!" she answered, teasing his ear with the tip of her tongue.

Hugh set her on her feet and stripped off his shirt immediately. He stopped there, coming to steal another kiss before he finished undressing himself and his lover.

Anna Rose felt his strong hands tremble as he removed her riding habit. But his nervousness was nothing compared to hers. She felt as if this were the first time they'd been together. Only their knowledge of each other's body—what pleased, what inflamed—was proof they knew each other well.

Hugh had his lover soaring long before he joined her in their total embrace. Her breasts, her thighs, her very soul ached with a maddening need for him when he finally entered her with a torturously slow thrust.

Anna Rose felt her senses reel as he filled her, ever so gradually, but, oh, so fully. Her muscles contracted, trying to draw him in quickly. But he would have none of it as he eased into her, inch by throbbing inch. She held her breath until she felt his heat searing the very heart of her. Already, the blissful end was beginning, and he rode her quickly to a soul-shattering orgasm.

But it was a long while before he was done with her. Miraculously, holding himself in check, he brought her to the brink again, then urged her over, to dizzying new heights. Finally, they collapsed together in sheer, ecstatic exhaustion. They lay in each other's arms, panting between kisses.

Not until they were dressed and ready to ride their separate ways did Hugh break his awful news to her. She was so happy, so filled and satisfied by him, that what he said all but shattered her.

He stood very close, his arm around her shoulders, his lips against her temple. "Darling, I have to go away for a time."

She pulled out of his embrace and stared at him, hoping she had heard him wrong. "No, Hugh!"

He nodded, unsmiling. "I hope it won't be for long. I've already talked to Angus about this."

A cold hand seemed to close around her heart. "You mean he's sending you away? But he can't! Not now, not after he brought us together!" She threw her arms around him sobbing against his chest. "Oh, darling, I can't stand it! Please, please don't go!"

He lifted her chin to look into her teary eyes. "Anna Rose, listen to me. Angus has nothing to do with my going. I spoke to

345

him about letting Charity stay with you while I'm away. So, you see, you can't blame your husband. In fact, he did everything he could to keep me here, even offering to pay off all my debts. But I wouldn't hear of that. A man must take care of his own."

"Hugh, where are you going? For how long?" she begged.

"I've taken a position as captain on one of the coastal steamers that plies the route between Savannah and Key West. I need the money, darling, if I'm to save The Highlands. Unfortunately, I'm not the planter Angus is. I made some disastrous mistakes with my crops last year. I risked almost everything, hoping to make a great deal of money, and I lost. As for how long I'll be gone, I can't tell you. A few months, a year perhaps."

Her voice trembled as she asked, "When do you leave?"

"That's why I had to see you today. I leave tomorrow morning." Reading her intention in her eyes, he was quick to add, "Don't come to see me off! I've always hated dockside fare-wells."

He kissed her once more, deeply, thoroughly. Then he lifted her onto her horse and gave the animal a slap on its flank.

"I love you, Anna Rose!" he shouted after her as her mount broke into a gallop.

Anna Rose, in spite of her promise to Hugh, slipped out in the cold mist of early dawn the next morning, unable to let her lover leave without setting eyes on him one last time. She rowed herself across the river and stood above the docks on the bluff at the edge of town, watching him secretly through her tears and wondering if she would ever see him again. She stood there, feeling empty and alone, until his boat was only a faint speck on the horizon. Then with a heavy step and a heavier heart, she headed home.

The fast-fading autumn gave way to the short, chill days of winter. With the cold weather, Angus was reduced to a near-invalid, sitting before the fire all day, wrapped in a shawl and blanket. Anna Rose tried to cheer him, but the old bright spirit had flown from him. It was as if the betrayal of his son had wounded him mortally. The only thing worse to ponder than Weyman's last visit was the thought that someday he might return. Without ever saying it aloud, Anna Rose and Angus shared the fear that he might come back one day to have his revenge upon them both. It was not a calming thought.

As for Hugh Sinclair, he wrote often to his daughter and to Angus, always sending along some friendly message for Anna Rose. Anna Rose understood his reluctance to proclaim his love to her directly, but the absence of such declarations pained her deeply.

Once Hugh managed a few hours off while his steamer was in for repairs at Savannah, and he came riding up to Rosedhu unannounced. Anna Rose came alive for the first time in weeks. However, it was a strained time. The love, the need, the passion were still there, all too evident, passing between them with the intensity of a bolt of lightning flashing through the sky. But in deference to Angus, Anna Rose and Hugh kept their distance. When he rode away the next day, the emptiness she felt was worse than ever.

Then on a frost-white morning shortly after Christmas, Pride brought exciting news from the mail boat, a letter from Margaret Mackintosh.

October 24, 1838
Inverness, Scotland

My darling Anna Rose,

How long I have waited to write you these tidings! At last, my affairs are in order, our tickets are in my hand, and we are preparing to come to you! You cannot begin to imagine my joy at this prospect! We sail on the first day of the new year, bound for the port of Savannah, and, with God's guidance, will be on your doorstep by the middle of the following month. All will be coming, including Iris and Shane, who is much stronger now.

Can you possibly imagine how I rejoiced to receive the news, first of baby John, and then of your dear little daughter? It is indeed a miracle that mother and child have been reunited. It will be good when the news can be told to all, but I will keep your secret for now, as you asked. I long to hold both of my sweet grandchildren very, very soon!

I do hope Angus is improving every day. Tell him that when I arrive I will brew him a Scotch broth sure to restore him. It is the least I can do, considering all that he has done for this family.

My dearest love to each and every one of you. Brothers and sisters send hugs. Until we meet again . . .

Your grateful mother,
Margaret Mackintosh

Anna Rose read the letter aloud to Angus, carefully avoiding the part about her daughter. She had yet to tell Heather or her husband the whole truth. When the time was right . . .

Her excitement over her mother's news was contagious, and soon Angus was laughing and crying right along with her.

"Well, bless me!" he said, hugging his beaming wife in his thin arms. "I was beginning to believe we'd never see this day! I can't tell you, Anna Rose, how happy I am for you. And for myself! That family of yours will certainly put some spirit back into this old house."

Anna Rose laughed. "Once Cullen and Ewan have their first go-around under this roof, you'll probably think my family has brought you more spirit than you bargained for, dear. You'll be hailing the first boat to send them back home!"

"Never, Anna Rose!" His voice was tender. "I want you all close to me."

For the first time in more months than she could remember, Angus drew his wife into his arms and kissed her, truly kissed her.

Even with all the preparations that had to be made, the weeks before the Mackintosh family's arrival passed all too slowly, it seemed to Anna Rose. But finally the happy day arrived.

As she and Angus stood with the children on the dock at Darien watching the boat draw nearer, it seemed that the little steamer took forever to creep up the river.

"Oh, Angus, I'm so excited!"

He squeezed her hand. "You have every right to be. And I must admit to more than a touch of nervousness. What if your mother finds her newest son-in-law lacking?"

Anna Rose gave her husband an appraising glance. The last weeks had restored some of his vigor. Now, dressed in his kilt for the occasion of the family's arrival, despite the whip of the chill wind about his bare knees, he looked every bit the noble Highland warrior. The clan colors gave him a decidedly distinguished air.

"My mother will love you, Angus, just as I do."

He smiled at her quiet words, acknowledging with a nod that he loved her, too. They had yet to discuss the situation with Hugh Sinclair, though Anna Rose took Angus's silence on the matter as approval of the arrangement. Anna Rose, knowing that he wished not to talk about it, kept her peace on the subject and went out of her way to be the perfect wife to him, in gratitude and in genuine affection for the man who was her husband.

"Oh, look! I can see them!" Anna Rose cried excitedly.

The little steamer chugged up the Altamaha. Even from a distance the knot of Mackintoshes clustered at the forward rail was easy to distinguish. They caught sight of Anna Rose and waved.

"Oh, Angus, I'm going to cry!" she said, clinging to his arm for support. "What'll they think when they find me all red-eyed?"

He patted her hand solicitously. "My darling wife, I doubt that yours will be the only tears this day."

The barrage of embraces and flood of happy tears soon proved Angus right. He felt quite overwhelmed to receive such a large and boisterous group into his quiet world.

There was the mother, Margaret Mackintosh, a beautiful, stately woman whose eyes alone betrayed her age and the sorrows she had endured. He was surprised to note that his mother-in-law was still so young, so lovely. Iris's letter had painted her as a weary and aging widow. She looked more like one of her own daughters than their mother.

The boys, Cullen and Ewan, were strapping lads, crofter's sons, indeed, and full of the devil, he could tell. Cullen, at seventeen, reminded him of a big, friendly sheep dog wanting to be scratched behind the ears. A year younger than his brother and not so forward, Ewan held back, watching all that happened with a keen eye, but not really joining fully in the happy celebration.

The young ladies would no doubt be turning many a head in the district. At fourteen and twelve, they were both beauties, but very different. The older sister, Laurel, had a quiet, haunting loveliness about her, while the younger, Fern, was as bright and vivacious as the first rays of the rising sun striking the velvet petals of a buttercup.

Only when Angus's gaze fell on his wife's oldest sister, did his smile fade. Iris Mackintosh Kilgore had the face of an angel, but the eyes of a wanton. Even though he knew she was a year younger than Anna Rose, Iris looked older, hardened by life. While all the other Mackintoshes exuded love and warmth, Iris stood motionless on the dock, as if she'd been chiseled from cold Georgia granite. When her young son Shane whimpered at her side, she shushed him harshly, jerking his thin arm until he howled. Angus watched the boy's grandmother bestow a chastising look on her daughter as she swept the weeping child into her arms.

So, this was his wife's family, his family now, Angus thought. Anna Rose had told him right; there would be few dull moments from this day forward.

* * *

The next days and weeks were filled with so much happiness and activity that Anna Rose lost all track of time. Had it not been for the nagging, little empty spot in her heart, she might not even have missed Hugh. But, of course, she did.

Her mother proved a tonic for Angus. Margaret, no stranger to pain herself, kept her son-in-law so busy explaining the workings of his plantation and showing her his holdings, that he had hardly a moment to think of his "wasting palsy." Anna Rose felt almost jealous that her mother was able to work such a miracle where she herself had failed. But she was too delighted with his seeming recovery to feel anything other than gratitude for her mother's healing talents.

Pride took her brothers under his dark wing. They hunted rice birds, quail, and dove, then moved on to bigger game, bringing in turkeys, wild boar, and deer. When they weren't hunting, they were out in the boats, fishing for hours at a stretch. They even left off their brotherly bickering when Pride set them to work burning out their own boat from a huge cypress trunk.

"Aye, this is the life!" Cullen told the assembled company one night at dinner. "My future's decided. I'll take my part of our money from the sale of the croft and sink it back into the land. Angus, do you know of a plot of rice land hereabouts that might be bought, but not too dearly?"

Anna Rose felt her heart swell when she saw her husband's expression. He was beaming at his young brother-in-law, pleased not only that the boy had planter's blood in his veins, but also that he had invited the older man's advice.

"Well, lad, I might just know exactly the place," Angus answered. "We'll go tomorrow and let you look it over."

Angus, who had resumed sharing Anna Rose's bed since her family's arrival, confided in her that night that he wanted to sell off a few acres of Rosedhu to Cullen. "I'd willingly give the land to the lad. But a man needs to feel he's worked for what he gets. I wouldn't deny a fine young man like your brother that pleasure."

Ewan surprised them all a few days later by announcing that he'd like to go away to school. After talking to some of the plantation sons about his own age at a Darien social, his mind was made up. "I want to attend Franklin College. Then perhaps I can come back to McIntosh County and read law with one of the local barristers."

Anna Rose watched her mother's pleased expression at Ewan's words. He had seemed to be such an unsettled lad a few years back. She knew her mother had worried no end over his fate. But

Ewan had grown up. He knew what he wanted and he meant to go after it. There was a lot of John Mackintosh in his second son.

Laurel and Fern spent their hours happily playing house with Charity, Shane, and little Johnnie. As the weather grew warmer and they could move their play outside, Angus had his carpenter construct a playhouse beside the huge fig tree near the kitchen. "It will double as a schoolhouse as soon as I find a proper tutor," Angus told Anna Rose. "Your sisters are as bright as they are beautiful. It will give me great pleasure to see them well-educated along with the younger in our brood."

Anna Rose could hardly contain her pleasure at his words. Angus had taken all the children under his protection. He was a born father. What a pity that his first son had turned out so badly! Surely it could be through no fault of his.

Charity adored her new relatives. She took a special liking for her shy cousin, Shane. He obviously worshipped the ground she trod, and under her guidance, he began to emerge from his shell. The two shared a close family resemblance, looking, Anna Rose thought, almost like twin brother and sister. They were beautiful children, both fair and blue-eyed. It was a special joy, seeing them together.

Only Iris marred the perfect tranquility at Rosedhu. A restless, tormented soul, she paced the halls at night, then slept most of the days away. She seemed totally uninterested in joining the others on any sort of outing. She spoke seldom and never pleasantly.

"What's wrong with her, Mother?" Anna Rose asked one especially lovely spring morning when they were planning a boat trip to Saint Simons to picnic on the beach and to gather shells.

Margaret shook her head tiredly. "Heaven only knows, my dear. I've never understood your sister. I suppose she misses her gay social life back home."

Anna Rose could hardly believe her ears. "A social life? On the croft? I never knew one existed."

"You never set out seeking adventure like your sister."

Anna Rose gave a wry laugh. "I never had to. It always found me!"

Her mother covered her daughter's hand and squeezed affectionately. "That's not what I mean, Anna Rose. Iris would never want the kind of life you've had. She couldn't handle it. What she does seek is male companionship."

"Oh!" Anna Rose sat up straighter, a sudden look of awareness on her face. "Why, of course! Why didn't it dawn on me? We'll plan a party, Mother. Angus knows everyone in the district. Don't you worry. We'll have Iris so busy with invitations soon that she won't have a moment to brood."

The invitations that Anna Rose and Margaret carefully lettered by hand, then sent to all the plantations in the district by slave messengers, announced a "Planting Season Ball" to be held at Rosedhu. Angus, much in the spirit of the frolic, sent Anna Rose, Margaret, and Iris to Savannah to have new gowns made for the occasion. The lavish ball was the talk of the entire district. Everyone who was anyone would be there. The plan seemed to be working already. Iris had lost some of her dour outlook and even offered to help with the preparations.

By midmorning of the appointed date, plantation boats were arriving already at Rosedhu landing. The early comers were invited to a picnic on the grounds before the main social event got underway that evening. Anna Rose noted with pleasure that Iris was swarmed by handsome admirers. It was no wonder. She looked ravishing in the lavender Swiss dress that she'd had made for the occasion.

After the picnic, the ladies adjourned to the bedrooms at Rosedhu to rest before they dressed for the ball. Anna Rose invited Iris to accompany her to the master bedroom for her nap, hoping they would have some time to talk. Bad feelings had existed between them when Anna Rose had left Scotland. She hoped they could smooth out any lingering misunderstandings once and for all.

Anna Rose was undressed, down to her camisole and pantalets, and had stretched out on the great rice bed by the time Iris extracted herself from the charming company on the lawn.

"Well, there you are!" Anna Rose said as her sister entered the room. "I've been wondering what was keeping you."

"This is really a foolish, tiresome custom, you know," Iris said in a disgruntled tone. "Finally, there's a reason to get out of bed in this deadly dull place, and what do you do? Order all the women to their rooms! I'd planned to stay down there with the men. But your prudish husband told me it would be unseemly! Anna Rose, I don't see how you could have married such an old fuddy-duddy! Why, he's older than Mother and twice as priggish!"

Her sister's words angered Anna Rose deeply, but she forced herself to remain calm. "Age means nothing when you are in love, Iris," she replied.

"In love?" Iris cried. "With that fossil? Please, Anna Rose, spare me! Why, if it weren't for your son, I'd doubt he could even perform any longer!"

Again Anna Rose felt the coldness touch her heart. But she refused to allow herself to lash out at her thoughtless sister. Instead, she changed the subject. "Have you never thought of marrying again, Iris? It's been some time since your husband passed away. I should think you'd want a father for Shane. He's such a darling boy, but so withdrawn. He needs a man's influence in his life, that's very plain."

"You sound just like Mother!" Iris snapped. "She's always badgering me about the boy. Well, he'll grow up one way or another. I certainly don't plan to wet-nurse him all his life. As for my marrying to provide him with a father, that's the most outrageous thing I've ever heard! If I marry again, it will be for myself alone! And I know what I want in a man this time: wealth, good looks—"

Anna Rose was frowning. "What about love, Iris?"

"Oh, don't give me that!" Iris whined. "We both know that love is just some fantasy invented to make women stay virgins half their lives. Well, it certainly didn't stop me!"

Anna Rose felt herself blushing at her sister's forthright speech. "You did marry very young, Iris."

"Ha! That's not what I mean." She stared hard at her sister, smiling cunningly while her gray eyes remained cold. She'd been waiting a long time to spring this secret on her sister. No one, looking at Shane Kilgore's light hair and blue-blue eyes, could doubt for an instant that Rory McShane had been his real father. It was time Anna Rose learned the truth. "You still believe I was a virgin on my wedding night, don't you? Well, I fooled you all, even my husband. I was already carrying Shane by the time I married Jaimie!"

"Iris!" Anna Rose gasped. "You can't mean what you're saying!"

"Why not, when it's the truth?" Iris sounded subdued suddenly, but she recovered her feisty temper quickly and flounced toward the door. "I can't stand being up here a minute longer. I'm going back downstairs. I don't care what your husband thinks!"

After Iris left, Anna Rose lay on her back on the bed staring up at the canopy and mulling over all that had passed between them. She tried to think who Shane's father might be, if not Jaimie Kilgore. She and Iris had always been together before they were wed. Under their parents' tight rein there had been no occasion for Iris to indulge her passionate inclination.

Suddenly, Anna Rose sat bolt upright in bed. A scene, like a misty vision, materialized before her eyes. A moonlit night, two figures huddled close, Iris with twigs in her hair and Rory looking no less a shambles. The two of them coming together, kissing in the moonlight outside her window.

Anna Rose pressed her fingertips to her lips to stifle a cry. Tears flooded her eyes. Could it be? Had Rory and Iris . . .

"No!" she said in a fervent whisper. "Never! It's not possible!"

But even as she spoke the words aloud, the memory of Rory's dying words came back to her. Iris's name had come to her on his final breath. The start of a dying man's confession? Pain tore through her heart. She knew it was true. Even her young nephew's name was a slap in the face to her pride—Shane, named for his father, Rory McShane. Iris had wanted Rory all along; she had sworn she would have him. And she had made her threat good!

How could Anna Rose ever face Iris calmly again?

Somehow she would have to for Shane's sake. The boy was a troubled child as it was. Knowledge of his true parentage might do irreparable damage. If Rory was really the boy's father, all the more reason for Anna Rose to protect him.

She rose from the bed and rang for her maid. It was time to dress for the ball.

31

Angus Campbell sloshed more brandy into his glass and continued pacing the library. He was drinking against doctor's orders, but tonight he needed more strength than he could find within himself alone. He glanced at the door. Where could Anna Rose be? He hoped she would come down before their surprise guest arrived. On the other hand, he half-hoped his carefully laid plans fell through.

He had been so sure this was the right thing to do. But as he waited downstairs for his wife to join him, he began to experience the old pangs of jealousy. He damned himself a thousand times over for the way he felt. Anna Rose had given him everything— her love, her comfort, a fine son, a family. Why, then, could he not give her the one thing she craved without harboring such grudging thoughts?

He had always considered himself a sophisticated and civilized gentleman. Hadn't he made a similar and equally sensible arrangement when his first wife was ill, when he'd been forced to abandon her bed? But he had not lost his affection for Clara when he had turned to one of the slave women for his carnal gratification. Dahlia had accepted him stoically. And their union had produced a fine son in Pride. So, some good had come out of the bad situation, he reasoned.

Now, the tables were turned. Anna Rose was the one who needed a lover. She was young, vibrant, passionate, as he well remembered. It would be dastardly of him to deny her the physical love she needed.

Could he have lived all these years without the comfort of a woman to hold? No! And he had no right to enforce celibacy upon Anna Rose simply because he was no longer the man he should be. He had done what must be done and his flaming jealousy could just be damned!

"Angus?" His wife's voice at the library door made him turn. "Oh, there you are!"

"Darling!" He smiled and went to her, bestowing a kiss on her cheek. "You look ravishing this evening, as usual."

She turned to give him the full effect of her new gown of pale rose tissue silk, trimmed in lace shot through with silver. When she faced him again, his smile had faded and she glimpsed the pain in his eyes.

Anna Rose hurried to him and gripped his hand. "Angus, you aren't ill?"

He shook his head. "No, darling. It's just that you look almost too lovely. I don't know how I'll bear sharing you with anyone else tonight."

She hugged him, pressing her cheek to his. "Dear Angus, you say the sweetest things."

Moments later, their guests, decked out in all their finery, began arriving downstairs. Anna Rose stood at her husband's elbow, acting the perfect hostess as she welcomed each couple. But her eyes strayed time and again to Iris. Like a brightly plumed bird, she preened and fluttered in her shockingly low-cut scarlet satin creation, attracting the attention of every man in the room. The glances she received from the ladies were anything but approving. Anna Rose noted with horror that her sister went in to dinner on the arm of one of their married guests, whose wife was left to fend for herself. Angus quickly sized up the situation and escorted the lady in, while Anna Rose took Cullen's arm.

Dinner seemed to be going well. But Anna Rose was conscious of a certain amount of strain radiating from her husband. Several times, Angus motioned to Pride, who nodded, then left the room only to return a short while later with a negative shake of his head. Anna Rose guessed that something was going on which she knew nothing about. It seemed almost as if Angus was expecting someone else to arrive. She glanced about the table, taking a quick inventory. All their guests were here.

Not until after dinner, when the ladies were making their exit to leave the gentlemen to their cigars and brandy, did Anna Rose have a chance to question Angus. When she passed his chair, she leaned down and asked, "What is afoot, my dear? You've been as nervous as a hare at a fox hunt all evening."

Angus offered her a wan smile. "Nothing to worry about, my darling. You'll see soon enough. Now go along and entertain your ladies."

Anna Rose had no more interest than Iris did in entertaining the other female guests after dinner. Something was going on and she very much wanted to be with her husband to find out exactly what it was. The spate of gossip in the parlor quickly bored her. And Iris's endless pacing annoyed her even more.

Finally, excusing herself to look in on the children, Anna Rose escaped the chattering females. Upstairs, Johnnie was fast asleep, one chubby thumb stuck in his mouth. She reached out and stroked his cheek. What a love he was!

Tiptoeing out of the nursery, she went to the room Iris shared with her son, where Shane should have been sleeping in his trundle bed. Anna Rose's heart all but stopped when she saw the little cot empty. For the first time, she realized how much difference it made that Shane might be Rory's son. Her fright was the same as if it had been one of her own children missing in the dark of night.

She fled the room, searching for the servant who should have been with him. But the upstairs hall was quiet and empty. Then she noticed that Charity's door was open.

"Oh, God, not both of them!" With a sinking feeling, she imagined the pair of them sneaking out for a late-night stroll along the dike. Anything could happen to them out there.

Clutching her breast, trying to keep hysteria at bay, Anna Rose rushed into the room. She expelled a long sigh and felt the dread draining away when she looked at the bed. Charity was there—safe, sound, and sleeping—with Shane, his golden hair tangled with hers, snuggled as close to her as he could get.

Anna Rose started to call the servant to take the boy back to his bed. But the children were sleeping so soundly and they looked so content, like two pink and gold cherubs. She tucked the covers up about them, kissed their foreheads, and left quietly.

She was almost down the stairs when she heard the front door opening. "Welcome, sir. The Major's been worried you might not get here." Pride's words drifted up to her, but she couldn't hear the other man's reply.

Who on earth? she wondered. All the guests had arrived long since. She hurried down the stairs to see who this latecomer could be. Halfway down, she stopped cold, hardly daring to believe her eyes.

"Hugh?" she asked, her voice little more than a whisper.

In answer, he smiled and came to where she stood. His eyes never left her as he climbed the stairs to meet the woman he loved. When he stood directly before her, he glanced over his shoulder to make sure they were alone, then took her into his arms.

Anna Rose had never felt anything like the sensation of this long-awaited embrace. For so many months, she had tried to push Hugh to the back of her mind, to keep him locked away in her heart until his return. That was, of course, impossible. Now the moment she had dreamed of for so long was actually here. She was in his arms. His lips were kissing hers. His body was pressed close, sending its heat to warm and caress her very soul.

Only as he was pulling away from the deep, thorough kiss did they become aware of their observer.

"Well, Sister dear, aren't you going to introduce me to your *friend*?"

Anna Rose gasped softly at the sound of Iris's voice. She tried to compose herself, but she knew her face was as bright a scarlet as her spying sister's gown. She was conscious of Hugh's movement at her side. He had tried to put some distance between them, but it was too late.

"Iris," Anna Rose said in an almost steady voice, "I'd like you to meet Captain Hugh Sinclair. He was a friend of Rory's and the captain of the ship that brought me to America."

Iris positively glowed for the man. "I believe I remember the name. Rory often mentioned you to me, Captain. Somehow I'd pictured you as much older, more the age of Anna Rose's dear husband."

"Mrs. Kilgore," Hugh answered with a bow, "I'm delighted to meet you at last. I've heard a great deal about you as well."

Iris offered him an enchanting trill of laughter. "None of it good, I'm sure, if my sister is the one who's been telling you."

357

Before their conversation could become any more uncomfortable for Anna Rose, the doors to the parlor and library opened and the guests converged once more.

"Ah, Hugh, you've made it!" Angus called. "How was Key West?"

"Hot!" Hugh called back over the babble of conversation separating them.

"And Savannah?"

"Wet, my friend! Very wet and unpleasant. I've longed for home. Thank you for giving me an excuse to visit."

"You need neither excuse nor invitation, Hugh. You're always welcome at Rosedhu. You know that."

Hugh moved down the stairs to clasp Angus's hand. Anna Rose stood watching, aching, knowing that she would try before the night was over to be alone with the man she loved, knowing also that her husband expected that she would and had brought Hugh here for that very purpose, as much as it hurt him.

Suddenly, music swelled through the hall. Angus, smiling in a strange, sad way, motioned Anna Rose to come have the first dance with Hugh. But before she could reach them, Iris flashed in like bright red flame to capture Hugh's arm.

"Captain, I'm sure you're a wonderful dancer. Therefore, I've decided that you and I shall lead out."

Hugh glanced up at Anna Rose and gave her a helpless shrug as her sister tugged him toward the music.

Anna Rose felt her blood go cold. Iris's plan was all too clear. Realizing that there was more than friendship between Hugh Sinclair and her sister, Iris meant to keep them apart if she could. Or more likely, she meant to have him for herself if she could manage it. Well, her little scheme wouldn't work. Hugh would have none of her false charms and falser words, Anna Rose was sure.

Suddenly, Anna Rose felt a warm hand on her arm. "Come along, my dear," Angus said soothingly. "Dance with me and don't fret over Iris. You'll have him away from her soon enough."

Anna Rose tried to laugh off her hurt and confusion. "If Hugh wants to dance with my sister, that's perfectly all right with me. They make a charming couple."

Angus leaned close and whispered, "My dear wife, you needn't try lying to me. And there's no need either in trying to protect my feelings in this matter. I love you more than life itself, Anna Rose. That is precisely why Hugh Sinclair is here tonight, why he has been here, with you, many times before. You're a woman who

358

needs a great deal of loving, more than I can give you these days. So let's be honest, shall we? You want him and so you shall have him!''

Anna Rose was speechless by the time Angus swept her onto the dance floor. She'd known that she had her husband's blessing all the while. But to have him state matters so bluntly made all the difference in the way she felt. It was almost as if she and Angus had suddenly become conspirators in the same wonderfully devious plan.

It wasn't easy to get away. Without Angus's help, the two lovers would have spent another long, frustrating night, staring at each other across a crowded room. And, undoubtedly, Iris would have been clinging to Hugh the whole while. As it was, she claimed Hugh for dance after dance, never letting anyone else get near him. Anna Rose was nearly out of her mind by the time Angus himself decided to intervene.

"My dear Captain," Angus said, tapping Hugh on the shoulder, "I'm afraid I can't allow you to monopolize my charming sister-in-law for another moment. The other poor chaps deserve their chance at her."

Before Iris could object, she was in Angus's arms and sweeping across the floor. She forced a bored smile, waiting for the end of the dance so that she could recapture her chosen prey.

Pride immediately met Hugh as he came off the dance floor, telling him that a boat had arrived at the landing with a message for him. Afraid that he'd been called back to Savannah prematurely, Hugh glanced about the room, anxious to have a final word with Anna Rose before he had to leave. But she was nowhere in sight. Annoyed beyond words, he turned and strode out, headed for the landing.

She was waiting there in the shadows, ready to come into his arms.

"Darling!" Hugh whispered between kisses. "What an awful night this has been!"

"Up till now," she replied breathlessly, before their lips met once more.

They went to the boathouse not far away. There was the scent of spring in the air, of new beginnings, of planting and growing. And so their feelings had grown in the months they had been apart. It seemed to Anna Rose that there had never been another man in her life, but after Hugh had loved her well, after the euphoria began to fade, a sadness descended over her.

359

Still lying naked in his arms, feeling his lips at her breast, she sighed and asked, "Darling, what's to become of us? I can't bear having you leave again, never knowing from one day to the next what will happen."

"Hush, love!" he soothed. "We aren't meant to know what will happen tomorrow or next week or next year. Someday things will be right for us—the right time, the right place. As for my going away again, it's better that way. It tears me up to see the look in Augus's eyes. I know he arranged this whole thing because he loves you and that only makes it harder. If I were in his place, I'd never have the strength. I'm a jealous man. I'd kill before I'd see you with another."

Anna Rose was crying softly, feeling every word Hugh spoke in the deepest part of her heart.

"Maybe this should be the last time, Hugh," she said quietly. "I don't think he can take it much longer. I'm not sure I can either."

Before Hugh could answer, a conch shrilled from outside.

"What the hell?" Hugh said. "A boat coming in this time of night?"

But the repeated blasts, they knew, signaled no boat. Something was very wrong.

"That's the fire signal!" Anna Rose cried, horrid visions of the night in New York rushing back to haunt her.

"No! Too many blasts," Hugh assured her. "But it is an alarm."

They dressed quickly. Anna Rose stayed inside while Hugh went out to see what was happening. When he returned, his face was pale.

"What is it?" Anna Rose demanded.

"Charity's missing." His voice was cold, toneless.

"Oh, no!" The picture of her daughter and Shane snuggled close in bed flitted before her eyes. "But I checked on her. She was sleeping soundly. Have they searched the house, Hugh?"

He gripped her shoulders before he broke the next news. "Now I don't want you to panic, Anna Rose. It seems young Shane was in her bedroom. He says a man came in and took her away."

"What man?" Anna Rose's mind was whirling. She could make no sense of any of this. There were twenty or so male guests in the house. But why would any of them go upstairs? Why would any of them take Charity from her bed?

Anna Rose pulled away from him and lunged for the door. "I have to find her, Hugh! My baby, my little girl! She's out there somewhere! She needs me!"

A grim-faced Angus met Anna Rose when she arrived back at the house. Her mother stood beside him, white with shock and fear. She took her daughter into her arms.

"Hush now, Anna Rose," Margaret said. "Angus says he won't get off the island with her. All the man are going out to search along with the servants. She'll be back home, safe and sound in no time. He wouldn't harm a child!"

"Who?" Anna Rose demanded of Angus, fearing she knew the answer already. "You must tell me! She's my own baby."

Angus Campbell's face was like hewn granite as he took his weeping wife from her mother. He had known the child was Anna Rose's for some time, since Hugh had confided the secret. But he'd said nothing to his wife, knowing she would tell him when she was ready. "Weyman came back tonight, Anna Rose," he said gently.

Through the long, dark hours, torches flared in the night. The armed men searched tirelessly, combing the dikes, the outbuildings, the rice swamps. But Weyman Campbell and the kidnapped child seemed to have disappeared. Anna Rose wanted to join in the search, but Angus forbade it. He was all too afraid of what they might find. He and Hugh went with the others, leaving Anna Rose in her mother's care.

It was near dawn when the two men, accompanied by Pride, found the first sign. One of Charity's pink ribbons waved like a flag from the broken branch that had torn it from her hair.

"This way," Angus commanded, taking his pistol from his belt.

The three men tramped into a palmetto thicket that swarmed with mosquitoes. The ground underfoot was soggy and uneven. They stumbled time and again, the sharp edges of the scrub palms slicing their faces and arms like razors.

Finally, up ahead they spotted a copse of bay trees. Beyond lay an open rice field, flooded with the spring flow.

"They have to be in those trees," Hugh whispered to Angus.

"Aye!" the older man answered. "You and Pride go around either side to the back. I'll wait here in case he makes a run for it."

Hugh gripped his friend's arm for a moment. "Angus, what if he doesn't give up?"

"Then shoot!" Angus answered grimly. "But mind the child. No harm must come to her."

"We'll try to take him peacefully," Hugh said, hoping to spare Angus any further trauma.

When Hugh and Pride were in position, Angus shouted, "Weyman Campbell, this is your father speaking. We have you surrounded. Send the child out and you won't be harmed. You have my promise on that!"

Weyman's voice, high-pitched with hysteria, answered back. "And you have my promise that if you come in here I'll slit her throat!"

Angus gripped his pistol tighter and edged toward the trees. "You're being foolish, Son! Leave the child be. What do you expect will come of this?"

"You'll tear up the new will and leave everything to me, your rightful heir, or I'll kill her."

Angus heard a rustling in the bushes behind him and turned. Anna Rose had disobeyed his orders and followed. He motioned for her to remain silent.

"How do I know you even have the girl?" Angus called.

Weyman appeared in the shadows among the thick bay branches, holding Charity before him as a shield. Her face was scratched and bloody from having been dragged, protesting, through the swamp, and her eyes were wide with terror. She saw Anna Rose and screamed her name. Angus heard a muffled sob from his wife.

Anna Rose, standing a few paces behind Angus, shivered with fear. It seemed that all the horrors she had lived through had been nothing compared to this. Her own little girl in the clutches of this madman!

"Please, God, don't let him hurt her!" she whispered.

She spied two dark shadows moving around the copse toward Angus. Hugh and Pride. They were closing in from both sides, evidently attempting to take Weyman by surprise and rescue Charity, while Angus continued talking to divert him.

"Why did you take the girl instead of Johnnie, if you meant to get at me?" Angus asked evenly.

Weyman laughed humorlessly. "You guessed my plan. It was your other son I was after. But that stupid idiot Dahlia was in the room with him. So I figured I'd get *her* daughter. That little bastard in bed with her almost fouled up the whole scheme, though. I meant to strangle him to shut him up. But there wasn't time."

"You've done a lot of unfortunate things in your life, Weyman. Don't add a child's blood to your hands. Think of your dear mother."

Angus's mention of Clara seemed to push Weyman over the

edge. "I *am* thinking of her," he yelled crazily. "She wanted me to have what was rightfully mine! You think she cared about you, old man? No! Never! She only loved me! She told me so! She said Rosedhu would be mine because she wanted it that way. And now you bring that woman and her bastards here and—"

It was all over quickly. Even as Angus moved closer toward the trees, Pride and Hugh charged in from either side. Anna Rose stood frozen with fear. She heard an angry snarl from Weyman, a scream from her daughter, a shot, then her own mournful cry.

A moment later, Hugh rushed toward her, carrying Charity in his arms, her face burrowed into his chest as she whimpered pitifully. Anna Rose, even as she took her little daughter, glanced beyond her husband to see Weyman Campbell's still form on the ground, a red stain blossoming on his breast. Angus stood motionless, the gun with which he had killed his son still smoking in his hand.

"I'm sorry, Clara," she heard Angus mutter. "I had to do it."

Anna Rose hurried to him. "Oh, Angus, you saved her life!"

Just as she reached her husband, his shoulders sagged, then he slumped to the ground.

"Hugh, help him!" Anna Rose screamed.

The doctor from the mainland could do little more than shake his head. "I warned him this might happen," he told Anna Rose.

They were standing in the hallway just outside the bedroom door. She could hear the ragged sound of her husband's uneven breathing from where he lay, pale and motionless, in the great rice bed.

"Isn't there anything we can do?" she begged.

"Nothing I can do, I'm sad to say." He patted Anna Rose's hand solicitously. "As for you, dear lady, go and sit with him. It may ease him some to have you close."

And sit she did, through that long, dreary day and far into the night. Dahlia brought food to her, but Anna Rose couldn't eat. She held her husband's hand, praying silently that he would live. But his face remained ashen, his eyes closed, and his breathing grew more labored with every hour. Anna Rose felt as if she were watching, helpless, while her dearest friend slipped away.

Finally, near midnight, when the house was quiet, the guests long gone, Angus's eyes flickered open and his lips moved soundlessly. Anna Rose gripped his hand tighter and leaned forward to hear whatever he might say.

"Hugh," was the only word Angus spoke, over and over as if he were calling for him.

Anna Rose turned to Dahlia. "Go fetch Captain Sinclair. Quickly!"

When he arrived from his guest room down the hall, Hugh was still wearing the same clothes he had worn the night before while they searched the island for Charity. A dark stubble of beard covered his face and his eyes were sunken with weariness.

"What is it, Anna Rose?" he asked quietly.

"He's asking for you," she answered.

Hugh came close to the bed to stand beside Anna Rose. Both of them stared intently at Angus.

"Charity?" Angus asked weakly.

Hugh forced a smile. "She's fine, Angus. No harm done apparently. She's sleeping soundly with Shane."

Angus closed his eyes and took a deep breath. Anna Rose leaned close, speaking his name, terrified that he had slipped away again.

"Anna Rose, my dearest love." The words came out quite plainly and his blue-gray eyes looked clear as he gazed at her.

Anna Rose brought his cold hand to her lips and kissed it. "Oh, Angus," she sobbed. "Don't go!"

"My time, child. A season for all things . . ."

Anna Rose thought her heart would break as he spoke those words. He had accepted his own death. But how could she?

Her pulse quickened with fear as she felt his fingers slipping from hers, but he had only reached for Hugh's hand and was now placing it over Anna Rose's.

"Take care of her, my friend."

A deeper silence settled over the room. For a moment, Anna Rose thought the wind had stopped blowing outside. But then she knew. His breathing had stopped. Angus was gone.

Feeling lost and alone, Anna Rose turned to look for comfort in Hugh's grave face. He closed his arms around her, feeling in his own body the sobs that racked hers. He smoothed her hair and held her gently, trying to soothe her grief. For a long time, her weeping was the only sound in the room. Then that too faded.

"What now, Hugh?" Anna Rose asked in a quiet voice, when she was calm enough to speak.

Still holding her, he looked down into her misty-green eyes that seemed to hold all the sadness in the world.

"Now, Anna Rose? First, we shall mourn our good friend properly. After that has been done, I plan to do as I promised Angus I would. I'll take care of you."

Hugh's words made Anna Rose feel as if another season was

coming on. Gone was the cold, harsh winter of her life, giving way to the promise of spring and an endless golden summer.

"He was our friend, wasn't he, Hugh?" Anna Rose whispered.

"Yes, my darling. Our best friend!"

EPILOGUE

"Hugh, I wish you'd tell me where we're going."

"Then it wouldn't be a surprise, would it, darling?"

Hugh cast a mischievous glance at his wife as they rode side by side along a wooded trail. She had never looked lovelier, he mused. Wisps of her long chestnut hair blew free from her braid in the warm, salt-scented breeze and the spring sunshine brought a high tint to her cheeks. The pale blue muslin gown she wore clung to her full breasts and tiny waist. In spite of the two children she had borne, she looked hardly more than a child herself. Only when he stared deep into her misty-green eyes could he detect a hint of the scars on her heart, on her very soul. But those would heal in time, Hugh was sure. After all, there was no greater balm for pain than love.

Hugh and Anna Rose had been man and wife for almost two years now, since the year after Angus Campbell's death. Still, every night when he took her in his arms, every morning when he awoke to find her next to him, Hugh marveled anew at his good fortune. She was like no other woman he had ever known. *And she was his*. What more could any man ask for?

She knew he was watching her, caressing her with those storm-dark eyes that always captured her even if he was across a crowded room from her. And that look never failed to bring a warm blush of longing to Anna Rose's cheeks. She had trouble understanding her own reaction to her husband. He was like a fever in her blood. Perhaps it was because they had been apart so long, had endured so much together and separately. Now, she could never seem to get enough of him—his kisses, his embraces, his just being there. Each night was a new and wondrous experience, each day an exciting adventure as Hugh Sinclair's wife. Anna Rose had never dreamed it could be this way. And soon, their life together would take on even more meaning.

She glanced at him and caught him staring at her as if he thought he might strip away the muslin from her breasts with the very heat of his gaze. One slender hand went to her bosom

366

protectively. She could feel her heart pounding beneath her palm. She felt quite breathless suddenly.

"Is it much farther?" she asked softly.

She knew that dark scowl on his face. He wanted her, now!

"It had better not be," he answered, shifting uncomfortably in his saddle.

Suddenly, Anna Rose smelled a familiar scent in the air—sweet, spicy, bringing back a rush of achingly fond memories and a touch of sadness as well. She raised her head higher, closed her eyes, and inhaled deeply.

"Oh, Hugh, the pride-of-India trees are in bloom! Why, it's just like that first day we came here and . . ."

Her words trailed off. Anna Rose lowered her eyes, shy suddenly. Hugh reached out a hand to cover hers as he finished for her. "And we made love, my darling."

"We came here often to make love. But the last time you went away."

Hugh could feel the pain in her words stabbing at his own heart.

"I never wanted to leave you."

At that moment, Anna Rose knew the surprise Hugh had in store for her. This was where they had come when she was still Angus Campbell's wife. This had been a lovers' secret rendezvous. Since Angus's death—it seemed so long ago—they had avoided the River House. Somehow it seemed a haunted place, tainted by the love they'd had no right to share. Today Hugh meant to put the old doubts, the old guilts to rest once and for all.

As if reading his wife's thoughts, Hugh said gently, "I didn't tell you where we were going because I was afraid you'd refuse to come, darling."

She turned to look him squarely in the eye. Her own misted with tears. "Oh, Hugh, you know I love this place! It's just that I never wanted to dredge up the past."

He squeezed her hand and brought it to his lips. "It's time we put the past to rest, darling."

They were in the clearing now, staring out over the broad river that danced with silver ripples beneath the blue, blue sky. The lacy, lavender blossoms of the pride-of-India trees nodded their delicate heads high above. Somewhere near, a palmetto rattled its fronds lazily in the breeze and birds called from the thick foliage of the ancient oaks. Everything looked cool and green and welcoming.

Hugh dismounted and lifted his arms to help Anna Rose down. She gripped his muscled shoulders as he clasped her about the waist. But instead of setting her on the ground immediately, he pulled her close, cradling her body against his urgent heat. Her toes barely touched the ground as his mouth came down on hers, searching with an intensity that she knew and welcomed.

"I brought a picnic basket earlier," he said in a husky voice, "but first . . ."

Without giving Anna Rose a chance to answer, Hugh lifted her in his arms and strode across the grass of the clearing. He had brought a blanket, too. It was spread in the shade beneath the pride-of-India trees. Gently, he placed his wife upon it.

"Here? Right out in the open?" Anna Rose said, half-rising.

Hugh pressed her back, coming for her lips again. "Here!" he answered firmly.

By the time he finished kissing her, Anna Rose could find no voice for further objections. If he wanted to make love out in the open . . . if he wanted to dive into the river and take her there . . . it made no difference. She wanted him as much as he wanted her!

But he didn't come to her at once. Anna Rose marveled for a moment at Hugh's way of leading her to the brink of ecstasy with a mere kiss or a stroke of his hand.

She watched, smiling, tingling, as he leaned back and gazed up at the unblemished sky, a look of deep contentment on his face. A moment later, he drew a wicker hamper from the bushes and poured them each a glass of wine. They sipped slowly, drinking in the sight of each other at the same time.

"Ah, Anna Rose, you can't begin to know how much I love you!" Hugh let his hand drift up her bodice as he spoke. It came to rest on the bone button at the top, which gave way to his will at once. A moment later, Anna Rose felt a rush of warm air over her breasts. A new kind of excitement flooded through her.

She cupped his cheek with one cool palm and smiled into his eyes. "I love you, too, Hugh Sinclair. I have for a very long time."

He laughed softly. "It must be the real thing. It's certainly survived a lot. But did you ever dream it could be this right? This good?"

"Perhaps when I was a very young, very romantic maiden back in Scotland. We girls believe in fairy tales, you know."

His hand slipped inside her bodice to cup one firm breast. "I never knew. I never guessed. I still find it hard to believe."

"We come of lucky clans, the Mackintoshes and the Sinclairs. Perhaps our lives are charmed."

"It would almost seem that way." He sighed and laid his head in her lap, staring up into her eyes. "Sometimes it almost frightens me."

"What do you mean, darling?"

"Well, life just seems too good right now. I've never been one to trust fate. Here we are together, almost too happy for words. Your mother and sisters are all being courted. Your brothers are set, Ewan in school and Cullen doing wonders with the rice swamps Angus left him. And Heather and Johnnie and little Shane fill the old castle with laughter. Why, even Iris seems to be settling down. It can't be real, can it?"

Anna Rose, still smiling, leaned down to kiss her husband tenderly. "Are you afraid it will vanish like a mist in the Highlands, darling? I don't think so. Besides, we deserve a bit of peace and happiness, don't you think? We've been through a lot, you and I."

"Aye, we have that! More than our share!"

Anna Rose lifted her glass in a toast. "To long happiness and to long lives with each other."

Hugh clinked his glass to hers and started to drink, but Anna Rose stayed his hand. "I haven't finished yet. There's more to my toast."

"Then by all means!" he said, his spirits high.

"To our child!" Anna Rose said, the words coming in a breathless rush.

For a long moment, Hugh only stared at his wife. Then, slowly, his puzzled expression gave way to a smile. "You mean . . . ? We're going to have . . . ? A boy or a girl, Anna Rose?"

She laughed and hugged him, rocking back and forth and feeling her whole body tingle with happiness and new life. "Now how would I be knowing that? And what does it matter anyway?"

Hugh brought her close and buried his face in the warm fragrance of her breasts. "Ah, darling, you're right. It makes no difference! A child of my own flesh and blood. One we've made with our special love. It's a wonder, a miracle!"

In moments, their happiness turned to something else—something wilder, more urgent, electric in its intensity. They kissed, they touched, they gloried in their love for each other.

When husband and wife were both dressed only in the lacy shadows from the pride-of-India trees, Hugh kissed Anna Rose deeply and let his hands tangle in her thick braid. When he released her lips, he still kept his hold on her hair. Anna Rose shivered as he slowly undid the braid, running his fingers sensuously through her long hair until she felt faint with wanting him.

He made her wait no longer. As the breeze teased the surface of the river with light kisses, sunlight and shadow caressed their entwined bodies. Hugh rode his wife gently, not wanting to disturb their sleeping child, but determined to love the mother well.

Anna Rose had never felt so loved, so cherished. It was as if Hugh Sinclair had been made for her, to have and to hold, when the great scheme of the universe was being formed. When the final moment of ecstasy came, tears rushed to her eyes. How could any man be capable of bringing such pleasure, of giving such love?

Long after their loving, they lay together beneath the trees, drowsy now and lulled by spent passions. The river sang on, the breeze kissed their bodies, and the spring sun went from golden yellow to muted shades of mauve and lavender.

At length, Hugh whispered, "Darling, will you come with me again to this place?"

Anna Rose turned to cling more closely to her husband. "I will come here whenever you ask. I will do whatever you want. Only hold me, darling. Make love to me in the sunset."

"In the sunset, by the light of the evening star, in the dead of night or the bright eye of noon."

He took her to him once more, and the ghosts of their past lives were banished by love. Gone was the pain of separation, the ache of loneliness. This was their place and their time. Hugh and Anna Rose were one . . . for now, for tomorrow, and forever.

ABOUT THE AUTHOR

BECKY LEE WEYRICH, named for Daphne Du Maurier's *Rebecca*, is the author of two volumes of poetry and twelve novels, including *Detour to Euphoria*, a Bantam Loveswept romance. A native of Georgia, Ms. Weyrich lives on St. Simon's Island with her husband Hank, a retired Navy pilot. They have two children—a married daughter and a son in college.

Special Offer
Buy a Bantam Book
for only 50¢.

Now you can have Bantam's catalog filled with hundreds of titles plus take advantage of our unique and exciting bonus book offer. A special offer which gives you the opportunity to purchase a Bantam book for only 50¢. Here's how!

By ordering any five books at the regular price per order, you can also choose any other single book listed (up to a $5.95 value) for just 50¢. Some restrictions do apply, but for further details why not send for Bantam's catalog of titles today!

Just send us your name and address and we will send you a catalog!

DON'T MISS
THESE CURRENT
Bantam Bestsellers

☐ 26807	**THE BEET QUEEN** Louise Edrich	$4.50
☐ 26808	**LOVE MEDICINE** Louise Edrich	$4.50
☐ 25800	**THE CIDER HOUSE RULES** John Irving	$4.95
☐ 25801	**DARK GODS** T. E. D. Klein	$3.95
☐ 26554	**HOLD THE DREAM**	$4.95
	Barbara Taylor Bradford	
☐ 26253	**VOICE OF THE HEART**	$4.95
	Barbara Taylor Bradford	
☐ 25432	**THE OCTOBER CIRCLE** Robert Littel	$3.95
☐ 23667	**NURSE'S STORY** Carol Gino	$3.95
☐ 24184	**THE WARLORD** Malcolm Bosse	$3.95
☐ 26322	**THE BOURNE SUPREMACY**	$4.95
	Robert Ludlum	
☐ 26056	**THE CLEANUP**	$3.95
	John Skipp & Craig Spector	
☐ 26140	**WILD MIDNIGHT** Maggie Davis	$3.95
☐ 26134	**THE EMBASSY HOUSE** Nicholas Proffit	$4.50
☐ 26142	**MATINEE IDOL** Ron Base	$3.95
☐ 25625	**A CROWD OF LOVERS** Laddie Marshak	$3.95
☐ 26659	**DREAMS & SHADOWS**	$4.50
	Rosemary Simpson	

___

Prices and availability subject to change without notice.

Buy them at your local bookstore or use this convenient coupon for ordering:

Bantam Books, Inc., Dept. FB, 414 East Golf Road, Des Plaines, Ill. 60016

Please send me the books I have checked above. I am enclosing $_____
(please add $1.50 to cover postage and handling). Send check or money order
—no cash or C.O.D.s please.

Mr/Ms_____

Address _____

City _____ State/Zip _____

FB—10/87

Please allow four to six weeks for delivery. This offer expires 4/88.